ATB & EBS hit will fines totally
almost £100 million over Trecker
kontoyer scandal - journal

NOW

AND

FOREVER

A spellbinding historical saga packed with danger,
drama and romance

MARGARET SCUTT

JOFFE
BOOKS

Joffe Books, London
www.joffebooks.com

First published in Great Britain in 2021

Cover art by Dee Dee Book Covers

ISBN: 978-1-80405-041-5

CHAPTER I

On the fourth day of June in the year 1682 my brother, Ralph Carey, brought his bride to our home. It was not a bright day. As I recall, it had rained since early dawn, and the trees hung dripping all around the house, and the hall was dark and forbidding as she entered it that first time. I have never forgotten any detail of this, my meeting with Frances, my brother's wife. I had waited, half sick with apprehension, wishing only for the moment to be over and past.

Now, on a gust of damp air, the door had opened, and the new mistress of the Grange was here at last. She threw back the hood of her travelling cloak, and hair so fair that it seemed silvery sprang out around her pale pointed face. Shimmering hair, brilliant eyes, the whole effect was of something all aglitter, so that the gloomy hall seemed darker in contrast, and she herself a thing of light. The little group of servants stared and murmured in admiration. For myself at that moment I could have given you no detail of her face or figure, I only knew that she was most beautiful, so much so that I shrank back into the shadows, wishing that I might never be called from their protection to stand beside her. But Ralph stamping in, ordering back the dogs and their clamour of welcome, roared out my name so that I could hide no more.

"Cat! Catherine! In the devil's name, where is the wench? Catherine—!"

As always with my brother he strove to veil discomfort with noise. Poor soul, he could not have been happy as to this meeting either. I knew that well enough.

"I am here, Ralph," I said, coming forward, my sympathy for him lost in the familiar dread of his displeasure. That I had incurred it once again was plain. The contemptuous curl of the full lips as I limped towards him, the scowling glance so quickly averted, these signs I knew so well that by now they should have lost the power to wound. But today the old pang was sharpened when I saw how differently he looked at his wife.

"Frances, my sister Catherine."

He had no time to say more. His wife came to me swiftly, both hands outstretched, smiling, yet with something appealing in her face.

"My sister, too, as I believe, sir," she said, with a quick backward glance at him. "I never had one before."

That was all she said, but as she took my hands, she laid her cheek against mine in the most confiding gesture. She was taller than I had thought, so that she bent slightly to me, but there was nothing of condescension about the caress. Her cheek was softly warm, and about her was some perfume I did not know, faint but subtly disturbing. It was long since a stranger had touched me, and I stiffened uneasily, but I did not draw away from her.

"You are welcome, sister," I said, and my voice in my own ears was cold and hard after the warmth of hers. "All is prepared for you."

She drew back a little with her hands still clasping mine, and her lips drooped as if she were a child unjustly scolded. Behind her I saw Ralph scowl, and waited for him to speak, knowing myself ungracious, unable to appear otherwise. But it was Frances who broke the silence.

"Will you see to it that Jennings has help with my gear, Ralph?" she asked, giving my hands a faint pressure then releasing them. "I am assured that Catherine and I will do very well without you for a space."

He looked at her, and I caught my breath. Long before, when life had seemed bright to me, I had seen Ralph's face unshadowed by bitterness. Now, with his eyes on his wife, the years had rolled away, so that I marvelled at the change in him. He had blamed himself so much, though God knows I had forgiven him — it was little enough to forgive. The sorrow of it was that he could not forgive himself, and so hating himself had grown to hate the sight of me. I suppose a limping ghost with a marred face, a constant reminder of a moment's drunken folly had been enough to sour him. I was glad to see him look at her so, to know myself and all the world forgotten, truly glad. And yet a most cruel pang pierced me as I watched. So much for her standing there unblemished, beloved — so little for me. I turned from them and their happiness.

"I will take you to your room," I said.

The old servants, who had assembled to greet her, bowed and curtsied. She gave them a careless nod and followed me in silence walking lightly up the wide stairs. I opened the door of their chamber, saying: "I think there is all you need."

She glanced around with little interest and gave a low laugh. "I am assured of it. But for one thing."

"Yes?" I paused in the doorway.

"Can you not stay a moment? It is probable that we shall not be long alone? And I wish to speak with you. Pray do not remain in the doorway like a bird about to take flight!"

"Very well," I said, and closed the door.

She said swiftly: "Ralph has told me of your misfortune, Catherine. I am truly sorry."

I felt the tide of red that swept me, scorching neck and cheeks.

"I have never asked for pity!"

"No. That I can understand. But friendship — does what has happened mean that you close the door on that?"

"I had not meant to do so?" I said, with discomfort.

"No?" Her sudden smile showed small very white teeth. "'You are welcome, sister!' But you might as well have said, 'Have a care, Frances — keep your distance!' And I had meant so well!"

She looked at me, spreading her hands and slightly raising her delicate brows, as if deploring her own failure. The faint warmth which I had known when she first ran to greet me came creeping back, and with it a kind of wonder. I had been so sure that my brother's wife would afford me at best pitying distaste, I the skeleton at the feast, who having no other place to go must needs ease an unwanted third in her home. I could not imagine that she would offer me a friendship which seemed frank and free.

I searched for words that would not be over cold. "I am sorry. I have been much alone and I fear my social graces are few."

She said sadly, as if I had hurt her: "Ah, Catherine, do not mind so much!"

I put my hand to my cheek, feeling against it the puckered skin round the scar which ran from eye to lip, drawing up that side of my face in a kind of dreadful smile, and looked at her. Eyes of a deep and lovely blue, white skin without flaw. "Do you think you would not mind?"

I had never meant to say it. I heard myself with horror and disgust, yet the words came tumbling out, hot and bitter, laying bare all that I would have kept hidden in the secret chamber which housed my hurt.

"You—" I heard myself continue "—beautiful, admired, loved — would you not care if that smooth skin were puckered and hideous, so that those who looked on you looked once and then away? If even your own kin shrank from the sight of you—?"

She shook her head, and I fell silent, appalled at what I had disclosed to her, a stranger, God knows without intending it.

She said, very gently, "I am assured that in like case I should long for death and turn against all the world, as

4

you have done. But I did not shrink at the sight of you, Catherine."

I recalled the feel of her cheek against mine and the way she had come to me, and I thought with a kind of wonder that it was truth she spoke. I held out my hands to my brother's wife and kissed her. It was the first time I had kissed anyone save my old nurse since the day when the world crashed round me in a red mist of pain.

"I wish you very happy, Frances," I said.

She gave a strange little sigh, almost, it seemed, of satisfaction. At the time I took no heed, but later — much later — I remembered it.

"I could show you a way of dressing hair which would hide much," she said. "You have beautiful hair, Catherine."

I suddenly felt old, ages older than my comforter, standing there in her beauty and assurance that all could be so easily set right. A new mode of hairdressing — a sugar plum to dry the tears of an unhappy child. Yet it was kindly meant. Looking back I am glad to think so, and that I accepted it as such.

"We will see, Frances," I said.

There was the faintest sound, scarcely more than a slight scratching on the door, Jennings, the maid, moving softly as any cat, came into the room.

* * *

I went early to my bed that night, knowing that Ralph and probably Frances also would be glad to have me go. It was natural enough, nor did I blame my brother for showing his feelings so plainly, but I could not help but feel that my position in his home would scarce be a happy one. I could, it was true, retire to my chamber and to the small store of books which had become my companions. I would have preferred to do this straight away, only I would have seemed ungracious to Frances who, throughout the evening, had continued to make overtures of friendship.

I pondered for hours over what I could do, coming to the uneasy conclusion that in fact there was nothing, for what could any woman do without money, friends, or any prospect of marriage? In twelve months' time when I should be one and twenty, some money would come to me, but it would need to be a great amount to throw a veil over my marred face and halting gait, new style of hair dressing and all. I did not pity myself in knowing this, simply realising that it was a fact impossible to overlook. Catherine Carey at seventeen might have taken her pick; Catherine Carey at twenty would be no man's choice.

And it was not only the change in appearance, though God knows that would have been enough. I, who had consciously feared nothing, now walked in dread, dread of meeting strangers or friends, of showing my changed face, of hearing what they whispered of me. I was as vulnerable as if some protective shell had been ripped away, leaving a quivering creature cruelly exposed. Shelter was only to be found in solitude, and until now this had not been denied me. But Ralph had married, and all was changed.

Frances. Again, I see her as I had seen her that evening in the candlelight — saw Ralph's dark face also, bemused, utterly lost in love for her. She had been gay, bubbling over with plans for the future, for filling the Grange with guests and laughter. And it would be so good for Catherine — Catherine would find so much pleasure in it all.

"I am afraid," I had muttered, clenching my hands under the table, "that I have lost the habit of pleasure."

The first words that came to my mind could scarcely have been more ill-chosen, savouring as they did of self-pity and reproach. I knew it as I saw Ralph bite his lip and caught the resentful glance he shot at me. Frances, seeming to notice nothing, hastened on with her soft flow of speech. She had a pretty voice, gay and lilting, with an intonation I did not know.

"Why, then, you will find it again, my dear, and this I promise you! I could never be glum for long, nor allow those around me to be so. Merry I must be, and as for you, Catherine, I will not have you a recluse at twenty."

Ralph looked at me again, this time without anger but with a kind of pleading that was half ashamed. There was nothing I could say, but now, tossing uneasily on my bed I felt that it was hard. I asked for so little, only that he left me in peace while Frances drove her triumphant chariot where she willed, just so long as she did not drive me captive at the wheels.

All in a moment from being broad awake I must have fallen heavily asleep, for instantly, it seemed I was in the midst of the dream. It was long since it had troubled me, and now, as if refreshed by the lapse of time was the more vivid, it brought back the past with an aching clarity.

It seemed that I was in the stable yard as I had been on that April morning three years past. It was bathed in sunlight and dappled shadow, the air filled with the vigour of spring. I was in my green riding gear, the centre of a laughing group. In my dream I was there, yet also in some strange fashion an onlooker, so that I saw myself as in a bright mirror. A slight figure, a dark, laughing face, like the face of a younger Ralph only softly curved, framed by black hair tossed in the breeze — a charming picture, so filled with confidence, with joy of living that in the dream my eyes pricked with tears. Then I was no longer looking on but myself, Catherine Carey, standing laughing in the sunlight.

"Why are you so doubtful?" I asked. "Ralph and I know what we are about."

The young man beside me laid a hand on my arm as if we two stood alone. In the dream I felt my arm most conscious of his touch.

He said urgently: "Ralph would know well enough were he sober. Catherine, for God's sake do not do this. I beg of you—!"

It seemed then that I saw him as clearly as I had seen myself. He was not much older than I, and taller even than Ralph, so that he bent his troubled face to mine, his grey eyes as imploring as his voice. It seemed I might have heeded him but Ralph came from the stable leading the great black horse and none too steady on his feet.

"I saddled him myself Catherine," he said, "since those louts were afraid. But you are not afraid, are you Catherine?"

I laughed and shook my head. There was answering laughter and talk of wagers. The young man arguing with Ralph, was pushed roughly aside. In the confusion of sound I was in the saddle, hooves lashing out beneath me and scattering the group before we shot away. I felt no fear, I was assured of my mastery of the great horse as the wall rose before us.

The black gathered himself for the leap. I heard Ralph's triumphant cry behind me. All in a flash the saddle slipped, dragging me with it. The world revolved around me and crashed with a blinding shock.

Shaking and drenched with sweat I awoke, heart thumping and my face wet with tears. Over and over again, I found myself saying, "I am not afraid. I am not afraid."

Slowly and painfully the dream receded. I came back to reality, to consciousness of what I was saying, and a bitter laughter shook me. Truly, I had not been afraid then — better for me if I had! — but I had been the veriest coward ever since, unable to move fast enough in my shameful and fearful retreat. And now here was Frances set on dragging me out, and I sick with terror at the mere prospect. It seemed to me in this moment of enlightenment that my spirit bore scars more ugly than the one which showed on my face.

I turned over uneasily. The bed was hot, and sleep felt far away. The memories recalled by the dream troubled me. Again I saw the face of the young man who had, in truth, striven to stop me. Martin. Martin Lacey, who had been part of my life, and who was now gone like all the rest. He had been brought up by his uncle, Colonel Gray, who had fought under Cromwell, and whose lands marched with ours. Martin had been one of the gay crowd which filled the Grange with laughter, and indeed, as children we had seldom been long apart. At that time he had looked down on me, and I had been honoured at being allowed to fetch and carry for him, but in the days before the crash the tables had been changed. It was part, and no small part, of my hurt that he had not come to me. Colonel Gray was dead, his home empty save for an aged couple of servants, Martin thought to be overseas. After the crash I had lain ill for weeks, knowing nothing of the world around me. Later, though I wondered at his absence I shrank from meeting Martin again, who had once looked on me with wondering admiration to see his despised playmate blossom overnight. I did not wish to think of him, since even now the memory brought pain.

Impatiently throwing back the coverings, I left my bed and went to the window. The rain had ceased, and a young moon hung in the sky. Beyond the trees a glimmer showed from the surface of the lake. It was very still.

From out of the stillness, slowly, peace came and enfolded me. The quiet night looking down on so many sorrows, passions and joys made me seem of little importance. The coming of Frances, the dream, the re-awakened memories had shaken me from the dumb and lonely endurance to which I had schooled myself. Now, in the silence of the night, I took courage. Catherine Carey was as she was. Life, that sometime gay adventure had turned drab and shot with pain, yet with courage all need not be lost.

I said, as I had said in my dream: "I am not afraid." And I returned to my bed, and almost at once fell asleep.

CHAPTER II

Frances, whatever she might be, proved true to her word. Before it seemed possible, the Grange, like myself, was roused from its dreaming solitude and filled as of old with noise and laughter. New servants appeared in the house, new horses in the stables. Fine ladies came, who looked on me with curiosity; fine gentlemen who looked once but seldom looked again. True to my resolve of courage I moved amongst them, answered when they addressed me, and continued my management of the household, in itself no easy task with the new servants looking down on the old and the old puzzled and shaken yet clinging to their rights. Frances should have dealt with such matters but when I suggested as much she refused with the liveliest horror.

"I am no housewife, nor do I intend to become prisoner of a bunch of keys. Take that much out of my hands and I shall be forever grateful."

"But it is your place!" I insisted. "'Tis you are mistress of the house."

She turned to look at me. She had the most wonderful eyes, a very deep blue, sometimes glittering like dark jewels. They held a person captive, when Frances wished it, so that they could not turn away.

"You speak the truth, Catherine," she said, still holding my gaze. "I am, and will be, mistress of this house and of all in it. There shall be no question as to that. But as for spinning, washing, making of preserves, disposal of servants, what do I care or know of those? A maid of honour learns other things."

Her face changed, growing momentarily pinched and old, with a bitter twist to the lips.

"Were you not happy at Court?" I asked, somewhat surprised.

"From time to time. You learn, as I say, much."

"I have heard that the life is most gay."

She shrugged. "Now there, my dear, all hangs on the meaning you give the word. His Majesty yet takes his royal pleasures, 'tis true, yet from the look on his face one would say has found small satisfaction in the same. The queen, poor soul — her pleasures are few enough, and she takes them but sadly. For the rest, intrigue piled on intrigue, with no man whose word you may trust nor no woman neither. Smiles that hide malice — lips that kiss one day and drip poison the next. Gay, Catherine? 'Tis one long brilliant masque with jugglers keeping their toys spinning in the air knowing that the first slip means the end of the game for them—!"

She stopped abruptly, and turned from me to the window, gazing away, yet not, I thought, seeing much. I saw that her hands were clenched and that she was breathing fast. There had been such bitterness in her tone that I felt a vague discomfort, sensing something of a deep and angry hurt which one would not expect to trouble a loved and new made bride.

I said, half from a desire to know, half to end this uncomfortable silence; "You did not meet Ralph at Court?"

"Ralph?" She repeated the name as if I spoke of a stranger, then suddenly turned to me, and laughed. "Ralph and Court would scarce agree. No, I met him at the house of Colonel Sidney, and the talk there would have sounded mighty strange at Court. My presence there also, had it become known."

"Colonel Sidney!" He was my father's friend, and there was always talk of him in the house when I was growing up. He'd also been a visitor on more occasions than I could count. "He is very stern and cold, is he not?"

"His air can be frosty enough," she replied, "and he has pride enough for Lucifer, despite being republican through and through. The king holds him in detestation, but the one who took me there said his home was the one place remaining where men may speak their minds without fear or favour. But it cannot last."

"I do not see why."

"You will, my dear. We may be far removed from the heart of things here in the Dorset countryside with only gossip and the newsletter for a link, but I tell you, Catherine, news of trouble will reach us even here. Sidney may be virtuous and fearless, but he is a better friend to others than to himself, and he has never learned to temper truth with discretion. Sooner or later his enemies will drag him down. It is not a fortunate position now to stand confessed as a friend to Algernon Sidney: quite soon it will be as healthy to put one's head in a noose."

"But—" I stammered, "does Ralph know of this?"

"Ralph, my dear, has sat with the rest at Sidney's feet, absorbed republican sentiments, and seen no farther than his own nose. He is a great deal safer here with other matters to concern him. In London with affairs a veritable witch brewwell!" She lifted her shoulders in a way she had. "'Tis scarce fitting that I should be a widow yet," she said.

This conversation, which I recall so clearly, was one of the few occasions when we spoke together with no one by. I mostly recall her surrounded by a throng — and spent very little time, as it seems to me, alone with her husband. And in company there was nothing visible of the side which she had shown to me. Like a butterfly, it seemed, she revelled in the pleasures of the day, taking no thought for the morrow. For the life of me I could not tell whether she cared for Ralph or had merely used him as a refuge from a situation which had for some reason become intolerable. For Ralph himself there could be no shadow of doubt. He, who had been self-sufficient and ruthless in his dealings with women was utterly bewitched, lost fathoms deep in love. He would even glance at me from time to time, as if bidding me to take note of her beauty and charm, although he was never fully at ease with me, poor Ralph!

There were times when I was filled with pity for Ralph, though why a sense of foreboding should trouble me I did not know. It was as if his happiness was so bright, of so fine a texture, that it could not endure. I told myself that it must be jealousy which made me feel this way, and that my own lack of prospects made me see his own happiness as temporary, yet there it was. I could not hear Frances laugh, or see Ralph with his face so changed as he looked at her, without that aching pity coming to trouble me. I felt we moved in a bright bubble which one day would burst around us, leaving us naked to a reality which would extinguish the light and silence the laughter. But the laughter and the gaiety continued, and money, as I could not help but note, poured out as if from an inexhaustible spring as the months went by.

I cannot say when I first noticed the change in her. There were many things, each slight and meaningless in itself yet together building a veritable mountain, dark and ominous. Was it in her tone, a strange sidelong glance? At first they only brought me a faint unease, the knowledge that all was not well. Then, as if it had never been, Frances would become her old charming self again, and I would chide myself for having imagined slights where no slights were. But they came again, and yet again until I could not help but know that it was not only Ralph who looked on me with distaste.

It grieved me. It grieved me greatly. Ralph's attitude, however hurtful, I had always been able to understand, knowing well enough that my mute presence seemed ever to reproach him. But Frances — there was another matter altogether. She had seemed to like me, had drawn me to her by that same liking. To have her so changed towards me, and for what reason I was at a loss to know, was bitter to me as gall.

It was no help when I told myself that in truth it was clear enough — that my appearance had filled her with revulsion from the start, and that she found it impossible to keep up those first overtures of friendship. I wished that she had been the same from the beginning and that I had never been brought from my frozen solitude.

Whatever our feelings, we kept the days of Christmas together with laughter and merriment which I could not help feeling were meaningless, with reckless revelry which cloaked something unspoken and threatening — or so, looking back, it seemed to me, as I recalled the dying of the old year and the coming of the new.

The greater part of our visitors had been friends of Frances but one day, early in January, there came a gentleman to see Ralph. Or so he said. It so happened that my brother and his wife were from home. The roads being passable, they had gone to join the festivities at the Carew's three miles from us, and were not expected back until late that afternoon. I, of course had been bidden with them, but having suffered a feverish chill for the past week had thankfully made my excuses. It was very pleasant to be alone again, most especially since Jennings, a creature whom I could not abide, had attended her mistress. She was the least obtrusive of women, soft spoken, soft moving, with hooded eyes, and the whole household loathed her. Even the dogs growled at her passage, yet also seemed afraid, while Martha, my old nurse muttered of witchcraft and the like. She had a fashion of materialising beside me when I felt myself alone, always with some excuse, never the slightest shadow of impertinence yet I found her unbearable. They say there be some who cannot be near a cat without a creeping disgust of the flesh, and just such an unreasoning revulsion did I feel towards Frances's devoted maid. However, as I say, for once the house was free of her and breathed more freely so.

Henry came into the room where I sat dreaming over a fire of great logs and startled me into wakefulness by announcing a visitor who, indeed, himself entered hard on the old man's heels. Blinking half resentfully, conscious of tumbled hair and my sad coloured old gown, I rose to greet him. He bowed over my hand with a faint smile but seemed little more pleased to see me than I to see him. He was tall and heavily built, and his riding dress, though travel stained, was not of our local cut.

"I ask pardon, Mistress, for intruding on you thus, but I wish to speak with your brother. I am told he is from home?"

"I fear so, sir," I answered. "Is your business urgent?"

"Urgent enough for me to have made a journey in search of him which was plaguey long and plaguey cold." He smiled, instantly shedding some of the years with which I had credited him.

"Perhaps I could take some message?"

"No, that would not serve." The smile had faded and his voice was curt once more. I felt some indignation at this, though he continued courteously enough. "I thank you, but I should wish to see him myself. Is he like to be long away?"

"Why, no, unless the weather stays them," I answered glancing out at the lowering sky, "I expect them a few hours from now."

"A few hours." He repeated the words in a musing voice looking as I had done from the window. Standing so, I thought his face set in lines of weariness was harsh, yet not unattractive.

Breaking a silence, which seemed overlong, I said: "I fear, sir, that I did not catch your name."

He swung round, the smile lighting his face again. "Indeed I ask your pardon. You must think me an unconscionable boor, but the truth is I have matters on my mind. My name is Roger Frampton, very much at your service, and your brother knows me well. And so you are Mistress Catherine? I have heard him speak of you."

"Ralph spoke of me?"

It was the most unguarded query, and my tone must have betrayed far more than I had meant. The hot blood burned in my cheeks as I saw his gaze change and quicken to interest. A lock of hair had fallen over my disfigured cheek. I pushed it back, and waited, steeling myself to meet his gaze. The steady look of his brown eyes did not change, and with surprise and gratitude I let my looks drop forward again.

"Ralph was grieved, most truly grieved," he said, with unlooked for gentleness, "over a hurt to you for which he knew himself to blame. But pray forgive me, Mistress Catherine. I did not mean to speak of aught that would give you pain."

Strangely, I felt warmth, not pain. The deep voice was kind and sincere. I could not resent his words and felt a glow of liking towards him.

"It is of no consequence," I said untruthfully. "Indeed, it is I who should ask your pardon. Will you not take some refreshment? I have been sadly remiss."

"Thank you, no. I must be on my way, for night falls early. But if I may I will write a message for your brother."

I said that I would bring him writing materials, and with a swift change of mood again felt some indignation that he would not trust me to pass on a message by word of mouth. I curtsied distantly as he held the door for me. Despite my downcast eyes I was conscious that a flicker of amusement had crossed his face. Well, let him laugh, and let him write his secret and depart. That same Catherine Carey who had lately warmed to him would be well content to see him go.

I had barely stepped from the room when I found him beside me and halted in surprise as he laid a hand on my arm.

"Wait. No need for a message, I believe. Your brother is returning."

Even as he spoke the great door was flung open and Ralph's voice calling to the servants made itself heard. My companion nodded.

"Ralph and no argument!" he said, in a low voice. "His bull's roar has not changed or lessened in volume!"

Taken by surprise I laughed with him, and at that moment Frances fluttered in like a wind-blown leaf. She was so wrapped and enfolded against the cold that little could be seen of her but bright eyes and the tip of a nose. The man beside me uttered a little sound and I looked up at him curiously. Seeing us, Frances halted, pulling back the furred hood from her face.

"Catherine? You have company, I see."

The words were nothing. The tone, and the look which accompanied them made me conscious that Master Frampton and I standing close together in the shadows might well surprise her. I moved forward, angrily conscious that the red had come to my face.

"Frances! I had not expected you so soon."

"No, Catherine?" She smiled, and my face burned the more hotly. "Ralph feared that snow was on the way, and that we might be weather-bound if we delayed. I am rejoiced to find that you have not been lonely."

I said stiffly: "This gentleman wished to see Ralph and, finding him from home, was about to take his leave. He—"

Frances did not heed me. Her eyes had turned from me to Roger Frampton, who at that moment had stepped from the shadows so that she saw his face. Completely motionless she gazed at him, her eyes wide and in them a look I had never seen before. She said in the faintest whisper: "You?"

He came forward and bent over her hand, and I saw her lips quiver and part. She might have thought it strange to come home and find me entertaining a stranger, but God knew what Ralph would think if he came in now and saw his wife with that look on her face. I moved hastily between them.

"Then you already know Master Frampton, Frances?" I said.

It was plain that she had completely forgotten my presence. She started, and with what seemed an actual physical effort looked away from Frampton and at me. But her eyes turned back to him at once.

"Master Frampton and I have met," she said in a curious voice. "I did not think to see him now. As I had heard he was overseas."

"I returned a week past," said Frampton. "As Mistress Catherine has said, I came to speak with your husband. I am fortunate that you put forward the time of your return."

"You had heard of my marriage?" she asked, still with that devouring gaze on his face and speaking as if those two stood alone.

"I had heard," he answered, looking at her steadily and with no shade of expression in face or voice. She lowered her gaze and her lips trembled.

"Much has happened since you went away," she said, her words at once a reproach, a defence, and a cry of sorrow so poignant that my own heart ached with pity, not for her — what did I truly know of her, when all was said? — but for my brother, whose wife could speak so to another man.

Then Ralph came stamping in, swearing at the cold and roaring a surprised welcome at his guest, and the past moments might never have been. Frances, to all appearance with no shadow of trouble on her was seconding my brother in his insistence that Master Frampton should remain with us for that night at least, and between them overcoming his apparent reluctance. Looking at Frances with wonder I saw her face alight with laughter, heard her voice clear and gay. As I moved away to make arrangements for our guest, I glanced back at the three of them, Ralph with an arm flung about his wife's shoulders, Frampton smiling at something he had said, and so comfortable did they seem together that I might have imagined what had passed. But my heart was heavy as I went up the stairs, and when I came upon Jennings drifting like a black shadow along the corridor a shiver took me; as if she walked with heavy footsteps over my grave.

CHAPTER III

Despite the hurry to be gone of which he had spoken, Roger Frampton was still with us when a week had passed. To be fair he was unable to do otherwise, since snow had fallen heavily overnight, and we were all prisoners within the walls of the Grange until such time as the thaw might come. During these days it seemed that his bearing towards Frances was all that befitted a guest in her husband's house, nor did she give any token of the feeling which had so disturbed me on their first meeting. Again I tried to believe that imagination had misled me, and to blame myself for such distempered fancies.

Frampton was closeted for long periods alone with Ralph and passing one could hear the quiet flow of his voice, with occasional vehement interjections by my brother, but what it all portended I did not know, and Frances did not enlighten me. She was quieter at this period than I had known her, and seemed, despite our mighty fires, to suffer much from the cold. She would sit huddled over the blaze, spreading her delicate hands so that they showed pinkly transparent, as if she could never have enough. Thus illumined, and with that silvery hair falling around her small face she seemed more a creature of fantasy than a woman of flesh and blood. I thought her unwell, and offered her potions which she declined, saying that if she needed help Jennings was skilled in such matters but that she would do well enough when the weather changed. I could not but think that it would be better for her to bestir herself and show some interest in household affairs, but this seemed never to enter her head, and it was not for me to order her. She was pleasant enough to me at this time, but withdrawn, as in a small world of her own. In her highbacked chair with the flickering light on her face and her blue eyes dreaming I did not feel that I knew her at all.

When the thaw came it came swiftly, with masses of snow sliding from roofs and branches. Everything damp to the touch, runnels of water glistening like slugs' trails on the walls, and outside a sea of slush. All the beauty and mystery brought by the snow was lost in mire, and I felt limp and oppressed. Frances, in contrast, seemed to come to life, even as she had said. That last evening, before our guest went on his way she was so gay, in such beauty and so sparkling with wit that neither man seemed able to take his eyes from her, and Ralph's pride and happiness reached its peak. And all unbidden the dark foreboding, that certainty of ill to come, troubled me yet again.

The talk, I recall, turned to Court affairs, and Frances having related some tale of scandal which set the men laughing had asked for the latest news from town.

"For indeed, sir," she said, "your speech has been confined to my husband, and on such sober matters that I feared to ask you nothing of interest to myself."

"And you are not afraid now?" asked Frampton, looking across the table at her.

"Why, since you assure us that you must go on the morrow, I must speak now, or forever hold my peace. How could I endure it if I had suffered you to leave without learning who is Monmouth's latest love, or what is now the mode at Court?"

"The mode and I are none so well acquainted, I fear," Frampton replied. "For the rest — Monmouth, by his progresses has angered his father yet again and Shaftesbury, after quarrelling with him has gone too far for his own safety and fled to Holland. God knows who will take his place."

"Ah, but here be heavy matters ageing. 'Tis the other side I would wish to know — the latest scandal, the newest shades — who loves whom?"

"Love?" echoed Frampton, in a curious voice. "Does that not depend on what meaning you attach to the word?"

He spoke half dreamily, gazing down at the table as if his thoughts were far away, but the already bright colour deepened in Frances' cheeks, and I saw her bite her lip like one who had received a wound. Ralph, lounging full fed and more than half asleep noticed nothing, and Frampton continued lightly with his speech as if the air hadn't quivered between the pair.

"If scandal is what you wish for, His Grace of Monmouth, as ever, supplies it in plenty. However, at the end of the line comes Lady Henrietta Wentworth, and they say she has him on his knees for her favours."

"But is he not already wed?" I asked.

Frances smiled, looking at me with brows slightly raised, and Ralph, coming to the surface, guffawed, so that I wished I had kept silent, but Frampton answered me with courtesy.

"He was wed, Mistress Catherine, to a wealthy Scottish lady when both were of tender years, but the gentleman has never been fully content with his bargain, and looks for his pleasures elsewhere."

"True son of his father," said Ralph, pouring more wine with an unsteady hand. "'Tis a whoremonger of a fellow, and I would we had another on whom to pin our hopes."

"'Tis a pretty gentleman enough," said Frances indulgently. "And not one easy to refuse." Then she added hastily, as if the last words had been ill judged: "He is well loved."

"Why yes. The man in the street acclaims the Protestant Duke. Bonfires burn and church bells ring to announce his return from banishment. Such is his charm that his faults are looked on with indulgence, and his father dotes on him — but not enough, mark you, to acknowledge him as legitimate."

"Black box and all," said Frances, nodding. "Yet men will put their hopes in him, and belike come to an ugly end on his account."

Frampton shrugged. "As to that, soon or late a man's end must come, and 'tis little matter how. And one can only use the tools ready to one's hand."

There was a kind of brooding silence, then he seemed to shake off heaviness and turned to what Frances had wished, talking of great folk and of their affairs, which truly seemed far from great. Frances listened and laughed, capping his tales with others, and Ralph slumped in his chair and fell asleep. And I sat hearing the talk and laughter, feeling that it was but a cloak for something much more strong and real, and the deep chill in the air seemed to creep into my bones.

At last we went to our rooms, and I hoped to put their affairs from me, but whether because of my troubled spirit or from some bodily ill I lay wakeful, with a throbbing at my temples and feverish tinglings running through my veins. After a while I could bear it no longer. There was a posset of herbs in the closet where I kept such matters below stairs, I thought a draught of that might aid me, and wrapping a cloak round my night rail I set off in search of it. Needing no light to guide me I started down the silent stairs.

In the hall below there was yet a glimmer from the fire. Halfway down I halted, freezing like a hare in its form. Two shadowy figures stood close against that faint light. There they were, Frampton and Frances.

Now, I offer no excuse for my behaviour. Two courses in honour were open to me; I could have spoken to them openly or returned straightaway to my room. I did neither. Shrinking into the shadows shamelessly, I listened. I have often wondered at myself since, for eavesdropping is not, in truth, a habit of mine. At the time I can only say there seemed no choice. There was anger, disgust, again pity for Ralph, but more than all I cannot but admit, a devouring curiosity.

At first it seemed that this would not be gratified. So softly were they speaking that only the faintest murmur reached my ears. Then I did catch the tail end of a remark by Frampton.

"—such utter madness!" he said.

Frances gave a kind of half sob, and her voice was raised.

"What other could I do? All these days, and no word with you. I could not let you go—"

"Hush! You will rouse your husband."

"He! No fear of that as you know well enough."

"Yes. It is a pretty picture, is it not? A guest in a friend's house creeping out to meet that friend's wife. It may be your fashion, Frances. It is not mine."

Whether they had raised their voices or whether my straining ears had become more accustomed to their speech I heard him most clearly and could even distinguish the sound of angry disgust in his voice.

"No — your ways were never mine. You were ever apt to sit in judgement. I am what I am. And I did love you," said my brother's wife.

"Love! And what of Dalton and Lindsey and the rest? Even before Conway — though he was the final straw."

"But cannot you understand," she cried, "they meant nothing — less than nothing. You were the only one in truth. But you tried me, condemned me, and went away."

"And what did you?" he whispered back, furiously it seemed. "Leap into the arms of a country squire, whose life you will mar like all the rest."

"I had to escape. There was no longer a place for me. And I would have given him what he wanted. Only—"

"Only what?"

"Only you came," she said.

Frampton muttered something, as if driven past endurance and the two shadows melted into one. For what seemed an age there was no sound at all, only that I thought to hear the angry beating of my heart. And now I longed to be in my room, away from it all, yet it seemed that I had lost all power of movement.

Frances spoke first, clearly and exultantly. "I knew!" she said.

"Yes, you knew. And what of it? What do you gain by knowing me to be so great a fool?"

"I gain — why I gain the whole world," she answered, laughing.

They clung again, then it seemed that Frampton put her away.

"No, Frances," he said.

She sobbed: "You cannot leave me now. How could I endure it? Take me with you. I will go to the ends of the earth."

"Oh, no, Frances. My travels are not that far, nor have you a part in them. A man without money is of no use to you. It would be the same story over again."

She began to plead with him in a soft babble of words, into which he broke ruthlessly.

"No more of this. It has been madness as I said and is over now. I mean it! Frances. This is the end."

"But you! What will you do?"

He laughed softly. "Even as you did, my dear."

I heard her catch her breath. "What — what do you mean?"

"You found yourself a husband with money. A wife in the same happy position will do well enough for me."

I heard her gasp. "You cannot! You shall not!"

He laughed again. "My dear," he said, pleasantly. "Do you think that you can stop me?"

There was a sound from the room beyond. Frances turned and ran swiftly up the stairs, passing me so close that I could have touched her. Her face was turned from me, but I knew that she was weeping as she ran. I forced my stiffened limbs to move, dreading lest Frampton should find me there, but he stayed motionless by the dying fire, and I reached my room and crept into bed.

Later I heard Ralph's unsteady footsteps on the stairs and his thickened voice bidding his guest goodnight. Frampton's voice replying was as calm as if nothing had happened. For a while I lay burning with anger against them both, then that faded, and a creeping chill took its place. What the outcome might be I could not know, but I wished most devoutly that Frances, her beauty and her charm, had never entered into our lives.

CHAPTER IV

I had not known how I should face those two after what I had heard, but the morning found me in such a dreamlike condition that all seemed unreal. Except that Frances's eyes were shadowed she seemed as usual, and Frampton showed no sign of discomfort. He left early, bent over Frances's hand and then mine. I should have been unable to bear his touch but for that strange feeling of unreality as if one looked on at figures moving in a play.

He looked gravely at me. "It has been a privilege to meet you, Mistress Catherine. I trust that before long I may see you again."

I took the words as an empty compliment, but I saw Ralph give Frances a sidelong grin, to which she did not respond. Her eyes were on Frampton, then they moved from him to me, giving me a long, strange look. At the time it meant nothing to me. Frampton rode away and I moved to go about my household duties, still without truly coming to life.

It was Ralph who brought me back with so great a shock that it set me tingling from head to foot as if I had been plunged into a fire. He had been looking at me rather oddly and looking away, and on a sudden he burst into speech.

"So, Catherine, you have an admirer," he said.

For a moment I did not take his meaning, only glancing at him with faint surprise, thinking he meant some jest.

"If so 'tis news to me," I answered.

He gave a loud uneasy laugh. "Sly boots that you are, waiting for our absence to entertain—"

Frances interposed, that look of hers on me again. "Why do you not speak plainly, Ralph?"

He stamped over to the fireplace, pushing back a log which was toppling dangerously. A shower of sparks crackled up the chimney. Frances was still watching me. I wished that she would look away.

"Our guest, Roger Frampton, has looked on you with favour. Is that plain enough?" And he laughed again, "Pox on it, such news should not turn you into Lot's wife!"

But bathed in that burning heat for the moment I could neither move nor speak. I felt with incredulous anger, how dared he, how dared he think to use me so? And dearly I recalled his voice from the shadowy hall: "You found yourself a husband with money. A wife in the same happy position would do well enough for me."

I had been standing by the door. I sat down rather hastily and looked at my brother and his wife — Ralph red-faced and faintly ill at ease, Frances ever with that blue gaze on my face. I thought, what if I speak now, what if I tell Ralph all I know? And I could not — how could I? God knew his happiness was unstable enough. It was not I who could give it its deathblow.

Frances broke the silence, very softly. "Are you not pleased, Catherine? You seemed to like him well enough."

I turned my eyes on her, and for the first time in our acquaintance hers fell before mine and a faint tide of colour rose in her cheeks. Her hands, resting on the arms of her chair tensed and the knuckles showed white. Without one word spoken I was assured that she knew I had discovered her secret. I looked back at Ralph.

"I have no desire to wed Master Frampton," I said steadily. "I thank you."

Ralph stared, scowled, and gave an angry laugh. "God's wounds! To hear the wench one would say that she might take her pick!"

Coming from him to me it was so cruel that I felt a tide of most bitter desolation engulf me. It seemed abundantly plain that he had hoped to be rid of me, that it was his angry disappointment which had spoken. I thought of Frampton, needing money so much that even I could be part of the price, and of Frances who had seemed loving and sweet and who was so far from what she had seemed; then I thought finally of myself, ugly and unloved. In all the years I had spoken no word of reproach to Ralph, not one, and this was my reward.

I said coldly: "I am well aware that I have no attractions to offer, Ralph. Nonetheless, it is as I said. I do not wish to wed. But if you are so anxious to be rid of me——"

He swore, the deep colour darkening his face. "Of all the bitter tongues! In God's name, who spoke of that?"

I went on unheeding, "When the inheritance is mine I will leave here. It is not long now. You shall be burdened by my presence no more."

He started towards me with some look of trouble in his face which made it warmer, more as it had been in days gone by. If I had met him halfway then all might have been changed, but my hurt was too recent, too deep.

"My mind is made up, Ralph," I said.

The hand he had extended dropped to his side.

"Do as you will, and be damned to you," he said thickly. "I shall not crawl to you, never fear."

Glancing back from the doorway I saw them both as in a picture — Ralph gazing after me with anger and surprise. Frances utterly inscrutable with her silvery hair like a halo around her small face. Then I closed the door on them both.

I suppose the sting of my hurt anger had upheld me until then. Now, it was as if my strength died away like lifeblood ebbing from a wound. I felt a dizzy sickness upon me and put a hand to my forehead, surprised to find it wet. I thought if I could just reach the staircase, gain the sanctuary of my room, then I would be all right. But I knew that I could not. There was a pounding in my ears and a darkness before my eyes which grew and enfolded me, so that I was lost.

* * *

How much later I could not say I found myself lying on my bed, vaguely wondering why I was fully dressed yet with the bed coverings pulled over me. There was a smell of burning which caught my throat and made me splatter with distaste.

A voice with a pleased tone to it said, "Ah! She is coming to herself. There's naught like burnt feathers under the nostrils." I opened my eyes and looked up into the wrinkled face of Martha, my old nurse. She gave me a toothless smile. "Better now, my lamb?"

"What happened? Why am I here?" I asked, wondering that my voice should sound so faint and far away.

"You swooned in the hall, my dear. Do you not recall? Master Ralph found you all of a heap on the floor and carried you here. He was much troubled and indeed you looked like death. He will be glad to see you—"

"No," I said.

"What?" Martha looked at me with surprise.

"I will not see him or anyone but you."

I had remembered not only my sickness but what had gone before. Later, I supposed, we should meet and cast a decent veil over all, but not yet. I would have my little space of solitude, for surely that was not too much to ask.

"But my dear, what can I say?" asked Martha in a troubled tone. "They pay no heed to me — you know that well enough. I should have gone long since had it not been for you."

"Dear Martha, I know and am grateful. But for now 'tis easy enough. I am truly weary — tell them that I sleep and must not be disturbed."

She seemed doubtful but helped me out of my clothes. I buried my face in the pillow and closed my eyes. It was as well since no sooner had she hobbled from the room than the

29

door was opened and I heard Ralph's unmistakable footfall. Had he been alone I might have tried to put my hurt behind me and come to an understanding with him, but there was the whisper of silken skirts and that faint perfume which told me who entered with him. Like an obstinate child I lay still, breathing regularly, feeling their eyes on me, wishing desperately that they would go.

"The old woman spoke truth," said Ralph, his voice unfamiliar as he schooled it to softness.

"Yes, she is sleeping," said Frances. "It is best so."

"Thank God for it. When I saw her lying there I thought that she was dead." I felt him come nearer, knew that he was gazing down on me. He said, with a kind of break in his voice: "She looks as she did — before it happened."

My scarred sheen was hidden in the pillow. Some of my bitterness faded at his tone.

"You never knew her as she was — full of spirit and with every man who came near her bewitched—"

"Yet she seems to be casting her spells over one man even as matters stand," said Frances, softly. And through my closed lids I felt her gaze on me again.

"As to that Catherine will be wealthy in a few months' time. I would that I could say as much for myself."

"I also," said Frances.

Ralph forgot himself and swore in his customary tone. "If my breeches pockets be empty I am not wholly to blame. And if you are displeased with me, I have a grievance too."

"You shall have your child, but in my good time. And quiet, or you will waken her."

"Nonetheless—" he muttered resentfully.

"I have uttered no complaint, Ralph. As yet," she said. And, with a sudden change of tone, she added, "In this matter of Roger Frampton — do you think that she will wed him?"

"How can I say? You heard her, and she seemed to mean what she said. She had ever a will of iron."

There was a kind of admiration in his voice. Again, it surprised and touched me.

"Yet her life," Frances said, hesitating, "as things are, and without marriage, has little to recommend it. If I were in like state—"

"Well?"

"I would as lief have done with it," said Frances.

Ralph made no reply, and I heard them cross the room and the door close behind them. I lay still for a while, making certain that I was indeed alone, then I opened my eyes.

The room was very quiet now, though their voices yet echoed in my ears. I reflected wryly that I was gaining in prowess as an eavesdropper, yet I was not sorry to have heard Ralph speak of me with that tinge of pride and affection. It was strange that it should have been on the very day that his speech had so bitterly wounded me. I suppose there is ever that certain bond between those of one blood, never to be wholly severed however greatly tried. It tugged at me, despite my hurt. Then I thought with unease how the theme of money had seemed to run through what they said, and I wondered how much would be mine. Enough, it would seem, to render as acceptable to Master Frampton. And Ralph, as I had feared, was in low waters — not that it was a surprise. He had spent far too long from home and he and his wife had fairly made money fly since their marriage. Well, I would as happily hand over some part of mine when I had it to Ralph as to Frampton, but I must keep enough for myself. Where to go and what to do was a sealed book to me, but remain here as matters stood I could not and would not do.

The slow hours passed and still I was left alone. I wondered somewhat that Martha did not return, but presently fell into a doze. When I awoke I thought to see her bending over me, but before I saw clearly a sense of strong revulsion told me I was wrong.

"Where is Martha?" I asked.

"I do not know, Mistress Catherine," answered Jennings respectfully. "My lady sent me to you. I have brought you some broth."

I was hungry but I wanted nothing from her hands.

"Take it away," I said. "And send Martha to me."

She went, silent as a ghost, and I lay waiting. But the grey light faded, and shadows filled the room, and Martha did not come.

I had given her up and had resigned myself to the long night since sleep seemed far from me, when there came the faintest scratching on the door, scarcely louder than a mouse in the panelling. I said softly, "Who is there?"

"'Tis Martha," her voice whispered back. "Hush! I should not be here — 'tis the first chance I had," she said, still in that strange breathless voice.

"Why do you not come in?"

"I will, so soon as I know that creature is not on my heels."

There was a pause, then the door opened cautiously as if to admit a conspirator. I raised myself on my elbow, feeling somewhat lightheaded but otherwise well enough. The shadowy figure hobbled to the bedside, bending over me.

"Why do you not bring lights? Since when have you needed to creep into my room like a thief?"

She caught her breath in a sound like that made by a weeping child. "Since I left you before. Since Master Ralph bid me go."

I reached out and caught her hand in mine. It was cold and shaking. I recalled all that those same hands had done for me and anger and pity rose side by side.

"I never thought to leave you, my lamb," she whispered "but they say I am old and grow fractious and troublesome. There be others who can do more for you than I."

"I do not understand," I said, frowning. "Are you at odds with Jennings?"

Martha snorted. "No more than I have been at odds with her since the black day when her misbegotten foot first crossed our threshold. Oh, I am old, bent and cantankerous — I know that well enough — but I know more too."

"What more?"

"I know that she is evil through and through and what happens to those who cross her. Why is there no babe from this marriage? She knows, with her herbs gathered at full moon and her muttering of spells."

"I cannot bear her near me, 'tis true — but let that pass," I said, uneasily. "Why did you speak of leaving me?"

"Because I must. Because I am sent away."

I felt a tear on the hand which clasped her own and my anger flared.

"As to that, we shall see," I said, pushing the coverings away from me.

She gripped my shoulders with surprising strength. "No, my dear, no!" she panted. "I must go. What use to bide here if they will not let me near you? And with that creature against me—"

My anger faded, and a kind of wondering fear took its place. There was something here that I did not understand. Martha, who had in all the years been noted for fearing neither man nor beast was now much afraid. I could feel it like something tangible, and it communicated itself to me.

"But for Ralph to do such a thing!" I said. For indeed, with all his faults, it was not his way.

"Ralph has married a wife," she answered. "And is his own man no longer."

"But where will you go? How will you live?"

"He has given me money. He could put that in my hand, but he could not look me in the eye. I'll go to my sister Naomi — you remember her?"

"In the cottage near the Chase? I remember it well enough."

Indeed, in my childhood it had been a small treat to be taken there. The reddest apples grew in the orchard at the back of the cottage, and there was a tiny stream where fish no bigger than my thumb nail darted and glittered. Naomi was fat and rosy as the apples and her husband a forester, tall with a booming voice and a great black beard. I had not thought of them for many a day, and now they came clearly back from the past.

"They will be kind to you?" I asked.

"We shall do well enough. And if you should have need of me you would know where I could be found." Then she added bitterly; "That is if you, too, are not glad to see the back of me."

"You are, as you said, cantankerous," I answered. "But you know better than that." We clasped one another for a moment. "I shall not remain here. As soon as I may, I shall find a place for myself, then I will fetch you to it."

Suddenly she stiffened and drew away, laying a gnarled finger on my lips. I had heard no sound but there was a crack of light showing where the door was not quite closed. I did not know that Martha had moved from my side, so silently did she go, but when Frances and Jennings came into the room she was nowhere to be seen.

Frances came to my bedside and set down the candle she carried. Her face was tranquil, and her voice gentle and soothing.

"Dear Catherine, we have brought you supper," she said. "Jennings told me you were not hungry before."

"Did she also tell you that I asked for my old nurse to be sent to me?"

"Martha is unwell," she answered calmly. "She grows old, Catherine, and your sickness of this morning troubled her. But Jennings, who is most skilled in nursing will do aught you need."

I did not look at Jennings, but was most conscious of her still figure and hooded eyes.

"I need nothing," I said, turning away.

"But you must eat! You will never regain strength thus. If you have no wish for company we will leave the food here and you to yourself."

I did not reply and she signed to Jennings to set down the platter.

"Sleep well, Catherine" she said, and they went together from the room. I was glad to see them go.

Some cautious minutes later Martha crept from the shelter of the curtains, hobbled to the door and peered out.

"I would not put it past her to be lingering there like a cat about to pounce," she said, returning to me.

"She is but Frances's serving woman. I know not why we should fear her," I said. But the words were empty, for with incredulous anger, I knew that I also felt the shadow of that fear.

"She looked at me today," said Martha, and gave a shudder. "Indeed, it is as well that I should go."

"Have a care for yourself. You are all the mother that I have known."

She bent to kiss me. "A poor imitation of the real thing! I would that I need not leave you."

"I would that also," I answered. And indeed, when she had crept sadly away, I felt more alone than I had ever done before.

CHAPTER V

I thought that I should lie wakeful, but a most heavy drowsiness came upon me. I had drunk most of the broth and eaten a little bread, forcing myself to do so, since I vowed I would not lie helpless here to be tended by Jennings. It was my desire to rise early and confront Ralph, for Martha should not be sent away without a protest from me. The more I thought of it the more unthinkable did it become. But I slept with most unusual heaviness, waking with a dry mouth and aching head to find it broad day. Angry with myself I dressed hastily and went first of all to Martha's room. It was bare and empty and when I went in search of Ralph he was not to be found. He was not wont to lie late abed, unlike Frances, who never seemed to come to life much before noon, and in any case I was not minded to go to their bedchamber. Instead I went through to the kitchen, pushing open the door and standing for a moment unseen.

A small group of our old servants stood close together, like sheep huddled against a common enemy. There was Henry, Joan, his wife, John the stableman and Rachel the serving maid. Jennings and the new coachman were nowhere to be seen.

"And where will it end?" Joan was demanding. "Tell me that!"

Henry, his wrinkled face a mask of trouble, shook his head. I moved forward and they turned and saw me. They were all old in our service, like Martha cantankerous, and, I suppose, over indulged, but as their eyes fastened on me I felt their anxiety and grieved for them, foolishly enough, since what could I do for them?

"I am looking for my brother," I said.

"Master Ralph and his lady have gone into Wimborne on business, Mistress Catherine," said Henry. "I was to tell you when you awoke."

So Frances for once had risen early and I too late. It came to me that perhaps they did not wish to face me.

"And Martha?" I asked, knowing what the answer would be.

"They took Martha to leave her with her sister," said Joan with no expression in her voice. She added, her tone changing, "Mercy on us, you are white as tallow! Sit you down, my dear, and Henry shall fetch you wine. Or I will warm some milk—"

They fussed around me, settling me in a chair by the fire, and I sipped the warm milk and felt how natural it was to be there with them. I might have been a child again, when I used to enter the kitchen and Joan would find some treat for me, afterwards wiping my sticky face and fingers lest Martha's reproaches should be heard in the land. They had quarrelled, those two, like cats, on any pretext, yet at bottom had been good friends enough.

"I wish that I had been in time to see her before she left," I said, half to myself.

Joan's colour deepened. "As to that—"

"Hush, woman!" interrupted Henry, with sudden authority, "Least said soonest mended. And John, Rachel — have you naught to do that you stand idling here?"

"Aye!" said Joan, with heavy emphasis, "Work while you may."

I opened my lips to speak and found no words. I would have reassured them if I could but who was I to do so and what power had I in my brother's house? He had, as Martha said, married a wife.

"Was Martha much grieved?" I asked, when Joan and I were left alone.

"She did not show it, and she hobbled out bravely enough. But you know and I know, Mistress Catherine, what she felt."

"What I cannot conceive is why it should be done, and in such haste!"

She came close to me, glancing first at the door. "It was because of what she said. We all felt it — we have done from the first — but Martha said it, to her very face."

"Said what?" I saw that Joan like Martha the previous evening, was afraid. Her hands were shaking and the little red veins on her cheeks stood out against a sudden pallor.

"Said that she — that woman — should not lay a finger on you. That she had sold her soul to the devil."

She actually made a sign in the air, as if warding off the evil eye. Still without mentioning a name, she went on.

"Henry was there, just before they carried you to your room, and he heard it. He said she made no reply, only looked at Martha for a moment and then was gone. Martha went with you then, but it was for the last time. My lady told Master Ralph that Martha's wits were gone, and that she could have her here no longer. Henry heard it all. Master Ralph swore and bellowed, but she had her way. And Mistress Catherine, what I ask myself, what we are all asking is in God's name, where will it end?"

She broke off, trembling and wiped away the little beads of sweat which had appeared on her lip.

"Martha was wrong to say such a thing," I said feebly.

Joan shot me a glance which told me that she understood my position well enough.

"As you say, it was foolish of her," she said, and instantly, it seemed, withdrew herself from me.

"The small parlour is warm and pleasant as you are alone," she said, "Will you take your meal there?"

I rose, and agreed, but looking at her closed face was impelled to say something of what I felt: "I am truly sorry, Joan. I will do what I can."

"We know that, Mistress Catherine" she said.

I hesitated, finding myself foolishly reluctant as she, to mention a certain name. "Where is she?"

She spread her hands. "Who can say? An hour past she left the house on some errand of her own. She may well be outside that door now."

Again, she made that gesture warding off ill and such was the force of her feeling that I was hard put to it not to join her. But when I went out no dark figure lurked there, and I did not set eyes on Jennings that day.

It was late when Ralph and Frances returned and when I went towards them they both looked on me with surprise. Ralph had been wearing his most forbidding scowl, and no pleasure lightened his face at sight of me.

"Why, Catherine, we had thought you were keeping to your bed today," said Frances, throwing back her cloak. "Jennings said you were sleeping soundly when we left."

So she had looked on me, though I had not seen her. The thought was not a pleasing one and added to my determination that I would say something of what was in my mind.

"I slept late," I answered, looking not at her but at my brother. "Ralph, I wish to speak with you."

"There is naught so difficult in that since I am here," he said, "but make it short. I am cold, hungry and thirsty."

"It may be," said Frances gently, "that Catherine wishes to speak with you alone."

He swore violently. "Then Catherine must think again. There is nothing to be said to me which my wife cannot hear."

I went on steadily as if there had been no interruption: "Why has Martha been sent away?"

"Because she was losing her wits and causing trouble. She is cared for well enough; you need not fear for that."

"She had cared for me all my life, you also. And you sent her off without one word to me."

His colour deepened and for a moment he looked half ashamed. Then, as always, he took refuge in bluster. "Plague take it, am I answerable to you? I make decisions in my own household."

I looked at Frances and said nothing, but they caught my meaning well enough.

She said, in a voice like silk: "You were in no case to be troubled over the matter — nor do I think you well enough to be troubled now."

"But where was the need for such haste?"

"Damme, need enough," said Ralph brutally. "Since if we had let her come to you she would have bellowed over you like a cow with a sick calf."

A tide of anger rose in me, hot and bitter. For the moment I hated them both. I said in a voice which I could not keep from shaking: "You have done as you would, and behaved most ill to an old woman who had only love for me. You have had your way, but in one thing I will have mine."

Ralph opened his lips, but Frances checked him with an upraised hand.

"Yes, Catherine?" she said.

"While I am under this roof, which please God may not be long, I will not be attended by Jennings. See to it, Frances, since I mean what I say. I will not have her near me."

She looked not at me but at her husband, raising her shoulders in a strange fashion she had, and arching her delicate brows.

"You see?" she said, "'Tis plain that Martha let drop some of her poison before she left."

My anger had drained from me, and I felt limp and weak, but I repeated obstinately: "I will not have her near me. I mean what I say."

"Rest assured, Catherine," she answered, like one indulging a fractious child. "Poor Jennings, who is faithful as ever Martha was, shall be kept from your presence. Unless—"

"Unless what?"

"Unless the time should come when you find yourself in need of her," she said.

I went to my bed feeling that my protest had been of little avail, and I made merely to look obstinate and unreasonable. Frances had so many weapons on her side; wit, beauty, her husband's love — oh, that was true enough. He was wax in her hands and she, as to my sorrow I knew, head over heels in love with another man. That man's face rose before me in the darkness, and I actually toyed with the thought of accepting his proposal as a means of escape from a position which grew more and more intolerable. At least, it would settle the matter as far as Frances was concerned. And then I thought again and was not so sure. Frances, that creature of light and gaiety, had some inflexibility of character which took her to a desired goal no matter what obstacle stood in the way. What had been the trouble which drove her to Ralph I did not know, but it was clear that he had been used as a stopgap. I had liked her so well when first she came, speaking to me with kindness and understanding that now I grieved for her loss as a child grieves for a broken toy. It seemed to me that the only true feeling she had ever shown was when she clung to Frampton in the darkened hall. And with the memory a sudden sick revulsion against him took me, and I knew that I could never be his wife. Poor Ralph at least was ignorant of the fact that he was married to one whose love was not for him. I could not, even to make my escape, go into a like position with open eyes.

After the snow the weather had been good, and the roads passable. It may be that my brother, too, found the present state of affairs not to his liking – though Frances, except that she was now always cold to me, behaved as if nothing had happened. At all events towards the end of January they took advantage of the weather and went to friends near Dorchester, remaining for almost three weeks. As a matter of course Jennings attended her mistress and again all within the walls of the Grange breathed more freely on that account.

With the coming of February, the restlessness of spring was already in the air, communicating itself to me. It may be that the happenings of the past months, despite all the unhappiness had been a kind of rough medicine rousing me like a creature sleeping a winter away for far too long. It was time that I bestirred myself.

I went, one day to Wimborne to call on our man of business, Mr Uvedale. He was understandably surprised to see me, but greeted me with courtesy. He seemed very old to me, and his frail body as dried up as some of the dusty parchments around him. I had not seen him since the days after my father's death, when I was too young to understand the words uttered in his droning voice. Far more clearly did I remember the sweetmeat he had surprisingly produced from his pocket and presented to me.

"On my soul, Mistress Catherine," he said, sweeping a pile of dusty documents from a chair and gesturing me to it, "This is a most pleasant surprise. You were a child when last we met. And now—"

"I shall be one and twenty on the eighteenth day of June," I said.

His eyebrows were grey and bushy, and seemed to move up and down like two fuzzy caterpillars. That was another thing I recalled from the past.

"An important date, indeed," said he. "There will be celebrations at the Grange, no doubt." The eyebrows arched, as if they laughed at the thought but the small grey eyes of Master Uvedale held no hint of mirth.

"There will be no celebration," I said, firmly. "And it is my desire to leave the Grange as soon as I may."

"You are to be wed and set up your own establishment? Very right and proper," said he, nodding.

"That is not the case, in the matter of marriage. But my own establishment, yes. My inheritance will allow for that?"

"Your inheritance will most certainly allow for that. You will be a wealthy woman. But — forgive me — what are

42

your plans? If you leave your brother's protection where will you go?"

"I do not know. So long as I go, it matters little more."

His eyebrows hunched in a sudden frown. "It matters little? At one and twenty?"

I found that, without any conscious prompting from me, my hand had crept to my scarred cheek. I knew that he noted it, though his face did not change.

He rose and walked to the window, his hands behind his back. He gazed outside for a moment before turning suddenly, as if he had come to a decision, he said; "Mistress Catherine, I have known you since childhood. Will you forgive me if I speak plainly to you? For a woman, young, wealthy, to leave her home — except for the protection of a husband — is to ask for trouble. Now, I do not doubt there have been difficulties to face. I know, also that your brother's behaviour has not been all it should and that your life may not have been a happy one. Nevertheless, I do urge you most earnestly not to throw away ill-advisedly his protection. He has given you a home—"

"He could scarce do otherwise," I said, stung. "And if nothing else, I have ordered his household for him."

"I know it. And if the rest of his life had been ordered as well, he would be in a better position now. But I could never reason with him — and for all your quiet ways, it seems unlikely that I can reason with you."

He wandered back to his chair and sat down rather wearily.

"Indeed, my mind is made up," I said, "but I would not be ungenerous to Ralph. If I am in a position to help him—"

He interrupted me, not angrily, but with a kind of deep solemnity.

"Never think of it. Hearken to me in this much, at least! Hand over every jot of your inheritance to your brother and to what avail? It would go like all the rest. You might as well pour it into a bottomless pit." He shook his head. "But leave that, and let us return to your own affairs. Is there no relative to whom you could go?"

"None who would want me, nor do I wish to be in another's home. As matters are I shall not marry; that is not to say I do not desire a household of my own."

He looked at me gravely. "Do you not think that there be some who see more than outward show?"

"It is possible, no doubt. It is also possible that money would add attraction to me. But I am not minded to wed for that."

"Your father spoke truth of you," said Mr Uvedale, shaking his head. "'As sweet a little maid as one could wish'," said he, "'but set in her own ways as any mule'."

I laughed and took my leave; he promised to wait on me in the near future.

"And mule or no mule," he said in parting, "I beg of you to consider. Do naught in haste."

"I will consider," I said.

"And go your own way! Well, well, I will say no more."

I thought, as the old coach lurched over the ruts that he had been kind and speaking for my good. But it was not his advice to me which I pondered, since as I had said, my mind was made up. It was his speech with regard to Ralph which troubled me. Try as I might, I could not forget it. After all, perhaps I did owe something to him. If, during the time between my fall and his marriage my life had not been gay, at least I had done much as I wished. I would not leave his roof indebted to him whatever Master Uvedale might say.

CHAPTER VI

Once more, in the absence of Ralph and his wife, I had a visitor. Again I was sitting over a fire alone, and again Master Frampton was beside me almost before Henry had spoken his name.

It was early afternoon, and a blustery rainy day. He was splashed with mire and looked weary. I thought his need must be great to have come on such a day, and felt scorn for him.

"I fear you find me alone once more, sir," I said coldly. "My brother and his wife are from home."

It seemed to me that he was somewhat surprised at my tone. He moved nearer the fire, and a cloud of steam drifted from his garments. I would as soon have had him far away but common courtesy made me offer him dry clothing and refreshment.

His eyes steadily on me, he brushed it aside. "I knew you would be alone. I was with your brother yesterday. It is with his knowledge that I am here to speak with you."

"I do not know," I said, without truth, "that there is anything you can have to say to me."

His face changed, showing a glint of amusement. "You surprise me, Mistress Catherine. I understood from Ralph that you were aware of my intentions regarding you. Have I your permission to address you?"

"As you will," I said indifferently. An ungenerous desire that he should humble himself to me strove with another feeling — the knowledge that, had matters stood other than they did, I might have liked him well enough.

He seemed not to note my ungracious manner and seated himself opposite me. The firelight flickered on his dark face showing lines graven from nose to lips. I thought it a strong face and wondered that he, looking every inch a man, should yet be so base.

He began abruptly. "I have little to offer a woman and my feet are set on a dangerous path. None the less, if you would take me as I am, I should be most happy if you would be my wife."

I thought how sweet the words might have sounded and how empty and hurtful they were knowing what I knew. I meant to refuse him there and then, but thought drearily the play might go on a little longer. "We have scarce met. We are strangers."

"I do not think it," he answered gravely. "The first time I met you, in this same room, I felt I knew and liked you well."

He sounded actually as if he spoke truth. I might have softened to him had I not remembered the image of the two figures melting together by the fireside those weeks before. The memory was so vivid that my speech came easily as anger glowed in my veins.

"I thank you for your offer, sir, but I fear I must decline."

He moved away sharply and looked at me in surprise. I held my head high and looked back at him. It was plain that whatever Ralph might have said, Roger Frampton had thought the day won.

"You sound very sure," he said slowly.

"I was never more sure of anything," I answered.

"May I ask why?" He added, sounding for a moment like a boy whose pride had been hurt. "I did not know that I was so displeasing to you."

I had never meant to speak of it. The thought of bringing my knowledge to light had never so much as entered my mind, yet all in a moment it was done.

"Since you ask me why," I said, "I will tell you. I saw and heard you and Frances in the hall the night before you left."

There was a long silence. A log toppled to the hearth with a shower of sparks. Frampton picked it up and threw it back on the fire. A little piece of ash glowed on the floor beside me. I crushed it out with my foot.

"So that's why."

"That's why." I then added, half defensively, "I had not meant to listen or spy. You need not think that."

"Yet you did not tell Ralph?"

"I may have discovered a most ugly thing," I said angrily. "That is not to say that I would be a bearer of tales."

"In any case he would probably not have believed you" he said as if to himself, gazing into the fire. "He is well in the toils."

I sprang to my feet. "It ill becomes you to speak so of him! Let us bring an end to this."

"I meant no disrespect to Ralph," he said looking somewhat surprised, "Pray do not leave me before I have told you how matters stand. You owe me that much at least."

"I owe you nothing. And as I told you I saw and heard for myself."

"Yes, and I am sorry for that," he said.

I sank into my chair again, not that I desired to do so but my knees were shaking and I did not wish him to see my weakness.

I drew a deep breath. "Sorry! Are you not ashamed?"

Gravely, he replied: "I am, and have been very much ashamed. Ralph is my friend. My conduct was not that of a gentleman."

"For the first time," I said, "I find myself in agreement with you."

The colour showed in his cheeks. I was glad to think that I had touched him at last.

"Your tongue is apt to wound, I see."

"It is the only weapon I have," I answered, and for some reason, as all too frequently, felt like I was in the wrong.

"My sole excuse is that it — the meeting with Frances — was not planned. Indeed, it was the last thing I had intended. Believe me I had put all that behind me. There were other matters on my mind."

I was silent. Probably he spoke truth and the meeting was brought about by Frances, but I remembered too clearly what I had seen.

"It is the oldest excuse in all the world, and I am still much to blame" he said, "but like Adam, I was tempted and I fell."

"You had met before. There was something between you — Frances made that plain enough — yet you came here in search of her, knowing her to be my brother's wife."

He made a sudden angry movement. "I perceive that I might as well save my breath, since you are determined not to believe me. Yet I will say again this once more, that I came to speak with your brother and God knows not with his wife."

There was a ring of truth in his voice. I thought, for the first time with faint pity for him, that Frances was hard enough to resist. My own defences had crumbled before her easily enough: how much more those of a man who loved her?

He answered my thoughts as if I had spoken them.

"I did love her. I would have married her but I am not rich and she could not wait. The moment my back was turned, there were others. She cannot, it seems, help herself. 'Tis in the blood. Oh, I am no saint from a stained-glass window myself, but neither could I take her, knowing all."

"And it was Ralph's money — what there is left of it — that made her wed him?"

"That, and the fact that she had offended a certain great lady so bitterly that it was necessary for her to remove herself. Even she realised she had gone too far."

I saw again Ralph's eyes as he looked on her that first evening, his pride and delight in her. Even then I had felt pity for him, as if I had dimly sensed the background to that bright figure.

"I would he had never met her," I said, half to myself, and tears pricked my eyes.

"Ralph's welfare is very dear to you, is it not?"

"He is my brother. He is all I have, and there is nothing I can do to help him. Nothing in the world."

He looked at me gravely. "I fear I have distressed you. I did not come here with that intent."

I thought of his reason for coming, and how little meaning it had beside all this.

"It is no matter," I said wearily. "I had guessed it was thus already. You did but tell me I was right."

He stepped towards me, and took my hands in his. I made to withdraw them, then let them lie limply in his.

Urgently he pressed on: "Despite all that has passed, despite your scorn for me, I am assured we should do well together. Will you not reconsider?"

"I might have done," I said, "if I had not heard you that night."

He dropped my hands with a sigh and moved away. "Yet you are wrong," he said.

"Wrong to think it is only my money that renders me acceptable? Oh no. I am not wrong."

"And I say that you are! I need money and your money would do much for me — I would be but a fool to deny it. But seeing you today, talking with you, knowing how you have been hurt, I have felt—" He broke off abruptly, seeming to pull himself together. "I know you will not believe me, so what use is trying to explain? Farewell, and if you ever need help and could think of me with kindness, call on me."

"I thank you," I said coldly, "but I think there is little chance that I should need your help."

"Nonetheless," he answered, looking back at me from the doorway, "my offer stands."

"Which offer? That of help, or of marriage?"

He laughed and pulled his cloak around him. "Why both to be sure." And bowing, he left me without another word.

I sat on, gazing into the caverns of the fire and the more I thought of our speech together the less real it seemed. It was as if I had fallen into slumber there alone, and dreamed the whole affair. And in the dream there was a faint haunting regret, as if one had been offered something pleasing to have and had pushed it wilfully aside.

I moved, finding myself cold and put fresh logs on the dying fire. with the movement the dreamlike sensation vanished and I was myself again. I looked at the hands which he had clasped and remembered his face as he had looked down at me. And all in a flash that face was replaced by another, young flushed and gazing on me with wonder and admiration. Martin. Martin, whom I had never seen since that day in the stable yard. Why the memory should now come to trouble me I did not know, but of one thing I was certain. If it had been he who clasped my hands and pleaded with me I could never have sent him away. And since it was as little likely that he should come to me after the years as that the moon should drop into my empty hands it was a foolish enough thought, and did naught to cheer me.

* * *

It was the twenty-second day of February when Ralph and Frances returned, and in just over three months I should be my own mistress. I counted the days, for their return was not a happy one. Ralph was most plainly troubled and his temper worse than ever, so that the servants went in dread of him. Frances did not seem to fear his rages but would look on him with weary distaste. They quarrelled now and Ralph's angry recriminations echoed through closed doors. At such times the voice of Frances was never heard, though I doubt not her answers were cutting enough. And with it all he still worshipped her, and I believe half his roaring rages were brought on by the knowledge that wife though she might be, he truly had no more hold on her than on a piece of floating thistle-down. And there was still no sign of a child.

He spoke of Frampton only once, to ask if he had called on me. I answered that he had and that I had sent him away.

"The more fool you!" said he, and that was all. Frances on that subject said nothing at all. She was very quiet and withdrawn. It was almost the first time since her coming that the Grange had been empty of guests and as if she needed gaiety and admiration to bring her to life, her light seemed to be dimmed. Not that she was any less beautiful. She spent hours with Jennings, who cared for her skin, hair and clothing, and she was always fine enough to have graced a Court rather than a country house, but it was as if she moved through a masquerade. What with this, with Jennings like a black shadow, the servants cowering and uneasy, the days passed heavily.

Ralph rode off one day to see Master Uvedale returning with a brow black as thunder. I had just entered the room where Frances was sitting gazing into the fire and would have withdrawn on seeing him but he stood in the doorway, blocking my exit. She looked at him, her brows slightly raised.

"I gather you gained little satisfaction?" she asked.

"Satisfaction! 'Tis worse even than I thought. Your bargain is not working out well, I fear."

The tone was hectoring, but back of it I could sense he hoped that she might reassure him. She said nothing, only glanced at him with no more warmth in her face than if she had been a statue.

"Perhaps," she said, "it would be more fitting that we did not brawl before Catherine."

He swung round, scowling at me as if seeing me for the first time. I clenched my fists so that the nails cut into my palms and forced myself to look back at him.

"Catherine — yes, I have something to say to you." He rounded on me. "I hear you visited Master Uvedale during our absence."

"I did," I answered, somewhat surprised at his tone.

"You did not think fit to tell me of it!"

"I had not thought that it would interest you. In any case we have seen little of one another since your return."

"That be damned. You crept off secretly, whining to the old man, making me look a fool, and worse!"

He turned to Frances. "Do you know, she even told him that she was leaving as soon as the money was hers! Devil knows what other tales she spread. By God, Catherine, 'tis an ill bird that fouls its own nest!"

His taunts hurt me like blows and I could not keep from trembling.

"It is not right of you to speak so to me!" I said in a choked voice.

"God's wounds, I am wrong, as always!" he shouted. "Why did you behave so, and what right was there in that? I had never thought you to be sly or underhand."

"Sly?" A wave of anger stiffened my knees and burnt up my fear. That final insult had acted as a spur to a failing horse. I glared back at my brother every whit as fiercely as he glared at me. We must have looked to Frances like a pair of game cocks. I believe she sat as calmly gazing as if it were some show put on for her benefit.

"How dare you say that to me! How dare you!" I saw his mouth fall open in utter amazement, and swept on. "There was no slyness or secrecy. I but wished to know where I stood. And as to my leaving, you knew. I had told you—"

"I did not think you meant it," he muttered.

"Then you know it now! I do mean it — I do!

"Yes." He looked at me with the anger fading from his face and most unfairly, a look of hurt wonder taking its place. "Ah well, I have heard tell that rats leave a sinking ship."

Treacherously the emotion which had upheld me ebbed, and the colour stung my cheeks.

"You would have been content enough had I left as Roger Frampton's wife!"

"That is a horse of quite another colour. Even you should know that," he answered, and walking over to the fireplace turned his back on me. I paused for a moment but neither he nor Frances spoke, and I went unhappily from the room, leaving the door slightly open, not through design, but because I found myself shaken by what had passed, and our angry voices still seemed to echo in my ears. Before I had crossed the hall I heard Frances say, with a tinge of weary contempt, "How well you handled that."

I made blindly for the stairs, almost running into a dark figure creeping down. For once Jennings lifted her heavy lids and looked directly at me. Her eyes had no life in them, no life at all, and my flesh crawled. She stood to one side that I might pass, and as I went on my way I was filled with certainty that her gaze was still on me. But when I turned sharply and looked back the staircase was empty.

CHAPTER VII

Up till now my story has been crystal clear in my memory and as the years go by, indeed, events of the past are more vivid to me than the happenings of yesterday. They say with the old it is often thus; of a certainty it is so with me. But from this fidelity of memory I must except the days soon after my quarrel with Ralph since over them a kind of veil is laid, and there is darkness and confusion, and I was not myself but some lost creature, knowing little of what she did.

It began with a mishap that befell me and that I remember well enough. It was the second day of March and one of those cleanly washed fair mornings when you are foolishly persuaded that winter is truly past. The sky was a clear blue like that of a hedge sparrow's egg, with only little puff balls of white cloud, fluffing against the blue. It looked so fresh and inviting and so heavy was the close air within the house that I threw aside all I should be doing, took my old cloak and went out into the woods.

The air was chill but seemed to sparkle, and everywhere birds sang, darting here and there. The catkins on the hazels, so long tightly held and stiff, swung yellow in an abandoned dance, and wandering on I almost forgot past troubles and those which most certainly lay ahead, and some of the weight lifted from my heart. I had not been well, with a kind of low fever, and a heaviness of spirit. Now I thought: *not so long before I am away, and all is changed*. Among the moss, celandines held their burnished faces to the light, and I had the fancy that I, away from unkindness, might blossom likewise. Love, marriage, a babe at my breast, these would not be for me, and nothing could truly replace them, yet on a morning such as this one could not feel completely without hope.

I thought as I breathed the fresh scented air how pleasant it was to be away from the house, and from the presence of Jennings, who truly seemed to haunt me. I could scarce raise my eyes without setting them on her, and more and more did she fill me with sick disgust. She had not looked fully at me again, but it was a fact that life had not gone easily with me since the time she did. Joan, with her fearful look, said that it was so with man or beast after those eyes had rested on them. This I could not wholly believe but I was glad that Martha was out of her reach, angered though I had been at her banishment. I only longed to be away likewise.

Beyond the belt of woodland which surrounded the Grange there lay open country, falling steeply into a valley, at the back of which rose the hills. Through the valley ran a little stream, a winterbourne, vanishing in the heat of summer, but at other times babbling its importance as it danced over the gravel. It had been a favourite haunt of mine in childhood, long unvisited, and I thought I would renew my acquaintance with it.

I picked my way down the narrow path and found that it was flowing full and with a smooth, contented sound, like one well fed. There was a rough bridge here, of logs, and I remembered how the small Catherine would send argosies of twigs floating under it. There had been a companion most times on these occasions — that same Martin who in the days before my fall had looked on me with surprised admiration as if I had emerged like a butterfly from some dingy shell. As I have said, he could not then look on me enough but in our childhood it had been far otherwise and he, a gawky schoolboy, treated me not at all kindly while I trotted at his heels like a spaniel. I stepped on the bridge gazing down at the brown water and heard his voice, which had often played traitor to him, a manly growl changing without warning to a cracked squeak. I smiled to myself and looked more closely, leaning forward to watch the tiny whirlpools and eddies of foam which had been used to hold back those twigs we sent afloating.

I heard no sound, there was not the slightest warning. One moment I stood there lost in memories, the next a violent blow in the back sent me helplessly face downwards in the stream. I caught my breath and choked, gulping water instead of air.

The shock was so great and I so hampered by my clothing that I might well have ended my troubles there and then in a few inches of water, but I was so angered and amazed at this attack that I somehow found strength to struggle to my feet.

Dripping and gasping, pushing the wet hair from my eyes, I staggered round, looking wildly for the one who had done this unbelievable thing. But there was no one — no one on the bridge or on the path, or in the fields beyond. In the short space while I floundered in the water, my assailant had vanished.

The banks were steep and slippery and my skirts held me down like leaden weights, but after several vain attempts I managed to scramble out. My teeth chattered and my very bones seemed chilled. I was afraid. To get back to warmth and safety I must pass through the woodland. And, in the woodland, the one who had struck might well be lurking to strike again. Yet the attack, if of murderous intent, had been a feeble effort. Telling myself that an assassin would have finished the task, I resolutely set my face for home.

The path which had led me so pleasantly down to the stream was, a different matter altogether now. What with the drag of my clothing, the chill which made breathing difficult and a band, tight and painful, round my chest, I was in a sorry state. Yet I struggled most miserably on, and when I at last reached the woodland I was utterly exhausted, so that even now, on level ground, I could not move as quickly as I wished. The cold had set me shivering as with an ague, my bones ached from the uncontrollable shaking, and a sharp pain stabbed my side. But I was no longer afraid, since bodily discomfort had put all else out of my mind. Somehow, I limped and staggered on, hearing and seeing nothing of whoever had put me in this plight.

I scarcely knew that I had reached the drive and scarcely realised that a voice was calling my name. Afterwards I knew that it was John, the stableman, who had all but carried me to the house, set me on a chair and called loudly for help. Time passed in a whirl of faces around me, voices wondering, exclaiming. Something was held to my lips but my chattering teeth made it difficult to swallow and most of the liquid ran down my chin, as if I had not been wet enough already. One face came clearly out of the mist, looking at me steadfastly, and with a kind of speculation. Silvery hair, deep blue eyes — I looked back at Frances striving in vain to control my shaking.

"Alas, sister, you are in a sorry state," she said in a grieving voice, "What possessed you to do such a thing? We must get you to bed—"

"The poor lady has an ague," said another voice, "see how she shudders and quakes."

"Do not bide there croaking like a raven! Fetch warming pans and set bricks to heat."

It was Joan, I thought dreamily, but their worry seemed to concern me no jot. At times the voices pounded on my ears, at times were far away. Someone bore me to my room, I dripping all the way, and someone began to strip my clothing from me. I came to myself a little then and tried to push her aside, but I had no strength and she went steadily on. I began to feel so ill that even the fact that Jennings's hands were on me seemed to matter very little.

She put me to bed as if I had been a child and went away returning with a steaming bowl from which she tried to feed me. I could not swallow for my throat seemed closed and despite all the coverings and the care they took to warm me, the cold had come into the bed with me and nothing would send it away.

Very little of this time is clear to me, but one thing I do recall most vividly. It was the voice of Jennings who was bending over me. "You will have no trouble now," she said.

And later, the voice of Frances: "But why, Catherine, why did you do such a thing?" she asked as if in sorrow and dismay. And to someone who stood on the other side of the bed, "She has been most strange in her manner of late — but that she should do this!"

Bemused as I was I took her meaning and managed to speak in a strange, creaking voice.

"I was pushed," I said.

"You see?" said Frances, and I knew how she would be looking: shoulders and brows raised.

The mists rolled over me again and that was the last thing I remember, since there followed a jumble of pain and fevered images which jostled one another so closely that I, Catherine Carey, was lost as utterly as if I had breathed my last, face downward in the stream.

The first thing I recall when the fever left me and I was myself again was fixing my eyes on something dancing and golden on my bedcovering. I could not think what it might be and watched it wonderingly, like a babe that fixes its gaze on any matter strange to it. Then, I saw, beside this golden glint, a hand, spread limply as if without strength of its own. It was thin and white, and I did not know it for my own. Then the golden light moved, touched the pale hand, and I felt its warmth. I realised then that it was a shaft of sunlight shining through a gap in the curtains, and that the hand must be my own. I was lying in my bed, but of what had brought me there I had no knowledge, nor did I wish to know. When I tried to move my hand it seemed heavy and lifeless, but this did not trouble me. I felt myself as one drifting without feeling or will into a sea of sleep.

I do not know how long I slumbered thus, but when I awoke again my mind was clear and thoughts came crowding in on me. I remembered my fall into the stream and my return, and knew that I had been fevered and near to death. There was no pain or fever now, only the most consuming weakness. I could not so much as lift my head from the pillow, and the bedcoverings held my body down as if I were tied and bound. It seemed hard to be so weak and helpless and I was most sorry for myself, so that tears welled into my eyes and coursed down my cheeks. I could not even raise my hand to wipe them away and this made me weep the more, I, who was never one for tears. But they came as from an inexhaustible spring until I cried myself, like a babe again, to sleep.

When I woke it was to the sound of a man's voice. At first I could not call it to mind, and lay there with my eyes still closed, idly speculating as to who it might be. Then he cleared his throat with a strange chuckling sound and at once I remembered. It was Master Thomas Woodman, the surgeon, who had attended me after my fall. He had always that habit of uttering a little sound like "Aha". Half a cough and half a gasp. Like Master Uvedale's eyebrows, it had found a place in my memory.

"The fever has left her and she will recover now. This healing slumber does more than all the draughts or bloodletting." He made that sound again. "What say the Scriptures? 'If he sleep he shall do well.' Have no fear Mistress Frances, your sister is on the road back to health after all."

"Yet I am troubled," said the voice of Frances sounding indeed grave and perplexed. "Her bodily health may return, but what then?"

I wondered what her meaning might be, and almost opened my eyes, but for some reason did not.

"Aha! You mean those distempered fancies of which you spoke?" Master Woodman, too, sounded grave.

A vague memory came to tease me, and with it a hint of something ugly and threatening. I lay as if still sleeping and listened.

"She had been so unlike herself" said Frances sorrowfully. "She had turned against her brother and me. It has grieved us. And then — to creep off alone and cast herself into the stream — what can it mean but that her wits have gone?"

The words, uttered faintly as if so difficult for Frances to say, seemed to repeat themselves over and over again, beating on my ears unbearably, so that I had much ado not to cry out. The ugly thing which had lurked in the shadows was in the open now, and more ugly than I could have dreamed.

"It could have been the onset of the fever," said Master Woodman doubtfully. "You may find her mind as well as her body whole again."

"If it could be so!" breathed Frances "But I have the gravest fears. It has been long since she was truly herself."

"Well, well, 'tis a sad case, aha!" said Master Woodman. "But come what may the poor lady is in good hands. She may take broths and eggs with milk now. You will find her weak for some time—"

His voice faded and I heard Frances follow him to the door. It closed behind them. The room was empty and silent, but the voice of Frances yet echoed in my ears and I said to myself, you will never get away, Catherine, now. And the walls of the room seemed to close in on me slowly, menacingly, so that I gasped for breath and strove to raise my feeble hands to push them away.

Outside the house a man's voice called something and there was the trample of a horse's hooves. For some reason the sound brought me back to reason. The walls retreated, and I drew a deep breath. Sweat soaked me, and I was weak as a kitten, but my mind was clear, and I saw most plainly what Frances was about and why. Catherine Carey, witless and deluded would remain ever in her brother's home, her money handled by her brother. It was a pretty plan enough, and most devilishly contrived, since if I shouted my wrongs to the housetops it would be but to strengthen what they said of me, called yet another delusion. I thought how little joy the coming money had brought me — a suitor wanting only that, this final misery and fear — and wished that I had handed every penny to Ralph, going into the world a beggar, rather than this. I was assured that Ralph would never, do what I would, believe me before his wife. The creature who had sent me floundering in the stream, and whose identity was not far to seek, had done her work most cunningly. If I had died, well and good; if I lived it was as a witless thing, lost to reality. It seemed to me that it would have been better by far if I had indeed come to an end of it out there in the water.

CHAPTER VIII

For days after my return to life I sank into a kind of pit of apathy. I let them wash me, feed me, tend me as if I were a child, all in a heavy lethargy in which it seemed to matter not one jot what became of me. I have long been assured that Jennings, skilled in potions, used some witch brew to keep me in that state, since while my bodily strength increased my brain was sluggish and I had no desire for anything in the world. I might have drifted on for the rest of my life witless, as Frances had said, letting days, weeks, months slip by in a grey and endless dream.

It was the smallest thing which brought me to myself again. Of all people it was Ralph who chanced to hand me the key to my release. He came to my room one day and with him came something which pierced the heavy air, bringing clear and fresh the very fragrance of spring. It touched me so deeply, I who had felt nothing for so long, that the pleasure mingled strangely with some haunting pain was almost more than I could bear.

"Here, little one," said Ralph, his voice most unusually gentle, "make yourself a tossy ball." And he plumped a mass of cowslips on the bed.

I breathed in the clean unforgettable scent and I was a child again sitting on the grass making the yellow flowers into a ball, tossing and catching it in the sunlight. And for the first time since they had brought me here, I longed most poignantly to breathe fresh air again, to feel the sun on me. I picked up some of the flowers, holding them to my face and Ralph spoke with pleasure indulgently, as if to a child.

"I thought that they would please you, sister. The ground is yellow with them."

"I remember," I said. "It was kind to bring them to me, Ralph."

He looked down at me with something of discomfort in his face. He was no man for a sickroom in any event, also I suppose they had told him my wits were gone, so it was the more to his credit that he had done this.

"I should like well to see them growing — to sit amongst them again," I said wistfully.

"You see?" said a voice at my brother's side. "'Tis as I told you. She is as a child again."

Ralph swung round and his voice was muffled. "I would that it were otherwise," he said.

"Indeed, it is most sad," said Frances.

I turned my head on the pillow and looked at her. She had laid a hand on Ralph's arm and her face was sweetly troubled. The sunlight was on her and she was beautiful as a dream.

"I do not fully believe it even now," said Ralph. "She spoke to me like herself. She was pleased with the flowers."

"My dear," said Frances, "I would with all my heart that you were right, but there is no doubt. Do you think she would lie thus, taking heed of naught? Her strength is returning but her will has gone."

I thought how right she had been, until now. What she did not realise was that the witless one's will to live was returning, as if some stifling weight had been lifted. I spoke my brother's name, and he turned back to the bedside. "I have been fevered and ill, but I am myself again," I said. "I am weary of this room and of being treated like one whose mind is gone."

"We do but think of your wellbeing, Catherine. You are not yet strong."

"I am strong enough to know what is being done to me!"

Even as the words were spoken, I knew my utter folly. A glint of satisfaction lit Frances's face, and Ralph turned sharply away with a groan. I should find no help there.

He said with his back to me: "'Tis what you have done to yourself. To throw yourself into the stream—"

"You will not believe me," I said wearily. "I know, but I did not throw myself into the stream. I was pushed."

I strove to speak calmly, but despite myself I had begun to tremble. Frances turned to Ralph, without speaking, and shook her head. He said, in a choked voice, "I will hear no more," and blundered from the room.

When he had gone Frances came to my side and bent over me. We looked at one another, she and I, and despite all I knew I could see nothing but kindness in her gaze.

"Why are you doing this to me, Frances?" I asked. "What harm have I ever done you?"

Her face did not change in the slightest degree. Any onlooker would have said she grieved most truly for me.

"What we do is for your own good, Catherine," she said gently. "Put these vain fancies aside and all will be well." She rose, smoothing down her skirts. "I will take the flowers."

"No. Leave me those, at least."

"As you will. Try to rest, my dear," she said, and went quietly from the room.

When she had gone I drew a deep breath of the freshly scented air, and did not try to rest. As if the cowslips had brought me some message from the outside world, I knew that as soon as I could force my feeble limbs I must strive to find some means of escape, since if I remained there could be no hope for me.

I pulled myself up in bed, finding it a mighty effort, but managing to sit bolt upright at last. My heart was pounding, and I rested for a space before putting the coverings back. My head seemed strangely light, and for the first time

I discovered that my hair had been cut off, but this I did not heed, being filled with a consuming desire to reach the window, to look out on the lake, to breathe the open air. If only that much I could do I felt there might be hope for me.

I tried to stand but my legs buckled under me with no more power than if I had been a babe, and I sank in a crumpled heap to the floor. I might well have remained there had it not been for the scent of the cowslips, seeming most strangely to urge me to try again. Gripping the bedpost, I pulled myself up. The window was only a few short steps away. Gritting my teeth, I cautiously put forward a foot, though as yet clinging to my support. And in some way, being upright again, out of the stifling embrace of the bed which had been my prison for so long, confidence welled up in me, and I told myself, you can do it if you will.

With an effort I released my hold to stand, swaying dizzily, but still on my feet. So enormous was my pride in this achievement that I found myself smiling foolishly. I shuffled forward, falling once to hands and knees and having much ado to raise myself again, but gasping words of encouragement as I had, in days gone by, done to a weary horse, I was up at last. One more shuffling step, another and another, and I had reached the window.

I do not know the feelings of Lazarus when he emerged from the tomb, whether the world seemed new to him, the light too brilliant for his darkened eyes. I only knew that never in my life had I seen such an aching beauty. It was almost too much to bear, and for a moment all swam before me in a dazzling light, then my sight cleared, and leaning on the sill I looked out at the scene as if I could never have enough.

Indeed, it was worth all the struggle. Below me the lake rippled gently, all little diamonds and flecks of light. Trees which I recalled armoured in brown against the winter now were fully clothed in green, and birds were singing, as if for me, a most jubilant chorus. Taking deep breaths of the clean air for a moment I forgot all save thankfulness that I had, as it were, emerged from darkness into light. And it was as if the light poured into my being, filling me with a wonder and joy greater than I had ever thought to know.

All of a sudden it seemed that my strength drained away from me, and that the bed from which I had longed to escape now called me back again. I reached it, dragged myself up, and was asleep almost before my head touched the pillow.

It was still daylight when I awoke next, at first wondering if I had dreamed, then knowing that I had truly been on my two feet, had walked again. At first that knowledge was enough to uphold me, but soon I began to consider my position. Someone had been in the room while I slept, for the cowslips had been removed, and by the bed was a platter of bread and a bowl of broth. I wondered what would have happened if the visitor had discovered me at the window. Probably they would have all decided I was again attempting to take my life. It made me realise that I must proceed with caution, for they would never leave me to myself once they knew me able to move. And I could move, I could! The thought was precious and I hugged it to me, since whatever the obstacles, I was assured it spelt freedom for me.

Lying there, I began to plan. It was not yet that I could make my bid for escape, that was plain enough. It was also plain that I must seem to my visitors to be still sunk in that mindless sea while in secret doing all I could to exercise my limbs. Food, too, was a problem, since I was as assured as that night followed day that what they had given me had brought me to this pass. Yet eat I must, and even at that moment was assailed by pangs of hunger such as I had not known since the day they brought me here.

The broth was still warm and smelt savoury enough. I thought that I must take the risk, and submit to being fed. They would be back soon enough, Jennings with her catlike tread or Frances with her false care for me. I did not know which of the two sickened me most. But when the door opened to my surprise and joy it was Joan who entered the room. I was so relieved to see her that all thought of caution left me, I smiled and spoke her name.

Her round face, set in unfamiliar lines of trouble, lit up. She hurried to my side, bending over me, smelling of flour and herbs, and pleasant, homely things.

"My dear, my dear, you are yourself again! Praise God for all His mercies! Do but wait until I tell—"

"Hush, Joan!" I broke in urgently, clasping her hand to stay her. "Listen to me! Are we alone?"

She said with deep satisfaction, "You know who is sick of a tertian ague and seems like to meet her master soon. My lady tends her, and that is why I am here." Her underlip jutted. "They never let me so much as look on you before."

I said in a whisper: "Joan, they plot against me. I must escape from them. Will you help me?"

Her face closed like a shutter, and I thought how well they had done their work, since even she believed me to be under delusions.

She said gently: "Let me give you your food, and do not trouble your head with fancies. None shall harm you. You have nothing to fear."

"Nothing to fear? And I have been harmed already, and most unkindly. I have been kept here—"

"But for your own good, my dear. You were too weak to do otherwise. Also—"

"Also I might try to take my own life," I said with bitterness. "Oh, yes, I know that is the tale. But I did not think you would have believed it, Joan." and I added, half to myself: "Martha would never have done so. It was an ill day for me when they sent her away."

All unwittingly I had found the right words. Joan's face, always of a ruddy complexion, deepened in colour, and her bosom swelled.

"Martha would do as we all have done, Mistress Catherine what was said to be best for you. Nor, for that matter, were we given any choice." She snorted angrily. "When John brought you in more dead than alive it was not for us to care for you, we who had known you from a babe. Oh no, it was that black creature who must nurse you, tend you, even prepare your food."

"I knew it. I knew that was it," I said, and pulling myself up in bed and grasping her arm, I strove most urgently to convince her. For indeed it seemed to me that here lay my only hope. "Do you not see that is why I have been lying here like a log? You hate her, you said she had sold her soul to the devil, yet you will not believe she works against me."

"Of her I can believe anything," she answered with a shudder. "But then — oh my dear, why did you do it? What drove you to such a pass?"

I looked at her steadily. "You mean the stream?"

She nodded, her eyes round and fearful. "What took you there alone?"

A wave of anger took me, and I gripped her arm with such force that she gave a little cry.

"It was a spring morning. I wearied of the house and wandered as far as the stream. And, before God, I did not throw myself in. I was struck from behind and thrust into the water. Why will no one believe that I speak the truth?"

Releasing her arm I sank back, the taste of defeat sour in my mouth. How empty a tale it sounded, and what chance had I of gaining belief?

Fondling her chin, she asked in a troubled voice: "Did you see who did it?"

"No. By the time I dragged myself out no one was there. So you see, there is only my word for it. And my word, it seems, is not enough."

"'Tis not that," she muttered, half ashamed. "But we thought 'twas the fever speaking. And who would do such a thing?"

"Who, indeed?" I said and held her gaze.

It was as if she had known all along and feared to face it. She clapped a hand to her mouth as if to stifle a cry and looked fearfully towards the door. Then, seeming to come to a decision she turned to me.

"I know not what to say. We will talk of this later, since please God she will not be recovered for some days. But now take your broth before it be stone cold. You need have no fear, since no hands touched it but these."

She propped me up and fed me, without uttering another word, yet when she left me I felt a ray of hope. And I prayed that Jennings's malady would not quickly pass and was most thankful for it, to such a pass had she brought me, I who had never wished a fellow creature ill before.

Days passed, and I saw neither Frances nor her maid, and it was as if that space of time was a gift laid in my hands. Joan continued to tend me, and I ate and drank all she brought me with confidence, and my strength was renewed. I could walk around my room limping almost as quickly as of old two or three times a day, and though my limbs might protest they obeyed my bidding. I would stretch my thin arms like a bird trying its wings, and I told myself that soon, soon, this bird would be ready to leave its cage. For with deep thankfulness I knew myself to be no longer alone. Joan's doubts were finally overcome, and however fearful for my safety she might be I was assured of her help.

In our talks she had made clear to me what I had been unable to understand — the fact that all the household had without hesitation taken my fall to be no accident. What Joan told me made it certain that my own suspicions were founded on a rock.

Jennings, it seemed, had said that she went to the stream that day in search of some plant which grew near the water, and which she used in one of the beauty lotions she prepared for her mistress. As her story went, she had seen me on the bridge, wringing my hands and like one distraught. A moment after she had seen me throw myself in. Rushing off for help she had met John, herself continuing to the house to prepare for my coming, though she feared it might not be as a living creature.

"She did not, then, attempt to save me?" I asked.

Joan snorted. "As she said, she felt her strength not equal to the task. Where you fell the banks were steep. And there, at least, she spoke truth. But as to strength I think she has more than any of us would dream." And again I felt that violent breathtaking blow which had sent me toppling forward.

"With her master to aid her, God save us all!" said Joan, with one of her fearful glances towards the door. "And alas, 'tis plain he is not for taking her yet, since she mends apace."

"Then we must lose no time." For by now my plans were complete. "I must go. You will help me, Joan? I dare wait no longer."

"But, my lamb, how can you? Weak as you still are how far would you gain? You would fall by the wayside, and I with your death on my conscience."

"You would have worse on your conscience should I remain here. I thought that you, at least, would believe me and help me. And I am strong enough now."

"I do believe you, and I will help you, only let it not be yet. I beg of you, wait until the time is right. Then—"

"The time is now," I said. "Useless to argue — my mind is made up. I shall go as soon as Frances and Ralph are abed. All I ask if that you will tell me when the way is clear. You must know nothing — you understand? Nothing. I would not have you suffer for me."

Tears brimmed over Joan's eyes and ran unheeded down her plump cheeks. She looked at me piteously and clasped her hands.

"What shall I do? Either way there seems a bottomless pit. If you would but take one of us with you, or even tell me where you plan to go!"

"It is best that you should not know, and you must seem as surprised as the others. Now, here is what I need from you."

She hearkened, and mouth and eyes grew round and large as she wrung her hands: "They will bring you back. Your last state will be worse than the first."

"If I fail I fail, and I must take the consequences. But if my plan succeeds there is only one place where they will look for me, and they will not find me there. Only bring me the clothing and some food, help me to dress, and be sure the side door is open. Bolt it when I have gone, and do as I said with the window. I climbed down the ivy many times when I was a child. Ralph will remember. Break a little away — for the rest I will see to myself."

"The maddest of all mad schemes!" mourned Joan, shaking her head so that a large tear hanging from the end of her nose shot from its moorings to land on her broad bosom with a plop.

"And why should it not be, since my wits are gone?" I asked, laughing. For somehow with the thought of action my spirits had soared, and I found myself saying as I had once said to my brother. "I am not afraid."

At last I prevailed on Joan, though sorely against her will, and when she left me, lay running over my plans in my mind. A few hours grace was all I needed, and please God they would be deceived into granting me that. For some reason I thought of Roger Frampton and his offer of help, wondering if he would, indeed have helped me in my adventure. But the path on which Catherine Carey's feet were set she must travel alone, and if, as Joan feared, she fell by the wayside she would have only herself to blame.

Leaden footed the hours passed. I could not rest. My body, as if impatient for action, jerked under the covering and I was wrapped in tingling heat. When the door opened at last I almost wrecked all by leaping up and crying Joan's name. Just in time the whisper of silken skirts and that faint perfume saved me, and I closed my eyes.

Frances spoke my name. I made no reply, but it was hard to lie as if sleeping while, for what seemed an age, she stood there gazing down on me. That strange, sweet scent which ever hung about her hair and garments reminded me of that first time when she had bent to embrace me, and I had liked her well. I felt a pang of sorrow for that which was irretrievably lost, then sorrow was followed by fear lest Joan, thinking me alone, should come now and all be discovered. Under the coverings I clenched my fists, praying for Frances to go.

She bent over me so that I could feel her breath warm on my face and laid a hand on my brow.

"You are fevered again, Catherine," she said, as if knowing me to be awake. "'Tis well that Jennings is herself again. Tomorrow she shall return to nursing you."

The hand was removed from a brow which, in truth, was burning. The silken skirts whispered away. I longed to leap from my bed, to follow her, to assure myself that she was safely in her room, but I forced myself to lie still. And the moments passed, leaving me still alone.

* * *

Time went heavily by. I began to fret, telling myself that Joan, unwilling conspirator that she was, had finally decided against helping me, and the morrow, with Jennings on her feet again, would be too late. I could not know whether she had, in truth, put her soul in pawn, or if she had powers out of this world. I did know that her devotion to Frances was such that she would stop at nothing to aid her against me. I thought how strange a couple they were, like darkness and light, so that Frances herself might have been the witch, and that other her black familiar, so my thoughts were not much less hag-ridden than those of Martha and Joan.

Would she never come? I moved restlessly in my bed and felt the sweat trickle down my body. I heard Ralph stumble up to bed, then all the house was still, as if it waited with me. I had all but given up hope when the door was opened most cautiously and Joan, in a frightened whisper, breathed my name.

The reaction from my fears was so great that for a moment I lay with a pounding heart fighting for breath. Then I came to myself and threw back the coverings. The moon gave us light enough for Joan to aid me with shaking fingers, murmuring her fears the while. When we had done, a thin boy in hodden grey had taken Catherine Carey's place, and I smiled, thinking of all the heroines of romance who had set off thus disguised.

"I should never have helped you. May the good God forgive me! Oh, 'tis the most hare-brained scheme, madness!" wept Joan, wringing her hands again. "Will you not think again even now?"

Unheeding, I kissed her, put aside her clinging arms, and with my shoes in my hand and my night gear and bundle of food under my arm I crept out into the silent house and most cautiously down the stairs. The first hazard was passed.

Out of the darkness came a small movement, no more than a rustle, yet enough to freeze my blood. They knew. All the time they knew and lay in wait for me here. I shrank back, with difficulty repressing a cry, and something rough and warm pressed against my legs. It was Ralph's dog Garth, by reason of age allowed houseroom at night, as I should have remembered. Thank God he knew me and made only the faintest whimpering sound of recognition. Even that echoed most shockingly loud in the silence. I spoke to him in a whisper, fondling his ears and bidding him lie down again. He obeyed, flopping heavily with a sigh, and I moved like a ghost to reach the little side door.

It was a most calm and lovely night bathed in moonlight, more fitting for some beauty meeting a lover than to show up my uncouth form. But there was no time to think of my appearance or of aught else other than making good my escape while yet I might. I crept to the wall under my bedroom window, from there moving towards the lake walking in fear, since I imagined I felt eyes peering at me from every window.

At the water's edge I flung down my night gear all of a heap and pulled off my clumping shoes and woollen hose. It did not matter that the grass was trodden by my progress but now I must leave no further tracks. The lake was said to be, in the centre, of unknown depth, with tales that those lost there were never recovered, hidden forever in the green darkness. If, for the time it took me to gain a sanctuary they thought me thus lost it was all I asked.

It being the only way to hide my next movements, I stepped into the water, shallow here and so cold that I felt goosepimples start out all over me. Glancing back once I saw my heap of clothing, ghostly in the moonlight, then I was round the curve of the lake, and there was only myself, with nothing of my past to be seen at all.

I waded on until I reached a spot where bushes grew down to the water, and here, I thought, would be the spot for me to set out in earnest. I stepped out of the water and into the shadows.

Underfoot was still a carpet of last year's leaves. I sat myself down, rubbing my numb feet into a glow with my kerchief, pulled on the rough hose which wrinkled sadly about my thin limbs, and put on the heavy shoes. One thing remained. Pushing my hand under the leaves I scooped up the damp soil and rubbed it well into my face. A dirty youth might better escape notice if the dirt served to hide the fact that his face was scarred. I smoothed back the leaves with care lest the search should come this far and stepped on to a tiny mossy path winding its way through the hazels. The moss was springy and would leave no trace, and most fortunately I had played in these woods so much in my childhood that I knew the way. Stepping delicately like Agag I started off, knowing my goal and that I must reach it before dawn.

I found it much harder going than I had thought, nor had I ever known that a wood held so many sounds at night. There were rustlings and creakings, and once so heavy a crashing through the undergrowth that I shrank back in terror. But the sound died away, and no creature came to harm me, whatever it was being in all probability as frightened as myself. After all, it was I who was the intruder, and so long as no fellow-human crossed my path, birds and animals should cause me no complaint.

All of a sudden, I was swept by such exhaustion that I sank to the ground, dropping my head to my knees. I meant it to be a moment's rest, but it was a long time before I could force my unwilling limbs to move again. The breeches outgrown by Joan's son were lined with leather, and held me down like armour. I dreaded the thought of dragging myself up, and although I knew that by lingering I lost what advantage I might have gained still I sat. Indeed, if a great owl had not swooped by me so low that it all but brushed my bowed head I might well have stayed there until morning. As it was, startled, I got to my feet, and once up staggered on. And now I found myself in most strange case, for my body seemed to float while my feet were so leaden that to lift them at all was almost beyond my power. I think my mind wandered, for at times it seemed that I was again making the weary journey back from the stream, and I said, you put one foot before the other, one before the other, and at last you will find rest.

Quite suddenly I was out of the woodland and on a stretch of grass, all silvered by moonlight, and looking fit for a fairy dancing floor. My brain cleared, and I was filled with joy, knowing my goal was almost reached. A few steps more and I should see the house, long empty save for a pair of deaf old servants where Martin, my childhood playfellow, had lived. I knew the place as well as the Grange, and there were outbuildings where I could sleep without fear of discovery. I had Joan's bundle of food, and I knew where a spring welled up in a corner of the yard. I felt that here, at last, I might safely rest.

I crossed the grass coming to an overgrown drive, where the trees had crowded forward making a tunnel of darkness, curving to that empty house where Martin, I thought, would never have grudged me sanctuary had he known my plight. I rounded the curve, so full of thankfulness that even my weariness was, for the time, forgotten, and came upon the house. And from the house which should have stood dark and deserted there shone a blaze of light.

CHAPTER IX

At first I stared, incredulous, telling myself that it was the moonlight shining on the windows which had deceived me, but the moon was sinking back of the house, and the light truly came from within. Tears of weak anger ran down my face and were salt on my lips. It was too much, the cruellest blow that fate could have dealt me. For years the place had been an empty shell with Martin on his travels, wherever they might be. I had heard no hint of his most ill-timed return.

Judging by the number of lighted windows he was far from being alone, and I thought peevishly that he could not have done better had it been his wish to thwart me. When I looked again, some of the windows were now blank, though that of the hall, the largest, yet poured out its stream of golden light. As I watched that, too, became dark, so that now the house was as I had thought to find it. I had been, indeed, only just in time — a few short moments longer and my fool's paradise would have been untouched.

One thing was certain. I dare not now risk the outbuildings, nor could I go near the house without fear of discovery. It was equally certain that I could walk no farther, since I had much ado even to stand, so weak was I. I thought bitterly that I might as well give up my foolish bid for freedom here and now. And then, with relief and joy I recalled the sum-merhouse, where we used to play and the long-legged spiders which lurked in the corners most hatefully. Martin, devilish boy, had once driven me to the point of frenzy by putting one down the back of my neck. To this day I could feel the horrible crawling thing, and see his nose suddenly dripping blood as I swung my clenched fist at him. Well, there would still be spiders, but I had faced worse perils since then. The place had been rickety and was by now probably little more than a ruin, but it was far enough from the house and its mysterious company to spell safety. It would do for me.

The worst of it was that it meant another journey, uphill now, since it had been built to afford a view of woodland and river, but merely recalling it seemed to refresh me with the new hope it gave of shelter and, for a space, security. But the slope was steeper far than I had remembered, and before I gained the top my lungs seemed like to burst, and there was a darkness before my eyes, so that at first I was deceived into thinking that my refuge had vanished, like so many of my hopes. And then my sight cleared, and I saw it outlined against the sky. No palace could have seemed more beautiful. There was no door, only an opening in the circular walls roofed by thatch where the sparrows built their nests. I stum-bled in, stretched myself on the bench which, as I recalled, ran round it, sinking into the hard wood as if it had been a goose feather bed. Instantly I fell asleep.

* * *

When I awoke it was to sunlight and a chorus of bird song. At first I could not think where I might be, and lay wonder-ing why there were no curtains to my bed, and why it was so cruelly hard. Then I remembered, and was suddenly as joyous as if every bird stretched its throat for me. I had made good my escape, and pride filled me at my own enterprise and endurance. Foolish creature that I was and puffed with self-conceit, I thought that my troubles were over, and the path lay clear ahead. It was a bright bubble, and like others of its kind vanished all too soon.

Attempting to sit up I found my cramped limbs an aching torment. My lovely moment passed, leaving me chilled, hungry, and drained of all confidence. If I could not reach the Chase and Martha, as I had planned, there was little hope for me, and even if I did reach her, Ralph would doubtless think of her and come a-seeking. For now my scheme, the idea of his thinking me lost in the dark lake, seemed one that would not deceive a child.

Despair, I think, might well have had its way with me then had I not remembered my bundle of food. The very thought of it made me realise my utter emptiness, putting all else out of my mind. Groaning with pain I dragged myself up, to sit for a moment with a roaring in my ears. Then it passed, and I looked wildly around me. Surely in that last climb up the slope I had not let my bundle fall! But it was not beside me on the seat, and the dusty floor was empty too. So gnawing was my hunger that if I had felt able for the short journey I would have taken myself down to the house and begged for scraps, heedless of discovery. I dropped my hand heavily to my side, and it fell on the bundle, lying half under the seat, where it must have dropped the night before.

There was bread, meat, a lump of cheese and two large apples. They were the old greasy pippins from the orchard, those that kept until apples came again. Their skins grew thicker, more wrinkled, as the winter passed, but they still made very good eating, and that morning they helped to make me a meal fit for the gods. Recklessly I ate every crumb and both apples, down to the stems, and not in all my life had I enjoyed a meal so much.

With a full belly, despair was banished and I told myself that after all things might be worse. Already I was feeling less cramped, and with any luck might be able to set off shortly on my travels again. I could take to the woods, and the Chase was not so far away. Removed from the house as it was, I had chosen my hiding place well. No one would come here, and after a short rest I should be fit to go on my way. Fullfed and secure in my seclusion I stretched my arms and yawned. And from quite near to my refuge I heard a man laugh, the sound of voices, the barking of a dog.

It is well-nigh miraculous to what one can be driven by sheer unthinking panic. One moment I could scarce have put a foot before the other, the next I had leapt up, and, it seemed, in the same moment rolled myself under the seat, my face pressed to the wall. There was the chill damp of the floor seeping through my clothing, the smell of dust and decay and the knowledge that I must not move a fraction, must scarcely breathe to avoid discovery.

There was a sudden clamour, the dog barking with wild excitement, and I thought bitterly that I might as well have been taken on my feet as dragged into the open like some poor hunted creature. But a voice called imperatively: "Here, boy! Cease that damned clamour. Down, I say! Down!"

"What ails him?" asked another laughing voice. "A rat i' the arras?"

"Rats, no doubt. But as to arras! — see for yourselves."

The light was obscured as men came in. From where I lay I could see nothing, but from the tramping feet I thought there might be five or six of them. The boards creaked above me as they seated themselves, so that I was imprisoned by unseen legs, and thought with foolish inward laughter how amazed they would be if I chose to make my presence felt. For indeed it seemed the height of absurdity that of all places they should have chosen this.

"I grant you 'tis secluded enough," said a voice above my head, "but for God's sake let us make haste. This bench is most damnably hard, and I have a long ride ahead of me."

"Hard benches are as a bed of roses compared with what you might suffer in the future," said another.

"And sore buttocks little enough compared with a stretched neck, which friends of a certain gentleman must be prepared to suffer."

"Ah, well, while my head sits on my shoulders I am ever one for my small comforts," said the man who had spoken first.

There was a chorus of laughter. Under its cover I cautiously pushed a finger down the side of my face to brush away some loathsome thing. Rats or not, the spiders were still there in force.

"I think, gentlemen," said a new voice, deep and with a note of authority, "we should not waste time. We have far more urgent matters to discuss than plots which may or may not take place."

"Colonel Sidney is right. We are not here—"

The next words were lost to me. So many years since I had heard the last speaker, yet instantly I knew him. Martin, my old playfellow — there was no surprise in finding him here, since this was his home, but what company was he keeping, and what were the matters to be discussed which called for such secrecy? It seemed that he, like another, might be setting his feet on dangerous ground, and that once again I was to become an eavesdropper.

"Yes, but what if there be such a scheme?" a loud voice enquired.

"A fatal disservice to our cause. I would have no part in it," said Sidney's voice.

"Nor I. No part at all," said Martin.

There was a chorus of half jeering dissent.

"You are too nice by half."

"This is no time for Trimmers!"

"If it be truly in train naught will stop it now."

"Nevertheless, I hold to what I said," came Martin's defiant voice, and clearly as if I looked upon him, I knew his jaw must be jutted and his lips were obstinately set. Once his mind was made up it would take more than a jeer or two to move him.

"What you fear," broke in the loud voice, "is that it might not stop short at apprehending the king's person?"

"I do. And I am not one for murder, and that of a damnably coldblooded kind. Lying in wait—"

The chorus of expostulation swelled again, sinking into silence as a calm voice spoke.

"I agree. His death in such fashion would serve to make him a martyr and do untold harm to our cause, which is the cause of the land we love."

A new voice spoke bluntly. "Sidney is right, but here is a pother for naught. Assassination is no part of the plan. His Grace would not have it otherwise."

"Even so, it is a skulking business. I would that all could be in the open," said Martin.

The other man gave a short laugh. "Do not we all? That day will come, never fear. The thing is to be ready for that same day."

The voices went on, now a jumble to me, so lost was I in amazement at what I heard. Could it be true that they had spoken of the king, had here, in this quiet spot talked of plots to seize him, or worse? And not only was it true but Martin was in some way involved. I thought of what befell plotters who were taken, and a shudder ran through me, and I had to clench my fists until the nails cut into the palms of my hands to control it.

In the tumult of my thoughts I heard little more of what they were saying, until I found that they were rising to go. I lay scarce daring to breathe, realising for the first time what my discovery now might mean, for it seemed to me that men who spoke of such matters would give a listener short shrift. But they were clattering out, and I felt a glimmer of hope.

"I know, I know," said a hearty voice, apparently in response to some statement. "As I said, the day will come, and when it does, my stout fellows in the west will be ready, and so I told His Grace."

"True enough, Trenchard. In the west they love him, but what of London? No more Shaftesbury and his brisk boys now."

"Oh, as to that—"

The voices faded in the distance. The footsteps died away, yet still I lay like a hare in its form, afraid to make the slightest move. There were faint sounds, the creaking of boards, something rustling in the thatch overhead, a dog barking, God be thanked, in the distance. I would have remained in my coffinlike prison until dusk, but a villainous attack of cramp sent such spasms of pain through me that move I must. Gasping with pain I crawled from my hiding place, lifting my face to the light and blinking like an owl. Gripping the seat for support and uttering whimpering little cries of pain, at last I stood more or less erect. And, with a shock which seemed to stop my heart I looked full into the amazed face of a man who was stepping into the hut.

It was as if all strength left me. I did not swoon, was fully conscious of the man's figure, dark against the sunlight, of my own body sinking, quite gently to the floor. It was as if all hope had been removed, and without it I was lost, without power or will. If he had raised a hand to strike me I should not have so much as flinched, but for what seemed an age he stood silent and motionless.

At last he spoke, and I, who had not recognised face or figure again knew his voice. He said, quite calmly. "How long have you been there?"

I tried to speak, to tell him who I was, but I could find no voice. His calmness vanished. In two strides he reached me, took my shoulder in a most painful grip, and plucked me to my feet. It seemed a strange thing to me that he did not know me then, since his touch, rough as it was, sent a thrill through my body such as it had not known for years.

"By God!" he gasped, and his eyes blazed down at me. "You shall answer me. Creeping spy that you are, you need not think by feigning weakness to escape."

He raised his arm and I cowered away with a whimper of fright. His arm dropped, without touching me, but he still held me. He said, half with contempt, half with a kind of shame. "I shall not strike you, poor bundle of rags that you are, but answer me you shall."

I said hoarsely. "I am no spy."

"Then why are you here, and for how long? What did you hear?"

"I heard naught," I said sulkily. "I am running away from my master, who beats me. I came here a few moments back to rest awhile."

"You lie," he said. "None came here lately. You were here for a purpose, and I will know who sent you or you will wish you had not been born."

"As God hears me, no man sent me. I did lie in saying I was not here before, but I truly thought it but a place to rest."

I half choked back a sob, feeling a great desolation of spirit, part from sheer exhaustion, part because this, my first meeting with Martin after the passage of years should find him looking on me with scorn and suspicion. Oh, I know I should have revealed myself to him then, but I looked down at my dirty clothing now richly decked with cobwebs, and a foolish pride held me back. My scarred face would be enough. At least the first time he knew me it should not be in this guise.

"So!" he said, frowning. "You came here to rest. When we — my friends and I — came here—"

"I crawled under the seat."

"A very frank and open action for one who is no spy," said he, with an unpleasant smile.

I flushed angrily. "How was I to know for what purpose you had come here? I hid only because I thought that if found I should be sent back."

"That sounds reasonable. Nonetheless — send you back you say? Back where?"

"To my master. You would not know him," I muttered.

He laughed unpleasantly. "At last we are in agreement since I am assured there is no such person."

"Well, do not believe me! I am not answerable to you!" I said, a spark of defiance lit in me by his manner. He had often been unbearable as a boy, and as a man he seemed even worse, and forgetting my position I stared him in the face. It was a mistake. I saw the contempt in the grey eyes I knew so well change to a flicker of interest, and he frowned, as if trying to recapture an elusive memory. I hastily dropped my gaze, but could still feel his on me.

"This master of yours," he said softly, "what manner of work did you for him?"

"Anything I was bid," I said sulkily.

"Be more particular. Did you, for instance, tend the swine?"

"From time to time," I answered, for I had, indeed, had dealings with those animals though not in life, and I thought of hams hanging in the chimney, and even at that juncture my mouth watered.

"A swineherd," he said musingly. "Show me your hands."

Unwillingly I extended them, glad to see how grimed they were. He relaxed his grip on my shoulder and took them letting them lie palm upwards on his own wide palm.

"Here be delicate hands for a swineherd, in truth," he said. "There is dirt, but I warrant its removal would show no signs of toil. Master Spy, had I not known you for a liar before these would have betrayed you."

I snatched them away, feeling the blood burn in my cheeks, but I would not look at him.

"There is also the fact that I have most certainly seen you before," he said. "Though I cannot at present recall where. However, we shall have time to remedy that."

"What — what do you mean?" I stammered.

"Why, that you must be my — for want of a better word — guest, for the time," he answered, again with that hateful smile, for which I could willingly have slapped his face. "If you thought to leave here bearing the fruits of your spying you must think again."

The mocking voice changed, becoming laden with such menace that I shrank back. And again I thought how the years had changed him.

"You need not be afraid," he said, with contempt. "I shall not harm you. But neither, by God, shall you be allowed to harm my friends and me."

"And God knows I have no desire to do so," I told him wearily. "But do what you will — I am in no case to stop you."

"Now, where—" he began, to break off suddenly, swinging round to the doorway.

"Did you find my gloves? You were so long that I came in search of you," said a deep voice I had heard from my hiding place. "Have you fallen into a train of thought, or — great heaven, what have we here?"

It seemed that I had gained the power of the Gorgon's head to turn men into stone. For what seemed an endless space we stood there in the dusty sunlight as if we were effigies, I drooping and dirty in my uncouth garb, Martin with his mouth open as if to speak, and that other with eyes fixed on me which seemed to strip me bare.

CHAPTER X

It is strange to think how clearly I remember him. Exhausted, weak as I was, he impressed me so deeply that even now, after all the years, I see him standing there with that clear gaze on me. Men have miscalled Algernon Sidney, those not fit to blacken his boots have striven to blacken his name, and he was not perfect — who amongst us is? — but I saw it in him even then, an integrity of purpose, something in his spirit not to be subdued by anything which life could do to him. I longed only to tell him the truth, assured that he would not condemn me. But it was Martin who spoke first, and with bitterness.

"Of all places I would have sworn that this would be safe from spies. Yet this fellow, sent by God knows who, was hiding here, and must have heard our every word. I would have cut off my right hand—"

He sounded youthful again as he turned to the other, like a schoolboy expecting punishment. Sidney's face, stern in repose, lightened to a smile, and he laid a hand on Martin's shoulder.

"Do not blame yourself, dear lad. A listener was scarce what we desired, but at least he has been discovered and we can see that our words are not passed on." He looked me up and down, raising his brows. "If, indeed, this be a spy. To me he looks more like a beggar, and a half starved one at that. He may be here by chance."

"By pure chance," I said eagerly. "I came here but to rest awhile. I have told him so, but he will not believe me."

The two men looked at one another strangely.

"You see?" said Martin.

Sidney stroked his cheek which, I was to find, was a habit of his when perplexed. He looked at me again, this time with speculation in his gaze.

"Indeed I see, or rather, I hear. A strange manner of speech for one so dirty and ill clad."

"And under the grime hands smooth and soft enough for one who tends the swine," said Martin with a short laugh.

"You do not think," said Sidney, gently, "that it would be as well to tell us the truth?"

I knew it, and again pride held me back.

"I am no spy. For the rest what use to tell you, since you will not believe me?" And I shot Martin a resentful glance. Again, it was a mistake. He scowled, muttering that he knew he had seen me before, but where?

"Well," said Sidney, "if I might advise you, take him to the house, give him food, and cleanse him. That might well aid your memory." He turned to me. "You were in need of rest, were you not? Then you will not be averse to remaining with this gentleman for a time. You will not be ill-treated, but we cannot, for the present, let you go."

"It seems that I have little choice."

"None at all," agreed Martin. "Follow us, and do not think to escape."

He might have saved his breath. We went out into the sunlight, I stumbling at their heels.

"You are lame?" asked Sidney, turning. "Truly, Martin, our dreaded spy is in poor shape. Here, boy, take my arm."

I muttered that I had fallen and hurt my ankle, which was near enough to the truth, and took his arm with gratitude. It was as well, since earth and sky were beginning to whirl about me, and the latter part of our journey I do not recall at all.

When I came to myself I found I was alone, huddled in a chair. Looking round me I saw panelled walls, a long oak table thick with dust. A man's cloak had been flung over me, but I saw by my hands that I was still uncleansed. It was just as well, since Martin, who had forgotten so much, would know me when my face was clean. What would happen then I scarcely cared. It was enough to lean back and rest.

The window was open, and I heard the sound of hooves and men's voices.

"Farewell for a while, dear lad," said Sidney's voice. "And have a care. This is no matter for you to be caught up in. 'Tis far too haphazard, and I pray God will die stillborn."

"So long as I have not unwittingly involved you." I heard Martin reply. "I would die rather than bring trouble on you."

"I know, but put it from your mind," answered Sidney.

"If 'tis discovered I shall be brought into it as the scape-goat in any case. Why, I had only to put my head out of a window to be accused of inciting a riot. Where there is a plot there is Sidney the republican at its head. And plots I loathe like the plague."

"Perhaps you would be safer out of the country for a time. Would you not consider it?"

Sidney laughed. "Why, there is one matter on which His Majesty and I are agreed. We neither of us intend to go on our travels again. This poor land is my home, and when I leave it again it will be for my final journey." He spoke quite cheerfully, yet I felt a momentary chill. Outside Martin murmured something I could not catch, and I heard Sidney laugh again.

"Well, have a care of your captive — I fancy an innocent eavesdropper. We will meet again as soon as I am able. God keep you, and farewell."

I heard him ride away, but when, moved by curiosity I peeped from the window I saw Martin still standing there. Unseen I was able to look my fill, and I thought how greatly he had changed. He had been gay, giving little thought for the morrow; now he looked bowed down with care. I wondered what had so changed him, making him older than his years. As if he felt my eyes on him he turned suddenly, glancing up at the window. I shrank back, my cheeks burning, and returned to my chair.

I began to wonder what would be the best thing for me to do, knowing that now discovery would be forced on me. In any case, I could not long have continued thus, for I have never fully believed those tales of women masquerading as men. If no man was privy to their secret so many simple matters of everyday would serve to unmask them. It was not only the putting on of a manly swagger, a deepened voice. There was the problem of where I should be put for the night, the fact that sooner or later I must cleanse my face. Like it or not, Martin would learn my secret, and perhaps he would think me mad like the rest.

My fruitless thoughts were interrupted by the opening of the door. Expecting Martin I glanced up sharply, but it was a stranger who entered, and a grim looking one at that. If his face had been carved from rock it could hardly have looked more set in lines of disapproval. The most rigid of puritans would have found him well to their taste in his sober serving man's garb, his cropped hair, and lips that looked as if they knew not how to smile. In silence he set down on the table a platter of food and a napkin, together with a bowl of water.

"My master bids you eat and cleanse yourself," he said, in a disgruntled voice. "He will speak with you later." The door closed behind him, and I heard the turning of a key. Well, matters were decided for me now, and at least, thank God, I could wash a face stiff with grime. The water was jet black by the time I had finished, but it refreshed me, and I fell on the food.

The light faded, and still Martin did not come. Now that I had determined to throw myself on his mercy I longed to see him, for surely, surely he would not refuse to help me.

The solemn man came in, removing what he had brought without a word. The dusk grew thicker and the room was very quiet. I started violently as the door opened, and Martin came into the room.

"You are ready now to speak with me?" he said. "I will call for lights."

"No! Pray do not," I said hastily, and my hand went to my cheek.

"Why? I have a desire to see your face, my most mysterious guest."

"I beg of you!" I heard my voice rising, and even in the half-light knew he was looking at me with surprise.

"As you will," he said indifferently. "But speak to the point. I am weary and out of spirits." And I heard him sigh.

"Out there you said you had seen me before."

He said nothing and I, feeling as I was plunging into deep waters, spoke his name. He moved suddenly, gripping my shoulders, so close that I could feel his breath on my face, but still he did not speak.

I said in a shaken voice: "Martin, Martin, do you still not know me?"

His hands dropped from my shoulders. He staggered back, crashing into the table. Then, in a whisper: "Great God Almighty!"

"Do you not know me?" I asked again.

He put a hand to his eyes. "You speak with the voice of Catherine Carey. But Catherine Carey is dead."

"Is that why you are so much afraid? There is no need. I am Catherine Carey, and not her ghost." And since he still remained motionless I went to him and laid my hands on his breast. "You give poor welcome to an old playfellow, Martin."

He gave a kind of sob and crushed my hands in his. I raised my face to his without thought, and our lips met and clung. He was not so completely changed after all. We moved apart, both, I think, somewhat shaken by the fervour of our embrace. It was Martin who spoke first.

"Am I out of my wits, or do I dream?" he whispered. "You seem flesh and blood, you speak with Catherine's voice. But how that may be when I have this moment returned from the Grange, where they mourn your death — "

"Let me sit down," I said rather faintly, "And I will tell you how it befell."

I sank into the chair, trembling. When he had kissed me it had all seemed so easy, as if I had come home. Now I was not so sure, and if he did not believe me it would be more than I could bear.

"I planned it all, my escape, leaving my night clothes at the lake edge," I said. "I needed time, and it seemed thus I might gain it if they thought me dead."

"But in God's name, why? There is Ralph, scarce able to speak for sorrow, Mistress Frances blaming herself—"

"She? Blaming herself?"

"That she left you unguarded."

"Since, I suppose, my wits were gone and I might well try to end my life," I said bitterly.

I felt him start. "You knew? You knew they feared it?"

"I knew that so long as they could keep me helpless, supposed witless, my inheritance could be handled by Ralph. I knew that, Martin, if naught else."

"Ralph?" he said, with incredulity. "Ralph would do such a thing? Never in this world!"

"It was not Ralph. He was deceived, like the rest."

"Then who?" He stilled. "No, you need not tell me. You accuse his wife."

I said nothing, but desolation enfolded me. Martin had seen Frances. So well I could imagine how she had looked, her beautiful eyes filled with grief, and how all men would believe her and seek to comfort her.

"Then this masquerade of yours was brought on through fear of the lady I saw today," he said slowly. "Are you sure that you are not misled?"

I gripped the arms of my chair. "I am very sure. But if you, too, think me deluded—"

"I know not what to think. Do you realise that this is the second time I have been told of your death?"

"The second time?"

"After your fall I tried many times to see you, but they said you were too ill. Then I was sent to Holland, and there heard the report of your death. After that nothing seemed of particular consequence. If I had not met Sidney — but that does not signify. My wild oats were a sorry crop enough, but why I am talking of myself at this stage God knows. You must tell me more if I am to understand."

"To believe, you mean. If you remember me at all you should know I am not wont to lie."

"I know it well," he answered gently. "But they said that after an illness you had become distraught, turning against those who loved you."

"It sounds so much more real than the truth," I said wearily. "I doubt if I shall convince even you."

"You could try," he said.

I willed myself to calmness and told him in detail, only omitting the fact that Frances loved Frampton, but telling of Ralph's difficulties, of my treatment, and how I made my plan to escape. My voice seemed to go on and on, flat and expressionless, as if I spoke of one other than myself, and he heard me to the end, without a word.

"And so I came here. And the rest you know."

"Yes," he answered. "The rest I know."

I huddled back in my chair, convinced that I had made my throw and lost. With the die so heavily weighted against me what else could I expect? The room was now in complete darkness, and Martin's face only a blur. The silence went on and on. An owl called mournfully outside, but we two in the room were very still, and the house was still around us.

At last he spoke, and at his words it was as if I came back to life.

"I am glad," he said quietly, "that fate brought you here, and to me. For indeed, Catherine, I think I am the one man who would believe you are not deceived."

"I—" My voice broke off, and I could find no words. As if I had put the question he said. "Why? Well, let us say because I knew you of old, and cannot think you so greatly changed."

My voice returned. "I am changed, Martin, greatly changed, in my ways and in my appearance. You — you will not think me pretty now."

"Yet I fancy the Catherine I knew still remains," he said.

His words stung me into thinking what a coward I had become, yet I was most thankful for them. I held out my hands to him in the darkness, and he took them, holding them warmly to his breast.

"Call for lights, Martin, if you will," I said.

"Very woman that you are, you are still wondering what effect your looks will have on me, as if that mattered. But wait, I will not be long."

He went from the room. I put a hand to my cheek, feeling the puckered skin, thinking childishly that when he returned, I could thus hide it from him. But it would have to come, and I forced myself to sit upright with my hands clasped in my lap. I was more afraid than when I had crept from the Grange or lay awaiting discovery in the hut.

A golden light shone through the open doorway. Martin came in alone, placed the lamp on the table, and closed the door. Coward again, I dropped my eyes lest I should see revulsion in his.

"Now," I said, still without looking at him, "you will see why I preferred the darkness. My voice, at least, is unchanged."

He came and knelt beside me, so that his face was on a level with mine. Very quietly, yet so that I knew he would be obeyed, he said. "Catherine, look at me."

I turned my head and met his gaze fully. And it held no trace of what I had feared to see.

CHAPTER XI

I awoke wrapped in comfort, and lay luxuriating in the feather-bed under me, the linen sheets which smelt of lavender. The bedcurtains of faded rose were drawn, but the light seeping through them, the birdsong outside, told me that a new day had come. I stretched my arms above my head, yawning, sleek and contented as any cat before the fire. With no thought for the morrow I lay only half aware, drugged by comfort in the rosy light.

There was a gentle tap on the door, and I heard it open. Martin's voice said cautiously: "Catherine, are you there?"

I was at once broad awake. Looking down I saw that I was still wearing my shirt, but that the rest of my garments lay folded on the foot of the bed. How they had come there I did not know. I only recalled talking with Martin far into the night before being suddenly overcome by sleep.

"Come in, Martin," I said, pulling the coverings decorously up to my chin, though indeed, if he had, as seemed probable, put me to bed, it was a trifle late to lock the stable door.

I heard him turn the key before coming quietly to the bedside, drawing back the curtains to look down at me. He seemed taller than I remembered, and I laughed. "Pray sit down, Martin. You make me feel as if a giant hovered over me."

His face was lit by his old smile. He sat down on the bed, which creaked under his weight, and we stayed silent for a while, and that foolish spring of happiness sang and bubbled in my heart. I had no thought of my reputation or whether it was strange us being together. Indeed, it seemed the most natural thing in the world.

"Did you put me to bed?" I asked him.

"I did," he answered. "Since you fell as dead asleep as if overcome by drink there was little else I could do. It was too late to take you back—"

My happiness vanished, leaving me shaken and afraid. I echoed. "Take me back?"

"My dear," he said gently, "what other can I do?"

"I thought you would have helped me! Martin, Martin, did you believe nothing of what I told you? I cannot go back, I will not. Martin, you did not mean it? You were teasing me, as you were ever wont to do. If you ever cared for me, even in the least degree—"

He said in a muffled voice: "Care for you? I loved you with all my heart. When I thought you dead I think something in me died also. But this mad escapade of yours must come to an end."

"I understand," I said. "I take it that your love also died. Was that when you saw my face last night?"

He was suddenly enraged. "You dammed little fool. Can you think of nothing but that your face is scarred? Do you imagine that you are not the same to me? I thought you understood that last night."

"Last night I thought many things. I thought that I had found sanctuary, that I need fear no more. I thought that we two, so long apart, had bridged the years. And to what does it all amount?" I sat up in bed, forgetful of my gaping shirt. "All you wish is to be rid of me. Well, that is simple enough. I will go, and trouble you no more. But you shall not take me back."

"You know I cannot let you go," he said.

95

"Why? Do you still think me a spy?"

"You know I do not. But how can I have you wandering alone—"

The last word echoed in my ears most drearily. His face swam in a mist of tears. Burying my face in the pillow I was unable to check my sobs. I felt his hand on my shoulder and shook it off.

"Go away," I said in a choked voice. "Leave me. I wish I had never seen you."

"Oh, Catherine," he said, "what is this? I never saw you weep before."

"Then you see me now," I sobbed, "and much good may it do you."

He laughed, and I was so enraged that I swung round, all blubbered with tears, and thumped his chest with my fists. Laughing still, he caught them in his grasp.

"We are back where we started, true enough! You pummelling me—"

"I would, I could truly hurt you!"

"Could you, Catherine? Why, what a savage creature you are! And yet you weep. Dear Catherine," he added, in the very tones of Martha, when we were young. "Dry your tears. Ha' done, my pretty lambkin, do 'ee, now!"

I chuckled faintly and found that my tears were soaking into his shoulder, and that I was held most closely to his breast. I hiccupped loudly, and he laughed again. Warmth crept through me, and my tears were dried.

I said, against his shoulder: "'Tis as well you locked the door."

"It is indeed," he answered complacently, and turned my face to his. "Sweetheart, you have the reddest nose," he said, and kissed me in a fashion which took all my breath away. Through the tumult which seemed to rage around I heard him speak my name most urgently. His lips came down on mine again. My arms went round his neck and held him close. I felt love and joy and a kind of pity for him, most strangely mingled. In all the world there was only him.

There was a loud knock on the door. Martin said something under his breath and released me, so that I fell back amongst the tumbled pillows. His breathing was fast, but he said calmly: "It may be just as well." he added, raising his voice. "Is it you, Tom?"

"'Tis I, master. The horses are waiting, if you are of the same mind."

The voice, that of the solemn serving man, sounded suspicious, as well it might. Judging from his expression the past few minutes would scarcely have been to his taste.

"I am coming," said Martin, "but we will not, I think, leave today." Bending towards me he whispered: "Clothe yourself, abandoned female that you are. I will settle certain matters then return."

"Do not be long," I said.

"I will not. But we must be careful, so become a boy again, for both our sakes."

He kissed me swiftly and was gone. I got into my rough clothing smiling to myself, yet I was not altogether happy — or rather, my happiness that I loved and was loved again seemed threatened. For all his professed belief in me he had spoken calmly of taking me back, and I knew of old how inflexible his purpose could be. But then again I would feel his arms around me, hear that shaken voice speaking my name, and forget all my fears.

"Boy," said a voice outside. "Open the door — though why you should occupy the room prepared for my master, and why Tom Jenkins should be set to wait on such as you the good lord knows. Not that it is for me, or for any of us, to question His mysterious ways."

I opened the door and he handed me food and drink, looking me up and down and muttering of thieves and vagabonds, and of what he would do if he had his way. Charity, it seemed, did not take pride of place in his religion.

"Am I to remain here, in this room?" I asked.

"Yes, if your honour pleases," he answered. "True, 'tis but poor accommodation for such as you, but you must bear with it for the time."

"Where is your master?"

He scowled at me. "What's that to you?"

I did not reply, and muttering he stumped away. I closed the door after him without regret.

There was a window seat, and despite the grime on the glass the sun was streaming in. I carried my bread and bacon and my mug of homebrewed ale there, and was comfortable enough. I felt better and stronger than I had for a long time and was almost completely content. I wished only that Martin would come.

I made the meal spin out as long as I could, but at last the final crumb was eaten, the mug drained dry. The sun shone in no longer and a sullen bank of cloud began to form. My spirits, too, were clouded. I was at first merely indignant that he should leave me alone for so long, but then imagination began to work. I saw him riding to the Grange, telling all to Ralph, riding here again to take me back. I began limping uneasily about the room, troubled by a premonition of evil, as if Jennings and her dark powers could reach me even here.

Slowly and remorselessly the clouds had covered the sky, and the room was now almost dark. I went back to the window and, kneeling on the seat, pressed my face to the pane. Against a background of deep purple the trees seemed to start forth, as if outlined by vivid light. It was hot and airless. The birds had ceased their singing, and every leaf, every blade of grass was still, as if waiting like my impatient self.

So suddenly that I recoiled and almost fell, a brilliant line snaked across the sky, and vanishing left it even darker than before. Scarcely had it gone when the thunder crashed as if immediately overhead, with such violence that I clapped my hands to my ears. I, who had proudly claimed to be afraid of nothing, had never confessed my unreasoning fear of such storms, was now so frightened that I almost ran to the bed, hiding my head under the covers as I had done when a child. Only one thing kept me there at the window — the thought of Martin, who might well be caught by the storm. I strained my eyes in the gloom, but there was no sign of him.

Again the lightning, for a moment, set the world alight, and in that moment with deepest joy I saw him galloping towards the house. My fears faded as if they had never been, and I almost ran out, heedless of everything save the fact that we could be together again. Once more the lightning split the sky. And by its light I saw that he was not alone.

* * *

This time the lightning, by now almost incessant, and the answering thunder had lost their power to make me afraid. The flash which had shown me Martin's two companions had shown me also how completely I was betrayed. Without a word to me without even the grace to warn me, he was returning with Ralph, and with, of all people, Roger Frampton. He who had raised me to the skies had now cast me down to such depths that I felt it more than I could bear. For even more than the dread of my return was the thought that Martin could use me so. I flung myself face downwards on the bed, and stayed there motionless for a long, long time.

At last I raised my head and looked vacantly around me. Rain was streaming down the window, and the air felt fresh and cool. As I looked the clouds moved rapidly, disclosing a patch of clearest blue, which spread and spread. The rain ceased, and the sun shone brilliantly. In the distance the thunder muttered, a pale shadow of its former self. A faint haze rose from the grass, like steam.

> *Fear no more the lightning flash*
> *Or the all dreaded thunder stone . . .*

Some words I had once read in a book amongst my scanty store came into my mind and seemed to mock me,

Truly the storm was no longer to be feared, but what of my own clouded future? Here was I in the room I had thought a haven, most helplessly trapped. The key, it was true, was on my side of the door, but that could only delay the outcome. Still they did not come, and I thought bitterly could well afford to take their time. I almost toyed with the idea of walking out of my own free will rather than awaiting an ignominious capture, but something held me back.

There was a sound outside. I sprang to my feet and stood facing the door. I heard a clatter and the discontented voice of Tom Jenkins bidding me open up, since he had brought me more food. I did not answer, and at last, muttering angrily, he went. Somehow the interruption seemed to serve as a spur, and I wondered, though with little hope, if I was truly beaten yet. There was still the window, and ivy grew thickly outside, which might, or might not, afford support. I remembered a certain day in my childhood when some that had looked secure had given way leaving me flat on my back with stars before my eyes and Martin's jeering laughter in my ears. I would have risked it, nonetheless, had it not been broad day. If, by some means, I could gain time . . .

A vague plan was coming to life, something after the fashion of my previous bid for escape. Suppose I left the window swinging open and could conceal myself, only until nightfall, so that they might search elsewhere, then I might make my way to Martha, for whom, at that moment, I longed. It was as if I were a child again who had been hurt and ran to her for comfort. I recalled Martin's voice those few hours ago, speaking the words we had both heard her use so many times, and my eyes stung at the memory. But I told myself there was no time now for tears. Was there any place here where I could hide? In a romance I could have touched a spot in the wainscot and found a secret passage leading to freedom, and I actually prowled around tapping and pressing, but without success. There remained the fireplace and the bed. The fireplace I rejected, so I turned to my final hope.

I could crawl under the feather mattress and perhaps also quietly suffocate there. I could lie under the bed itself, but that would be the first place they'd look. I raised my eyes. The bed seemed to reach high, with no space between its top and the ceiling, but I remembered games of hide and go seek, when the small Catherine had found space in just such a dusty sanctuary. Pulling a chair to the bedside I climbed up, feeling with my outstretched hand. There was a gap, but one so small that I doubted whether, thin as I was, I could hope to squirm through. I set my lips and vowed that I would try.

First I set the window wide, with great difficulty and dislodging several angry spiders whose webs were thick around, then I climbed again on my chair and gripped the edge of the canopy, pulling myself up. The first thing that happened was that I cracked my head on the ceiling with force enough to bring the water to my eyes, but I did not let go. The bed was, by now, an enemy to be conquered, and this I vowed I would do, but the chair was not high enough for my purpose. Gasping and angry I hung, legs kicking in their wide breeches, conscious even then of what a figure I must present. I felt with my feet for the top of the chair back, balanced, and raised myself. The chair lurched, and my head shot into the space between canopy and ceiling. I jerked and wriggled like a hooked fish, my feet now kicking in space, unable to move either out or in. With my mouth and nostrils full of dust I eased one shoulder, then the other. Ever so little I was gaining, and now was into my waist. A final bitter struggle with my voluminous breeches almost parting company with me, and there I was, face downward, exhausted and all but choked, yet triumphant.

The canopy sagged in the middle, so that I had more room to turn, and was able to roll over on my back. This was a relief, since the dust was so thick, like a carpet, that lying face downwards one would all but stifle in the horrible soft stuff. Above me my friends the spiders had held carnival, festooning the ceiling, but I was not in such bad case as I had been on the hard floor of the hut. I was so weary, both in mind and body that I was content simply to rest, and, strange as it may seem in the light of my position, actually fell into a kind of half-sleep, through which stalked dreams, foolish and terrifying. In all of them I was running, running, with weighted limbs, sometimes along endless corridors, sometimes through dark forests, at last along a rocky shore where waves crashed on the stones.

Then I was fully awake, and the crashing a thunderous knocking on the door.

"Catherine!" roared Martin, for a moment ceasing his assault on the door. "Why the devil do you not answer? By God, if this be another of your tricks! This is no time for such damnable folly. Open the door, or by God I will break it down!"

There was another buffet which seemed to shake me where I lay, followed by a yelp of pain, then silence. I waited to hear the voices of those others, but now the only sound was that of footsteps rapidly retreating. It seemed strange that Ralph, if there, should not have made his presence felt, and for one sweet moment I wondered if I had misjudged Martin after all. But then I thought my brother might have been sworn to silence so that I might walk all unsuspecting into his arms, and the bitter certainty of my betrayal would not be denied.

If Martin had gone for weapons to help him in his attack on the stout oak door he was taking his time. But the next sounds I heard came from outside, a curious mixture of heavy breathing, scrabbling and scraping, followed by a loud and bitter oath. Someone was trusting himself to the ivy, and apparently finding it as insecure as I had feared. Turning my head I could see through the narrow space a small part of the window. Against the opening Martin's face, red and furious, appeared. He pulled himself up blotting out the light, and the next moment half fell into the room.

Now, lying motionless except that my heart seemed to shake my body with its beating, I could see him no more, but his movements were clear enough to my ears. He spoke bitterly and with threats as to what he would do to me when he found me.

"I know, you jade, that you are here," he said. "Another open window is not enough to deceive me. Oh yes, you are here, and by God, when I find you, you will wish that you were not. And as to those who call you mad—" here a footstool was kicked across the room with a crash — "why damn me if I do not agree with them, since none but a mad-woman would behave thus." The last words echoed with a hollow boom, and I guessed he was looking up the chimney where he seemed to crack his head, for a dull thud was followed by an anguished oath. Now he was at the bed, tearing down the curtains and buffeting it so that I rocked as if at sea. I thought he plumped down to look under the bed, then I heard him walk across the room.

"No," he said in a different voice. "It cannot be. I do not believe it."

I was filled with curiosity. Did he indeed think I had escaped? It was not like Martin to give up so easily.

"No secret panel," said he musingly. "No trapdoor in floor or ceiling. And as, my Catherine, I am assured you went not by the window, but one thing remains."

On the last words he moved swiftly, and two hands appeared on the edge of the canopy. The next moment Martin and I gazed into one another's eyes.

"You knew," I said angrily. "You knew all the time."

"Almost all," he assented. "I have played hide and go seek with you before, my dear, or had you forgot? After all you seem to have forgot so much. Gratitude, decency, any feeling for me—"

"I!" said I, feeling the colour burn my cheeks. "You dare say that to me! What of you?"

"What the devil you mean, and how the devil you got yourself through so small a space are alike unknown to me," he answered. "But since you got there let us even get you out again, then perchance we might talk like reasoning beings. Though, indeed, I doubt it."

"Go away," I said. "We have nothing to say to each other anymore."

"As you will. I can wait." His face vanished, and I heard him drop to the floor. From the sounds he settled himself in the chair and stretched out his legs. He also began to sing, most villainously off-key, like a great bumblebee.

"Her petticoat was crimson
She was a wanton jade
And from my purse she took her fill,
That greedy buxom maid."

"I should think," I said, "You had better things to do than to sit there singing bawdy rhymes."

"You should hear the rest," he replied. "And I should think that you had better things to do than to remain in so ridiculous a posture." And he went on with his infuriating humming. I thought how changed he had seemed when first I saw him, and how he now seemed to have reverted to boyhood, when he ever had the way to drive me to frenzy. Not that I could talk, since I, too was behaving like a child.

"Anything is better than being forced to hearken to you," I said. "I will come down."

"You may need my help," he said courteously. "I am, as always, at your service."

Opening my mouth to retort I was overtaken by a violent sneeze, and the dust rose round me in a cloud. I wriggled to the edge and eased out my head and shoulders.

"Oh, Absalom!" remarked Martin, leaning back in his chair and observing me with every evidence of pleasure. "I believe you are as much held prisoner as was that unfortunate."

I said coldly. "I got myself in — I can get myself out again."

"And land headfirst on the floor, breaking your neck in the process? Well, well, if that be your desire who am I to hinder you?" And he began his singing, if one could call it that, again.

In the midst of my anger I was shaken by laughter, and somehow the laughter awakened me to my own folly. Had he in truth betrayed me he would not have been behaving thus. I knew it and was ashamed.

"You may help me if you will," I said.

"Now there is generosity for you!" he said admiringly. "How can I thank you?"

"Please, Martin," I said, and gave a snort of that foolish laughter. There, spread-eagled face downwards, I was once more filled with happiness. I said, coaxingly. "Will you not help me?"

He rose and came to the bedside. "If I did as you deserved I would leave you there until you had given me some explanation of your conduct. However, as you are turning purple in the face — here, lay your hands on my shoulders."

As I obeyed, he reached up and clutched me under the arms.

"Now," he said, "much as I might desire it, I will not let you fall. Come, what is hindering you?"

"'Tis these damnable breeches," I gasped, squirming. "They take up more room than the rest of me."

"Well, there's a remedy for that," he said. "Had you not—" With a mighty heave I won through. Off guard he staggered, and the next moment we were both on the floor, Martin in a sitting posture, I sprawled over him.

"Good God, I told you to come, but need you make it so hasty a business?" He set me on my feet and stood up, rubbing himself.

"I did not mean — are you hurt?"

He felt himself with some care. "No bones are broken, but I am sorely bruised." He looked at me, no longer teasing. "And now, if you please, I will hear the reason for all this."

"I — I thought it would be a jest," I muttered feebly for I was ashamed to tell him, since I now looked back with amazement at my lack of faith.

He only shook his head and waited.

"You were so long gone," I said. "And when you returned you were not alone."

"Well?" said he, as I paused. "And what then?"

"Can you not imagine what I thought?"

"Oh, yes," he said. "It is clear enough. It also makes clear the kind of trust you had in me, the fact that you spoke truth last night."

"Last night?"

"When you said you were changed. The Catherine I knew was not filled with doubts and suspicion. This Catherine I find I do not know at all."

His voice held a kind of weary contempt which I found unbearable. He seemed, on a sudden, very far away. I groped for the chair and sat blindly down, unable to find words.

"How could you?" he said, looking down at me. "How dared you think that I would do such a thing?"

At last I was stung to my own defence. "Indeed, I am sorry now, but at the time, seeing them here with you — after all, you had said that you would take me back."

"I know what I said. But I did not mean simply to deliver you into their hands. I had planned otherwise."

"Then— then why bring them here?"

"I met them by purest chance. I had business with my steward and returning came upon them. It may have escaped your notice that something of a storm was brewing? They came to shelter, and when the storm cleared they left. It was as simple as that."

I was humbled. "I am sorry, Martin, truly sorry. I see now that I was wrong."

"And so all can be forgiven and forgotten, I suppose."

"You are not over-generous," I said, stung. "I think I am not the only one who has changed, Martin."

"Trust a woman to put one in the wrong!"

"And trust you to be always right!" I glared up at him as he scowled down at me. "You were ever so, puffed up, unable to see any point of view but your own!"

"Good God! That, coming from you—!"

In the midst of my indignation I felt a kind of warmth. Martin enraged, hurling insults at me, was a Martin returned from that cold distance. We were on our old footing again.

"In a moment I shall he expected to crave your pardon," he shouted, giving me a most venomous glance. "You will have a damnably long wait."

He stamped to the window and stood there with his back to me, rigid indignation in every line. Again that foolish laughter banished my anger. I buried my face in my hands, and heard Martin come towards me.

"You weep for shame, and well you may," he said, rather uncertainly. A sound which might have been a whooping sob escaped me. I felt his hand on my shoulder, and gasped, "I am not weeping," and whooped again with laughter.

His hand dropped from my shoulder, and he pulled mine from my face. I looked up into his affronted countenance.

"You — you! Is this a time for laughter?"

"I know," I said weakly, and laughed the more. He shook me violently. My laughter ceased, and I gave a little cry.

"You hurt me!"

"'Tis nothing to what you deserve!"

"I know. I am sorry. Martin, can we not forget my follies, and be friends again?"

"Friends?" he echoed in a curious voice. "When were we ever that?" And without warning he swooped over me, so that I shrank back, half expecting a blow.

"Friends?" he said again, and his lips came down on mine, and his arms went round me. The breath was well-nigh crushed from my body. He raised his head, remarking that I was a witch who should be burned, and kissed me again. I was pressed quite painfully against the carved back of the chair, but I uttered no complaint.

At last he released me, drew a deep breath, and said, not at all lovingly, "I suppose you are content now."

"Content?"

"To know how besotted I am. To know that you can twist me round your little finger."

"Can I do that indeed, Martin?"

He muttered something I could not distinguish, and was suddenly on his knees beside me, his face on a level with

107

mine. I bent forward and laid my cheek against his, and all the tumult and anger were as if they had never been.

"I am very content, Martin," I said, "if it be true that you are indeed my love."

"For what it is worth, and God knows, that is not much," he answered, "you have my love now and forever."

"And for what it is worth, you have mine," I echoed. "As, I think, you always have."

It was a long time until he spoke again. "When I planned to take you back it was not to deliver you up to them but as my promised wife."

"And you truly do not mind?"

He took my meaning, and drew a finger gently along my scarred cheek.

"Only for you. Catherine, I bear unseen scars which are uglier far. You do not know—"

"I know I love you, and I will go with you wherever you may go. Once we are wed will be time enough to tell Ralph. Do you not think that would be best?"

"Whether it be best or not I have grave doubts," he answered. "I only know—"

"Know what, dear heart?"

"That I cannot let you go, my Catherine," he said. "Until I must."

CHAPTER XII

When I look back my life seems to be divided in two parts neatly as a halved apple. The first part was all my own small affairs, with little knowledge of what passed in the world outside. The second I was to be involved in great matters, touching the wellbeing of so many. At times my past life at the Grange would seem dreamlike, unreal. At times it was my stay in London which seemed the dream, with its noise and cruelty and horror. But it was no dream, and part of the pattern of my life.

My meeting with Martin, my life laid in his hands, changed all my plans. I never reached that little cottage in the Chase where I had thought to find shelter, but came with him and Tom Jenkins to London, still pretending myself a boy. I rode pillion behind Martin, and was happy as a bird, while poor Tom could scarce have been more disapproving had he known the true facts of the case. He muttered of whipping posts and pillories every time he came near me, and with that spring of happiness within me it was most difficult to retain my secret and act as a hangdog captive. For all Martin's care to speak little to me and that roughly there were times when our eyes would meet, our hands touch, which made us forget all we should have remembered, and Tom, I think, was dimly aware of this undercurrent. He seemed to sense something not fully understood, and seldom left us alone, so the nights we spent on the way were highly decorous.

"Did you not sleep well?" I murmured to Martin, after the last night.

"With your snoring coupled with Tom's I did not," he answered sulkily. "And there was another reason."

"What was that?" I asked, smiling to myself.

"If you do not know I shall not tell you," he said. "But I have a very good notion that you do. And why you should laugh—"

"I am so happy I cannot help it."

"You had better, for here comes Tom."

"Like the poor, he is always with us," I said composing my features just in time as that worthy, his face a contrast to the bright morning, ranged alongside. I wondered if he would ever bring himself to think me a fit wife for his master, and the words "wife to Martin" sang in my heart, and the sunshine, the blue sky, the dog roses in the tangled hedge-row all made a background to my joy. For the days were fair and the air most pleasing to one who had been cooped up for so long. Yet I believe I should have felt the same had we ridden through tempest, to such unthinking bliss had I been brought.

The sun was low and shadows lay long on the grass when Tom, all unwilling, was given money and sent on ahead.

"See that the young huzbird does not vanish in the crowd," he warned, with his unpleasant gaze on me. "Not that it might not be as well to be rid of him."

"For God's sake save your breath and go. We shall be close on your heels."

Tom clattered off, his back rigid with offence.

"Have we far to go?" I asked.

"Not far, my love. Are you weary?"

I moved closer against his back. "Somewhat stiff, and my bones ache, but it is no matter. Where do we go in London, Martin?"

He glanced round, somewhat surprised. "Did I not tell you? To my house, by the river. It is empty but will at least provide shelter for the night. Tomorrow we will set matters right. You shall become a woman again and, as soon as may be, my wife."

"You were very sure of me, were you not? Now I come to think of it you did not so much as ask for my hand."

"I have been sadly remiss, I fear."

"It is no matter," I said, laughing. "With all that has passed I have small choice in the affair."

"At least, it does not seem to darken your spirits," he said, and his hand clasped mine, and he smiled over his shoulder at me, his grey eyes holding a look which seemed to twist my heart. Then he released my hand, shaking his head.

"If I look at you for long we shall never finish our journey," he said, and quickened our speed. Soon we were amongst houses, more and more, and there was steadily mounting noise, people, coaches, so that I began to feel dizzy and kept my eyes on Martin's straight back, taking in very little on this, my first visit to London. I became more weary than I had known for the noises seemed to blend into one strange roar, and this and the movement of the horse might have been a dream, and when at last we stopped I swayed, and almost fell. Dimly I heard Martin's voice and Tom's gruff reply, then the *clop-clop* of hooves as the horse was led away.

"Bear up, my love," whispered Martin, supporting me. "You have done well, and now shall rest."

"I fear I cannot walk. My legs are like jelly."

"Then I must even carry you," he said, and picked me up like a babe. Glancing round he kissed me swiftly, then carried me through some tangled bushes which brushed against my face and to a space where light shone from a doorway.

"And you had best remove your arms from about my neck," he muttered. "Or poor Tom will be given furiously to think."

He set me down on some kind of bench. It was hard, and I moved uncomfortably. Looking around me I wrinkled

111

my nose against the stale smell, the unwelcoming feel of a house which has been left unoccupied for a long time. I saw a room darkly panelled, furnished by a long table, benches, and a great press. There were platters and candles on the table, and by their light I could see a kind of bloom which overlaid the wood, and trickles of damp here and there. If Martin had not told me his house stood by the river I might well have guessed as much.

A feeble fire of logs strove for life with little conviction, now and then sending puffs of smoke into the room. Here there was no sound of voices, of busy people about their affairs, but a faint lapping sound, continuous and vaguely mournful. After my glad day it all seemed sad, and I felt suddenly cold, holding my hands to what feeble warmth there was. I felt it unkind in Martin to leave me alone and could have whimpered like a lonely child.

It was not for long. He and Tom came in together, Tom bearing a basket and Martin an armful of logs. He knelt at the hearth attempting to coax the fire, becoming angry at its lack of response and swearing violently and fluently.

"Foul language will be of no avail," said Tom sternly. And putting Martin aside he set to work on the fire himself, puffing at it like a hard-featured cherub, at last rewarded by a flicker, then another, which grew to a moderate blaze. He rose, dusting his hands on his breeches, remarking that there were those who wasted breath in profane language while others used it to some purpose.

With the flickering firelight and my solitude banished my spirits rose again, and even Tom's presence did not hinder me from making a hearty meal. He had brought in pasties, bread, and salt meat, which, with wine, tasted most pleasing. I was sore and unable to sit with comfort, but now warm and fed and filled with happy anticipation. It seemed not possible that a short time ago I had been held prisoner at the Grange. I was half asleep in my dreamy content when there sounded an imperative knocking on the door.

Tom paused, a crust with a great bite out of it halfway to his mouth and looked up in surprise. The knocking sounded again.

"Who the devil it can be!" said Martin uneasily, glancing at me. "Go, Tom, and see."

Tom rose, bolted what was evidently a good-sized mouthful and went out, closing the door behind him. We heard a murmur of voices, and I shrank back with visions of an indignant Ralph who had already tracked me down. Martin had risen and stood facing the door, his tall figure tense, his mouth set firmly. The door opened and I saw his face change, to lighten with pleasure and surprise.

"'Tis you, of all people!" he exclaimed. "I thought you still at Penshurst."

"I did intend to make a lengthy stay there, but I heard disquieting news." The newcomer, catching sight of me, broke off in surprise. "Why, you yet keep your uninvited guest. I had not thought to find him here."

I met the keen gaze of Colonel Sidney, and felt the colour burn my cheeks.

"As to that, sir, my spy proved other than I had thought. Come near the fire, which at least sets off some of the damp, and rest awhile."

Colonel Sidney sat down facing him and let the cloak slip from his shoulders. The smile with which he had greeted Martin had faded, and his face was grim and austere. His suit of brown was plain to the extreme, but there was something about his bearing which made me recall that he sprang from a noble line, and that the man who was a noted republican could have held his own with prince or king. Even I had heard tales of him — how he had fought on the Parliamentary side and been wounded in battle yet raised his voice against the execution of the King, had turned from Cromwell when he saw him as a tyrant, and lived long in exile. He was now, as I later discovered, something past his sixtieth year, and looked older, until he smiled, when the austerity was lost in warmth, and the grim face with its angular lines softened unbelievably. But it was not often that he did so.

Martin stirred up the fire and sent Tom for more logs. Sidney accepted wine and said. "I am weary, both in body and mind, but your spy, who is no spy, and who, now that his face is clean looks even less of a swineherd, intrigues me greatly."

Martin looked at me questioningly, and without words I gave my consent, to sit listening to my story as told by him with a certain wonder to think it truly concerned myself. When Martin disclosed my identity Sidney exclaimed in surprise and the colour stung my face again, but after that he hearkened in silence to the end.

"And so," Martin concluded, "knowing not what other to do I brought her here."

"You brought her here?" echoed Sidney, "knowing all the perils of the road, footpads, the ever-present fear of discovery. Well, well, it would seem the age of chivalry is not dead, since here we have damsel in distress, knight errant and all."

"You think I did wrong," said Martin, rather defiantly.

"I think the behaviour of you both has been imprudent to the last degree," he answered calmly, "but that you must already know. And it is possible that you found it not easy to do otherwise."

I spoke for the first time, not to defend myself, but on Martin's behalf. "He would have taken me back. It was I who persuaded him not to do so." Then I added, as if it made all clear, "We knew one another well in the past. I would not have asked it of a stranger."

"And, as soon as possible, we are to be wed," added Martin.

"All things considered that is probably as well," murmured Sidney. His face was unyielding, but I thought there was a hint of laughter in his voice. I looked at him resentfully, and he rose, and bowed over my hand.

"We have met before, Mistress Catherine, when you were but knee high. Your father, I recall, spoke of you as a self-willed puss who could turn men round her little finger. It seems to me you do so still." He released my hand and turned to Martin. "You are a pair of madcap children who should be whipped and given bread and water, but I wish you both very happy. I wish it with all my heart." And, as if to himself, he added. "There is little enough of happiness, God knows."

He sat down again and asked. "What are your present plans? You cannot keep the lady here."

"I thought to take her to my aunt," said Martin.

Both Sidney and I looked up sharply, I because this was news to me, he apparently with approval.

"My good friend the redoubtable dame!" he exclaimed. "Why, that is the best of plans. Henrietta Lacey will not so much as turn a hair." And for the first time I heard him laugh whole-heartedly. "You are fortunate in your relative, my boy," he said.

Tom's cough sounded outside. Martin laid a finger on his lips, and Colonel Sidney, his eyes still lit by laughter, nodded. Tom entered with the logs, remarking that he had put a room ready for me, so that their honours might talk in peace. There would be, he said, no reason to trouble themselves on my account, since he would lock the door and keep the key.

"You do very well, my man," said Sidney cordially, with a sidelong glance at me. "Master Lacey is well served by you, as I should expect from the son of the man who fought so bravely beside me at Marston Moor."

Tom's sanctimonious face relaxed to a pleased smile which made it unfamiliar. He jerked his head in my direction and I rose unwillingly.

"Sleep well, my lad," said Colonel Sidney blandly.

"Lucky if he do," said Tom darkly. "And more than he deserves."

When I was in the damp barely furnished chamber and the key turned on me I thought he was probably right, and I had so much to think of that sleep, in any case, would have been hard to woo. I thought of Colonel Sidney, and how he had wished us happiness while he himself was weary in mind and body. And I wondered what the disquieting news he had heard might be, and if it would affect Martin and myself.

CHAPTER XIII

"I do not see why I should be taken to this aunt of yours," I said, frowning. "Why cannot I remain here?"

"You know very well why not," said Martin. "For one thing you have to become a woman again. What would befall poor Tom if we sprang that on him is more than I can conceive."

"It would probably strike him dumb, and a good thing too," said I viciously, for I had suffered much from his tongue that morning, and from his infuriating habit of giving me scarce a moment alone with Martin. Back he came now, always with that bulging eye of disapproval and suspicion fixed on me. I glared back, and he muttered his opinion of me, which was hardly flattering.

Martin was giving him instructions, handing him money, adding that I was to be lodged elsewhere, and that he himself would see to it.

"Huh! Newgate would fit the bill," observed Tom, looking me up and down. "As hang-gallows a young rapscallion as ever I set eyes on, and no more than half a man."

Martin turned rather suddenly to the window, his shoulders shaking, uttering peculiar sounds. I looked at the speaker with burning indignation.

"You will have taken a chill, belike," he observed to Martin, who was still uttering strangled sounds. "'Tis not surprising in this place. Even at this season the damp strikes home."

"I do well enough," said Martin, controlling himself. "Take the money and get all we need — the house will soon be habitable again. I will ask my aunt to obtain a serving wench to help you."

"What do I want with that?" he snapped back. "We need no daughters of Jezebel here, hindering more than they help. Their eyes are lewd, and often as not their ways lead down to destruction."

"Why do you let him speak to you thus?" I asked Martin, when Tom had gone at last, piously thanking God that he had seen the last of me.

"Because he is true as steel, and those Puritan ways and speech clothe devotion. You may yet find cause for gratitude in his presence, Catherine."

"He will have cause for surprise when he knows who I am and will regret certain words he has said."

"He will consider them justified. And he will serve you with the utmost loyalty, have no fear of that."

I frowned. "I should not think he would accept me, knowing all this."

"You will belong to me; therefore he will accept you. And I fear, sweet, you must even accept him."

"Well, if we could leave Tom and all his virtues for one moment, what of this aunt of yours? Do you take me to her in this guise, and if so, what will she think?"

Martin laughed and kissed me suddenly.

"In this guise you go, and she will merely think you a maid of spirit. You do not know my aunt. And come, we waste time, and Tom will be returning."

"One thing before we go," I said, laying a hand on his arm. "Why was Colonel Sidney troubled last night?" And, as he said nothing, I added resentfully, "If I am to be your wife I have a right to know what concerns you. And it seems to me that something concerning Colonel Sidney touches you."

He sighed. "He had heard rumours which bode ill for those not of the King's party," he said briefly. And dismissing the subject, he took his hat and we went out through the tangled bushes, over a stretch of dewy grass, and to the river-bank itself. Here a path lay alongside the wide flow of water, just now dancing in the sunlight. Martin led the way, and I looked on his tall figure, the brown hair falling under the broadbrimmed hat, and thought how much a part of my life he had become in this short space of time. I spoke his name, and he turned to smile over his shoulder at me.

"What is it, my love?"

"But to remind you that I am here."

The pathway was narrow and deserted. Turning, he took me for a brief moment into his arms.

"I had not forgotten," he said.

Now the path widened, and we walked side by side, with the water lapping and babbling cheerily, and the sun warm on us. Leaving the river we came quite suddenly upon a street filled with shops and noise and people, more than I had ever seen together at one time. The shopkeepers were crying their wares, urging all to "buy, buy, buy", since nowhere else would be found goods such as theirs. There were brightly coloured signs and gaily dressed folk, but there was also a smell which made me wrinkle my nose. Ladies and serving women looked kindly on Martin, and with no interest at all on me. I dropped humbly behind him and was glad when we turned from the bustle into a quiet alley, stopping at the door of a house which seemed all a tiptoe, as if at any moment it might topple forward. It was much black by soot, as were its neighbours, and I learned later had narrowly escaped the path of that great fire which had raged through the city some twenty years before.

"Now," said Martin, stopping at the door and speaking in a low voice, "You may find my aunt a little strange in manner, but at heart she is the kindest of persons. At first sight—"

He broke off suddenly, but now the door opened a crack, and a voice declaimed loudly. "No beggars or vagabonds here! Take yourself off — begone!"

I was startled, for if the voice belonged to Martin's aunt it was more like that of a man. I looked at him and saw that he was laughing. He gently put me on one side. "Aunt, 'tis I. Martin. Will you not open the door?"

The resounding voice uttered an exclamation of surprise. There was a rattling of chains, then the door was flung wide and I saw Henrietta Lacey for the first time. If Martin made me feel small the lady now framed in the doorway dwarfed me. She was dressed, save for her petticoat, in a man's riding suit of Lincoln green. A kerchief was tied round her head, and, as if she were not tall enough already, this was surmounted by a steeple crowned hat. She fairly filled the doorway, so that even Martin was little taller and much leaner, and as she held out mighty arms to him, he was engulfed in a rib-cracking embrace. The deep voice rejoiced over him, and he was welcomed like the returned prodigal son.

"My dear boy, dear little Martin, after these many years!" Here he was kissed resoundingly on both cheeks, held away at arm's length and lovingly regarded, then clasped in that crushing embrace once more. "What best of winds blew you here? I thought you far away. And why does that beggar lad yet linger? Drive him hence, Martin."

"'Tis no beggar lad, Aunt, and comes with me. May we enter? I have a tale to tell. Also I need your help, which I am assured you will not withhold."

Brown eyes were turned on my shrinking form, looking me up and down before returning with amusement to Martin.

"Few seek out Henrietta Lacey without needing that. Well, well, I cannot hope to be visited for my own charms, which are something past their prime. Come in, then, both of you, and let me hear this tale. Malachi!" She raised her voice to a mighty roar. "Bring wine to the south parlour. We have guests."

She cast aside her hat as we followed her in, and the door was closed. A great tabby cat stalked towards her with tail erect. Martin bent to fondle it, but leaped back with blood starting out of his hand, and muttered an oath. His aunt laughed indulgently and picked up the great creature, settling it on her shoulder where it remained purring loudly and looking deceptively gentle.

"Methuselah will be touched by none but me, and is good as any watchdog," she said, leading us into a small room. "He grows old and ill tempered, like me. Think not too hardly of him, Martin."

Martin gave a rather sickly smile, bound a kerchief round his hand and made no reply. A smaller cat rose from the fireside and rubbed its head against my leg.

"I have but the five now," said Mistress Lacey. "Poor Jonah, alas, is no more." Her brow clouded and she heaved a sigh. "We think it was by poison, and could I find who did the deed he might yet rue the day. But here is Malachi. Let us forget our sorrows for the moment."

A small bent serving man tottered in, accompanied by two more cats. I began to feel that my stay here would not be a lonely one; that Martin might have warned me; and that a scratched hand was no more than he deserved. I am fond of cats in moderation, but enough is enough.

We drank our wine and ate some kind of sweetmeat, very sticky, and clinging lovingly to the roof of one's mouth, so that we were all perforce silent for a space. Looking around me I saw that it was a pleasant room, oddly shaped, and looking out on a small overgrown garden, but there was too much cat fur for my liking, and the legs of the table and chairs were scored by their claws. Also there was a smell.

Martin bolted what seemed to be an obstinate morsel and turned to his aunt. Forgetting the cats, I twisted my fingers together as he began to speak.

"Dear Aunt—"

She smiled and, leaning forward, patted him on the knee. Methuselah, swaying, leaped from her shoulder and sat down in a far corner, his tail waving furiously.

"'Tis pleasant to hear your voice again, dear boy. I have thought many times of you and wondered how you fared. See how Methuselah sulks yonder! He is jealous, and I must needs soothe his injured feelings."

"Let me speak first," said Martin, as she started to rise. "It will not take long."

"As you will." But she looked anxiously at her deposed favourite, now yowling softly to himself in his corner. "I am all attention."

"This beggar lad, as you thought him, is neither beggar nor lad," said Martin loudly. "'Tis Catherine Carey who escaped from various dangers thus disguised, and who is to be my wife."

Mistress Lacey's eyes were still fixed on Methuselah. She said calmly. "Is it so indeed?"

In the face of this lack of interest Martin ploughed desperately on.

"It is not fitting that she should remain with me until we can be wed. I have, therefore, brought her to you—"

"Wait! Let me settle this matter," she interrupted.

There was a short interval, after which she returned to her chair bearing Methuselah with her. Martin muttered a few words as to the animal's antecedents under his breath and gazed at the ceiling. A rhythmic rattling sound filled the room, and Mistress Lacey smiled.

"He is content again, and now I can listen to your tale, which I did not fully comprehend before."

Martin swallowed something and doggedly repeated his story, which this time had a most gratifying effect. Mistress Lacey clapped her hands together and laughed heartily.

"You two rogues! You sit there mim as a mouse and tell me of such matters! What have you been about, the pair of you? And what a maid of spirit this must be!"

"Did I not tell you?" said Martin to me.

I said, colouring, "I am aware that my behaviour must seem most strange, but there were reasons—"

"Reasons? I will be bound that there were. And as to strange behaviour, in this world where women are expected to sit meek and mim and never take thought for themselves, bowing in all things to their lords and masters, God save us all—!" She paused for breath, having apparently lost the thread of her argument, and turned to Martin. "'Tis time and more than time that you were wed, and I rejoice that it will be to a wench with a mind of her own."

"And Catherine may remain with you? There is clothing to be got, and other matters."

"She may stay and is welcome. And as to clothing, above stairs is all that belonged to Mary." Her voice softened, and the big figure drooped. "She and your Catherine were much of a size, and she would be well pleased for her to have them."

"You would not be grieved?" asked Martin gently, adding to me, "Mary was my cousin. She died at nineteen."

"I shall not be grieved, and if my Mary were here she would give them gladly." She nodded towards a portrait on the well above the chimneypiece. "See if you think there would be aught niggardly in her."

The painted face of the young girl smiled down on us, gay yet faintly wistful. It scarcely seemed the best of omens for me to step into her shoes, yet it was most kindly meant. I could not refuse an offer which would truly solve my present difficulties.

"But it may be," said Mistress Lacey, uncannily reading my mind, "that you shrink from such an idea."

I glanced at the portrait which smiled on me in a comradely fashion.

"It is most kind, and I accept most gladly," I said, adding diffidently. "She died young. I am sorry."

Martin pressed my arm as if in warning, and I said no more. Mistress Lacey rose, clutching the great cat with her face unchanged, but her hands were shaking.

"I will prepare for your stay. It is not, perhaps, the household to which you are accustomed, but such as it is I bid you welcome."

When she had gone, I turned to Martin, vaguely troubled.

"Did I say — was it wrong to speak of her daughter?"

"Her death was in a strange, cruel fashion and my aunt cannot bear to speak of it. The affair changed her greatly, but she is most good at heart. Your stay here will not be long."

His face was somewhat anxious, and I hastened to reassure him.

"We shall do very well. I have not behaved altogether like other women myself." And I looked down at my ugly garb and longed to change it.

Mistress Lacey, coming briskly back, remarked that all was in order, and Martin might now go about his business while we two became better acquainted. Martin meekly agreed and rose to go.

"You may kiss her if you wish," said Mistress Lacey indulgently. "The cats and I need not hinder you." And when we embraced in rather a constrained fashion under her eye she observed that they did it better in her day. I could not help laughing, and the other two joined me, so that the room, for a while, filled with our mirth.

"Well," said Martin, picking up his hat, "however unwillingly I had best go."

"An old friend sups with me tonight. You may join us if you will," said Mistress Lacey, accompanying him to the door and giving him a resounding kiss. "Knave that you are, I am right glad to see you and your maid. Come as soon as you may," she said.

She did not return at once, and I sat wondering at one who could not speak of her daughter's death, yet could hand over that same daughter's clothing to another, and the blue eyes in the portrait looked down sweetly on me, half wistful, half with a kind of lurking laughter. And I grieved for one whom I had never met — and one whose life had ended at nineteen.

CHAPTER XIV

I came down the stairs slowly, holding my wide skirts on either side. My gown was of violet, trimmed with pearls, the sleeves cut open to disclose an undersleeve of palest yellow, like the colour of a primrose. Stiff petticoats rustled as I moved and gave out a faint perfume. The gown fitted as if it had been made for me, as did the brocaded shoes, and against the deep colour my skin looked white. Never in my life had I owned such a garment. Even the lovely gowns which Frances wore, though they might be of a later mode, could not surpass it. I wished that my hair had grown enough to fall in ringlets round my face, like those of the girl whose dress I wore, and I wished I were not scarred. But, since I knew that Martin was my love, even that had lost its power to darken my spirit.

He was standing at the foot of the stairs talking with his aunt, and at the whisper of my silken skirts they both turned, and as I paused looking down at them, so they stayed gazing up at me, Martin with admiration and delight, the other with God knows what memories. But she spoke gallantly enough.

"Well, Martin, I have made your lad into a lass again. Does she please you?"

He said nothing but bent and kissed her. She gave a laugh and pushed him away, but I think she understood.

"Do not trouble yourself with a withered old woman when that awaits you!"

I came down, spread my skirts and curtsied to them both, then held out my hand to Martin. Smiling down at me he bent over it and kissed it.

"A very pretty picture," said a man's voice from the doorway, "And in truth the swineherd transforms most prettily." I turned and saw Colonel Sidney come forward. He, too, bowed in a most courtly fashion over my hand.

"A little more of this and I shall fancy myself at Whitehall," observed Mistress Lacey.

"God forbid!" replied her guest with feeling.

"Well, well, let us sup, and hear the latest news from the coffee-houses. Catherine and I have been about women's matters the livelong day. Let us hear what passes in the great world of men."

"So you yet scorn us, Henrietta," said Sidney, smiling at her as we sat down at table. "Well, perhaps you are not so far wrong. We are a poor crew enough, and truth and honour seem but empty words today."

"An honest man knows well what he may expect, since what match is he for the rogues who hold power today? Therefore, Algernon, take heed of yourself, for though stiff-necked, obstinate, with a head stuffed full as an egg with meat of strange notions, I yet acknowledge you to be honest to the core."

"I am, as always, grateful for your opinion of me," he answered gravely. And now Malachi, accompanied by a buxom girl brought in the meal, and I looked about me, taking little heed of the talk.

Even on this June evening the room was dim and shadowy, so that the log fire did not seem out of place. The long table at which we sat was of oak and so dark that it was almost black, and the wainscot was of the same sad hue, while the window was so overgrown on the outside that it let in little light. There was a portrait in this room, too. Not of a smiling girl but a grim-faced man with cropped hair, who held his

125

head with an air of command. Despite the harshness of the face and the deep lines from nose to compressed lips, there was something vaguely familiar which teased me. After a little, with a start of surprise, I saw what it was. The eyes of the portrait were like, very like, those of Martin.

The talk had flagged, and I found that I had been served with mutton. Glancing up, I saw that the others were watching me. I was somewhat discomposed, but Henrietta smiled kindly on me, and we set to. The food was good and plentiful, and I was glad that the cats appeared to be regaling themselves elsewhere. This evening my hostess, velvet gowned and somewhat neater than she had been in the day, seemed more as other women. It was plain that Algernon Sidney looked on her with affection, and if there was also a hint of amusement he yet listened to her views with respect. It had never before occurred to me that what she said held truth, and that the minds of women might well vie with those of their lords and masters, and I was much struck.

"Under whose reign did England reach the peak of her greatness?" she was demanding. "Which of your men ruled as did Elizabeth? — and that with no need of a man at her heels, mark that!"

"Not one man in particular, or at least, not for long," murmured Sidney, smiling. "But you will admit that around her there was scarcely a dearth of males."

Henrietta gave a snort which fairly set the candle-flames fluttering. "Yes, and she had the sense to use them, to set them all to do her bidding. Therein lay her greatness."

"Yet she was no common woman. Did she not herself say as much? 'I have the heart and stomach of a man—'"

"There are those who could make black white in argument," shouted Henrietta, her already high colour deepening. "Let her heart and stomach and any other parts be what they might, she remained a woman, and living proof that women are capable of more than bearing children and of keeping the household's belly filled." And she clapped her fist on the table so that the platters rattled.

"My dear Henrietta," protested Sidney, "I am assured that you are right. As you well know you preach to the converted. I have long held the view, and indeed, put it into writing, that women are more than chattels or playthings. When they are put in their rightful place, and when men achieve integrity, then comes Utopia. Pray believe me, before our good meal is bounced into the air or ever we have had time to savour it!"

His hostess relaxed with a half-willing laugh, and the talk was of small matters until the board was cleared. We sat on, and now it was Sidney who spoke and we who listened, and could not be unmoved by his deep sincerity. Henrietta forgot to champion her sex, and, arms on the table, her eyes only for him, listened while he spoke of government which held nothing of tyranny, of those republican principles which had ruled his life and made him, for much of it, an exile.

At length he stopped, smiled at me, and said, "I fear I have talked overlong, and that on matters which must seem of small interest to youth. Yet it will lie in the hands of the young. The future is theirs to make or mar."

"Yes. We shall not see it, you and I," said Mistress Lacey sombrely.

"Not in reality. In my writing, thank God, I have moved away from what is and entered my Celestial City. That, at least, can never be taken from me."

Glancing across at Martin I felt a stab of jealousy. He had completely forgotten me, and was drinking in every word, his face alight. For one unworthy moment I was hurt and angry, and looked coldly on the speaker. I have been sorry for it since, many times. At least I am glad that he and Martin, fortunately oblivious, never knew.

Colonel Sidney rose to take his leave, now looking sad and old, as if the forgotten cares of the present were closing in on him again, and the future of which he had spoken indeed was the promised land to Moses, not for him to see. He bade me farewell very kindly, thanked Henrietta for an evening which had, he said, given him true pleasure, and went with

Martin from the room. Just over the threshold I heard him say in quite a different tone: "You will keep your promise! It could well be the last thing I shall ask of you." Then the door closed behind them, and I heard no more.

* * *

So I stayed in the house of Henrietta, as she had bidden me call her, and grew to like her well. Despite her appearance, her houseful of cats, she had a keen brain, a dry and sometimes caustic wit, and the kindest heart in the world. Colonel Sidney was not the only man who visited her during my stay, for many noted Whigs seemed glad to talk with her, and to discuss the rumours which seemed to fill the air like a cloud of gnats. Some Scot had been arrested, and there was talk of a plot against the king. Despite what I had overheard in the hut, it seemed no concern of mine. So much was happening — shopping trips, walks abroad, rides in Henrietta's coach which was, I should think, the least comfortable in London.

Once, in Saint James' Park, we caught a glimpse of the king, walking with a small train of gentlemen and dogs, pausing to throw bread to the ducks. He turned once, so that I saw him clearly, and have ever since marvelled that he should be called the "Merry Monarch", for that grim face held little but a weary lack of interest. Yet he was king, and my pulses quickened at the sight of him, and I gazed at the bright clothing, the great periwigs of those who attended him, and thought they were like actors dressed for a play. For by now I had been to my first theatre, where a drama by Master Dryden had been shown and though I did not fully understand all the lines had been lost in admiration of those who spoke them. It seemed that some political meaning was there, and boos came from part of the crowd, and Martin muttered under his breath. I myself was so lost in a trance of delight that when we left and stepped into the coach I felt as if I, too, took part in a play, that soon the lights would dim and I should be myself again, all this no more than a dream.

But Martin's hand clasping mine, the way his grey eyes softened, despite his anger at the play, when they met mine, these were real enough.

I had seen little of him during the past days, and when he did come we were not often alone together. But it would not be for long now that we should be apart, and at the thought, my joy was so deep that I had much ado not to shout it to the world, and I am assured that my face which had been glum so long was now alight with smiles. This period before my marriage seemed to hold the shining beauty of early dawn when all lies waiting the glory of the sun, and it appears not possible that any cloud should mar the perfection that was to come. If I had never known happiness before I knew it now, and was filled with gratitude. I might have missed it so easily — a moment longer under the seat in the hut and we might never have met. Walking with Martin at my side, I shivered at the thought, and his hand tightened on mine. "A goose walked over my grave," I said, laughing at that which seemed so far away.

"Come in, Martin, will you not! I can give you something to wash the taste of that damned play from your throat", said Henrietta, as we reached the house. Martin agreed, adding that he wished to speak with me.

"And high time too, since the maid has not been over blessed with your company of late. Still, I must say she looks not ill on it."

"She looks gay and fair as the morning," said Martin, handing us from the coach. "And I am honoured to squire two such ladies." And he bowed with an air.

"You are out of your place, my lad. Courtly speeches butter no paws with me," said his aunt, but she had a pleased smile. "There, get along the pair of you. I must tell my children that I am returned."

Crying on her cats she left us in the little room where we had first spoken with her, and for a time we said nothing at all. Then I raised my head.

"What did you say, dear heart?"

"I said that I am glad you wear your own hair."

He laughed, marking that his desire was to please me in all things, also that his head was hot enough without a wig. Then he looked at me rather gravely.

"Catherine."

"My dear love?"

"You will not be pleased with what I have to say. I should have told you before, but there have been so many matters of business — I have been away overlong — but let that go. I have sent Tom on a journey." He paused, looking somewhat anxiously at me.

"I shall shed no tears over that, worthy though he be."

He frowned. "You do not understand. I have sent him with a message concerning you."

"You have sent him to Ralph," I said flatly, looking away. "You need tell me no more."

He muttered something and turned my face back to his. "Think, my love! He must know. It is unfair to him and to me as matters stand. I suppose it has never occurred to you that I shall be looked on as a fortune-hunter if not an abductor."

"Then you had best send me back and have an end to it since I am such a burden to you!"

He pulled me into his arms and murmured against my hair, "If I did not know that you are jesting, I would beat you for that. You are not truly grieved? I did what I must."

"I suppose you are right. Only—"

"Only?"

"Only we have been so happy, so far removed from the past. But you are right, and I would not wish Ralph to continue unhappy. And as to my fortune, I had meant to hand some part of it over to him."

"Do what you will — 'tis you, not your money, that I want. And you I will have. And do not fear — by the time Ralph knows you will be safely my wife."

"You sound as if I were all that man could wish for. It is past my understanding."

He laughed. "Who needs to understand? It is, as God knows, the truth. I lost you — I found you — and, finding you, have found all I need in this world, and perhaps the next."

After that we spoke no more until Henrietta and her train of cats came into the room. We moved apart, and she cocked an eye at us, observing that she trusted we had finished our conversation. And that mighty laugh of hers filled the room.

It was long that night before sleep came to me. I thought of my brother and how dumbfounded he would be, hoping that there would be a tinge of relief, a touch of his old feeling for me, but I knew that he would be justifiably enraged at the trick I had played on him. And to add to the cruelty there was my inheritance, snatched from the hands which had thought to hold it like fairy gold. I vowed that I would make it up to Ralph and rejoiced in the memory of what Martin had said. The words echoed most sweetly in my mind, and I recalled the way he had looked at me as he spoke.

There were times when the man he had become changed to the boy Martin, back from the past, so that the years between might never have been. I saw him as if he were there beside me — the grey eyes which could look so bleak but were warm enough for me, the straight black brows, the brown hair which, thick and springy, seemed to have a life of its own, a tiny white scar at the corner of his right eye. Martin. Martin, whose wife I was to be, and from whom I should not be parted any more. I was most happy, yet at the back of my mind was something vaguely discomforting, small as the cloud no bigger than a man's hand. I groped after it, at last tracking it down. It was another voice which I recalled, a voice echoing most earnestly: "You will keep your promise?"

"You look heavy-eyed," said Henrietta when we met the next morning. "Is your stomach distempered? If so I will give you a draught."

"I did not sleep well, that is all," I said.

"That's not surprising. As well now when you are man and wife, though I shall be sad to lose you. The cats, too like you well."

This was true, since I could scarce move without one or more of the furry bodies pressed against me. I did not tell Henrietta that I could well dispense with some of this affection, but said sincerely: "I shall never forget your kindness to me — the way you took me in without question, treating me as your own child."

Her eyes went to the smiling portrait, and for an instant their keen gaze softened, and her lips quivered.

"She would have liked you well," she said, and at once, as if to forbid questioning or sympathy became herself again. "I go to the fishmonger to tell him what I think of the stinking stuff he calls fish. You had best accompany me. Mayhap the air will refresh you."

We set out together. As always I felt dwarfed by her towering figure, and although she strove to accommodate her steps to mine, at times, forgetting me, she would stride on ahead. Finding me not beside her she would halt in some surprise, then the same thing would happen all over again. I was accustomed to it by now, and besides, was so much interested in all around me that I paid no heed. The hour being early not many folk were abroad, and I could gaze my fill while turning a deaf ear to those who implored me to buy.

I had lingered beside a mercer's all aglow with rich stuffs of every hue, and so beautiful that I longed to touch them, when I heard her calling me with a mixture of mirth and displeasure. Realising I had stayed overlong I turned hastily and ran full pelt into a man coming towards me. With a startled oath he held me, and I begged his pardon.

"As to that—" he began but broke off. "Catherine?" I looked for the first time into his face and saw it white and frightened, as I had not seen Roger Frampton look before.

I said, in a voice as shaken as his own: "I am no ghost, sir."

"No," he said, and the colour came slowly back to his face. "You are solid enough to have well-nigh driven the breath from my body. But how in God's name Catherine Carey who is dead and drowned walks and talks here today is past my understanding."

"A pretty state of affairs if a maid cannot walk two steps without being accosted!" Henrietta's voice boomed from behind me. "Take your hands from her, or by God, you shall feel the weight of mine!"

Roger Frampton gazed wildly at Henrietta's face, now crimson with rage, and stepped back. A small crowd gathered and he shot a hunted glance around. I was shaken by laughter yet I couldn't help but feel sorry for Frampton, who looked as if in the midst of a distasteful dream.

I said hastily. "This gentleman is known to me. It was my fault—"

Henrietta gave one of her mighty snorts, coldly asked those around if they had nothing else to do but stare, and fixed her gaze on Frampton.

"On my word, we too have met! At the house of John Strange, was it not? Master—"

"Frampton. Roger Frampton. And I well recall our meeting Mistress Lacey."

"So you and Catherine are known to one another? When I thought to see her in the clutches of some lewd gallant I came to the rescue. As well that I did not strike before I spoke!"

"Indeed, yes," he replied with feeling. I laughed again, and he looked at me with surprise and a kind of admiration. "For a spirit from the vasty deep you seem most gay."

I reflected that he had scarcely known me to laugh before, and found that Henrietta was inviting him to return with us once her affray with the sinful fishmonger was over. She strode off, and we followed more slowly. I could feel his gaze on me, the one unanswered question hanging between us.

"Have you seen Ralph of late?" I asked.

"A week past, at Glyn's," he replied.

"And he was well?"

"He was greatly saddened by the sudden and tragic death of his sister. Otherwise he was well."

The words struck me as a reproach, and we walked on in silence for a while. I did not feel it necessary to justify my actions to Roger Frampton, and I could net help feeling that if Ralph were so saddened by my death he might well have been gentler with me in life, but I was somewhat pricked by conscience none the less.

"I did not wish to hurt him," I said at last. "It seemed the only way. In any case, by now it is probable that he knows I am not dead. A messenger has been sent to him."

"Perhaps that is as well," he answered politely.

Then Henrietta returned triumphantly from her battle, handed her great basket to Roger as if it had been a posy, and we made our way back.

"You are in time for the wedding," she said.

"Wedding?"

"Did you not know? This Catherine is to wed my nephew Martin, so you are in time to wish happiness to the bride."

There was a short pause, then he said quietly: "I do, indeed, wish her every happiness."

I murmured my thanks, without looking at him. And when I recalled that his own offer to me had been prompted by self-interest it seemed hard that I should be made to feel sorry for him.

When we had reached the house and were alone for a while he said abruptly. "I suppose you do not wish to tell me the reason for your behaviour — if, indeed, reason there can be."

I flushed angrily. "I do not know that I am answerable to you, but my position in my brother's household had become impossible. I was treated as if half-witted, and had I remained would most certainly have become so."

"It is true they said as much," he allowed, frowning. "It surprised me at the time. But why?"

Reluctant to tell him, I remained silent.

"And this marriage of yours? A mighty sudden affair, is it not?"

"Sudden indeed," I said, smiling. "But we were friends of old."

He looked at me wonderingly, then sighed. "At least," he said, "'tis clear you are no unwilling bride."

With Henrietta's return the talk became general. But ever and again I caught him looking at me as if he could not believe what he saw.

He rose to take his leave, then turned to me as if with a sudden recollection.

"I had not told you of a happening at the Grange shortly after your — departure."

"No? Ralph is in no kind of trouble?"

"Not more than any of us who follow the unpopular line. No, there was a death, a real one, corpse and all. Do you recall a storm of thunder, very violent? Your sister's woman, Jennings, was out in it. She took shelter under a tree which was struck and she was killed."

He spoke briefly, but there was a look on his face as if he recalled something distasteful. Henrietta spoke of storms she had known, but I said nothing. I pictured that dark figure as the storm raged around her, and wondered if she had indeed gone in the lightning flash to render up her soul. And then I thought it might not have been so, that my dislike and repulsion might have misled me into thinking her other than she was. But I could feel no sorrow at her death.

"Frances will miss her," I said, half to myself. "The rest of the household will shed no tear."

He nodded. "I heard that you held her responsible for your sickness, and Ralph says there were mutterings of witchcraft and the like. Be that as it may, she has gone now, and I must do likewise."

He took his leave, remarking that it had been an unexpected pleasure, and Henrietta said that it would have been more unexpected still had she followed her first inclination.

So we parted laughing. But I thought he looked grim and old when the laughter died.

"I think," said Henrietta, returning, "we had best sing Haste to the wedding before other gentlemen from your past appear."

"He is not from my past. And his love was for Frances, not for me."

"Frances Leigh — that lovely creature whose face belied her nature? Not that one can blame her for being a wanton. Her mother was a notable French whore, and Gervase Leigh picked her up on his travels, prudently married her, and lived on her in comfort till the day of his death. And touching this Frampton, I had heard that he was besotted over her. The strange thing is that she was said to be heels over head in love with him. Not that it stopped her from adding Lord Conway to the list of those to whom she had been over kind. His wife returned without warning — well!" She shrugged her shoulders. "All town rang with the affair, and that was the end for Frampton. It was also the end for Frances here, and she was glad enough to wed your brother, God help him."

"From all I hear I should not have thought one scandal more or less would be of much account."

"True enough in general. But Jane Conway is the wrong person to cross, and that in her own home. She is mighty close to the queen. But were I your brother I would not have this Frampton too near. Frances Leigh might sell her favours to the highest bidder — to him she gave her heart. Although, so far as he is concerned, from the way he looked at you—"

"You deceive yourself. There is nothing between us — you have only to look at me beside Frances to know that."

"Well, well, it may be I was wrong," said she blandly. "But of one thing I am assured."

"And what is that?"

"That Martin, had he been here, would have thought as I did."

CHAPTER XV

"So," said Martin, "it is done, and none can change it now."

We were alone together in our own home at last, and we looked at one another half shyly, scarce able to believe that it could be truly so.

"Do you wish to change it? And so soon?"

"Not I! I am at this moment the very button on the cap of fortune. What the days to come may do to us, who can say? There is the matter of your curst temper—"

"And of your curst obstinacy!"

"Now here is talk for a newmade wife!" said he reprovingly. "Am I not your lord and master, and should I not be all perfection in your eyes?"

"And I in yours? Sauce for the goose is sauce for the gander, is it not?"

"Now I see that I have left you with my aunt overlong, and that she has imbued you with her sentiments."

I said, forsaking our light talk, which had served to cloak a certain embarrassment: "She has been as a mother to me, and I shall never cease to be grateful." I paused, hesitant yet curious. "Martin—"

"Yes, my love?"

"In what manner did her daughter die? She never told me."

He frowned. "'Tis scarce fit talk for a wedding night, but if you must have it, I will tell you. She was returning from a visit to her betrothed. They were walking with only a servant, since the way was short and the evening fine when they were set upon. Mary was seized and dragged into a doorway, the serving man and Richard, both trying to defend her were run through and left to die. When they were found, Mary was kneeling in the filth with his head in her lap trying to rouse him. They did all things possible, but she had been most cruelly used, and what with that and her grief she became fevered and did not linger long."

"Oh, Martin! But the men — could they not be found and punished?"

He laughed unpleasantly. "When the highest in the land join in like merry pranks? Can you wonder if we plan for a time when there will be law and justice? Is it not worth planning for?"

My heart ached for the smiling girl in the portrait, and I thought with Martin that this was strange talk for our marriage night. I wished I had not been moved to ask him for so ugly a history.

"I am very sorry," I said. "For her, for her lover, and for your aunt."

His arms closed round me, and he said, with a new urgency. "Forget it, sweetheart. Here is no time for sorrow."

And indeed, our happiness was most great. But since it belonged to us alone, I am not minded to write of it, but rather keep it like some jewel jealously locked away.

* * *

I awoke before my husband, and raised myself to look down at him. He was sleeping like a child, his lips slightly pouting, and I was so shaken by love for him that I bent closer, and without waking his arms came in search of me as if it were the most natural thing in the world that I should be there with him. Despite all the strangeness it was also thus with me. I lay back again, and he murmured most comfortably, and slept on.

It was little past dawn, and the air was fresh, faintly scented by the herbs which had been strewn over our marriage bed. Even here I fancied I could hear the voice of the river, but it no longer sounded sad as on the night of our arrival. The house had been swept and garnished since then, and no longer smelled of damp and decay. Henrietta had found us a couple of serving maids, sisters, the older, Tabitha, serious of mien, while Mercy had a roguish eye and a loud and ready laugh, with curls of hair ever escaping beneath her cap. Grave and gay, they both worked with a will, and I wondered what Tom would think of them, and for that matter, how he would meet me. I knew that Martin had told him the truth of the matter, and that after the first stunned silence Tom had delivered himself of such a spate of texts concerning scarlet women and their wiles that Martin had told him to hold his tongue if he did not wish them to part company. Tom had ridden off bitterly offended, but he would come round, said Martin, and that I should learn to value him. I had grave doubts.

The light grew stronger and I heard the sounds of movement in the house, but Martin still slept, smiling now. I watched him, and memories buzzed through my head like bees. I recalled Henrietta dressing me for my wedding as if I had indeed been that child she loved, and I thought if Martin and I had a child how could I bear to lose it? I remembered the wedding itself, with Martin most fine and unfamiliar in golden brown, myself in heavy amber silk, and how I had suddenly become much afraid, until Martin took my hand and I met his clear gaze and knew that all was well. The face of Colonel Sidney had seemed grave and worn, until it was lit by a smile as he wished us happiness, adding that there was small need for him to wish it, since he was assured that it would be ours. And Henrietta, for once most grand in pearl embroidered velvet had engulfed us in turn in her embrace without a word. After that it had been a whirl with nothing clear in my mind until we had come to our home and to be truly man and wife.

I thought of the strange road which had brought me to this, my bridal bed, and wondered how Ralph would have taken the news. I hoped that he would be reconciled to me, for my happiness made me wish to extend arms of friendship to him, but there were difficulties in the way great as those met by Master Bunyan's pilgrim. Frances was his wife, and I had accused her in a manner like to prove unforgivable. At least my marriage would assure her that I had no designs on Roger Frampton, and I was sure that it was his offer for me which had turned her finally against me. I remembered her wistful charm that first meeting, and still felt that she had meant me well. But she was so strange a mixture! The tale told me by Henrietta had been no surprise, but I could not think of it without a sick disgust. Loving one man, how could she give herself, with all that entailed, to others? And I recalled Roger Frampton's weary voice: "She cannot help herself. 'Tis in the blood."

For some reason with the thought of Roger Frampton came the recollection of the news he had given me, and at once the most vivid picture flashed into my mind. I saw it all, the dark figure cowering against a tree, face upturned, eyes glaring into an unbelievable horror, then the searing flash which blackened and destroyed. It was so real that I gave a little cry and Martin woke. He blinked then looked at me with surprise. In some dudgeon he said, "I did not think to see you looking so. In God's name, what is wrong?"

The picture faded as if it had never been. Smiling, I bent to kiss him.

"Why were you looking on me as if at a monster? Last night it was not so. Am I so repulsive in my sleep?"

"Most dreadful," said I, gently pulling his hair. "But I was not thinking of you just then."

"And that is a pretty confession for a newmade wife! What occupied those thoughts of yours? Some lover from the past?"

"You will never believe it, but I was thinking of that woman of Frances, and how Roger Frampton said the lightning struck her down. She was one whom I could not abide and, I believe, had all to do with my troubles, but I pictured her end, and it was horrible."

"You think too much, and at the strangest times," he said, looking bemused. "But speaking of this Frampton, how long had you known him?"

"Not long. He was with us some days at the Grange when the snow came. I had met him only once since until this last time." A teasing spirit moved me to add: "'Tis true he wished to wed me."

Martin raised himself in some surprise.

"The devil he did! May I ask why, since you were so unhappy, you did not accept him?"

"I might have done, but I knew he wanted only my money. Also — but let that go."

Martin looked at me searchingly and was apparently content with what he saw. "To the devil with Frampton, the past, dead wenches and all. Let us turn to our own affairs." And he stretched out his arms for me.

"I was driven to my thoughts having such a slug-a-bed for a husband!"

"And why not? Newly-wed, lie long abed. And we are very newly-wed — or had you forgotten, Catherine — Catherine?"

"No," I said. "I had not forgotten."

* * *

Back of the house was a little *pleasaunce*, overgrown and neglected, but filled with sunshine. Here was a sundial, and by the wall a stone seat, where we sat awhile that morning eating cherries which Mercy, the smiling maid, had brought in. I do not know why it came into my mind then warm and happy as I was, but I was moved to ask Martin what the promise he had given to Colonel Sidney might be. It was almost an idle question, but once asked it seemed to bring into the open matters for disquiet, which might well cloud our happiness.

"It is something which may never happen," he answered. "And there is no need in the world for you to trouble yourself over it, on this day of all days."

I persisted. "I am your wife. I should know all that concerns you."

He looked down at me, no longer smiling. "Can you not leave it, Catherine, and take my word that it is better you not knowing? Is not this, our life together, enough for you? I thought you happy."

I took his hand and held it to my cheek. "I am happier than I could have dreamed. My heart sings with joy."

"Well, then," said he, kissing me. "Let us leave it there."

But I could not leave it, being driven by some demon of curiosity mingled with a vague fear. I admired and respected Colonel Sidney, but Martin was my dearest love. If any promise he had made spelt trouble for him then I would fight it.

"I wish very much to know," I said, trying again. "Will you not tell me, Martin?"

I was sorry when I saw his face cloud, but I did not falter in my determination, and at last I had my way.

"I will tell you, daughter of Eve, since you persist. But mark this, Catherine, I shall not break my word. Even you need not think to persuade me otherwise."

"How could I think it? I know that if your mind is set on any course it would take a miracle to move you."

"A man must do what he feels to be right, whether mistaken or no. But I would rather you did not use your wiles to persuade me, my Delilah. I am weak as water where you are concerned."

Looking at him I thought there was little sign of weakness in his face, set now, and most like that of the man in the portrait. I knew, too, that if I did persuade him to break his pledged word he would hate himself for ever, and that in the end the blame would attach itself to me. I shivered, and he turned to me in surprise.

"You are not cold in this sunshine!" For indeed, the warmth in this enclosed spot was so great that the heat seemed to shimmer above the mossy paving.

"I am not cold. For a moment I was troubled."

"It is your own fault. You spoil our lovely day by curiosity, and then fear what you may hear."

"Yes, you are right. Let it go, Martin. I will ask you no more, and all shall be as it was before."

He kissed my troubled face gently, but said in rather a sombre tone: "The water has gone under the bridge, my sweet, and it will not come back. I will tell you, so that you may not imagine affairs to be worse than they are. My promise is only that should this crazy plot be discovered I should leave England before being taken."

"Leave England! Leave me! You cannot mean it."

"There's the rub," said he. "When I gave the promise, I was not a married man. Yet I gave it."

"But I do not understand. This plot — is it the same spoken of that time when you thought me a spy? Why, you and Colonel Sidney both would have no part in that."

"No part at all, God knows, but that will not stop those who would denounce Sidney and any known friend of his. They would step into shoes like those of Titus Oates, spreading the net far and wide to bring in innocent and guilty alike. We, who would have no part in this furtive business, can hardly hope to be untouched by it."

"Would they truly try to kill the king?"

"God knows. They say not, and it will not come to that, since undoubtedly the whole affair will be discovered. As Sidney said, there are far too many involved, and those with little sense or prudence. We only hope it will die unborn."

"But you — you say you plan for the future. What of the king then?"

"Not murder, believe me," he answered earnestly. "But the king, in nature will not live forever. We plan for one to follow him who would think for the people, not solely for himself, and would allow a representative government to hold sway."

Even I had heard enough to take his meaning. "Under Monmouth?" I asked.

"When the time is ripe, and not before." He turned to take my hands, a smile lighting his face. "My love, must we talk of politics now? Could we not have this small space for pleasure?"

"Small space indeed!" I echoed, shivering again. "Martin, if you do go, if it comes to that, you would not leave me behind?"

"Dear heart, if I went it would be in such haste that I must be alone. But I would send for you at the first possible moment. Do you think I would willingly be parted from you now? But after all, you would rather have me with my head, such as it is, on my shoulders, would you not?"

He smiled, but I shuddered.

"'Tis no laughing matter!" I protested. "And will not Colonel Sidney himself escape?"

"I have begged him to do so, but he says he is old and weary, and has lived afar from his native land too much. Come what may he will remain, and bid me go like a rat that leaves a sinking ship. He will have it so, and I have promised."

He shook his shoulders impatiently, rose, and pulled me to my feet.

"Again I say, it may never happen. Today, at least I will have no more of such talk, and I will have a wife who smiles. Come, my love, we will take a trip on the river and let tomorrow care for itself. No, I mean it! Not another word."

So we spent the sunlit day without speaking of serious matters again, and we laughed together and seemed as carefree as the midges dancing over the water. But when I slept that night I had a dream so sad that I woke sobbing and shaking, with a face wet with tears. And I clung to my husband as if to assure myself that he was still there with me, and had not gone to some untold danger leaving me alone.

* * *

The days passed like shining beads on a string, and my fears were pushed into the background, and Martin was ever at my side. We were so happy together that I could scarce believe it true. When we touched hands or kissed there was the most lovely feeling of completeness, of true belonging one to the other. When we talked it was of the past or the future, but our future, and that of kings, princes or conspirators seemed to mean nothing to us. Our laughter filled the house, and the two serving maids smiled indulgently on us, as if we were children whose happiness spread pleasure all around. We rode into the country, strolled by the river, saw the many sights of the city, all as if we had not a care in the world. At times we would argue as we had done so often, break off with laughter, recall the sins of our childhood — oh, it all seems a foolish tale enough, and I suppose we were foolish. But I shall remember those days for the rest of my life.

The fourth day after our marriage was the tenth of June, and I recall it well, for Martin, becoming somewhat more serious, took me to his man of business, instructing him that I should, if needful, be supplied with money by him. I looked at Martin with apprehension, but he only laughed, and stopped my mouth when I would have spoken.

"There is no sinister background to my behaviour, and you need not look as if the worst had happened," he said. "But our days of holiday must some time come to an end, and matters of business claim our attention. There is, for example, the manor."

"The manor," I echoed eagerly. "Shall we live there?"

"I think so. We are Dorset folk and cannot be mewed for ever in the town. And when our children come it will be best for them." He looked at me inquiringly with his head on one side like a bird, and I laughed, and told him he would have to wait awhile. And the thought of one day holding his child to my breast was so sweet that it was almost too much to bear.

We returned late one afternoon from seeing Henrietta, who had been so pleased with our company that we had stayed longer than we meant. When we entered we were laughing over something she had said, and at first did not see that Tabitha was waiting to attract our attention, and looking somewhat discomposed.

"A gentleman is waiting for you in the south parlour. He gave no name, but said that you would know him."

I knew at once who the visitor would be, and the enormity of my conduct rose before me, and I was afraid to face him. I turned to Martin, and he put his arm around me and gave me a reassuring hug.

"Was there ever such a wench as you for meeting trouble more than halfway? 'Tis probably no one of importance, and in any case there is no need for you to turn pale and tremble. You have a husband now, as I have so often to remind you."

We heard the sound of a chair pushed roughly back, an inpatient oath. I had made no mistake as to the one who awaited us.

"Oho!" said Martin, enlightened. "I see. You remain here or go above stairs. I will see him first."

"No. I will come with you," I said.

"There is my girl! We will face the outraged brother together."

We went into the parlour. Ralph, who was standing at the window swung round at out entrance scowling formidably.

"I am sorry to have kept you waiting," said Martin courteously. "It was a poor welcome, I fear."

"To the devil with that!" roared Ralph. "You have been a damnably long time, but I would have waited longer to see the pair of you."

"Why, that is most kind and forgiving of you, and more than we deserve," said Martin cordially.

Ralph stared like an enraged bull and turned an alarming shade of purple.

"God's teeth, you take it calmly enough! You abduct my sister when her wits are gone and marry her out of hand. You know what men call such as you?"

"I know," said Martin gently. "But I should not advise you to say it."

There was more menace back of the quiet voice than in all Ralph's bellowings, and I caught my breath.

"Ralph, it is not as you think," I said hastily. "Martin had nothing to do with my leaving home. The plan, the deceit, were all mine."

"That be damned for a tale! What kind of fool do you take me to be?"

"A very loudmouthed one," murmured Martin. "But I admit you have been ill-used and deserve a full explanation. Will you not cease ranting, sit down, and let us discuss the matter calmly?"

Ralph opened his mouth. I went quickly to him, laying a hand on his arm.

"Please, Ralph," I said.

He swallowed what he had been about to say and looked down at me, the angry resentment in his face mingled with a certain wonder. I went on before he could speak again. "I am truly grieved for the sorrow I caused you. It was all I could think to do at the time."

He said, not shouting now. "We thought you dead. You made it appear so. And you expect me to forgive that?"

"It is more than I deserve, but what is done is done. And I shall no longer be a burden on you."

I meant no harm, but he leaped as if stung.

"Burden!" he roared. "Did I ever call you that?"

"No, but I was not a happy member of your household. It is understandable. I fear I behaved ill after my fall."

"I felt," he said, looking at me as if we two were alone, "that you blamed me with every breath you drew. And God knows with reason, since it was my drunken folly which marred you. That damned horse — I would have killed him had he not made straight for his old stables. Not that the brute was to blame. It was I, and I alone."

"I never blamed you," I replied, looking straight back at him. "I was — not happy, that was all. My limp, my scarred face, seemed to matter so much."

"And do they not matter now?"

"Since my husband can bear them, why shouldn't I? I am very happy, Ralph. I know I did wrong, but indeed, I cannot regret it."

He sat down without a word. His face was grim and forbidding, but I was no longer afraid. Martin drew up a chair for me, and I sat down also, spreading the cherry skirts of the new gown he had bought me.

"You will take some refreshment?" I asked.

He snorted impatiently, but Martin went to the door and called for wine. Tabitha, bringing it, looked somewhat alarmed. Ralph's voice would not have confined itself to the one room. He was quiet now, but not mollified, and if his look turned towards me had softened it was otherwise when his eye lightened on Martin.

"I shall need a deal of convincing, and so I warn you," he said heavily. "But as you ask it of me, Catherine, I will listen and reserve judgement. And by God, if matters are as I thought, you and I, Lacey, will have a reckoning."

Martin went rather white round the lips, but not with fear. "I told my wife what would be said of me, but since she and I know the truth it does not trouble me. I will, however, tell you that her money is that to me!" And he snapped his fingers. "I would have married her without a shift to her back. Indeed," he added, with a sidelong glance at me, "I almost did."

"She is fine enough now, at all events," said Ralph drily. "And if it is not too much to ask, I should wish to hear this tale of yours from the beginning."

"As far as I am concerned, Catherine made her way to the manor not knowing that I was there. When we met she asked for my protection. I thought at first to take her back, but when I saw how matters stood I decided otherwise. I brought her to London—"

"Giving no thought whatever to her good name."

Martin flushed, and I laid a hand on his knee. "I gave every thought. She went to my aunt, who cared for her like a mother — during the journey, also, we were not alone. In any case, your sister would have been safe in my hands, as you should know."

Ralph moved impatiently. "Let that be as it may — you spoke of protection. Protection from what? She had a home with me and all her wants supplied. If she could not be content was I to blame?"

"You know best as to that. I know only that when I found her, rightly or wrongly, she dreaded to return to your roof. And we were not strangers, after all. Had I not been away and deceived into thinking her dead I should have asked for her hand long since."

Ralph looked at me uneasily. "This matter of your dreading to return, of preferring to leave like a thief in the night, and worse! Dear God, when I recall that heap of night gear at the lake's edge, and how I felt—"

"I am truly sorry," I said.

"Sorry! The only excuse I can find for you is that you were out of your wits, as they said. I tried not to believe it, but if you had seen her, Martin, you could scarce have doubted the evidence of your own eyes. She lay not moving, caring for nothing and nobody." He paused, adding heavily. "Besides, she had tried to take her own life. And she had turned against Frances. Why did you, Catherine? When first you met it was not so, and she liked you well. She says you blamed her—"

He broke off and looked fully at me, with some hurt in his eyes, as if he dreaded what I might say. His high colour had faded and there were lines in his face which I did not remember. I felt that one way and another, despite his faults, he had been most ill-used, and knew that I could not speak against his wife to him.

"I had been fevered and, it may be, imagined some part of my wrongs," I said. Martin looked at me with surprise, but Ralph's face brightened, and I added, "But one thing I know, the woman Jennings was my enemy. It was she who pushed me into the stream, and after put some witch's brew into my food, taking away all my strength and feeling."

"Jennings!" he said, and a look came into his face which I had not seen before.

"Master Frampton told me she was dead."

He nodded. "And in a fashion so sudden that all the talk is that she was sold to the devil and he claimed his own. We found her, Frampton and I, when we rode back from the manor that day." He broke off suddenly to look accusingly on us. "I suppose you had her hidden away even then, and let me go still thinking her dead. By God, you should answer to me for that!"

"Whenever you wish," said Martin pleasantly.

"Tell us more of Jennings," I said hastily.

Ralph removed his bulging gaze from my husband and continued, rather unwillingly.

"You recall the little clearing at the edge of the park, where the great beech tree grew? It was there. The storm was over and the sun was shining, and the birds singing as we rode back. But not in the clearing. No bird sang there."

Into the pleasant room, like a creeping mist, came the memory of something which had shaken him so greatly that we, too, seemed to share his fear. That it was Ralph speaking, Ralph who was never noted for sensibility, made it the more strange and horrible. I gave a shudder, almost as if I had seen the sight which even now took the colour from his cheeks.

"It was the stench we noticed first," he said. "A kind of bitter burning, which caught the backs of our throats and all but choked us. Then the horses shook and sweated and refused to move. Frampton said the lightning had struck the tree and went to see. I heard him cry out, left the horses and followed him. The air was full of evil smelling smoke, and it was dark, though outside the sun still shone. Frampton pointed to something and I saw her. Dear God, I saw her, and I wish that I had not."

There were beads of sweat on his forehead. Martin pushed a filled goblet over to him, and he drank thirstily.

"The beech had been struck right down the middle of its great trunk and was smouldering still. She lay at the foot, her arms spread wide, and all one side was black and charred. But her eyes were open, and in them and on her face was a look — oh God, I cannot describe it. I only know that if what they said of her was true she might well have looked into the hell that awaited her before she died."

Martin's hand closed on mine, and he said in a matter-of-fact tone, "To be struck by lightning is horror enough, I should think. For myself I take little heed of tales of witch-craft, souls sold to the devil and the like."

"You did not know Jennings," I said, darkly.

"And you did not see the look on her face," added Ralph.

Martin rose. "In any case, she is with us no more, and we can forget her. Will you not also forget your wrongs, Ralph, and be on good terms with us? We desire it greatly, my wife and I."

The last words were spoken with pride, and we smiled together, half forgetful of Ralph.

"Well—" said he.

"You have drunk with us, after all!"

Ralph looked at his empty glass in some surprise and gave a short bark of laughter.

"None the less," he said, in a grumbling tone, "'Tis a most damnable coil, and will take a deal of unravelling."

"Yet if we set our minds to it I think it can be done," said Martin. "In particular if we talk together as friends — or rather, brothers," and he looked impudently at Ralph with his eyebrows raised and his head on one side in that way he had. It was touch and go. For a moment I thought that Ralph would drive his fist into that smiling face, and where would any hope of agreement be then? But he relaxed and spoke calmly enough.

"I shall never cease to think that you played me a damned scurvy trick, but what's done is done, and we must make the best of it. But brother or no brother, Master Martin, 'tis no words of yours that make me say so."

"What, then?" asked Martin with interest.

"'Tis that she looks—" Ralph stopped, looking at me "—as she did before."

He muttered the words as if half ashamed, and I went to him and kissed him. It was for the first time for many years.

"Dear Ralph, I am most happy," I said.

He held me closely for a moment, then turned to the table and asked for more wine. Leaving them together with a light heart I went to see to our meal. And I wished that Ralph, who had been moved by my happiness could find happiness also, and was glad that I had refrained from miscalling Frances to him.

Ralph remained overnight, setting off early the next morning to join the companions with whom he was riding. Before he left we spoke alone, and I told him of my wish that half my inheritance should be his. He swore and protested, but somewhat half-heartedly, and in the end said candidly. "To speak truth I should be damnably glad of it, but it is not right."

"It is my wish," I said. "And that of my husband also."

"'My husband! My wife!' The two of you linger on the words as if you could never have enough."

"We are but newly-wed," I said in apology.

He sighed and said. "Hold you happiness while you may, little sister. 'Tis not a thing that lasts."

I said nothing, for I was assured that our happiness would be no passing thing, and again I was sorry for him. I told him to make any arrangements, and that I would sign all necessary papers, and gave him a letter saying this. Then Martin joined us, and we made our farewells.

"We came out of that with more ease than I expected," said my husband, when Ralph had gone. "You have a persuasive tongue, my love. Left to ourselves there would have been bloodshed, his or mine."

"And to what avail?" I demanded tartly. "That is where men are such fools."

"True, true. And how much of your inheritance have you promised him?"

"Only half." I added defensively. "You said you did not mind."

"I am making no complaint. And neither, I dare warrant, is Ralph."

"He swore a little—"

"And held out his hand at the same time."

I could not help laughing. "I am very sorry for him."

"Why? Because you give him half and not the whole?"

"For that matter, thinking me dead, he had every right to consider it his. No. I was thinking that he has not found what we have found."

He kissed me, teasing no longer. "There are few, my sweet, who have."

And for three more carefree days we went our merry way, and the storm that was brewing grew and grew, and in our happiness little did we reck of it.

CHAPTER XVI

Tom, who had been doing business for Martin at the manor, arrived back on the fourteenth of June, and with his coming it seemed that we returned to care. It was nothing that was said, and he carried off our first meeting by simply ignoring the fact that we had met before. Yet after he had spoken alone with Martin, I felt in my bones that trouble lay ahead. Martin, when I asked him, said that there was no definite news, only rumours which might or might not be true, but there was something, some slight change in him, which I could not help but sense. It was not that he was less loving towards me, but as if — how can I put it? — our time of holiday was over, and affairs which had been set aside could be ignored no longer.

On the day we met again with Colonel Sidney at the house of Henrietta, though no word was spoken of plots in my hearing, I felt or imagined the same air about them which I had felt in Martin. They were both most kind and indulgent towards me, Colonel Sidney complimenting me on my looks and Henrietta on my gown, but all the talk that evening was of the past. Colonel Sidney, I recall, spoke of his family home at Penshurst, the park, the quiet there, as if he had small hope of seeing it again, at least so it seemed to me. Henrietta spoke of her dead husband, the stern-faced man in the portrait, he whose eyes were like those of Martin, recalling how he had been thrown into prison for refusing to pay a tax he thought unjust and had died there.

"Ever stubborn and stiff-necked," said she, with a sigh. "But one whose word was his bond."

"The salt of the earth," said Colonel Sidney. "What said Master Bunyan of his Valiant for Truth? 'So he passed over. And all the trumpets sounded for him on the other side.'"

"Valiant for Truth!" echoed Henrietta, flushing, and with sparkling eyes. "A title grander than that of any king!"

The two men smiled at her enthusiasm, but I said, "It seems hard to die, even for the truth."

Sidney looked on me very kindly. "Death is not the worst enemy, Mistress Catherine."

"But the final one! The end of all we know."

"That, perhaps, but there is more to come." Then he added softly, as if to himself, "'My soul there is a country, Afar beyond the stars.'" There, surely, all our doubts may be resolved, all our shortcomings forgiven. Death is but a way through the dark valley into light. My sins are many, but I do not fear to travel that road."

"But not yet!" said Martin leaning forward. "We cannot lose you yet."

His voice was urgent as if he spoke of that which he could not bear to contemplate, and Sidney smiled.

"My dear lad, I assure you I do not imagine that the day is imminent. Look not so solemn and downcast! I say only that when the time does come I trust I shall face it with fortitude, knowing that my work will be carried on, if not here, at least in my friend's settlement beyond the seas."

And partly, I believe, for my sake, he began telling us of this friend, whose name was Penn, and who in a far-off land was practicing those principles of government in which he himself so passionately believed. He spoke of vast tracts of land, lakes, painted forests. Gloomy forebodings were forgotten, and I, even as my companions, hung on his words. It

155

seemed to me most fine to brave the dangers of that wild land and starting from nothing to carve out a way of life in which merit should count for more than riches, true worth more than hereditary titles. But it all seemed almost as remote as that country beyond the stars.

He paused at length, observing that he became garrulous with age, and would weary us with his talk. Henrietta echoed my own feelings.

"You know you have not wearied us, Algernon, but that land is far removed from this."

"I cannot argue with you there. Justice a travesty, virtue a jest, the English pensioners of the French—"

His face, so lately bright, became a sombre mask of disgust, and he shook his shoulders impatiently. "None the less, a day will come!" he said.

"With Monmouth!" asked Henrietta.

"He has his following and is loved as the king's brother is not. But his time is not ripe. Those who seek to hasten it could ruin all."

Henrietta snorted. "Monmouth! The son of a woman who—"

Sidney interrupted her. "Who was the prettiest creature." There was a certain regret in his tone. He looked down at the table as if forgetful of us, remembering something long past.

"Her end was not pretty!" said Henrietta, with two spots of colour burning high on her cheeks. Sidney glanced quickly at her and seemed about to speak, but she, as if anxious to cover her last remark, swept on.

"Monmouth, from what I hear, is too easily led. And besides — you may rail against divine right, Algernon, but one in his shoes has no rights at all." For the first time I saw Colonel Sidney angered. He bent his brows on Henrietta, who was unabashed. "Oh yes, you can frown on me," she tsked. "'Tis your great fault, my friend, that all must needs think as you do. Well, here is one who says what she thinks, tread on whose corns she may!"

The table rattled, and Sidney relaxed. Smiling at her, he said, "You hit off my weakness shrewdly enough, but 'tis the pot calling the kettle black. What say you to that?"

"What can she say?" said Martin, laughing. "'Tis true that you are a pigeon pair. But to return to the matter of Monmouth, he is the king's son—"

"What's remarkable there?" asked Henrietta. "Old Rowley!" I did not take her meaning, but the two men laughed.

"His firstborn, at least."

"So you say. There are doubts even as to that."

"Well, then, his best beloved son."

"David and Absalom. Dryden hit it off well, one must admit."

"The original Absalom in plotting against his father came to a bad end," observed Henrietta, pursing her lips. "And he, at least, was legitimate."

"Touching Monmouth, none know the rights of that," said Martin, somewhat annoyed.

"I do," said Henrietta. "Had he been born in wedlock his father, doting on him as he does, would have acknowledged him long since. Answer that if you can!"

"'Tis unanswerable," admitted Sidney. Martin scowled and said nothing.

"Well, then."

"Well, then!" echoed Sidney. "His birth, at least, is no fault of his. And if he be the man to unite the country and rule with a temperate government — and here the weakness in his claim may be of help — I should favour him."

"I too, and many another," said Martin. "The west is for him heart and soul."

"And where the west leads the rest must needs follow?" asked Henrietta gently.

"God knows," he answered, with a sigh. "But one day it will be resolved."

"To our sorrow," said Henrietta heavily. "Monmouth's way will be no flowery path. Blood will be shed, brother turn against brother, and when, or if, he is king, will it be so different?"

Martin and Colonel Sidney both tried to break in, but Henrietta's mighty voice beat them down.

"It needs a woman to set matters right — one who would see beyond a pretty face and figure and a charm without depth. You make him what you would have him be. A woman would know better."

"There have been women enough," murmured Sidney, as she paused for breath. "No man could call him an anchorite."

"I did not speak of women in that sense, as well you know. But it is of no avail to talk. Your minds are fixed, and like the Gadarene swine you make haste to your destruction."

"No, no, Henrietta!" protested Sidney. "That is unfair. I, at least, make no haste, and you will admit I said but a short space past that Monmouth's time has not yet come. And when it does I doubt if I shall be there to see it."

There was that boding note again. Henrietta glanced at him uneasily.

"Alas, poor greybeard! Surely not one foot in the grave already!"

He made no reply, only gave her that fleeting smile which so changed his face, making him seem far removed from what she called him. We parted soon after, and Henrietta waved us on our way with Methuselah on her shoulder and his companions weaving about her legs. I thought what a strange figure she presented, and how fond I had grown of her.

Colonel Sidney, before we went our separate ways, echoed my thoughts. "One may smile at her and her cats, but there stands a good woman and a true friend. There are not so many such."

We agreed with all sincerity, and he bent over my hand, clapped Martin on the shoulder, and bade us farewell. For some reason I looked back once at his slight erect form. He was walking swiftly, but as if he felt my gaze he turned and raised his hand in a friendly gesture. I have recalled it often since.

* * *

"The whole town is buzzing with it. They say 'tis the beginning of another affair like that of Titus Oates, and that many a head must needs sit uneasy on its shoulders."

I had been on my way to the parlour with my hands full of roses, red and white and most sweetly scented when Tom's voice, unusually raised, came to my ears. I halted, knowing at once of what he spoke, and my grip tightened on the rose-stems, and a thorn ran into my finger.

Martin was standing by the window, his eyes on Tom, who had his back to me. For the moment neither man saw me, and I stood listening.

"Not so loud!" said Martin. "What else did you hear?"

Tom obediently lowered his voice, but there was still a breathless quality of excitement about it.

"The plot, they say, was to kill the king and the Duke of York at the Rye House as they returned from Newmarket. It was to start a great rising in favour of the Protestant Duke. He, they say, is in hiding, though others think him already taken, or dead."

"Tales!" said Martin contemptuously. "Told by a pack of old apple-women, with a grain of truth to a mountain of imagination."

"That's as may be. There was a plot, and the plot has been betrayed. That, I should think, is enough."

"More than enough," said Martin, and his tone was such that I caught my breath. It was a tiny sound, but they both glanced at the doorway and saw me standing there, roses and all. Their faces changed instantly, Tom's becoming an expressionless mask, and Martin's shedding its look of trouble as he smiled at me. But I could not return the smile.

"Why, sweetheart, you are white as your roses," said he in a rallying tone. "Have you been listening to Tom's budget? 'Tis naught but hearsay, and no need to take it to heart."

Tom said nothing, but turned to go. I put up a hand to check him.

"No," I said. "Do not go before you have told all you heard."

Tom cocked an eye at Martin who nodded, not smiling now. He set a chair for me, standing behind it so that I could not see his face. I laid my roses on the table, and their scent filled the air. It was sweet, and I have never cared for it since.

Tom began his tale. Martin, still standing behind me laid a hand on my shoulder, and so we stayed, not moving, our eyes on the speaker. I remember it all very well, how the sun was shining outside the open window, and how a bee droned in buzzing angrily against the glass, too foolish to go out the way it had come. Sunshine, roses, the babble of the river and Tom's voice going on and on, as if he spoke the prologue to a play. All men know now what he had heard, and the whole thing has been given a name to carry into history together with the Gunpowder Plot, the Popish Plot, and many more which had led men to most ugly deaths. We did not give it a title then.

It seemed that at this Rye House lived a man named Rumbold. A maltster, his dwelling, lying as it did on the road which the king and the duke would have taken on their return from the horseraces at Newmarket, was ideal for the purpose. Whether that purpose meant murder or, as some passionately declaimed, merely holding the royal brothers until certain demands had been met, I do not know. Martin said, long after, that with every party there are extremists, men who love violence for its own sake, and for these their fellows must pay the price. However that might be, this plot was betrayed by two brothers named Keeling, and, said Tom grimly, the hunt was on, and hats worn with the Monmouth cock might well prove a curse to those who wore them. As for the duke himself, it was said that unless he gave evidence against the plotters he would never again dare show his face at Court. And it might come to much worse than that.

"The plot was none of his," said Martin positively. "And if he knew anything about any conspirator he is not the man to betray them. He would never turn informer to save his own skin."

"Time will show," said Tom, shaking his head. "Many a pretty gentleman is brave enough in battle, but when the shadow of the Tower comes nigh—"

I shivered, and Martin's hand closed on my shoulder. "That will do, Tom. I know his nature better than you."

Tom, seeming to feel himself dismissed, turned to the door, but as if remembering something, paused.

"I did not tell you who they say is to be taken."

Martin's grip suddenly tightened, so that I almost cried out.

"Well, who?" He demanded. "For God's sake do not stand there as if savouring it. Devil burn you—"

"I do not. You should know better than that," said Tom. Sounding more hurt than angered. "And there is no need to use such words, and in the presence of your wife."

"I will use worse if you do not speak!"

"The talk is all of him, poor gentleman," said Tom, shaking his head, "And all men say it will go hard with him."

I felt Martin take a deep breath and interposed, fearing this maddening behaviour might lead to violence.

"With whom, Tom?" I asked quietly.

"With Lord William Russell. May God have mercy on him," he answered, and went out without another word.

Martin's hand fell from my shoulder. He walked to the window, and standing with his back to me, muttered that he was sorry he had shouted, but that Tom was enough to try the patience of a saint, which he was not. I went to him, and he put an arm around me, and we stood silent for a space.

"You were afraid that he spoke of Colonel Sidney, were you not?" I said at last.

"If Russell is taken so will he be," he said, wearily. "There is no reason for either to be touched by this plot — 'tis a mere excuse, and Sidney is as far removed from it as light from dark. But he is so disliked by the Court party and has been blamed for so much. Yes, you are right. I did fear it."

"I also," I said, "and for more than the one reason. You think only of him, I for what it could mean to us and our life together."

"God knows I think of it too. You are my most dear wife, and I would never willingly bring you a moment of sorrow. But he—" He broke off suddenly, as if unable to find words, and I moved a little away. He drew me back, and into his arms.

"You need not withdraw yourself from me," he said. "You know that you have no cause for jealousy, Catherine."

"Do I?" I saw the hurt in his eyes and relented. "Dear, I am sorry. I am not jealous, or only from time to time. I know he is your friend, and I would not have it otherwise."

"You do not know what he has done for me. No one does, save the two of us. I am proud to know him as my friend, but there is more, much more."

He paused, with a faraway look, so that I felt, even touching him as I was, that he had left me. Indeed, I think that is the strangest part of any relationship, how, while knowing one another to the extreme of intimacy, two people can yet be remote, each tied like a bundle in his or her inmost feelings. I loved Martin, I knew most confidently that Martin loved me, yet I knew there were recesses in his being to which even I could not penetrate. Perhaps it is wrong to wish to possess a loved one utterly, yet it can be most hurtful to be shut out.

Martin became conscious of me again, and smiled, as if echoing my thoughts.

"The closed door must be opened, must it, my sweet?" he said, smiling, yet with something faintly regretful in his voice.

"Only if you wish it," I said hastily. "I do not wish to pry."

"In actual fact there is little to tell. I thought that having met him you would understand." He looked at me, half wistfully. "Did he not impress you?"

"He did. Who could hear him without being moved by his sincerity? Whether in agreement with him or no."

"His views are too advanced for this age of ours. But he came to me like a breath of truth, of reality in an ugly and unreal world. I will tell you how we met, though even then you may not understand."

"At least," I said, "I could try."

"Let us go out into the sunshine," he said, not adding "while yet we may." But the words came to my mind.

The stone seat was warm in the sunshine and winged creatures droned drunkenly amongst the flowers. The birds which we had fed were now so tame that they hopped or strutted almost at our feet. Martin began almost at once to talk of the past, half reluctantly, yet, I have thought since, finding a certain relief in the telling.

"'Tis not a pretty story, and I have no excuse to offer. Had I not thought you dead — but that does not alter it. When my uncle died I was sent overseas to complete my education. I did, but scarcely as he had intended. Then came the tale of your death, and there was I with more money than I needed and nothing to anchor me. Then, when I was sick of myself and should have returned home, I had an engagement to keep. It almost ended my career for good, and but for Tom and his care probably would have done."

"I do not understand," I said frowning.

"It was a duel," he said.

"A duel? But why?"

"It was with the husband of a certain lady, and he had cause to think I had injured him. The lady, in fact, told him so."

"And had you?"

"I told you it was not a pretty story," he said. "Do you wish me to go into detail?"

I shook my head, and my hand went up to touch my scarred cheek. It was something I had not done of late.

"The lady convinced her husband that her virtue, though assailed, was intact, tossed me aside, and turned to fresh conquests. It was, it seemed, a habit with her."

"And you loved her? You cared?"

"Love!" he said violently. "That had no part in it. I was first flattered, then— but you would not understand. I would never have mentioned it except that it added to my feeling that nothing was of consequence. I came to London feeling thus and at once found my feet amongst those who felt likewise. Nothing was real, nothing mattered, therefore night in night out you drank yourself into forgetfulness. Only day came, and you could not forget. My friends and I were as vicious a band of drunken sots as you can imagine." He paused, adding. "That was what I was when he came upon me."

My thoughts had been with that unknown woman, and far from Sidney, while Martin had forgotten everything save him. The angry shame had left his face, and it was lit by a remembering smile.

"His coach knocked me down — I was very drunk at the time," he said. "My leg was broken, and he took me to his own home, tended me, and brought me by degrees to see what I had become. It was not that he preached at me or looked on me from a cold and virtuous height. It was — oh, how can I tell you? — as if a wanderer in the wilderness had come upon a spring of clear water. He made me feel that every man was responsible for his own life, and that it could be worth the living. In the midst of vice and intrigue he was untouched. His love for his country, his hatred of the way it had been brought low, touched me also, and I began to share his plans for the future. He's like a father to me. Now do you understand?"

"But why did you not come home before?"

"Because I was sorry and ashamed. As I still am."

"And she? Were you still thinking of her?"

He turned, catching my hands in his.

"Sweetheart, will you not forget her? God knows I have done so long since. Most men, I suppose, have matters for regret in their past lives. I would I were an exception, but what is done is done."

He spoke truth, and I thought how lightly others would have dismissed it all. But there was a Puritan streak in Martin, and it was not only in appearance that he resembled the man in the portrait.

He said, urgently. "Do not look at me so! Say that you will forget."

I knew that I should not forget — how could I? I hated that unknown woman and the thought of what had been between them. But Martin was mine, and we might be parted soon. I could not let our last hours together be marred so I said steadily: "We all have matters in the past of which we are ashamed. The present, and please God the future is ours. We can put the past behind us."

He murmured something and took me in his arms, holding me close. And he said that in all his life there had been but the one woman for him.

"Scarred face, limp, and all?" I asked.

"You," he answered, with such pride and love in his voice that it was my turn to be ashamed, and I pushed the ghost from the past into the background. So we stayed for a while, not speaking, undisturbed in our sunlit solitude. Not far away the city buzzed with speculation, and men walked in fear, but for that little space we did not allow it to touch us. And the knowledge that our peace could not last made it all the more precious.

At last Martin raised his head and put me gently from him. A light breeze had risen, and the soft air struck cold.

"Sweetheart, I could stay thus forever," he said. "But I think I should find what is happening for myself."

"I will come with you," I said quickly.

He shook his head. "For this once, love, I will go alone, but I promise I will not be long."

I clung to him, suddenly afraid. "You cannot be touched by this plot? You had truly no part in it?"

He smiled at me but loosed my hands. "You need not ask me. The spy hidden under the seat should be convinced of that."

"Well, then! In that case they cannot touch you or Colonel Sidney. We need not be troubled, need we?"

He rose, put out his hands, and pulled me up to face him.

"That sounds reasonable, my love. Let us hope you may be right."

But when he had gone all the reason in the world could not allay my fears. I could settle to nothing when I returned to the house, where the walls seemed to close in on me, and I thought of many things. There was the Duke of Monmouth, who had once been pointed out to me in Gray's Inn Gardens, where wealth and fashion were used to promenade. He had been laughing, a darling of the gods from whom adversity seemed far removed. I wondered if the handsome face still smiled. Martin had shown me the great house in Soho where he lived as a prince, if not acknowledged as one. If half the rumours repeated by Tom were true he would not be there now. I was sorry if he had been brought innocently into this matter, but he was nothing to me. For Colonel Sidney, though without the near idolatry felt by my husband, it was otherwise. Most clearly I recalled his voice as I had heard it from outside the window at Martin's home. "*I shall be brought into it, as I am the certain scapegoat.*" He had sounded, as I recalled, quite matter-of-fact. And if he were taken in then Martin also would be either captured or a fugitive. By whatever path my thoughts travelled they returned to that sad conclusion.

There were some papers in a folder on the table, written in a clear, beautiful hand. I turned the pages idly and came upon the words. "Mankind is inclined to vice, and the way to virtue so hard that it wants encouragement, but when all honours, advantages and preferments are given to vice and despised virtue finds no other rewards than hatred, persecution, and death, there are few who will follow it."

Hatred, persecution, and death. The words echoed my thoughts most heavily. I turned to the beginning and was not surprised to see a written inscription. *To my friend Martin Lacey, from Algernon Sidney.*

The title was written with a flourish. *Discourses Concerning Government. By Algernon Sidney, Esq.* I turned the pages with ever growing disquiet. At a time like the present the writer, scholarly and sincere though he might be, was most criminally careless of his own wellbeing. Phrases leaped from the page.

> *No man comes to command many unless by consent or by force . . . The ancients chose those to be king who excelled in the virtues most beneficial to civil societies . . . all just magisterial power is from the people . . . They who have the right of choosing a king have the right of making a king . . . Kings . . . can have no other just power than what the laws give, nor any title to the privileges of the Lord's Anointed.*

There was more, much more. With shaking hands I put the papers inside the folder and carried it to our bedchamber wrapped it in one of my bedgowns and laid it in a dark corner of the press, laying other garments over it. This I did in a fever of haste, for I recalled tales of searches for treasonable writings and the like. My husband was already compromised enough. At least, the republican writings of his friend should not be laid out for all to see. But the knowledge of its presence, hidden though it was, gave weight to my fears. When Martin at last returned I ran to him, holding him as if to assure myself that he was truly there with me.

CHAPTER XVII

There followed on Tom's news a kind of lull, a few days in which nothing happened to touch our friends or us. It had a breathless quality, as I recall, something like the time in which one awaits the breaking of a storm. Martin was out and about a great many times without me, and I asked no questions as to his business, only welcoming him back with relief and joy. But on my birthday he made holiday, and we forgot, or tried to forget the witch's brew that was coming to the boil. I had almost put the date which once seemed all important to me out of my mind, but Martin had not forgotten.

I awoke that morning to find myself alone and was instantly certain that the time of parting had come. For a time I lay most desolate, then I climbed from the bed and hastened to the door, telling myself that he could not be long gone, that I might catch him and at least bid him farewell. I flung open the door, and there he was, coming towards me, his hands filled with flowers. He halted in surprise.

"And where might you be hastening, barefoot and in your night gear? It is most unseemly in a wedded wife, in particular one of your advanced years."

He laughed down at me, but I could not yet laugh back. I was shaking and cold, and I laid my hands on his breast.

His laughing face changed, and he put an arm around me, half carrying me back into the room.

"Why, love, what is wrong? You look as if you had seen a ghost."

"I woke, and you were gone." With a kind of anger born of relief, I added: "Why did you go without a word to me?"

"You were sleeping soundly, and I was not far away. I did but go to the garden to pluck a birthday posy for you, that you might find it when you woke. It seemed a pleasing conceit at the time."

"Oh, Martin!" Remorsefully I took the little knot of gilly-flowers, rosemary and lad's love, still wet with dew, and smiled at him. "Thank you. I am sorry to have been so foolish."

"Most foolish," he assented. "Did you think your spouse had been spirited away forever?"

I did not tell him that I had, indeed, thought as much, but he knew well enough. He knew my thoughts almost as soon as I myself, and I leaned my head against him without speaking.

"You look like some small bird fallen from its nest, feathers all ruffled and bright eyes gazing. Back to your bed and get yourself warm, shaking creature that you are."

"I am not cold now," said I, snuggling against him. "Do you go abroad, Martin, that you rise so early?"

"Today I will go nowhere without you," he answered. "This is your day, my love, and we will eat, drink, and be merry — no, devil take it! That is scarce the happiest choice of words."

I finished the phrase for him, clinging to him, and he said reasonably, "After all, it is always so. From the cradle onwards there is the one certainty."

"But death is so final! One cannot help but fear it."

"Final? Why, I think there is more to it than that. I think that we two shall not be separated merely by the dissolution of our bodies. Somewhere, somehow, we shall be together, you and I."

"And — you are not afraid?"

"Of death? Not a whit. If one can face up to life and what it can do — now there's another matter, and I no braver than the rest. If one can bear with that in all its ugliness what remains? Only a door through which all of us must pass in turn."

"How can you talk so?" I asked in a muffled voice, my face still pressed to his chest. "You sound as if you cared nothing for leaving me, while I cannot bear even the thought. It is here I want you, not in some shadowy future."

"Dear heart you know me better than that. I am of the same mind, and for all my high-flown sentiments have no intention in the world of leaving it or you before I must, which I trust is not yet. I mean to become at least a grandfather — with your assistance, of course."

"And now you are laughing!" I said, taken aback yet pleased as his change in mood. "Indeed, I do not know what to make of you today."

"Nor I," he agreed cordially. "Why I should be talking like a preacher on any morning I do not know, and most certainly not on your birthday. What I had meant to say was that I wish you very happy, my dear and only love, now and in the years to come."

"You have given me more happiness than I had thought possible. You know that," I said.

He kissed me, and the rosemary and lad's love, crushed against my breast, filled the air with fragrance.

"And what you have given me, my Catherine," said he, not laughing now, "is more than I can ever say, and God knows more than I deserve."

"We might never have met again," I said, after a time. "Had you ever thought of it? The chance that you should have come to the hut that day."

"The day when an uncouth boy thought fit to come back into my life! Oh yes, I have had the same notion. But meet we did, and if my lady wife were to look under her pillow she might — one can, of course, be certain of nothing — but she might find something to take her mind from other matters."

I hastened round the bed, thrusting my hand under the pillow. Pleased and excited as a child I drew out a flat package and, looking at Martin, saw him smiling at my pleasure as if he had never a thought of care.

"Open it my love," said he indulgently, and in a would-be offhand manner. "'Tis a small matter, but one I thought might please you."

Within the wrapping was a leather case. I raised the lid and drew a deep breath.

"Please no! I never saw anything so beautiful. Dear Martin—"

"It was my mother's," said he. "She would have been happy for you to wear it."

I drew out the shining chain, marvelling at the great red stone set in gold which hung from it and seemed to hold a living flame. It was true — never in my life had I seen anything to rival it, and I turned it this way and that and the stone flashed up at me as if it were truly alight.

"Look at the back," said Martin. "I had a posy put there for you. Can you make it out?"

The back was a flat round of gold with a border pattern of tiny leaves. In the centre entwined initials, his and mine, were engraved. Close to the leaf design were words, the letters so small that I could not at first decipher them, then it was as if they sprang out at me. I repeated them slowly. "Now and forever."

I turned to my husband and could not speak, but he seemed content with what my look expressed. Laughing, he said, "Do you intend to remain in your night gown all day? It is, of course, entirely as you wish. I shall make no complaint." And he gave me that impudent birdlike look of his, head on one side, and eyes alight with teasing.

The day which had begun so strangely continued in the gayest fashion, and I wore Martin's gift, and we, as he had said, made holiday and were merry together. I have only to look at my locket, at the inscription, for the years to roll away, and for every detail to stand out in my memory. It is as if I see two tiny far-off figures crystal clear in the sunlight, and I hear the echo of their laughter. For we allowed no speck of care to mar our day, speaking of nothing connected with heavy matters, only continuing with delight to discover one another.

He took me, I remember, to Islington, and we saw the rosy milkmaids and drank foaming warm milk, and ate the biggest strawberries, all swamped in cream. There were many fine ladies there, and the sight of them — all aglow with beauty and youth and happiness — made me sigh with longing for what I used to be.

"Bah!" said Martin when I told my thoughts. "You are spreading your net for compliments."

"Compliments? Me?"

"You know well that since you have learned to smile the scar is hardly to be seen."

I was much struck, hopeful, yet scarcely able to be persuaded.

"In any case," I said, "As I told Ralph, I do not mind now — or at least, only a little — since you do not."

"I am glad," said he, "That you have realised it at last. For God knows it is the truth, and if I did not fear to puff you with overweening conceit I would tell you that you are the prettiest enchantress, with none to hold a candle to your charms."

"I am puffed already," said I. "Tell me more."

"You have had sufficient strawberries and pretty speeches for one day. Where is your moderation, and your modesty?"

"Gone, all gone. And unregretted. Though I must say I fear you look on me with partial eyes, and that few would agree with you."

He scowled at me. "Shameless woman! Is not the love and admiration of your lawful wedded husband enough for you?"

"More than enough," I said, and softly repeated the words he had set on my gift.

His gaze dwelt on me. "I shall always remember you as you are today." And he, too, spoke the words as I had done.

"How do you wish to end the day?" asked Martin, much later. We were sitting on the grass in as secluded a spot as we could find, or at least I was sitting with my back against a tree while my lord and master took his ease full length, with his head in my lap. I had been tickling his nose with a long blade of grass to make him sneeze, and we were altogether as foolish a pair as you could wish to see. Voices and laughter from others enjoying the sunshine came faintly to us, blending with the hum of insects to a drowsy chorus. The air was full of country scents, crushed grass and small flowers yielding their sweetness.

"I do not wish it to end at all," I said, sighing.

"Then we will purchase a cow and set up here. And the sun will always shine—"

"And our cow never go dry!"

"An idyllic prospect, my milkmaid," he said, yawning and stretching. "Nevertheless, I fear we must remove ourselves or night will be on us before we know."

I leaned over him, and the ruby swung out on its chain catching the light.

"Then let us go home," I said.

"You are sure? No further junketing? How pleasant to know that my company is still enough for you after our long space of married life! It suits me well, my dear."

I have wondered since what might have happened had we not returned when we did. It was with no thought in my mind save that we should end our happy day most happily in our own home together, and during the long ride back I had not the slightest presentiment, no shadow fell across our path. I am glad of it now, that our happiness lasted at least that long.

Martin lifted me down at the gate, called for Tom, but received no reply. Muttering something touching the antecedents of that worthy he told me to go in while he stabled the horse himself. I said that I would wait for him, having no wish to go in before I must, since the evening was fair.

I wandered between the tangled bushes, humming to myself, counting over the pleasures of the day like beads on a rosary.

All in an instant the song died on my lips and with it went my content. I had heard no movement, to all appearance nothing stirred in the undergrowth, yet I was coldly certain that I was not alone. Somewhere, hidden but near to me, someone watched and waited. My hand went to my ruby, closing round it, but I think that even then I knew I need not fear its loss, and that it was for Martin that the watcher lurked unseen.

With the first warning I had halted, as if turned to something without power of movement, but now my brain began to race. If I remained Martin would come here to join me. Would there be time to warn him? How long I had stood motionless I did not know. It seemed an age, but I could well be mistaken. And then another thought struck me — whoever waited most certainly wished to do so unseen. Would it be possible for me to frighten him off, if only for the moment?

Drawing a deep breath, I called as loudly as I could. "Who is there? Tom, hasten — bring the dogs. Someone is lurking here."

If I had hoped imagination had played me a trick I was at once taught otherwise. My cry met with an instant response, a heavy crashing through the bushes to my right as if the watcher fled with more haste than discretion. At the same instant pounding feet heralded the arrival of Tom, bellowing threats and brandishing a cudgel. His face was red with rage, and I saw that one eye was swollen and almost closed. He pulled up at sight of me, peering at me lopsidedly.

"Tom," I said, scarce able to find a shred of voice, for all that I had called so loudly before, "There was someone hiding in the bushes."

"Again!" he exclaimed. "I feared it when we heard you call, but I thought we had seen the last of that misbegotten son of Belial."

"You mean he was here before? And oh, Tom, what has happened to your eye?"

"And what goes on here? Catherine, I heard you cry out." Martin, somewhat out of breath, had come on the scene. "Are you hurt? What has happened?"

"I am not hurt, but someone was hiding here. When I called he made off — and Martin, Tom has hurt his eye."

"Good God!" Martin stared at Tom, who looked affronted. "What have you there?" He added, putting an arm around me. "Do not be afraid, my love. 'Tis probably some shabby footpad you scared away."

"He was here before. Tom—"

"Tom appears to have had the worst of any encounter," said Martin lightly, hoping, I think, to make little of the matter to me.

"I did not," Tom defended himself sulkily. "He had me by surprise, but he felt the toe of my boot none the less."

"Perhaps," suggested Martin gently, "you might care to tell us how it befell. Although, unlike yourself, I have two good eyes, I confess to finding myself somewhat in the dark."

His tone was still light, but the arm around me was tense and his face unsmiling. I did not think that a common footpad would give him cause to look so, and I caught my breath.

"Tabitha thought she saw a fellow creeping through the bushes an hour back," said Tom briefly. "I came to look."

"With more zeal than prudence, I should imagine. However—"

"He rose like a serpent from under my feet," said Tom indignantly. "He caught me this blow before I saw him. I tried to hold him, but he was slippery as an eel, and made off."

"Aided by your boot, as you said. And you did not follow?"

"I did, but he was too quick for me. When I got through the bushes there was no sign of him. But I heard a horse gallop away."

"A horse! I knew it was no footpad," I said. "I knew it all the time."

"Hush, my sweet. Let us take you in, since our bird has flown. Tom and I will look around, and you have nothing to fear."

"I am not afraid for myself," I said, though I was shaking.

175

He made no reply, only the arm round my shoulders tightened. We went to the house, finding the two maids peering from the doorway, and he made me drink some wine. Then he and Tom went out into the garden.

I said to Tabitha. "You saw this man?"

"Not clearly," she answered. "He seemed to be bent double, creeping through the bushes. Then he stopped, as if watching the house, and I called Master Jenkins."

"Poor soul!" said her sister, shuddering rather pleasurably. "He came back dripping blood, and his eye like a filled bladder."

"And all to no purpose, since the villain made good his escape."

"Go to the door, and see if you can hear them," I said, more because I wished to be alone than for any good reason. There was a tightness in my breast, and I found it difficult to speak. I did not think that they would find the watcher now, but I was assured that he and those who sent him would return. And my thoughts went to that folder of writings, hidden away above stairs. I thought, too, that with Martin's presence known we should not have long to wait. For somehow, from the moment when I felt those eyes on me from the bushes, I never doubted but that Martin and I might bid farewell to our days of happiness together.

I moved restlessly about the room, which had seemed so damp and unwelcoming on the night of our arrival, and was now shining, smelling not of damp and neglect but of beeswax, herbs, and flowers. Tabitha and Mercy were good and willing workers, and under their ministrations the house had bloomed anew, somewhat as I myself had done. It was a happy place, and every surface which could be polished winked back the light and the small panes of glass in the window shone likewise. I wandered over to it, pressing my face against the cool glass.

My heart first leaped, then seemed actually to stop its beating, and I shrank back with a gasp of fear. I had gazed into a face which, as if it mirrored mine, was pressed against the outside of the window.

CHAPTER XVIII

I do not know why I uttered no cry, except that the shock seemed to have taken away all power of speech and movement, so that I could only stand with my hands to my breast striving to collect myself. There was a darkness before my eyes and a pounding in my ears, but at last I drew a deep, painful breath, and recovered myself. I thought that the prowler, probably startled as myself, would have vanished by now, but when I looked his figure was still there, dark against the setting sun. Far from being startled at the sight of me he was now tapping on the glass to attract my attention. Amazed at his effrontery I opened my lips to call Tabitha and Mercy, but my cry died unuttered. The man at the window had turned his head so that the light, for the first time, was on his face. It bore a look I had not seen on it before, but I recognised him and opened the window. Roger Frampton swung a leg over the sill and stood before me.

He made no apology or explanation, only saying in a low and urgent voice. "Your husband — is he still here? If so I must speak to him, and at once."

I looked at him without replying, and saw that his face was of a curious grey pallor, and that his left arm was thrust into the breast of his cloak. There was a dark patch just below the shoulder as of damp, but I knew what it was, and caught my breath.

"You are hurt," I said quickly. "Drink this."

Some of the wine which Martin had poured for me yet remained. I handed it to him, and saw a little colour creep back into his face. He looked at me with a shadow of his old smile.

"I will call for water and linen. Let me tend your wound."

"No, no," he said hastily. "There is no time for that, and besides, the fewer who know of my presence here the better. 'Tis only a scratch, and the bleeding has stopped." Rather remorsefully, he added: "You look in need of care yourself. I am sorry to have frightened you."

"I was frightened before you came. There was a man hiding in the garden, seeming to spy on the house. Martin and his man are out there now."

"Yes, I knew the house was watched," he replied. "That is why I came to the window. I—"

He broke off suddenly, raising his hand. From outside came the sound of voices, of steps approaching. Frampton moved swiftly and silently to stand in the shadow by the door. I had a sudden memory of the way he and I had stood in the hall at the Grange, and of the way Frances had looked when we stepped out into the light. It seemed a long time ago.

Martin's voice sounded clearly, apparently in answer to something that Tom had said.

"No. You will remain with her whatever happens. You know very well that my trust is in you."

"You may well need me," muttered Tom in a discontented voice. "I should be with you."

"You heard me. For God's sake, cease making objections and do as I say with a good grace." He laughed suddenly. "A cross-grained, churlish, argumentative fellow, yet I shall be happy to know you are at her side."

"But where—?"

"Holland, probably. I am not sure, but in any case it will not be long before you can bring her to me."

"As to that, only the good God knows. But I will do your will. You know that."

"I do know it. Now go and clap something to that eye of yours, which is a sorry sight."

We heard Tom's footsteps clump away as Martin came into the room.

"The bird, once again, has flown, my love," said he, lightly. "Think no more of him."

"Martin," I said, and moved my head to indicate the figure by the door. Martin swung round, and Frampton stepped forward.

"Good God! You! But how came you here? And what has happened to your arm?"

"A slight scuffle with those who would have hindered me. Never mind that — I come to warn you. There is no time to lose."

"To warn me?"

"I thought you would have heard, and be already gone, then I had word that they were looking for you."

"We were out of town, and have heard nothing. What is it?"

For the moment I was forgotten, and I knew something of Henrietta's resentment at the treatment of our sex. Here were men's affairs, and the woman left outside as if they did not touch her, but they did, most cruelly.

"The informers are out in force," said Frampton bitterly.

"Nine names are added to the list, with yours — and mine — amongst them. There is a warrant out for our arrest, and a reward offered."

"But Martin had no part in this plot!" I cried, not able to keep silent.

"Nor had I, or many another who will he named," said Frampton, in a matter-of-fact tone. "That will make not the slightest difference. They are out for blood, and any of our known sympathies will serve as a sacrifice."

I turned blindly to Martin, who held me closely for a moment before putting me gently aside.

"Sidney?" he asked.

Frampton shook his head. "Not yet."

I heard Martin's sigh of relief and thought bitterly how little he cared for himself so long as his hero remained untouched. Frampton was speaking urgently of the need for haste, and I looked up at my husband.

"Sweetheart," he said, bending to me. "I am sorry your day has ended thus."

I clung to his hand and said in a choked voice, "Only take me with you. Do not leave me here alone, not knowing whether you live or die."

Over my head I saw the two men exchange a swift glance. Frampton walked to the window, standing there with his back to us. Martin knelt beside me and put his arms about my rigid body.

"It is not possible, my love. Do not make it harder for me! Tom will care for you, and my aunt is your good friend."

"I do not want them," I said childishly. "I want only you."

Frampton moved as if in discomfort. Martin kissed me, put away my hands that would have held him, and rose.

"If they come tell them I am in the country, for how long a stay you do not know. It may hold them for a time. And do not grieve, dear heart. I will return or send for you as soon as I may. God knows I want this parting no more than you." He turned to Frampton and said, in a new, brisk voice: "What's the plan?"

"There is a boat waiting, and horses downstream. If we leave now we can be aboard ship and sail with the tide. 'Tis our only chance."

He came to me, taking my hand. In the midst of my sorrow it came to me that he must have risked his own safety to aid Martin, and I tried to thank him. He smiled, but said nothing, only bending to kiss my hand.

It was all a whirl from then, and I recall nothing clearly. I know that Tom was sent out, returning to say that all was well as far as he could see, then we were all in the garden, shadowy now, and making our way along the path which led to the river. Frampton, who was ahead, whistled softly, and a boat rowed by a bearded man came without a sound, like a shadow.

Tom gripped the side of the boat, Frampton stepped in, and my husband kissed me and held me, and of all that was in our hearts we spoke not one word. Then they were gone, with only the faintest splash of the oars to tell of their going, and the dusk swallowed them up, and Tom and I were left standing there together. I think we stood silently for a long time, with the river murmuring at our feet and no other sound at all.

At last Tom cleared his throat with a loud rasping sound and asked if i would not go in, since the mist was rising. I turned obediently, for it seemed to matter little what I did, and we went back to the house and into the empty room.

I sat down at the table, gazing vacantly around me. As I recall it, I felt no pain, only a queer numb blankness, with nothing to care for anymore. It had all happened so quickly at the last that it might have been a dream from which one could awaken, to shake it off with a laugh. I should probably have sat on in my apathy had I not become conscious that Tom was standing at my side. Somehow the sight of his solid figure, so far removed from any dream, brought me back to reality, and to the first stab of pain. I wondered why he, always so distant with me, should remain now when all my desire was to be alone. Looking up at him, I saw that his eye was turning all colours of the rainbow, giving an unusually rakish air to his sanctimonious face.

Clearing his throat as if in some discomfort, he said gruffly: "They will be away, I have no doubt, and safe. It is unlikely that we shall be troubled before morning, and that should give them the start they need."

I realised with faint surprise that he was trying to reassure me, and that his open eye was fixed anxiously on me. For the first time I felt the truth of what Martin said of him, and that, for all his disapproving air, I was now in the care of one reliable as a rock.

"Is there anything we should do?" I asked. "My husband is supposedly in the country, but they will find his horse in the stable."

Tom nodded. "I had thought of that, and wondered if I should take it elsewhere, but the risk, with watchers around, is too great. We must let that go, and events will take their course."

"I suppose so," I said wearily.

"You should be in your bed. Shall I send Mercy to you?"

"Not yet. I will wait awhile." As he turned to go, I added, "I am glad to have you here with me, Tom, and I know you would have wished to be with my husband and not here. I am grateful."

A slow tide of colour rose in his dark face, but he made no reply. He was halfway through the door when a thought struck me, and I called him back. He was beside me in an instant.

"What now? Someone at the window?"

"No, not I have this moment remembered — Tom, when the sheriff's officers come, will they search the house?"

"Without doubt. Those gentry leave naught to chance. Why, Mistress, is there aught for them to find?"

"There are some papers — some writings of Colonel Sidney's. I have them hidden, but if the search is thorough—"

"Give them to me," interrupted Tom. "There is the kitchen fire, and I will send the wenches to bed."

"But Martin — he would not wish them burnt."

"Better that than found. You had best look through his baggage to see if there is any matter there, but I do not think it. He has been prepared for this."

I thought of our carefree day, and how little anyone seeing him then would have thought him prepared for flight. I had a picture so clear that my heart twisted with pain, of his laughing face as he fed me with strawberries, reproving me for gluttony as Martha had done when I was a child. But there was no time for fond memories now. I went swiftly to

182

my room, found the papers, and handed them to Tom, who told me I need trouble myself no more over them, at least.

"It will be no easy matter to burn," I said.

"Little by little and bit by bit," he answered. "I have the night before me."

Soon after he had gone the two girls came to me, asking if I needed them. They sounded subdued, and had lost their bright colour, and I thought the events of the past hour must have given them food for thought. I told them that my husband had found it necessary to leave in haste.

"It is probable that men may come searching for him," I said. "I shall tell them that he had affairs in the country. But there is no need for you to be drawn into the matter, and if you wish to leave, I shall understand."

There was a moment of silence. They looked at one another then at me, and Tabitha, the elder, spoke for them both.

"If you please, we would rather stay."

"I do please, very much," I said truthfully. "But I must warn you, there may be unpleasantness to face. My husband has done no wrong—"

I found myself unable to continue, and they both made clucking sounds of sympathy, as if to comfort a child. I controlled myself, continuing: "You will have heard talk of a plot?"

"Oh yes," said Tabitha, nodding solemnly.

"One hears tell of little else," said Mercy cheerfully.

"My husband had no part in it, but we have been told that he is named in it."

"There be those," said Tabitha darkly, "as would accuse their own grandmothers for sixpence."

"Far less than that," observed Mercy, shaking her head.

"Well, now you know all. And you still wish to stay?"

They nodded in unison, like a pair of dancers, and Tabitha, in a motherly tone, urged me to get some rest.

"I would bring you some warm milk," said she with some bitterness, "had I not been as good as ordered out of my own kitchen."

"I also," said Mercy, with a snort.

"Tom has his reasons," I said. "Like you, he is aiding me, and I am grateful for you all."

They glanced at one another, and again Tabitha spoke for both.

"We have been happy here, and we wish—" she paused, seeming to grope for words, and added triumphantly. "We wish you a happy issue out of all your afflictions."

"Amen," said Mercy fervently.

As if feeling, with some reason, that the last word had been spoken, they left me, and I went about my task of searching Martin's belongings. But when my search was ended and nothing found, and I lay at last in the bed which seemed so coldly empty, the words came back to me, bringing a little comfort. And I prayed for my husband and myself that it might indeed be so.

CHAPTER XIX

I had at last fallen into an uneasy doze when I was rudely awakened by a thundering on the door below. I shot up, at first forgetting I was alone and turning to Martin for reassurance before the truth came flooding coldly back. It was to be the first of many like awakenings in the days to come.

The noise was continuing, now accompanied by a loud voice, bidding us open up in the name of the king. With a pounding heart I looked around me, to see that it was barely light, and I wondered if Tom, whose grumbling voice I could already hear, had been given time to complete his work of destruction. If the pages were discovered half burnt they might well prove the more damning, and I wished I had let them take their chance. Pulling a bedgown round me I hastened barefoot to the head of the stairs. Tabitha and Mercy were peering from the door of their room, their round faces fearful. Without speaking to them I picked up my skirts and sped down.

"Cease your plaguey clamour!" Tom was saying. "Am I not coming as fast as my legs will bring me? No need to rouse my lady."

"Hold your tongue and open the door, or we will break it down!"

Muttering, Tom bent to the bolts, and I slipped past him unseen, and went straight to the kitchen. The flagged floor struck cold to my bare feet, but I paid no heed. Gazing with sick dread into the grate I found it empty save for innocent ashes. No sign that any papers had been burnt was there at all.

My first moment of pure relief faded almost at once. If they had not been burned, if Tom had delayed and they were yet intact, what then? I looked feverishly around me, but saw only the homely matters of everyday, and of papers, incriminating or otherwise, no sign. The outer door opened and I heard a loud, authoritative voice in the hall. Slipping without a sound into the garden room I sat down, pulling my skirts around my feet.

"You lie, fellow," said the harsh voice. "The approach to the house was close watched, and we know our bird has not flown."

The door was flung open and a tall man, black-bearded and angry-looking, came stomping in. There were raindrops in his hair and beard, and his boots were mired. In the midst of my fears I took note of the marks he left on the floor, and was displeased.

Without noticing me he turned, bellowing. "You, fellow — what are you about? You need not think to go slinking off!"

"I am not slinking off," said Tom, in a tone of dignified reproof. "I do but go to acquaint my lady with your presence."

"There is no need, Tom," I said. "This — gentleman — had already made his presence known."

It seemed that the room was now filled with men. Besides the black-bearded leader there were two rough-looking figures. Tom entered behind them looking not a whit guilty, but outraged.

"You are wife to Martin Lacey?" asked the first man, offering me no courtesy but looking me up and down in a fashion which made me very conscious of my attire. I forced myself to meet his gaze without flinching. "I am. And I wish to know for what reason, in my husband's absence, you break thus rudely into his home."

He laughed, not pleasantly. "In the first place I am assured that despite what you say his absence is a tale. In the second I have to inform you that I hold a warrant for his apprehension."

"A warrant? But what is the charge?"

Without replying he snapped his fingers at the two men who disappeared, apparently taking his meaning without need of words. Then he turned to me.

"My fellows are at front and back, so if you plan to hold me in talk while your husband makes good his escape, think again. The charge, as I have no doubt you already know, is of being concerned in a plot against the persons of His Majesty the King and the Duke of York."

"My husband is concerned in no such plot, nor is he here. He was called to his home in Dorset late yesterday, or he would tell you as much himself."

"Would he, by God! He has primed you well enough, it is plain." The jeering tone changed to one of menace. "Those who think to hinder us in the apprehension of traitors would do well to have a care, be they wife, Mistress, or light o' love. Remain where you are, and you, fellow, also. Miles, stay with them. I will look above stairs."

At his raised voice one of the men came in and stood grinning cheerfully at Tom who, standing within a few feet of me was as little able to relieve my fears as if he had been miles away. We heard those booted feet pounding up the stairs and a duet of high-pitched indignant cries from Mercy and Tabitha. A moment later they scurried into the room. Tabitha was fully dressed, but Mercy still in her petticoat. The man called Miles looked at her plump charms and gave an appreciative whistle, and Mercy folded her arms across her breast and glared at him.

"It has come to something when decent women are not so much as given time to get into their bodice!"

187

"Bless you, my chick, never give a thought to me," he said in a hoarse voice. "We see many a sight, and some not so well blessed in the matter of flesh as you."

Mercy turned with a flounce and came to kneel beside me, taking my hands and rubbing them between her own. From above thuds and crashes told of an unavailing search. Tabitha folded her hands before her, compressed her lips, and stood like a statue of disapproval. At a particularly heavy thud Miles grinned and jerked a dirty thumb upwards.

"Master Felton does not waste time," he observed confidentially. "He hath an eye like a stinking eel for them as think to hide."

"He will find nothing here," said Tom calmly.

I shot him a quick glance, and for one instant his eye met mine. His face might have been a block of wood for any sign of expression, yet his message reached me. I gave a little sigh and relaxed.

"She is faint, poor lady," said Mercy to Tabitha. "And small wonder!"

"Small wonder indeed," echoed Tabitha. "If my master were here he would have something to say! I will fetch her some water," and she turned to the door.

"No," said Miles, raising an enormous hand and grinning still. "You will bide here, or Master Felton will skin me alive."

Tabitha tossed her head indignantly and began fanning me with her kerchief. I was not faint, but I lay back and let them fuss over me.

A torrent of oaths and crashing footsteps heralded the return of Master Felton, red-faced and scowling. I put Tabitha and Mercy aside and sat erect.

"Are you satisfied now, sir?" I asked coldly.

"I am very far from satisfied, but I am assured that he is not above stairs," he answered. "There are still places for him to be holed like a rat, and like a rat we will dig him out."

"You could tear the house to pieces and still not find one who is not here," I said steadily. "You might save yourself the pains."

He stared at me rudely. His eyes, slightly bulging, were reddish-brown in colour, and I disliked the look in them greatly.

"And you might save yourself the pains of lying," he said with contempt. "What you think to gain I do not know. He returned here and did not leave again. We shall find him, never fear."

"You will not find him," I said. "I do not lie, and he is not here. But since you will not accept my word—"

"By God, you are in the right of it there!" he interrupted, with a short bark of laughter.

I continued as if he had not spoken: "At least my maids and I might be allowed to go to our rooms. Your rude arrival brought us from our beds half clothed."

He actually looked half ashamed. "Go, if you wish. It will leave us the more space here. Miles, wait at the foot of the stairs."

I rose, forcing myself to hold my head high, and went to the door, followed by Tabitha and Mercy. He kept his scowling gaze on us, as if to cover his momentary weakness, and as Mercy drew level with him shot out a hand and gripped her wrist. She gave a little cry, and I turned indignantly.

"It is no part of your duty to mishandle women, sir! My maids have done no wrong."

"You would be surprised," he answered, his eyes not on me but on Mercy's plump bosom. "At what our duty embraces. But you need not fear for the wench's virtue — I do but wish to put a question to her."

"Then you can keep your hands and eyes to yourself," said Mercy, flushing.

"Let the maid cover herself," said Tom, in solemn reproof. "'Tis not seemly."

"Hold your noise, you sour faced oaf. And you, girl — where is your master?"

"You know if you be not deaf. My lady has told you time and again," said Mercy defiantly.

He dropped her hand with an oath and stamped over to the fireplace, peering up the chimney. As we went up the stairs we heard him knocking on the panelling, I suppose hoping to find a secret room.

Tabitha helped me to dress, for which I was grateful, since my hands were shaking. She smoothed my hair, and the face which looked back at me from the mirror was not like my own. "Since you have learned to smile," Martin had said, "The scar is scarcely to be seen." I was not smiling now, and again it showed clearly, lifting one side of my mouth as if in mockery.

"Do not fret yourself," soothed Tabitha. "That loud mouthed bully can do naught."

"I know," I said, and indeed, I could not have been more thankful that my husband had gone in time. But I hated the uproar, the violation of our serene little home, and I hated the man with his swagger and hot brown eyes who had treated us with such lack of common respect. The room was a shambles. Clothing, Martin's and mine, was flung here and there, bedding strewn on the floor. It was as well that nothing had remained hidden in the press, which had been ransacked. Tabitha, her lips set in a line of disapproval, began folding and putting everything in order, and Mercy, now clothed and decorous, came to aid her. My jewel box was open and flung to the floor, and with a cry of distress I picked up the gold chain which Martin had only yesterday fastened about my neck.

"My ruby! It has gone!"

I began scrabbling about in the litter on the floor, half sobbing, and the two girls came to help me in the search.

"We will find it, never fear," said Tabitha, who seemed to have made herself my comforter. "The room is in such a cagmag that forty such might well be hidden under it."

"It was only yesterday he gave it to me," I said. "I cannot bear to lose it."

"It could well be in that man's pouch," said Mercy viciously. "I would not put it past him."

"Oh, no — he would not! It must be here if only we could find it."

Mercy, now flat on her face under the bed gave a loud sneeze and wriggled out. Her face was red, and dust and feathers ornamented her head, but she looked most beautiful to me. Smiling, she held out her hands, and on the palm my ruby winked and glowed.

"There, my dear," said she, as indulgently as if handing a sugarplum to a child.

I threw my arms around her and kissed her hot face. Taking my jewel I saw that it was unharmed, and the tiny inscription seemed to come to me like a message from Martin. I slid it back on to its chain and fastened it about my neck, seeming strengthened by its presence there.

At last there came a lull below stairs, and we heard voices raised outside the house. We went down and saw the sorry wreck of what our pleasant home had been. Tabitha observed, rather aptly, that the heathen raged together, and instantly, with her sister, began to work. I walked to the back of the house, meeting Master Felton who, returning from his fruitless search, looked even more like an angry bull than before. Tom's face was wooden as a ship's figurehead, and the villainous countenance of Miles still wore its gap-toothed grin.

"Well, sir?" I asked. "Now are you satisfied?"

"That your husband is not here, yes," he replied sullenly. "But I doubt if he is far away."

He began questioning me as to Martin's estate, and I said he might well be on his way back now, to which he answered that if he knew what was best for him he would so do and give himself up. This struck me as being so much a case of Dilly, Dilly, come and be killed, that I could scarcely keep from smiling.

"We may now be relieved of your company?" I asked.

"I am going, certainly. My time is precious, and I cannot kick my heels here. But I shall leave a man for the time being."

"Why?" I asked resentfully. "You burst into my home, behave most ill, find that what I have told you is the truth — cannot we now be left in peace?"

"I fear not," he said, with sarcasm. "When your husband returns from the country, whither, it seems, he has travelled on foot, I should wish to be informed, lest he set off on his travels again. Miles," he gestured to his man, "you will remain here."

I said no more and went back to the house. After all, it was no matter. Martin, please God, was safely away by now, and would not return. And mingled with thankfulness at his escape came the chill consciousness of my own loss.

It seemed quiet with Felton's voice no longer raised, and when Tom came in alone I started violently.

"That man—"

"He is in the stable," he answered. "He will remain there, and is asking for food and drink. I will take it to him, since he is a lewd fellow, and not to be trusted with women. See to it, Tabitha."

"Tom," I said softly. "You did not burn it?"

He shook his head, and a look of complacence crept over his battered countenance.

"I changed my mind, which was as well, since they came earlier than I had thought."

"But where?"

He bent his head to my ear, whispering, so that his beard tickled my cheek. "Weighted and at the bottom of the river." And without waiting for a reply, he stumped off, bearing meat and drink for our unwanted guest. I watched him go with a dawning affection. How simple, and how effective! Once again words of Master Shakespeare's came into my mind.

And deeper than did ever plummet sound
I'll drown my book.

Well, the river would hold its secret, and had thus a second time come to our aid. Felton had been foolish not to think of it, but I supposed had been blinded by his stubborn certainty that Martin was still here. And then, to trouble me, came the thought that perhaps he was not so lacking in sense, that perhaps even now ships were being searched and fugitives discovered. Yet it should have sailed, and in any case it availed nothing for me to torment myself with fears. I made myself eat some of the food which Tabitha had brought me and began repairing some of the damage the visitors had done, but the morning seemed endless, empty as the house without Martin. Tom came in once to say that Felton had ridden up, spoken with the man Miles, and ridden off again. This we both felt to be a good sign, since with Martin taken surely Miles would have been removed. The girls went marketing and returned with no fresh news, and the laggard moments crept by. Tom, who had a deep distrust for the morals of Miles, kept one stern eye on him as far as possible, and, for all his vaunted dislike of wenches in the house, was obviously constituting himself their protector. I wondered if that grim exterior concealed a weakness for one of them, thinking, half-smiling, that I must tell Martin, remembering in the same breath that he was no longer there to tell. I longed to go out, to find for myself what might be happening, yet felt I should stay lest Martin might have been able to send some message to me. He would, I knew, set my fears at rest if he could, and I chided myself, saying that the fact he had not been taken should be enough for me, but it was of no avail.

What made matters worse was a horrible sickness which came upon me from time to time, and which I could not shake off, try as I would. The hot bitterness would rise in my throat and I would be retching and miserable until it passed. It was, I supposed, due to the emotional upheaval of the past hours, and very unpleasant it was. I was in my room crouched over a basin in one of these attacks when I heard a voice I knew.

"No, I will find her for myself. If she sleeps I will not disturb her."

I raised my sweating face and turned eagerly to the door. Footsteps approached, and a deep voice called my name. I strove to reply, but could only manage a gasp. The door opened, and like a ship in full sail Henrietta strode in. At first she did not see me, and with a muttered unladylike word was sweeping out again, but I managed to speak, and she swung back.

"What's this, what's this?" she demanded, seeing my shaky form. "They did not tell me you were ill. What the devil are they about to leave you here alone?"

"'Tis but a queasy stomach, and is passing now," I said, pushing back the hair from my wet forehead. "I would rather be alone."

I stood up, finding that she was looking at me in a strange fashion, her lips pursed.

"Queasy stomach?" she repeated slowly.

"Yes. Never mind that. Oh, Henrietta did you know? Martin has gone."

"I know, my poppet, I know," she said gently.

I was not conscious of making any movement, but I found myself in her arms, my damp face against her breast. She held me most lovingly, and I clung to her.

"Listen, love. All is well. I have a message for you," she said.

I raised my head, half incredulous. "He sent a message to you, and not to me?"

A flicker of amusement lit Henrietta's face. "For matters of policy only," she said drily. "He thought this house might still be watched."

I was ashamed of my pettiness and said humbly: "He was right. Forgive me — and oh, what is the message?"

"Only this. The boat sailed safely with the tide."

"Thank God," I said, on a deep breath. "Thank God! I had been so fearful — and men have been here already."

Then she said something which roused me as if a trumpet call had sounded. I gazed at her, mouth and eyes wide, and she nodded with a pleased smile.

"Had you not thought it for yourself? There is naught so surprising in it, after all."

"But — but it is so soon! Surely it is not possible to tell as yet!"

Again she nodded, with pursed lips. "Those who live longest will see most," she said. "But for myself I have no doubt. No doubt at all."

CHAPTER XX

I think a week had passed with no word from Martin when Henrietta, now a daily visitor, came to me with a face so changed that I felt the strength drain from me, and clung to her for support. In a whisper I spoke my husband's name, and she was swift to reassure me, though her mask of sorrow did not fade.

"No, no, poppet, there is no ill news of Martin — but he would be grieved, as I am, at what has befallen." She went to the window and stood with her back to me, her tall figure slightly bowed, as I had not seen it before. "Sidney is taken."

"Sidney!"

We had both known that it must be so. The events of the past days had led inexorably to that conclusion, yet to know it an accomplished fact was as if to receive a crushing blow. It was, I suppose, something of the same way that we regard death, of all things the most inevitable, a shock when it comes to those we love, having without all reason regarded it as something which happens to others, leaving ourselves untouched.

"When did it happen?" I asked her, feeling cold. "And where is he now?"

"Yesterday. He was at his home, about to dine. And he is in the Tower, as are Lord William Russell and Wildman."

She swung round suddenly, adding with bitterness. "The man who placed his country before life and safety is now held a traitor and will suffer the fate served out to such."

She uttered a strange sound between a snort and a groan, and her lip trembled like that of an unhappy child. She did not weep — I never, in all the years I knew her, saw her weep but once — yet my heart ached for her. I went to her and she put an arm about me, but half as if she were not fully conscious of my presence.

"Dear Henrietta, sit down. Let me give you some wine." For I was troubled by her look of stony despair. She shook her head, but seated herself wearily, brushing a hand before her eyes as if cobwebs clouded her vision. I seated myself at her side, striving to find words.

"Dear, it may not be as bad as you fear. He had no part in the plot—" she gave a short bark of completely mirthless laughter, and the well-meant words of comfort died on my lips.

"When they have longed to find a handle against him? With Jeffreys, a packed jury, and the king behind all? He is tried and condemned as surely as if the trial were over. There may be hope in heaven for Algernon Sidney. On earth there is none," she said.

The words hung heavily on the air. I shivered, again, and for the first time she seemed to realise my presence, looking down on me with a shadow of her old smile.

"Poor Catherine! I am an ill-starred visitor with my load of woe, but I thought you would wish to know. Also, I wished to be with one of my own." She added, stroking back my hair. "For indeed, you have become to me as a child of mine."

"I am glad," I said truthfully. "As for me, what I should have done without you I do not know." And it was a fact that since the time, so short in actual days, so endless to live through of Martin's departure, I had come to depend on her more and more.

"How did you hear of it?" I asked her, when we had sat silent for a time.

"His man came to me early this morning," she answered. "It was Algernon's wish. He had not been unprepared, and our friendship is of long standing."

"He spoke of you in glowing terms," I said.

"God knows why! A loudmouthed termagant of a woman—"

"Whom he knew he could trust in all things."

"Well," she allowed in a softened tone, "there is that, at least, and in a society where every man turns to bite his neighbour it is, I suppose, worth something."

"I know it was worth a great deal to him."

I thought unhappily that I was speaking of Colonel Sidney as if he were already dead, and wondered how he would be faring in that grim building where so many had eaten out their hearts in captivity. I had known him for so short a time, my feeling for him was so slight compared with that of Martin and Henrietta, yet I was filled with aching pity. I recalled him laughing at Henrietta's table, wishing us happy after our marriage, talking with his grave face made youthful by enthusiasm of that land beyond the seas, and all that his friend was doing there. I did not care to think of him daunted and brought low. And even with the thought I knew myself most foolish, since no adversity would have power to darken the light which burned so clearly in his spirit.

Henrietta began to talk, at first in snatches, with some difficulty, then more easily, as if she found some solace in the telling, so that I had a clear picture of Colonel Sidney's last hours in his own quiet home. I tried to take in every word, not only for myself, but for Martin, too. I knew he would wish to know all, grieving as he would be at his absence from his friend's side at such a time, most urgent desire of that same friend though it might be.

"He was wise in that, at least, God be thanked," said Henrietta.

I was ashamed to find that in my thought for Martin I had lost the thread of the conversation, and looked at her inquiringly.

"Yes," said she, observing this. "It is small wonder that you look puzzled, since I am before my tale. The truth is my poor brain is in a ferment, and it is hard to put matters in order for myself, let alone you."

She sighed, and again passed a big hand over her eyes in that strange gesture, as if brushing away cobwebs.

"You are weary and troubled," I said gently. "Why do you not rest now, and we will talk later."

"There's no rest for me, child. No, I am better talking, if you can bear with me."

It moved me to hear her speak so humbly, so unlike herself, and I knew not what to say to comfort her. I laid my cheek against her hand in silence, and after a little she began to speak again.

"When I said just now that he was wise, it was in the matter of his papers. They took all they could lay hands on, and asked him to put his seal on them. But this he would not do."

"And you think he was wise to refuse? Surely his own seal would have been a safeguard."

"To be sure," said Henrietta drily. "One would think so. Unfortunately, my dear, in the past it has proved otherwise. There are those who can most cunningly remove seals unbroken, replacing them when certain matters have been added — that is, if treasonable papers had not been already inserted unseen. It has been known, and men have died because of it. Algernon, I think, recalled this, and refused in time — not that it will avail him in the event. He has written against the divine right of kings, and that will be enough to damn him. Writings are an abiding witness, and his pen may well be turned to an edged weapon that takes his life away."

I remembered the words which had come to my eyes on those papers left with Martin, and thought her not far wrong. I almost told her what had become of them, but bit the words back lest the knowledge might displease her, for I felt a certain guilt at what I had caused to be done. Not noticing me, she went mourning on.

"Years he spent over his *Discourses Concerning Government.* Filled with wisdom, and truth, and nothing on God's earth would have stopped him from writing them." She smote her hands together with such force that I jumped. She said bitterly: "Men! They must be ever striving to put the world to rights, and missing what lies under their foolish noses."

I looked up at her and saw the dark colour rise in her face, settling in patches on her cheekbones. She stared back at me, half with defiance, half with a hint of shyness, and she said, as if I had spoken? "Oh, yes. Had you not seen it before?"

"I — I knew you to be close friends — that he looked up to you—"

"How can men do other to a maypole? True enough, he did look up to me, while I, God help me—" She broke off suddenly, rose, and went again to the window. "Laugh if you will," she said in a choked voice. "I know well it gives food for mirth. And as for him, I doubt if he would credit it did the angel Gabriel come to tell him of my folly."

"I am not laughing," I said. "And he, if he knew, would not laugh either."

"He would probably, with the utmost courtesy, put as much space between us as possible. And who could blame him? And why I am prating of what has been and should have remained my shameful secret only God knows."

"There is no shame," I said, seeking for the right words. "And I am glad you told me."

"Well," she said, in her old loud voice, "what's done is done, but we will speak no more of it."

It was at once a plea and a command, and indeed, through all the years to come we never did, and while she lived I told no one, not even my nearest and dearest, since I felt it belonged to her alone. But it cannot harm her now since the affairs of this world have no power to trouble her anymore, and as I write I see her most clearly, and think her outward appearance hid a true and loving heart. And I think if the man she loved had been able to bring his lofty plans and grand ideals for mankind down to earth he might have found with her unthought of happiness.

As if to forget this baring of her inmost thoughts, Henrietta ceased talking of Sidney, and turned to me with the questions which now came at every visit. Each time I laughed at her, saying, with reason, that it was far too soon to be certain, but nothing would move her, and with a warmth which seemed to come from within flooding my whole being, I hoped that she would he proved right. And Martin's laughing voice would echo in my ears: "I hope to become a grandfather — with your assistance, of course." There he would be at my side, head tilted and eyebrows raised, so clearly that I would almost stretch out my arms to him before the sense of loss came coldly back again.

Having exhausted her questioning Henrietta rose to go, still feeling, I think, a certain discomfort. I asked her to stay longer, but she replied that the cats would be missing her, also that there might be more news. I felt that she probably wished to be alone, and she gave me one of her bear-like hugs and departed. I went into the garden where Tom was working and told him the news. He paused in his labours, not ungratefully, since he had small love for his present occupation, and his face took on an even graver air.

"The ungodly flourish, and the righteous are brought low," he said, before adding more practically: "A pity that he, also, had not fled from the wrath to come."

I was of the same opinion, but I suppose there comes a time when one wearies of being banished, even for one's safety's sake.

"It will go hard with him," said Tom, shaking his head. "They will make a clean sweep now. Essex, Lord Russell, Colonel Sidney — God be thanked he is not here to be added to the list."

"I only hope he is safe," I said uneasily. "If he could contrive to send word—"

"He will do so, never fear," he answered gently. "The house is still watched, and there cannot be too much care.

Trust in the Lord, Mistress, and all will yet be well. But as for Colonel Sidney, he had best get to his prayers." And he bent to his weeding again.

I went back to the house, unhappy and again troubled by that vile nausea which so often came to plague me now, and, horrible as it was, making me hope that Henrietta might be right. It did not last long, and I wiped my face and longing for air wandered out again, since the walls of the house seemed to enclose me like a prison. I went through the garden taking care to be unseen by Tom, whose face was hidden and broad rump upraised as he toiled. Had he known he would either have hindered or accompanied me, and though it was most ungrateful there were times when his diligent care seemed to well-nigh smother me, and it was with a half-guilty sense of relief that I made my way out of the garden, and to the riverbank.

It was a calm and sunny day, and the river flowed gently, dappled by the light, and making small gurglings and cluckings in a contented manner, like a babe fullfed. There was a fresh, tangy smell from some water plant growing along the verge, and swallows swooped and dipped tirelessly over the surface. It was all most peaceful, and almost impossible to believe that so near the city was filled with bustle and noise, with men walking in fear of an ugly death. Again I pictured the Tower, and the new captive within its walls, and all the warmth of the sun could not keep me from shaking.

Stone walls do not a prison make
Nor iron bars a cage.

The lofty words of Lovelace came to my mind, but I could not, just then, share the sentiment, feeling that the prison which held poor Sidney was grim and real enough, and his cage like to be one from which there could be no hope of escape.

Lost in my thoughts I had wandered farther than I meant and was assured of a scolding from Tom if he should discover my imprudence, as he would doubtless term it. Though since, until now, I had not set eyes on a living soul, I felt mutinously that I was unlikely to come to any harm, and might even go a little farther while I was about it.

Now I did see another person, a boatman by his dress, whose small craft was tied to a tree which overhung the river. It appeared to have taken in an uncomfortable quantity of water, which he was occupied in dipping out. I had seen no sign of a watcher, and did not think this could be one, so far from the house, and I glanced at him incuriously as I passed. His back was towards me and a woollen cap pulled down over his head, and for a moment I thought there was something vaguely familiar about him. A few steps on I turned to glance back, finding that he was also gazing at me, though at once he bent to his task again. For the first time I felt that Tom might be in the right, after all, for there was something furtive about the quick movement, as of one who avoided recognition, and I thought with weary disgust that he could well be a spy. I turned back decisively, my head held high, passing him without a glance, when in a low voice he spoke my name.

Whirling round I gazed with disbelief. It was not possible, a trick of the imagination. The crouching figure, still diligently bailing out the boat was not, could not be that of Roger Frampton. But he had spoken with Roger Frampton's voice.

Still with his back to me, he said. "Do not look at me or seem surprised. Wander to and fro, as if you had heard nothing."

Forcing my trembling limbs to move I went a few paces, then turned negligently back to lean against the tree near him. I did not look at him, and any watcher would have seen nothing out of the ordinary, and in any case I did not believe that we were observed, but I had been impressed by the urgency in his low-voiced commands. But when he continued his work in silence I could bear it no more.

"How come you here — and oh God, where is Martin?"

For the first time, after glancing swiftly to left and right he turned to look fully at me. He was so changed that had I not recognised his voice I doubt if I should have known him. A stubble of grizzled beard covered his face, blurring its lines, and a bandage round his forehead, grimy and stained, obscured the sight of one eye. He looked a ruffian, and a ruffian who had been in the wars.

I said in a faint voice, "Martin?" and clung to the tree trunk for support.

"There was a collision at sea, in thick fog," he said. "Our ship was sunk. I was picked up and brought back to Poole. I made my way here to see you."

I tried to speak, but my lips were stiff, and I could utter no sound. I gazed away at the dancing water and thought how it had taken my love away from me, but as yet I did not fully understand, only it seemed that somewhere near me was pain and loss which none could help me to bear.

I had closed my eyes, and when I opened them it was to find that Frampton, now heedless of watchers, real or imaginary, had left his boat and come to stand beside me. I looked vacantly at him, and he made as if to touch me, but his hands fell back.

"We were swept apart. God knows I would have saved him if I could," he said in a muffled voice.

"I know it also," I said steadily, remembering how he had come to warn Martin. "And you are still in danger, are you not?"

He looked at me, with a kind of wonder that I should give a thought to him.

"I shall do well enough, but you — you look—" He broke off, adding bitterly: "I cannot even see you safe home. Are you faint? Can you reach it?"

"Oh, yes. Do not trouble yourself over me. And in any case, I shall not be alone."

His eyes followed mine to a burly figure, approaching us with haste. Tom, like a faithful hound, had tracked me down.

"Thank God," said Frampton, recognising him. "At least I shall leave you in safe hands. And do not give up all hope — Martin, too, may well have been picked up. We were not far from the coast. It was that damned fog — I will make inquiries—"

Tom, puffing from his haste, was beside us, the words of angry reproof dying on his lips as he saw Frampton, and the look on our faces. Frampton hastily told him what he had told me and turned back to the boat.

"But shall I not see you again?" I asked selfishly, since I could not but know that by remaining he was in the more danger. But there was so much that I wished to know, and he, now, seemed the one point of contact with Martin.

"If all is well and I am able to come after nightfall, I will tap on the window," he answered. "But do not count on it."

"And have a care," warned Tom. "Put not your feet into the snare of the ungodly."

Frampton replied that he would make every endeavour not to do so, and seemed to send some wordless message to Tom, who nodded, and put a heavy arm around me. I was grateful, for my body seemed not wishful to obey me, and there seemed to be a mist before my eyes. When it cleared I saw that the river was empty, and that the boat had vanished like a dream. Tom, looking anxiously at me, besought me to come home, and I went obediently, with the coldness round my heart spreading and spreading, until I thought I should never know warmth again.

CHAPTER XXI

Tom took me back with, what was wonderful for him, no word of reproach. Indeed, I do not think we spoke at all, until we were entering the house, when it came on me like a sickening blow that Martin might never cross its threshold again, and the stab of pain was so sharp that I could not keep from uttering a faint whimpering sound. Tom muttered something and guided me to a chair, looking down at me with the colour drained from his broad face.

"You cared for him too," I said, looking up at him, and was ashamed of my selfishness, but only for a moment, since I had little thought just then for any other than myself. I saw Martin's face, white and lost, with the dark waters swirling around it, and the same dark waters seemed to engulf me, so that I gasped for breath. The waves pounded in my ears, and I went down, down, in the roaring blackness.

Far away I heard a voice which seemed to be calling on me. I tried not to heed it, but it came nearer, nearer, and most unwillingly I opened my eyes and came drifting back to a world in which Martin was not. The faces round me, at first hazy as if seen through mist, steadied and became clear. There was Tom, still with that strange, mottled pallor, the two girls, both tearful, both breaking into smiles as they met my gaze.

"There, there, my dear," said Tabitha, who was rubbing my hands between her own. "You are better now."

"I thought you were dead," said Mercy, with a loud sob. "So white and still—"

"Hush, foolish one, and bring wine," reproved Tabitha. "Can you sit up, my dear? 'Twill be better so, but do not hasten. Take your time."

I thought, all the time in the world, and wished that Mercy had been right. But I let them tend me and drank some of the wine.

"Do not trouble yourselves further," I said wearily, longing, for all their goodness, only to be left alone. "I will rest awhile."

They seemed to take my meaning, and after settling me more comfortably went out, followed by Tom. I was ungratefully glad to see them go, and when I became conscious that he had turned back and was standing beside me I gave him no welcome.

He said, without any of his usual Biblical turn of speech, "The news is bad, but do not give up hope, Mistress. There is no certainty that he is dead. All may yet be well."

I shook my head. "If he were alive, he would have sent word. He would not let me suffer like this."

"Have you not thought that he may have had no opportunity as yet? One was picked up and brought here, but there may have been other boats making for Dutch or French ports." Surprisingly, he gave a gruff bark of laughter. "He was not born to be drowned, that one. No weakling, also he could swim like any fish. Not so easily overcome as all that!"

For the first time I gave him my full attention. It was true, Martin was a great swimmer, and had once, for a wager, gone thrice round our lake, no mean distance. But the lake was not the open sea.

"You are trying to comfort me," I said. "It is too much to hope. I cannot believe it — I only wish I could."

"Oh ye of little faith!" said Tom sternly, returning to his customary manner. "Have trust in the Lord, and if it be

His will, all shall yet be well. If Master Frampton comes this evening we may learn more to the purpose. For myself, I will not believe him dead until I know it for a fact, and you should do likewise." And, having said his say, he departed without more words.

When he had gone the room seemed very still. I closed my eyes, and memories came flooding. I remembered our journey to London and my happiness, and how we had come back to this house on our wedding night. I remembered our laughter, the piercing joy we had known, the sense of comradeship as well as bodily love. And I thought of that last day together when we were so joyous, and my hand closed over the great ruby lying on my breast. I turned it to see the tiny inscription on the back, again hearing Martin's voice most clearly as he repeated the words. For the first time tears came to my eyes, and I wept for our lost happiness.

What followed I can never hope to explain, but will simply tell it as it happened. In the midst of my weeping, as if from far away, there came the strangest feeling that someone, somewhere, was striving most earnestly to reach me. I sat up in my chair, my tears forgotten, my whole being tense and agonising to receive the waves which seemed to clamour on me, bearing a message if I could but understand. Stronger they came, until it was almost more than I could bear, and all in an instant ceased. I sank back, shaking and half afraid, yet with a conviction steadily growing which set a glimmer of warmth where only cold had been before.

I said, as if I spoke to one standing at my side; "I know, dear heart. I understand."

Looking back I find it strange that I did not then wonder if Martin, breaking those most powerful bonds, had called to me after death. At the time no such thought came to me. I felt only that he had thus assured me that he lived, and that his thoughts were of me. And of my thankfulness I can find nothing to say, since it was beyond the reach of words.

After a time I went to Mercy and Tabitha, who looked at my changed face with wonder.

"The news was bad, but not final," I told them, adding as Tom appeared in the doorway. "I was at first too shaken to hope, but now I do not believe him dead."

"Nor I," he replied, actually with a smile. "Did I not say so? Though you were even as a doubting Thomas before."

"The shock was great. Little wonder if she feared the worst," said Tabitha.

"I will try not to do so again," I said, not knowing then how hard it would be, and how many times my faith would falter and all but die.

The day limped heavily on its way, since despite my newfound hope I could apply myself to nothing, longing only for nightfall and the coming of Roger Frampton. Somehow I never doubted that he would make his way to me, although the house was still watched from time to time. Miles's dirty self and perpetual grin was no longer with us, but every so often a slinking form would appear, hopeful, I suppose, to handle the reward set on the heads of the accused. Their bullying leader I had not seen since the day he came to find his bird flown. I wondered if the men who took Colonel Sidney had been as rude, then recalled that Henrietta said he had been courteously treated, save for their anger when he refused to set his seal to the documents they took. It seemed an ugly world to me, where justice could be travestied, and men not hope for a fair trial. I was glad that Ralph was far enough away not to be another victim, since I knew well where his sympathies lay. I thought a little of him and of Frances, wondering how matters stood between them, then dismissed them, only able to think, with foolish lack of patience, that night would never come.

At last the shadows crept into the house, and the mist, which often came with evening, rose over the river and closed in on us. Tom waited with me, and I was glad of his company, since the slightest sound seemed to set my body jangling like a set of bells, and I could not keep still. It was growing late, and my hope had almost died when a shadowy figure came catlike, on silent feet, through the open window.

Tom closed it after him, saying quietly: "As well if we went to the kitchens. The windows are shuttered, and any prowler would see little and hear naught."

We followed him, finding the cooking fire still alight and seeing one another for the first time. Tom cast on some small billets of wood which flared and sent our shadows dancing on the walls. Frampton stretched his hands to the blaze, and I saw that they were grimed, and had suffered rough usage. He was shivering, and his face, under the unfamiliar stubble, looked old and weary, and, unless the flickering light deceived me, of a deadly pallor.

"The river turns cold of nights," he said, as if in apology. "And I have a curst ague about me, which does not help matters."

"You are ill," I said, for the first time forgetting my own affairs, and taking note of his breathing which came with a rasping effort, the shaking which he seemed unable to control.

"It will pass," he said, with chattering teeth. "It must, indeed, since I need be on my way before dawn."

Tom, who seemed to have taken command of the situation, brought him a mug of ale and a hunk of mutton pasty. He drank thirstily but pushed away the food and was taken by a fit of shivering so strong that it fairly convulsed him. Tom and I glanced at one another over his head.

"He should he abed to sweat it out. 'Tis bound to take its course," said Tom, in a low voice.

"No!" gasped Frampton, raising a ghastly face. "I must go. I did not intend—"

He strove to rise, but the dreadful shivering took him again, and he fell back on the settle, gasping for breath.

"Oh, God!" he said indistinctly. "I knew I should not have come."

Laying a hand on his arm I said, striving to comfort him: "You came out of kindness for me, and you cannot leave thus. Tom will see to it." And I thought, gratefully, that the one I had miscalled would, indeed, see to all.

"My bed," he said briefly. "All the warm coverings we can muster, and the sooner the better, or he will be past moving."

Frampton muttered something quite unintelligible and tried again to rise. The shivering was less, and this time he got to his feet, though with a hand on the back of the settle for support. With an effort he said, "Do not trouble yourselves. I will go now, while my legs will carry me."

"You will go to bed, and at once," said Tom sternly. "And save your breath, for you will need it."

He looked wildly at me, but I said: "Indeed, you must do as Tom says. You are not fit to do otherwise — you must know that."

The shadow of his old smile crossed his face. "I fear I must agree with you. I am sorry—"

After that he spoke clearly no more, neither during the difficult passage of the stairs nor when he lay at last in Tom's bed, shaking so that it shook with him, and muttering in a queer gabble of which we could make neither rhyme nor reason. Tabitha and Mercy, wakened by the noise, went hastily for more coverings, for warm bricks, but despite all he leaped like a landed fish, and was not for a moment still. I had hurriedly told the girls that he was a friend of Martin's, whose presence must be kept secret, and was grateful for the calmness with which they accepted him. Indeed, Tom giving up his bed without a murmur, Tabitha and Mercy uncomplainingly roused from sleep, seemed to me to show such simple goodness that I felt pride in them. For with all the cruelty, self-seeking and treachery in high places one would lose faith in human nature were it not for such as these.

We needed all the assistance we could find, for the sick man, as the night wore on, grew steadily worse. The incessant shaking, the hoarse gabble of speech, gave him no rest, and his face was ghastly. When my father died I, as a child, was taken to look on him, and I had never been able to forget that grey, shadowed face, so different from the one I had known. The face of Roger Frampton under the soiled bandage which we had not paused to remove looked sadly like that other face, touched by the hand of death.

There was little we could do for him, save that Tom held him down, lest his convulsive movements should throw him from the bed, and he seemed not to know us, but to have removed himself to some dark land of trouble and pain. Tabitha and Tom, meeting one another's gaze across the tumbled bed, shook their heads.

"He should have skilled nursing," I said. "But what can we do? I dare not reveal his presence here."

"That would be a poor physic for him," agreed Tom, rubbing a sleeve across his sweating face. "No, Mistress, it will take its course, and end one way or t'other. It is in the Lord's Hands, and must be as He wills."

"Amen," said Tabitha, adding to me. "You should rest. This is not right for you."

I realised that she, who had never mentioned it by word or glance before, held the same opinion as Henrietta touching my condition, but gave little thought to it at the time.

"We could take turns to be with him," I suggested. "Tom cannot go on forever."

"For this night at least," he answered. "No wench at this juncture would have strength to hold him. Woman's work will come later, when he is recovering — if, that is to say, he ever does."

Tabitha took command. "I will remain while Mercy rests, then she can take my place. Do you rest, also Mistress — you look fit to drop."

Tom muttered ungraciously that he had no need for any wench, but it struck me there was a faint look of pleasure in his weary face. I agreed, rather unwillingly, and on condition that I was also called when Mercy took her turn and paused by the bed on my way out. Frampton's sunken eyes looked up into mine without recognition, but when I laid my hand, for a moment, on the restless head, he seemed to lie more quietly before a fresh fit took him. An arm was thrown wildly out, and his hand closed on my wrist with such force that I gave a little cry. His grip did not relax, and was of an amazing strength. I could not find it in my heart to force apart the fingers which held me as if they would never let me go.

"It is best if I stay, after all," I said. "Bring the stool here, Tabitha, and I shall do well enough."

She demurred, but finally obeyed, and the three of us with the man on the bed settled to what the coming hours might bring. Whether it was his hold on me that calmed him, or simply that his distemper was taking its course, the fits of shivering were now interspaced by intervals which grew longer as the night wore on. It mattered not if he lay like one already dead or jerked like a thing on strings, still he clasped my arm, and if I made the slightest move would grip the more fiercely, as if I were his last hold on life. It grew more and more hard to bear, that grip, with my hand growing numb and rivulets of pain running sickeningly to my armpit, but I set my teeth and vowed that I would not weaken.

At some time Tabitha went silently out returning with warm milk, which I drank gratefully, and every so often she would try to make me more at ease, propping me with pillows, and tucking covers from my own bed round me. And at last it seemed the ague itself had passed, though that difficult breathing still seemed to fill the room.

Tom straightened himself wearily and went out. I was troubled lest Frampton should need holding down again, but Tom was not long gone, and I looked at him with gratitude as he took up his old place at the bedside. The sick man was still enough now, and I told myself that the worst was over and thanked God. Utterly exhausted though he seemed to be, he still maintained his hold on me, and despite my discomfort I had half drifted into sleep when I became conscious of a change. The hand which had been cold was on a sudden burning, and the face which had been white as the pillow on which it lay was now darkly flushed. I did not know whether this could be for good or ill, and hastily drew the attention of the others.

"A fever," said Tom gloomily. "Bad now, in his weakness. He should be cupped."

"Stuff and nonsense," said Tabitha, with asperity. "The letting of blood one way or another is all that men can think of. What he needs is a cooling draught, and I have the very thing." She went hastily from the room.

"Mistress Know-all," said Tom sourly, but with a faint admiring smile, so that even then I thought it was clear which of the sisters had found a chink in his armour, and how tickled Martin would have been at the notion. But I was quickly recalled to the sick man, who, without warning, called in a loud, hoarse voice: "Have done! What use to plead or deny? I loved you, loved you, while you—! Do not dare to speak of your love to me!"

There was something so shocking in the sudden outburst that Tom and I both started, and he looked at me strangely.

"Oh no. He is not speaking of me," I said, as if he had accused me. I knew well enough who haunted that fevered mind, and for a moment I saw that sweet and lovely face as if she stood beside us, watching us with her great eyes.

"'Tis strange that a man's mind should turn to carnal lusts when his end is near," said Tom, drawing down the corners of his mouth. "Rather should he be calling on the Lord for pity and forgiveness."

I bit back a rejoinder, recalling how selflessly he had striven that night, and again we listened to the man who, from some strange borderland, recalled his onetime love.

"Frances, Frances," mourned the hoarse voice. "So beautiful, so untrue. Wanton and greedy, yet with it all, God help me, a very part of me. I pluck you from my heart and you return and will not be denied. Dear God—"

His voice trailed off to an unintelligible murmur, and he fell silent, struggling for breath, and moving his head restlessly from side to side, his clasp burning into my wrist. And even then I thought with faint indignation that it was well I had rejected that proposal of his, since though he might have a certain fondness for me there was little enough left for any other woman after what my brother's wife had done to him. Tabitha returned, bearing a cup from which a faintly aromatic steam arose. She nodded reassuringly to me, remarking in her calm voice that I was to be of good cheer, since this had been handed down from her great granny, and had never been known to fail.

"It needs be a corpse-reviver then," muttered Tom. "He is far gone. That outcry was his last."

"You will see," she answered. "Raise him, and steady his head."

Tom slid his arm under Frampton's shoulders. I saw his head flop to one side and felt with a catch at my heart that he had indeed gone beyond the reach of any remedy, save that he still maintained his hold on me. His mouth was slightly open, and as Tom supported him Tabitha tilted her cup to it. Some of the liquid, which was green, ran down his chin, but some made its way to his throat, for he uttered a choking sound.

"There, there, my dear," said Tabitha, in a motherly tone. "Take it, now. Do as I bid you — 'tis for your own good."

As if returning to childhood, Frampton obediently swallowed, until the cup was empty.

"You may lay him back now," said Tabitha, "and wait."

The sick man, silent now, sank back into the pillows as if utterly spent. The flush had faded, leaving mottled patches of colour which stood out in an ugly fashion on the shadowed pallor of his cheeks. His breathing, that sound which had been a background to the night, seemed even more difficult, with ever longer pauses between each rasping inhalation, so that one waited for each to be the last.

"I told you," Tom said to Tabitha. "He was too far gone. As well try to raise the dead."

"And I tell you that you are well named," she answered. "Have faith and cease your croakings. You prophesy doom like any raven."

I leaned my head against the pillows and thought that it was the doubter who was right, and that Roger Frampton had come to the end of that dangerous road on which he had once told me his feet were set. Much as I grieved for him, who had risked himself to come for Martin, I also grieved more selfishly, feeling it hard that he could not have told me more before he died. In the closing hours of that long night my faith in Martin's survival flickered like a dying flame and was almost lost. And I wished that I too might be going to that country of Algernon Sidney's far beyond the stars, since the world I knew would hold only emptiness for me.

Outside a bird called sleepily, then another. The night which had seemed endless was coming to an end at last. Tom put out the candles, which had burned low, and drew back the curtains. A faint light crept into the room. Roger Frampton gave a long sigh, and his hand dropped from my wrist. The breathing sounded no more.

My arm fell heavily and without feeling to my side, and desolation swept over me. For some reason I had felt the two lives, his and Martin's, to be in some way bound, that if Frampton recovered I might hope the more. Now all hope was gone, and I lost in the slough of despond.

"What did I tell you?" came the voice of Tabitha, clear and triumphant, so that I wondered to hear her.

"Praise God for all His mercies!" said Tom. "And that draught of yours has wondrous powers. You spoke no more than the truth."

I raised my head blinking at them vacantly, amazed that they should be so misled.

"What do you mean? He is dead."

"Dead? Far from it," said Tabitha, laughing.

"His fever has broken. He sweats like a pig," said Tom.

"But — he does not breathe!"

"See for yourself, my pretty. Believe me, he will do well now. He sweats, and sleeps, and will live."

I did as she bade me. The first rays of the sun crept into the room, and I saw Frampton's face all pearled with sweat, and almost imperceptibly the rising and falling of his breast. He looked as if he had fought with demons, but they were right, and it was I who had been deceived. The sun shone more warmly, and the bird song rose and swelled, and we looked at one another with hollow eyes and smiled. Then my numbed arm came alive with such a stab that I cried out. Looking down I saw it marked and puffy from his hold.

Mercy was summoned and we went to our rest. The last thing I knew before I fell on my bed and into a pit of sleep was the sound of a loud and smacking kiss. At the time I thought nothing of it, but later I marvelled that Tom should have been so moved, and I thought that it was not only in nursing the sick that Tabitha had triumphed.

CHAPTER XXII

When I awoke the sun was high, and at first, as often on waking I thought Martin was aside me, and stretched out my arms for him. One felt stiff and heavy, and at once I recalled what had happened and sat up. Henrietta, who was sitting by the bed, nodded with pursed lips.

"And here's a pretty coil!" said she, without greeting.

"You know?" I added, rather defensively, "He came out of kindness to me. Henrietta, the ship was lost."

"I know that also. But until we are persuaded otherwise we may still hope."

There was little conviction in her tone, but I said steadily, "I believe him to be alive."

She patted my hand, looking at me kindly, then with a return to her usual brisk manner asked. "And this other — what's to be done with him? Had you thought of that?"

"He will leave as soon as he is able. We had much ado to make him stay last night, ill as he was."

"At least he had the consideration not to die here," said Henrietta unkindly. She had, I think, taken it into her head that his liking for me was more than proper, and I thought she needed only to have heard him the night before to have known otherwise.

"Well," she continued, rising. "It seems he was not followed here, else you would have had visitors by now, but for God's sake have a care. You have more than yourself to think of now."

I said, with a secret smile: "I begin to think you may be right."

"And high time too! Did I not tell you?"

"I must go down," I said, refusing to continue. "What is the news?"

"His Grace of Monmouth has retired. Colonel Ramsey has given himself up. Lord Russell is for trial on the thirteenth of July?"

"And Colonel Sidney?"

She shook her head. "Nothing as yet. He is most strictly kept and allowed no visitors. None can help him now."

As if unwilling to say more she took her leave of me, again counselling prudence, and I rose to go in search of food, finding myself greatly in need of it. Tabitha greeted me with the news that our visitor yet slept, and that Mercy was with him.

"And Tom? You both must be weary."

"He is in the stable," she said, and I saw a tinge of colour rise in her cheeks. "We are well enough."

"I did not know that you had such skill in nursing," I said, eating hungrily.

"Not skill — I would not say that. But my great granny was a wise woman, and some of her matters have been handed down. Dried herbs and the like I keep ever by me. There is great virtue in—"

She broke off suddenly with a violent start. I, with a hand halfway to my mouth was alike struck dumb. Loud and imperative the knocking on the door sounded again. All in a moment I imagined the sick man dragged from his bed to meet a shameful death, and thought with bitterness that we might have saved our efforts of the previous night.

Tom looked in at the door, his face as troubled as ours. There was a pause, then the knocking sounded again.

I came to myself and spoke swiftly. "Do you keep yourself out of sight. I will say 'tis you who lies sick abed. It may serve. Tabitha, let them in."

Tom vanished, and Tabitha, all her colour gone, went to the door. I heard a murmur of voices, but not the shouting or stamping footfalls I had feared. Almost at once Tabitha returned.

"'Tis but a lady who would speak with you. She waits in the garden room."

The relief was so great that I had to pause and take a deep breath before going to see who my unexpected guest might be. The door of the garden room stood open. A faint remembered scent drifted out to me, and I knew.

She was standing gazing out of the window. I had made no sound, but she swung round suddenly and we stood face to face. As always, she was fine enough to have graced a Court in her gown of rich amber silk, the bodice close to her figure, the sleeves ending above her elbows and frothing with lace. Jewels glittered at her breast and around her white neck. She held a pair of perfumed gloves sparkling with embroidery silver and gold, and, as that first time I saw her, she seemed a thing of light. Standing there in the sunshine she was even more beautiful than I remembered, and again I felt drab beside her.

"Frances?" I said uncertainly. "How come you here, and where is Ralph?" And remembering I was in my own house, I added. "Will you not be seated?"

A flicker of amusement crossed her face, but she sat down, laying her gloves on the table. I took a chair opposite her, feeling her gaze on me.

"Ralph remains at home," she said. "I came with my friend Mary Stainer, who has been visiting in our neighbourhood, and whose home is but a short space from here. You have changed, Catherine."

"You have not," I said truthfully.

"No," she agreed, this time with something strange, almost fierce in her eyes. "I do not change."

Considering all that had passed I thought it surprising that she should have come to me, and even more surprising that Ralph should allow her out of his sight. I offered her refreshment, which she declined, and asked after him.

"He is well," she answered, "Or was when I left."

"He is not in trouble?"

She shook her head. "All is as usual with him — except, that is, for one thing." Calmly as if she spoke of something not of the least importance, she added, "I have left him and shall not return."

I gazed at her stupidly, unable to believe my ears. Then a wave of anger swept me, so that I pushed back my chair and stood over her. She looked faintly surprised, and again I pictured Ralph as he looked at her that first day, and recalled how I had pitied him, even then.

"You cannot! How could you? You are his wife—"

"I was his wife. No more," she answered, with that slight dismissing movement of the shoulders which I had seen before. "We have come to the end of the road, he and I."

"You never cared for him," I said bitterly. "You took him, used him, and now you throw him aside. Are you not ashamed? And he — does he know?"

"Not as yet," she answered indifferently. "Else would I have him pounding like an enraged bull at my heels."

The contempt, the utter lack of feeling, were too much for me. I raised my hand and struck her across the cheek. She made no movement, and my hand fell to my side, but on her smooth face its mark showed red.

"I am sorry," I said unsteadily. "I should not have done that."

"No," she assented. "You should not. I am sorry that Jennings is no longer here. She had better means than I of avenging my injuries." And for one strange moment it was as if the dead woman stood before me, raising those hooded eyes to fix them on my own.

I sat down rather suddenly, and a great bluebottle which had been droning about the roof flew almost into my face

221

before making its way out of the window. Remembering tales I had heard I could not repress a shudder. I saw a faint smile stretch Frances's lips, but she said nothing, and angry with myself, I pushed my folly aside.

"What I cannot understand," I said, "is why you should come to me. Apart from all else, as Ralph's sister you could hardly expect me to welcome you."

"As Ralph's sister — no, I did not come for that," she answered, again with that slight gesture, as if poor Ralph and all concerning him were of supreme indifference to her. "I came to you for news — news of one we both know — since I am persuaded you can give it to me."

As if her eyes on me could read of the man lying above stairs, I dropped my own, and felt the colour burn my cheeks. She saw, and for the first time showed emotion.

"I knew it! I always knew that I was right. Ralph might prate of your devotion to this husband of yours, but I knew better. Though what Roger could see in you beside me—"

She broke off panting, looking on me with hatred. I was as angered as she, since I could not bear to hear her speak of Martin. "You deceive yourself completely. Unlike you, my husband is the only man in my life." And half unconsciously my hand went to the ruby pendant at my breast.

"He would have wed you," she snapped, "and not for the money only, no matter what he might say. He would not listen to me."

I looked at her changed face with wonder. She had utterly dismissed Ralph, as if only her passion for Frampton held meaning. Whatever else in her life was unreal that was real enough, and had it not been for my brother I might almost have pitied her.

Rising, I said coldly, "We have nothing to say to one another. You had better go. Why you should have come at all is past my understanding."

"I came because I had news of his father's death. All will be changed for him now."

"So that is it!"

222

"That is it. And I will not go until you tell me where I may find him."

"Have you no shame?"

"None at all. And if you wish me to go you had best tell me." Her eyes narrowed suddenly. She said, very softly: "Do you know, Catherine, I have the strangest feeling that he is not far away."

My treacherous colour rose again, but I managed to keep my voice steady. "If you know so much you must know that he was wanted in connection with this plot. He, together with my husband, escaped overseas."

She looked at me searchingly, and frowned. "You seem to speak truth, yet I could have sworn . . . However—"

She sighed, picked up her gloves, rose, and turned to the door. Mercy's voice came clearly from the kitchen.

"Sister, he is awake, and asking for food."

Frances shot me one look, and before I could make any attempt to stop her, she was past me in a swirl of silken skirts and running up the stairs. I followed with what haste I could, but I knew that nothing would stop her now. She did not even try the wrong door, but as if by instinct darted into Tom's room. I heard her cry of triumph, then no other sound. When I reached the doorway she had flung herself down at the bed-side, those silvery ringlets spread like a curtain, her face hidden her whole body shaken by sobs. Across her, Frampton's eyes, with God knows what look in them, met mine.

There was a gasp from behind me. I turned to meet the scandalized gaze of Tabitha and Mercy and could find no words.

Frances spoke first in a sobbing voice. "My dear love, I have found you. As soon as you are recovered we will be together. I will never leave you again."

He said faintly: "You should not have come. Your husband—"

"He is nothing to me. There is only you."

Tabitha, looking outraged, stepped past me and into the room. She was bearing a bowl of broth, and her colour was high. Ignoring Frances, she spoke directly to Frampton. "You will take this, sir, and then you should rest. You are not out of the wood yet."

Ashamed of my inaction, I laid a hand on Frances' shoulder. "Tabitha is right, and Master Frampton has been near to death. You should not trouble him now."

To my surprise she rose obediently, bent to give him a lingering kiss, and with one devouring look came away. At the doorway she turned, said, "I will return. Until tomorrow, my dearest love!" and as calmly as if her visit had been all that was decorous and right lifted her skirts and walked down the stairs. She simply ignored the rest of us. I believe she would have gone without another word had I not overtaken her.

"Frances," I said, urgently. "You will not come here again."

"Do you think to stand between us? You lied to me once, and you lie again," she answered. "Can you not see that nothing will stop me now that I have found him again? Neither God nor man." And she actually laughed on a low exultant note as she went out into the sunshine.

I stood there in the doorway, shaken and unhappy. What could I do? If I sent word to Ralph he would come storming up, probably thirsting for Frampton's blood, and all to no avail, since his wife was undoubtedly lost to him. Yet I could not allow her access to her lover under my own roof, as if encouraging her — not that I cared to keep them apart. Ralph would be well rid of one who had never been truly his. I thought wearily that my own troubles were more than enough for me, and I wished, as I had often wished before, that she had never entered our lives. As for Roger Frampton, it was perhaps unfair, since this visitation was none of his doing, but I felt small desire to see him now, only for what he might be able to tell me of Martin. And with the thought my longing for him was so great that I put a hand to my heart to hold back the pain.

"I do not know the lady," said Tabitha from behind me, "but she has done neither you nor the sick gentleman good. You look like a ghost, and he, who should be resting, is now all agog to be gone."

"She is my brother's wife," I said.

Tabitha looked as disapproving as Tom. "Then why—?"

"Do not ask me," I said wearily. "She has left my brother, it seems, but how she came here I do not know. It was as if she were certain that I should have knowledge of her—" Swallowing the final word, I cried childishly. "I wish it had not happened, and I know not what to do!"

Tabitha's mass of outraged virtue relaxed, and she said in a motherly tone: "Do not trouble yourself — he mends apace and will soon be fit to go." The corners of her mouth turned down again. "And with such lewd and godforsaken behaviour the sooner the better," she muttered.

The later part of the day was lost to me, and my anxieties forgotten as I slept the hours away. When I saw the evening shadows lying on the grass I could scarce believe it, for it seemed but a moment since I had closed my eyes. I stretched, yawned, and was still only half awake. Tabitha looking in, remarked that I seemed better for my rest, and I remembered all that had passed, and marvelled that I could have slept.

"How is Master Frampton? And has she returned?"

"He does very well, and is asking to speak with you," said Tabitha, setting her lips. "And the lady has not returned. I should not trouble yourself with him — I told him how you had been beside him all the night."

Against her disapproval I went up the stairs, which still seemed to echo the flying footsteps of Frances. He was lying with his face to the door, and his sunken eyes lit up at sight of me.

"It is good of you to come," he said. "I would ask your pardon could I find the words."

"Did you know," I asked, "that Frances had left my brother for you?"

"God knows I did not — how could I? I cannot conceive how she found me — and to come here! I will be gone as soon as I may."

"And what of her? And of my brother? It seems he knows nothing as yet."

"Then it may not be too late. If I go, she may return to him."

"That will be pleasant for Ralph," I said coldly. "A wife who yearns only for another man."

The colour stained his cheeks and faded, leaving him so white that I felt compunction. After all, her coming had not been at his desire, but I wearied of the whole business.

"You were to tell me more of Martin," I said.

"It is little enough," he answered. "The fog came like a blanket, and this ship was on us without warning. There was no time — one minute he was beside me, the next we were swept apart. I clung to some wreckage and a fishing vessel picked me up when the fog lifted. By then there was no sign of him. But there were other boats."

"He may still have been picked up?" I said hopefully.

"I will go in search of him. We cannot have been far from the Dutch coast." Then he added, with difficulty, "You are angered, and I do not wonder. Believe me, I am sorry. How she knew I should be here — but she could not! It must have been the merest chance, and before God, I would have given my right arm that it should not have happened. And why now?"

"She had heard that your father was dead."

"Oho! So that was it!" An ugly look crossed his face. "She might have saved herself the trouble. My father was estranged from me to the last, and there will be precious little for me. But let that go! I have not so much as thanked you for your care of me."

"I did nothing. It was Tabitha."

He shook his head. "It was not Tabitha whose touch kept me from going into the darkness," he said.

* * *

Henrietta came the next morning as usual. I, who had waited with every moment for Frances to keep her word, poured it all out to her at once.

"Poor little one," she said, stroking back my hair. "Troubles come in battalions, but do not be cast down. 'Tis none of your doing."

"But Ralph! What will he think of me?"

"What he does not know will not hurt him," she answered. "And after all, she may not come again. A wanton such as she may well have had second thoughts."

I shook my head. "If you had seen and heard her—"

"Well, well, short of barring the doors you cannot keep her out. But if you wish I will remain and give my fine lady the rough edge of my tongue. Not that I am likely to bring her to her senses, and as for your brother, he is well rid of her."

"Ralph will not think so," I sighed.

Henrietta remained until noon, and Frances had not appeared, though I had thought to find her at my door long since. Henrietta finally left, saying that Frances had probably come to her senses, and with Frampton on his way I should be able to forget the whole matter. I thought otherwise, and she had not been long gone when, with a sinking heart, I heard the expected knocking on the door. Thinking I would make, for Ralph's sake, one final appeal, I went to admit her myself. But it was not Frances. Instead a solemn-faced man whom I had never seen before awaited me.

At first I was so taken aback that I gaped at him, then my thoughts flew to Frampton. But the newcomer bowed politely and was altogether unlike those who had come before.

"Your pardon, Mistress, but might I speak with Mistress Carey? I have a message from my lady."

"Your lady?"

"Lady Mary Steiner. Mistress Carey was with her until she came to you, and my lady wishes to know if she is returning or wishes her gear brought here."

I stared at him. "But — but I do not understand."

He said, looking surprised. "I accompanied her here myself yesterday. She dismissed me, saying she was not sure how long she might remain. When she had not returned by nightfall my lady guessed that she would be spending the night with you."

"She came, as you say," I said uneasily. "But as for remaining, she was here less than an hour in all."

A flicker of surprise crossed his smooth face. "She did not leave alone?"

I nodded, and he shook his head reprovingly. "No lady should walk without escort," he said.

I gazed at him, taking in the implication, and that last sight of Frances came to me. There had been gems at her breast, rings on her fingers. I remembered those men who lurked about the house.

"Surely no ill can have befallen her! It was broad day when she left, and she said it was not far."

"Upwards of quarter of a mile," he assented. "Yet far enough for footpads and the like." Again he shook his head, making a faint sound of disapproval, tongue tapping against his teeth. "I had best go and inform my lady."

He bowed, and was gone, leaving me troubled and uncertain what to do. I turned to Tom, who heard me in silence, then remarked briefly that he would take a look around. It seemed a long time before he returned, and by then I had told myself that there could be some simple explanation. Frances was so much a creature of her own desires that the fact she had not returned to her friend might mean little.

And then I saw that Tom was holding something between finger and thumb which caught the light. I had last seen it on her hand. The gold and silver embroidery had lost something of its glitter, and the pale leather was streaked with damp. Tom looked questioningly at me, and I nodded.

"She dropped it on the path?" I asked. "It must have lain there all night."

Tom shook his head. "It was not on the path. It was within the laurels. I should never have looked there, but I saw marks on the ground, and broken twigs." He frowned and said heavily: "The way of the light woman leads down to hell. I fear she has met with her deserts."

"No, it cannot be! So near the house, and in broad day! We should have heard."

"A hand clapped over her mouth would see to that. And if she struggled she would probably be silenced for good."

I shuddered, seeing all too clearly my brother's wife, the smile struck from her face and terror stamped in its stead. She had given me little cause to love her, but God knows I would not have wished her this. A thought struck me.

"Are we still watched?" I asked, turning to Tom.

"I saw no sign. Nor do I think it likely the watcher will return," he said, with dark significance. "I must waste no more time — I but wished to be certain that the glove was hers." He looked down at the pretty thing in my hand, muttered that all was vanity, and returned to his search. A movement behind me made me whirl around. Roger Frampton, fully dressed, one hand on the door as if for support, was standing there, Mercy wringing her hands at his side.

He said, brushing aside her tearful expostulations. "I heard some talk of Frances. What has happened?"

"You should not be out of your bed! Suppose you are seen?"

"What of that! For God's sake, tell me!"

"He would have his clothing, say what I would" sobbed Mercy. "And he more dead than alive."

"You show small consideration for yourself, or, for that matter, for me," I said indignantly. Then I met his gaze and my heart smote me.

"Frances, it seems, is missing," I said reluctantly. "We know nothing more. Will you not wait in your room?"

He shook his head impatiently. "I told you I would leave as soon as I was able. That has not changed, but I must know what has befallen her." Rather indistinctly, he added, "I beg of you to understand. Indeed, I cannot help myself."

"At least, until Tom returns wait within, and out of sight." Then, for he looked fit to drop: "Mercy, bring food and wine to the garden room."

He followed me, not willingly, and we were scarcely in the house when there came the sound of voices, of heavy footsteps outside.

"Stay where you are," I said, hastening out to find Tom, and with him the serving man who had come already, and another, more roughly clad, beside him. Tom met my eyes and shook his head.

"My lady bade me help in the search," said the first man. "She is greatly troubled."

"There be some signs," said Tom obscurely. "If you, Master—?"

"John Ffookes is my name. And this is Obadiah."

Obadiah, who had a strong smell of the stable about him smiled and ducked his head. Tom said something in a low voice and they moved off, turning from the tangled bushes and towards the river. And as I watched them go I knew, and the knowledge caught at my heart.

I felt faint when I went back to Frampton and was at first unable to speak. "Dear God! What has happened?" he asked, putting wine to my lips.

"Nothing," I said faintly. "Men are helping in the search. They have gone to the river."

"The river!" he echoed. We gazed on one another, and I saw what little colour there was in his cheeks drain shockingly away, until it might have been a dead man who gazed on me from hollow eyes. Then, putting me aside when I would have stayed him, he was gone, and I heard his footsteps on the paved path outside. I hastened to the doorway, calling on him to stop, but he paid no heed, and my voice was echoed by a more distant cry. At the sound he stopped dead, then, unbelievably, began to run. There was another shout, then silence.

I found Tabitha and Mercy beside me, and we stood like a group of stone figures, so intent on listening that we spoke no word, seeming scarcely to breathe. It is so long ago, yet I shudder at the memory even now.

Our time of waiting was not long. They came into sight, their faces solemn, even that of the smiling Obadiah, walking heavily, bearing a burden between them. And that was how Frances kept her pledged word and did, indeed, return, though not as she had planned. For though the man she loved walked close beside her it meant nothing to her, since no affair of this world could touch that passionate, wayward heart of hers anymore.

They laid her down, looking at her with pity and with awe. Her silvery hair was darkened by the water and on her forehead a great bruise showed, but except for that she might have been asleep. They had found her, like the lost girl in the play, near the willow which had checked her with its branches, else the river might have held its secret, and carried her away.

What happened after is a blur to me. I recall bustling low voices, talk of what must be done, Tabitha and Mercy working together. Tom left with the other men, after speaking aside with Frampton.

When they had gone, he came to me, saying without preamble.

"I will tell Ralph."

"What?" I asked drearily. "That she left him for you?"

He shook his head. "That I can save him at least. But the rest he must know."

"Then you are going now?"

"I must. Tom will be returning with others, and I will be discovered. I should like to see her once more, then I will go."

There seemed little feeling in his voice, and we went together to the room where she lay. The girls had removed the marks the river had left and folded the quiet hands on her breast with a spray of rosemary between them. She looked touchingly young, and still most beautiful. We looked down on her, he and I, and what thoughts were in his mind I do not know. He did not speak or touch her, only stood gazing down for a long time, and her laugh seemed to echo in the room. Her words, the last I ever heard her speak — "Nothing will stop me now that I have found him again. Neither God nor man" — seemed to hang between us.

CHAPTER XXIII

Following the death of Frances with all the inquiries and troubles which it set in motion, there came a lull in such matters as closely touched myself. Days passed into weeks with no word from Frampton and no news of Martin. Sometimes, sick at heart, I called myself a fool not to accept his death as a fact, yet somehow the spark of hope would never allow itself to be wholly extinguished. Somehow, somewhere, I knew I would see him again, and not I alone, since now there was no doubt that Henrietta was right, and I was to bear his child. Now, looking back, I feel I could never have lived through the endless waiting without that sweet certainty to uphold me, and yet I do not know. We are so apt to cry of what we cannot endure, yet when the time comes, from some unknown fount of strength we do endure whatever fate may bring to us.

I think of Ralph when he came to me, and of how grief had changed him, giving him a kind of quiet dignity. Once, when we were alone together, he said abruptly, "When first I heard of the river I thought she had died by her own desire."

I looked at him, reading the hurt, the humiliation in his altered face, and for a moment in pity for her was lost in anger. He had loved her so dearly — she might at least have left him his self-respect.

As if echoing my thoughts, he said, "She never loved me as I loved her. I knew it from the first, but I would not admit it, even to myself, and I thought children would come, and make all right. It is no pleasant thing for a man to be looked on with contempt by the one person—" He broke off suddenly, and turned away.

Knowing what I did I could find no words to comfort him, and that was the only time he spoke of his hurt to me. More like himself, he raged against her murderer, saying what he would do could he but lay hands on him, but of Frances he spoke no more. And despite all efforts and offers of reward time went by, and the lurking brute who had spelt fate for her was not found.

With Ralph's departure, as I said, my own affairs were quiet enough, but in the world outside it was not so. Algernon Sidney yet lay in the Tower awaiting trial, but Lord William Russell was tried — if one can call it that — condemned and mangled on the scaffold. Lord Essex left the Tower by another route, preferring, it seemed, to take his life by his own hand rather than wait for what his fellows would do to him — if, indeed, it were suicide, of which there was some doubt. It made sickening hearing for Sidney's friends, and Henrietta lost her high colour and grew so thin that she seemed taller than ever, the maypole that she had called herself indeed. I was so grieved for her, for Sidney and for Ralph, my constant longing for Martin was so great, yet with it all there was something of comfort when I thought of the child to come. It was so wonderful a thing, that growing life within me, part of us and of our love, which I should someday hold to my breast.

For Henrietta there was no such aid, except that she was as careful over my wellbeing as if I had been her own lost child. Perhaps it was some slight help to her, after all. I should be glad to think it, since, as with my brother, I could offer her no comfort in words. For Colonel Sidney, though innocent as my unborn babe, we knew there could be no hope. If the dice had not been heavily weighted enough against him before, there was the Lord Chief Justice Jeffreys to contend with, who, men said, had openly sworn to have his life. Lord Russell, tried on the thirteenth day of July, executed on the twenty-first of that same month, told how swiftly such travesties of justice could take their course. And I could almost be grateful that Martin did not return, since to do so would be to walk into the jaws of a trap.

It was soon after poor Lord Russell's execution that the first move was made, and Colonel Sidney, before the king and council, accused of treason. He refused, as he said, to fortify evidence by speaking at that stage, so the proceedings were quickly over, and he returned to the Tower. Henrietta, in constant touch with his man, was told of this, and also that already his master's house had been ransacked, his coaches and goods confiscated.

"As if," said Henrietta bitterly, "he were now tried and condemned. Not but what 'tis good as done now."

"The Duke of Monmouth may intercede," said I, striving to find some shred of hope.

"He? He is most diligently trying to save his own skin," she answered. "Though I may do him some injustice. He did write to Lord Russell from his place of hiding offering to surrender himself if that might in any way contribute to his service."

"Surely one can but give him credit for that!"

"No doubt you are right," said Henrietta, with little conviction. The popular duke had never found favour in her eyes. "He might have guessed what the reply would be."

"Lord Russell refused?"

"He said, 'It would be no advantage to me to have my friends die with me.' Probably he was right."

"It all seems so great a waste! A few men plot, and many who had no part in it die or are in hiding. And to what purpose?"

"To a great deal for the king, since this plot, far from harming him, was a gift placed full in his greedy hands. Do you not see it has given him such an ascendancy over the

Whig party as he might never have hoped for otherwise? Speak of a plot to an Englishman and he bands with his fellows like a pack of hounds, eager to run down anything in their path. The small fry went quickly, and the bigger game must follow. Oh yes, my dear, 'tis as you say, the most damnable waste, but men are men. Women know better."

"I wonder how Colonel Sidney fares, and if they treat him harshly?"

She shook her head. "How he feels only God knows. But if they grant him writing materials he will care little what bodily suffering he endures. His writing — did you know that his dearest wish is to see those Discourses Concerning Government made public? He trusted Martin to see to that."

I gazed blankly at her, and she asked what ailed me.

"Nothing," I said untruthfully. For I felt a burden of remorse at the thought of those writings and could not bear to tell her what had been done, feeling that neither she nor my husband would forgive me. "I did but wish that Martin were here."

Henrietta patted me indulgently on the shoulder, but her face was grave.

"Dear child, are you still convinced he will return?"

"He will return," I said.

"Frampton is long in sending word," she said uneasily. "He promised, did he not?"

"You know he did. Do you not think I find it hard waiting, waiting, as the days go by?"

She held me, muttering that she was a clumsy old fool, who had not meant to trouble me, and that she would try to share my faith. And I did not tell her how often I all but failed to keep it myself.

"Do not miscall yourself," I said. "You know well that you are the greatest comfort I have."

Henrietta, who ever shied away from expressions of gratitude, cleared her throat loudly, and changed the subject.

"There is something I wish," she said, in rather a high voice.

"Something I can do? Tell me." She had fallen silent and was twisting her fingers together, for all the world like an embarrassed child.

"'Tis in the matter of Algernon," she said. "When he is brought to trial — there is so little one can do — but if, in passing, he could but glimpse a friendly face! There will be so many to stare, and jeer."

"You would be there, and you wish me to go with you?"

She nodded, humbly. "It is foolish, I know, and selfish to ask it of you."

"It is not, and I will. You do not need to ask."

She crushed my hands, her worn face alight with gratitude. But it was not only for her, loving her though I did, that I made the promise. Once again, for the merest shred of time, I felt that Martin was near, and that I had pleased him.

The trial was fixed for the seventh of November, and it was Henrietta's consuming hope to see him enter the Hall, and that, God willing, he might see us. With this in mind we made an early start, escorted by Tom. Now I was taken from the kind of bubble which had lately enclosed me with my own hopes and fears, I began to feel keenly for the man who had lived through those weary months and was now approaching an ordeal fit to break the strongest.

It was a gloomy morning as we drove through the streets, early as it was alive with folk all heading the one way. Poor Henrietta, between her longing to see her friend once more and the feeling of guilt, which, it transpired, afflicted her at having brought me in my present condition, was far removed from her usual self. I was unable to calm her. For myself, that early sickness being happily past, I was in as rude health as I had ever been and was now active, the growing babe gave me no trouble. But it was not possible to convince her.

"I should never have brought you!" She muttered for the third time. "Most arrant selfishness—"

"Do not think it," I begged her. "In any case I should have wished to come, if only for Martin's sake. And with you and Tom to care for me, how can I come to harm?"

But when we left the coach and went on foot, I began to see that her misgivings might be justified, and this no place for a woman with child. Already the crowd was dense outside Westminster Hall, and a rough and motley gathering it was. There was no giving way, no hint of courtesy as they elbowed their way forward with oaths and rough laughter to see the sight. It seemed hard that he should be made a show for those who gaped and grinned without a thought of sympathy for him. It was strange, since so much of his thought had been for the betterment of others. Yet it was not wholly so, for amongst those faces, empty or brutish, were others with steadfast eyes and set lips, and these, I was certain, had come like ourselves, from different motives.

All the while we had been moving steadily, I so shielded by the bodies of my two companions that I felt no touch from the crowd, which was growing denser, and from time to time objected loudly to our progress. Paying no heed to comments unfavourable or worse we pressed on, at last finding ourselves almost beside the great doors, and in as good a position as we could have wished. At my side Tom stood rocklike. Behind me Henrietta had ceased to think of me.

There was a constant bustle in and out of the doorway. Glancing in past the soldiers on guard I could catch a glimpse of the lofty hall where a king had spoken unavailingly in his own defence. Names were bandied among the more knowledgeable of our fellows. We caught glimpses of some connected with the trial, but Jeffreys we did not see — though his name was on every lip. A man nearby was telling his neighbour of Lord Russell's trial and his conduct of it, fairly smacking his lips over the recollection. But behind him I heard a voice say, "A bad day for the liberties of England, when her justice is administered by such hands as those."

There were some murmurs of agreement, but these were drowned by noisy protests.

"Watch your words! There be pillories—"

"God save the King's Majesty, and to hell with all traitors. Jeffreys is the man to deal with them."

"One of the damned plotters yourself, belike."

"Oh, no," said the first voice, with a hint of amusement. "Merely a student of law."

"Law! Master Algernon Sidney, pox on him, will soon know what the law means!"

I felt Henrietta stiffen, but at that moment a deep hum, as of pleasurable anticipation, rose from the crowd, and all heads turned in the same direction. There were soldiers gathered in Palace Yard, and now, as the crowd surged forward, a group of them came briskly forcing it back, their eyes keen and suspicious. We held our ground, and the officer in charge looked us up and down but said nothing.

A shouted command was followed by the tramp of feet as a party of soldiers marched towards the door. Quite unconscious of her neighbours Henrietta was muttering a desperate prayer, and they, for their part, were too absorbed to notice her. For in the midst of the armed men walked the one we had come to see.

"Dear God! Dear God!" breathed Henrietta.

I knew for what she begged and thought there was little chance it would be granted. Colonel Sidney was so closely guarded, so hemmed in by the figures in their brilliant uniforms that all I could see was the plume of a hat, a touch of brown against the scarlet which, in a moment, would be engulfed by the great dark hall, and lost to view. My heart ached for the woman who had asked so little and was to be denied even that.

As the marchers drew level with us some persons at the back of the crowd, angered, it seemed, at being unable to see, pushed forward with such determination that, like a wave, all of us in the front were forced forward also. An officer snarled a furious order. The soldiers halted, and almost opposite us Algernon Sidney halted too.

He was looking straight ahead, and about him was an air of the deadliest weariness, only held in check by an inflexible determination. It was as if I could feel the gripping effort with which he held himself gallantly upright, ignoring the babel around him, the curses of the soldiers forcing us back, the complaints of the crowd. Like a man of stone he stood, so near us, so infinitely far removed. They were forming up again, and in a moment he would be gone.

Quite suddenly, as if in answer to a summons, he turned, and looked fully at us. He was most sadly changed. Years, not months, might have traced those new lines of endurance on the face which was overlaid by a kind of shadowy pallor. He saw Henrietta and gazed, as if unable to trust his eyes, then the smile which I remembered transfigured that weary face. His lips moved, but what he said we could not hear. It was all over in a moment. The soldiers closed round him, and he was gone.

I turned to Henrietta. "It was worth it. He saw you. He knew."

"Yes," she said, her eyes not on me, but on the great door. Her lips trembled, her face was contorted like that of a child. And that was the time, the only time, that ever I saw her weep.

CHAPTER XXIV

It was as well for Algernon Sidney that he had known that moment when he turned to see the face of a friend, for he was to know little of comfort after. That first hearing, to be followed in a fortnight's time by another, was a mockery of justice, every plea he attempted to make in his own defence met by ridicule and rude scorn. We were told that his bearing under this treatment was of such dignity that he shamed those who sat in judgement on him — that is, if they were able to feel shame, of which there is grave doubt. Of Jeffreys, even now, I cannot think without a shudder. It was not his appearance, for I saw him once, leaning back in his coach, and it was a handsome face, which seemed strange to me, for had his face matched his soul he would have seemed a monster. Men said that his determination to leave no loophole for one whose nature surpassed his own as light to darkness lay in his desire to please the king. If so I trust His Majesty was able to find pride in his tool.

It was not only the friends of Sidney who felt the cruel injustice of his treatment. At this time men in the streets spoke their thoughts aloud, many adding that if the verdict were returned against him, it could not be carried out. But, as we heard long after, Jeffreys had sworn a mighty oath, saying that either Sidney or he must die, and all men know to what lengths he went that the innocent blood might be shed.

The jury was packed, there was no witness, not one, who could say of his own knowledge that the prisoner had taken any part in the plot. Indeed, it was rumoured that one Howard of Escrick, he whose evidence had cost Lord Russell his life, murmured of a sham plot, a monstrous bubble. Yet he gave the same evidence as he had done at Lord Russell's trial, and I could imagine Sidney's look of haughty contempt as he said he had no question to put to such a witness. Sidney's devoted man, who was present, and told Henrietta every detail, said this silence was held against his master, but he remained unmoved.

Unable to find the proof they needed, they now brought up Sidney's writings, claiming them to be an incitement to rebellion. This the defence tore to shreds, saying that all being written before the king even sat on the throne it could not possibly be designed against him, adding that almost all the circumstances of the trial were originals, the summing up barbarous, and composed merely of invectives. There was, said Sidney's man, a buzz of agreement at this, instantly checked as Jeffreys glared around him. Only the defence counsel met those deadly eyes, and continued, pleading that it had been said that the prisoner was not only guilty but that he could not be otherwise because his principles led him to it.

Here Jeffreys flung himself back in his seat with a loud laugh, of course echoed by his fellows, but the defence went steadily on: 'It might with as good reason have been urged that he not only was become but had been born a traitor. High treason must be proved by an overt act and proved by two witnesses.'

I am no lawyer, and often as the finer points have been explained to me I cannot pretend to fully understand them, even now. What does stand out in my memory with the very ring of truth are the words spoken by Sir John Howles who, in the face of Jeffrey's dangerous anger, said, "That it was strange to see what progress was made in resolutions of points of law to take away a man's life, as if, in Colonel Sidney's words, the court and council thought it their duty to take away a man's life anyhow."

Whether this plain statement troubled the Lord Chief Justice, not with remorse but with fear lest it might sway the verdict, none know. What is known is that he, against all precedent, actually went himself to those sheep, the jury, to assure himself that they should not stray from the fold. Thus persuaded, they did his will, bringing in the verdict which will remain a stain on English justice to the end of time.

Henrietta had known all too well what it must be. She was yet shocked most cruelly when it became an accomplished fact. Again, I could not hope to comfort her, could only listen, my heart aching for her as well as for him.

"He objected to the verdict, or tried to," she said bitterly. "Time and again he tried to speak. Jeffreys gave him the lie in open court, and finally, knowing all hope was gone, he fell silent, and bore the insults, Pierre says, with patience. So Jeffreys has had his will. I wonder if he can sleep at night with what is on his soul — if, that is, he has one, and it be not already sold."

There was no hint of the old vehemence in her tone, only a kind of dreary resignation, as if an end had come to all striving and hope. Even that tall body, used to be proudly erect, now drooped as if under a burden too great to bear.

"Will it be soon?" I asked fearfully.

"Not for three weeks. He means to send Halifax a paper with his main points of defence to be laid before the king, appealing to him to review the matter."

"Then it is not over! Even yet there may be hope."

She only looked at me and shook her head.

"But you say all are shocked at the manner of his trial. The king may be moved—"

"Oh no," she said, quite calmly but with a look in her eyes which pierced my heart. "Jeffreys is the king's creature, else even he would never dare to do as he had done. As well appeal to him as to his master. I hope only for one thing

— that someday the Lord Chief Justice himself may cower in fear and know what it means to beg for what is denied him."

"But does Colonel Sidney hold any hope?"

"He?" There was actually the hint of a smile, and her voice was touched with pride. "He knows. Algernon, with all his faults, was ever clear-sighted, not to be deluded by vain hopes. But he will set out his defence in a fashion which is indisputable and having acquitted himself to his own satisfaction will face without flinching what is to come." Her voice changed, and she added, most sadly, "It is I who have nothing to uphold me now."

Again my heart ached for her, and again I could find nothing to say. Yet she was wrong, for next time I saw her she was upheld by some purpose which had, it seemed, brought her back to life. She was so changed that I thought for one moment a miracle had happened, and then I saw it was not relief which had brought that new look to her face, but an inflexible determination.

"There is news," she said, "but not good news. It is as I said."

"But — the king? Surely, surely, he was not unmoved!"

"He! Did you yet cherish hope of him? The date of execution is fixed. It is for December the seventh."

Her voice was level, but the hand I clutched in mine was cold and shaking. "I shall be there."

I gazed at her aghast. "Henrietta, you cannot! How could you bear it?"

A queer smile crossed her face. "He will bear it, Catherine, and as for me, how could I bear it otherwise? I have told him."

"Told him! You mean you have seen him?"

"Last evening. All hope being at an end they have at last allowed his friends to visit him. And I shall remember it — yes, until the end of my life." She gazed away, pride mingled with the sadness in her face. "None knew his faults better than I, his pride, his hatred of contradiction, yet with it all I knew him to be a man. God knows he has proved it now.

Steadfast, inflexible — Catherine, when Algernon Sidney is brought to the scaffold the shame will not be his. And one day his name will he cleared to all the world. He knows it, and so do I."

I thought that it could be small comfort to one awaiting death and marvelled at her courage. For I could not, just then, look beyond what was to happen three weeks from now.

"He spoke of you and Martin," said Henrietta. "He sent his greetings to you and prays that the child to come will find better days than we have known. He is confident that Martin lives, and that you will be reunited."

My eyes stung with tears. "At a time like this he could think of us?"

"You may well wonder. His serenity is such that all who see him are moved by it. Why, one of the sheriffs who brought him the news was so affected that he actually wept. He is writing what he calls his Apology and making his peace with God. And if all men could face death as he is doing—"

She broke off suddenly, and I sobbed, clinging to her, "I will come with you. You shall not go alone."

"No, my love. As matters are, it cannot be. Remember, you have your babe to consider. There are many who would escort me, but if Martin's man, who knew him well, could be at my side, that would serve me best of all."

"Tom will go — you do not need to ask. But Henrietta—"

She rose, shaking her head. "No, Catherine. My mind is made up, and you know that I am right."

I did know in my heart, and was conscious of relief, since I dreaded the thought of what she would see. I could not but marvel that she could bear it. As if reading my thoughts, she said, "He told me that seeing me that day as he went to trial had upheld him through it all. This time he will not see me, but he will know that I am there. It is the last thing that I can do for him in this world, and God knows little enough."

So when that Friday came I remained at home with Tabitha and Mercy, and Tom went with Henrietta as she had wished. Since all London would be gaping at a free spectacle he was not, for once, afraid to leave me, and apart from all else I felt he would represent Martin, of whom there was still no word. He had now been gone from me for a longer space than that of our married life together, and it was by now almost impossible to believe he lived. Almost, but not quite, for still at times there came that strange certainty that despite all, he was alive and thinking of me.

The day, though cold, was clear, and the sky just flecked with cloud. I was foolishly thankful that the walk to the scaffold from the Tower would not be through rain, on such trivial matters does the mind run, even at such a time as this. In my mind I saw Sidney most clearly, and wondered if he would walk briskly, as they say King Charles did, or take with a measured step his last short journey on earth. I knew that, apart from his two servants only officials would accompany him, and I thought of another who would have been there if he could. So my thoughts crowded in on me as the sands of Algernon Sidney's life ran low.

I began to pace restlessly back and forth, wishing that despite all I was there, rather than here, imagining every detail. The hour drew slowly, inexorably close.

The girls came quietly in, Tabitha with her Bible in her hand. She handed it to me, nodding wordlessly. I felt the book's comforting weight in my hands, as Tabitha began to quote from memory.

"'Yea, though I walk through the valley of the shadow of death I will fear no evil, for Thou art with me . . .'"

The well-known words meant more to me than ever before.

"'Blessed are the dead that die in the Lord,'" said Tabitha. "'For they shall see God.'"

"Amen," said Mercy, bowing her head.

Their voices were filled with the calmest confidence. I tried to speak but could not. So we waited together while the last slow moments passed.

It was long after I looked for them that Henrietta and Tom returned, for the streets had been so crowded that progress was well-nigh impossible, but at last I hastened to meet them. They were both white faced but calm, and Henrietta held me lovingly, saying that I had been distressing myself, and should not do so. And for a while she said nothing of what had happened, speaking only of myself. It was as if she had closed a door on something belonging only to herself, and I felt it was not for me to try to open it. But at last she began to tell me, quietly, but painting a picture for me so vividly that I might have been at her side.

She and Tom had stood at the window of a house hired from a dweller on Tower Hill — there was a brisk traffic in such that day. Outside the crowd, ever swelling, waited with greedy eyes on the black draped scaffold, murmuring like a great swarm of bees. They were so densely packed that it was an indeterminate mass that Henrietta saw, a sea of faces, all turned in the one direction, and even the rooftops were occupied, every window lined with watchers who came to see how a man would die.

"We watched for him," said Henrietta. "For a long time we watched. Then all the packed bodies seemed to sway, and there was a sound like a deep breath, almost a groan. I looked at the scaffold and saw the executioner standing there."

I shivered, and she patted my hand, as if it were I who stood in need of comfort.

"And not long after he came. He came quite steadily, with all eyes on him. I saw him clearly, and Catherine, for those who loved him there could be only pride. Had he been walking to all honour he could not have borne himself more gallantly. His face — the look on it — I cannot describe. It was — not happy, but composed and confident, as if he had fought his last fight, and there was nothing left to fear. He came to the foot of the scaffold, and paused there, looking up at the sky, and I think he smiled. I am not sure, for I was not brave as he was, and there was a darkness before my eyes. When it cleared I saw that he had mounted the scaffold, and there was a hush, since men waited to see if he would speak. But the time for that was past."

She was silent for so long that I thought she had told me all, and was silent also. But she went on, speaking for the first time with difficulty, as if the telling was almost more than she could bear.

"He gave some papers to the officer, made his farewells to his servants, handed money to the executioner. Oh, yes — it is expected that it should be given to the one who will strike the blow. I watched him, Catherine, as he made his final preparations and bowed his head in prayer. And then I turned coward and closed my eyes. Not for long — I told myself that I must see him once again, whatever the cost. But when I forced myself to look again — he had already gone."

CHAPTER XXV

I slept badly that night, and woke with a heaviness of spirit. There seemed little need to rouse myself, and I lay thinking of Henrietta, who had refused to remain with me or to accept my offer to accompany her, since I felt she should not be left alone. I have thought since that in this I was wrong, and that probably, like some wounded creature solitude was her one desire. In any case, she left me, making her farewells steadily enough, as if to match the bearing of the friend she had lost. It seemed strange to me that she, who had wept to see him pass to his trial, had now no tear to shed. I was young then and had not learned what has come home to me since, that there be sorrows too deep for tears.

My thoughts turned from her to the man who had died, and I marvelled at the power he had owned to attract love. Austere, stern, neither handsome in face nor outstanding in affairs, never, despite his birth, cutting an outstanding figure in the world, yet owning something, some shining integrity of purpose which none who knew him could deny. Why, even I, despite my jealousy, had felt it during our brief acquaintance, wishing that I might stand well in his eyes. And he was gone, while Jeffreys and his like lived on, to wax and grow fat on the fruits of corruption.

There have been martyrs since time began, and I fear, since human nature changes not, it will be so until the end. I wished I could have felt pride, as Henrietta did, but at this time I could feel only bitterness. Dark sorrow enfolded me, and I thought drearily that Sidney was gone, and that Martin, for all my faith, was probably lost also. Even the thought of our coming child had, for once, no power to cheer me.

However, life goes on, whether worth the living or not. I rose, ate, drank, went about my usual household duties all with that weight on me. It was a gloomy day, with none of the pale sunshine which had lit Sidney's path to the scaffold. Even Mercy was subdued, and Tom's face grimmer than ever. When Henrietta arrived for her morning visit, for the first time I forgot myself in a surge of gratitude, that even now she could bring herself to think of me.

She looked older, and a kind of grey shadow overlaid her face, yet it was composed and save for that look of deathly exhaustion she seemed not unlike her usual self. She shook her head at my appearance, rousing herself to cheer me, so that I, who should have been upholding her, was ashamed. For a while we spoke only of certain physics which, she said, would be of great help to me, but later she told me that Sidney's man had come to her bearing a copy of his last writings and a letter for Martin.

"Martin! I begin to wonder—" I said.

Laying a hand on mine she said gently. "Do not lose hope now. You have held to your faith so steadfastly, and I told you Algernon was convinced that he lives." She looked away. "They say that those about to die sometimes see clearly."

"Please God it may be so. What is in his writings?"

"A plain statement of all that befell him, and of his complete innocence. You shall read it — indeed, I think everyone in England who can read English will do so, since already it is being copied and spread abroad." And in a low voice she repeated sentences from the closing lines of the words written during those last weary hours in the Tower.

"'. . . Stir up such as are faint, direct those that are willing, confirm those that waver, give wisdom and integrity unto all. Order all things so as may most redound to Thine own glory. Grant that I may die glorifying Thee for all Thy mercies, and that at the last Thou hast permitted me to be singled out as a witness of Thy truth . . . I know my Redeemer lives, and as He hath, in a great measure, upheld me in the day of my calamity I hope that He will still uphold me by His spirit in this last moment and giving me grace to glorify Him in my death receive me into the glory prepared for those that fear Him when my body shall be dissolved. Amen.'"

The quiet voice ceased. We were silent for a long time, and the words seemed to echo in the silence. Then she turned to me. "He was upheld. I thank God for that. And while his writings live on he is not truly gone."

And she kissed me and said farewell. I watched her tall figure and recalled how Sidney had once spoken of her, and felt that I, too, was proud to know her.

I sat thinking only of her, yet vaguely conscious of voices somewhere in the background. Henrietta's coach could scarcely have gone from sight when Tom came into the room, so hastily that I looked up in surprise. His face was flushed, and there was about him an air of great, if suppressed, emotion. Scarcely knowing why, I found my heart beginning to beat unsteadily. He came close to me, bent his head and muttered in my ear.

"Do not be alarmed. I have a message."

My lips moved, but without sound. I gazed into his changed face, my eyes seeing the question I could not speak.

"'Tis from him — Master Frampton. He has sent word that he is near and wishes to speak with you. And — there is news."

"News!" I found my voice, a queer croak. Tom looked at me uneasily.

"Is all well with you? Shall I call Tabitha?"

"No, no, no! For God's sake, Tom, what news? Is it good or bad?" I caught at his arm, half crying in my impatience.

He said, with what seemed maddening deliberation, "The message was this: the wanderer is found."

I saw Tom's face swell and swim before my eyes, seeming to fill the room, then dwindle to a mere speck. The walls tilted and whirled around me. I heard his voice upraised and came dizzily back, to find him clasping me closely with a look of outrage on his face. I remembered what he had said, and the joy, the wonder, were so great that I turned and kissed him, which seemed to frighten him, for he called piously on the Lord.

I sat up, striving to collect myself, wondering if I were in the midst of some dream.

"Oh, Tom, you are sure? Tell me again."

He did so, watching me warily the while, and I repeated the words, for the time being unable to think of anything but the glorious knowledge that my husband lived, that I should see him, talk with him, hold him once more. It was almost more than I could bear, and I clasped my hands over my heart.

"Where is he?" I asked, now feeling that I could not waste another instant, so much time had already been lost to us. "I must see him, and at once."

"Patience," counselled Tom. "The place is a rough tavern, and not fit for you, I will go first—"

"Fit for me? What does that matter? Do you not understand? He is alive and will be waiting for me. Wherever he is I cannot delay seeing him."

Tom still demurred, but I overrode him, as just then I would have overridden the king himself if he had thought to stay me, and we set off on foot, since he said it was not far. I wrapped my cloak round a figure much changed from the one Martin would remember, pulled the hood over my flushed face, and we left the river, passing through one narrow alley after another. Tom steered me along, keeping me from splashing unheeding through the filth in the gutter, and at last we came to a mean-looking inn.

"Wait!" said Tom. "And speak no names."

251

I had actually forgotten that both Martin and Roger Frampton were both wanted men, for the news which had sent new life bubbling and dancing through my veins had crowded out all else. Now I glanced round me uneasily, seeing a group of men a few yards away engaged in some drunken argument but they were paying no attention to us, and other than for them the alley was empty. Tom tapped cautiously on the door and straightway opened it, taking my hand so that I went with him, as if there were any need for that, when I was afire with impatience. A huge man lurched forward, and Tom muttered something I did not catch. He looked me up and down, nodded, and led us into a small room, close-smelling and dirty, leaving us there without a word. His looks did not inspire confidence, and I wondered if we were deceived. My heart sank. The door opened and Roger Frampton came into the room. He was alone.

I had been so sure that there would be no more waiting that my newfound happiness vanished like a burst bubble. I looked at him and said nothing, for I was afraid. He came to me, taking my hands, and saying quickly, as if he read my fears, "Martin is alive."

It was as if I, too, came back to life. I clung to his hands, ashamed of my lack of faith.

"Where is he?" I turned blindly to the door.

He held me gently back, and I said, half sobbing, "I must see him. You cannot keep me from him now."

"You shall see him," he answered. "But there is something I must tell you first. I beg of you, sit here and listen. I promise it will not take long."

Unwillingly I obeyed, gazing up at him. My cloak had fallen open, and I saw first surprise then what seemed to be pity in his face.

"If Martin lives," I said, "That is all I need to know."

"Not all," he answered, still with that pitying look. "There is something more."

Beside me I felt Tom stiffen, as if he, too, was troubled by a certain note in the speaker's voice. It seemed a tedious time before he continued, haltingly, as if searching for the right words.

"Martin was picked up, as I was, only his boat was engaged in some smuggling enterprise. It seems they ran into trouble. The rights of what befell I do not know, only that Martin took a blow on the head which all but killed him. From what I gather they ran into a deserted beach on a Dutch island and left him there."

"Left him!"

"They themselves were in danger, and thought him dying, if not already dead. They were not far out, and indeed, but for the kindness of some poor folk who found him and took him to their home he could not have survived. I do not know how long it was before he showed signs of life."

"But he did recover. He did!"

"Not wholly," he said. "There are moments when he is his old self, but for most of the time he remembers nothing. Do you understand what I am trying to say? You must be prepared — it is possible, almost certain, that he will not know you."

The words sounded in my ears, but I heard them with complete disbelief. I grieved for my husband's sufferings, but I had no shadow of doubt that he would know me. How could it be otherwise when we were each part of the other? He would not have been brought back to me for this.

"How did you find him?" asked Tom, speaking for the first time. "And does he know you?"

"I found him, after following many false trails from a word here, a rumour there. At last there was talk in an inn of a man found on a beach who seemed witless, and knew not even his own name. I thought it another empty tale, but I followed it up, and so found him. And at first he did not know me. Much of the time now he still does not."

I rose. "May I not see him now?"

"So long as you are prepared. I fear it will not be easy."

"I am prepared. Only I can wait no longer. Do you not understand?"

Despite myself my voice rose, and for all that Roger Frampton had done at that moment I almost hated him. I saw him glance at Tom, and he said gently: "I do understand. Wait here."

I stood forgetful of Tom, forgetful of everything, save that Martin, my husband, was coming to me. My heart was beating heavily, almost painfully. I could not take my eyes from the door.

There was a movement outside, the sound of voices, not Martin's. The door opened and he came into the room.

As if surprised to find it occupied, he checked, turning back to Roger Frampton, seeming to seek reassurance. Frampton laid a hand on his shoulder and urged him gently forward. I clasped my hands at my breast and looked into my husband's face, seeing how greatly he had changed. It is so hard to describe. It was not his pallor, that look of one who had been near to death. It was as if behind the features I knew, was a lost creature, so far removed from me that I could not hope to find him.

He said, still looking back at Frampton, not at me, and in a faintly troubled voice, "I am sorry. I did not know anyone was here."

"Do you not see who it is?" asked Frampton.

He did look at me then, and from me to Tom, with a troubled air but no hint of recognition. He half bowed to me. "I am sorry."

"It is not a good day," said Frampton, shaking his head. "Will you not leave it for now? Truly it would be best."

"No. Let us be alone together. He will know me," I said steadily, my eyes on the face of Martin, who was not Martin, but someone wandering in a dark world apart. Whether Frampton demurred or not I do not recall. I only know that we were left together, as I had wished.

There was a settle by the chimneypiece. I took his hand and led him to it, and we sat there side by side. I laid my hands on his arm and said, "Martin. Look at me."

With a kind of touching obedience he turned to me, and we gazed on one another, he and I, and there was no change in his face, no gladness, no sorrow, only that faintly puzzled look. He sighed and turned away.

"Martin, Martin," I besought him. "Do you not know me? Have you forgotten?"

He shook his head, half impatiently. Again he said, "I am sorry."

Against that wall between us it seemed useless, almost cruel, to persist, yet I could not leave it so. I leaned closer, thinking that his body might recall mine, if all else were forgotten, and I put my arms around him, and laid my cheek against his. And it might have been a stranger to whom I was offering advances, received with a faint discomfort and not the slightest hint of response. My arms fell away, and desolation swept over me. My head drooped forward, and the ruby pendant swung out from my breast. I remembered the morning he had given it to me, our happiness together, and it was more than I could bear. Frampton had been right, and I most sadly wrong. For that day, at least, I would strive no more.

In the very moment of my decision, I felt a change. He had been rigid at my side, as if amazed at my behaviour, looking obstinately away. Now he had turned his head and was gazing, not at me, but at the great ruby winking and glowing in its circlet of gold. His forehead was wrinkled, and again he gave that slight impatient shake of the head. I held my ruby out to him, and still he gazed.

"Dear, do you remember?" I asked him, trying to keep my voice from shaking. "Your gift to me, that last day we were together. I have worn it ever since."

He seemed not to hear me, and I ceased speaking. He slowly reached out a hand, touching the ruby gently, as if to assure himself that it was real. I sat motionless, every atom of my being striving to get to him, to break through the barrier which separated us even while our bodies touched, and I could feel his breath on my face. With a great leap of my heart, I saw that he was turning the pendant, so that it lay on his palm, the golden back uppermost, with its tiny wreath and inscription. He was bending over it, his brow furrowed as if with the most deep and painful concentration. Scarcely daring to breathe I waited.

His lips moved, but he uttered no sound. There was sweat standing out on his brow, and his body was strained, as if he fought for remembrance. Then it was over. As if he could strive no more he slumped back, the ruby falling from his hand to swing in a flashing arc before it settled and was still. He brushed a hand across his eyes, and yet again uttered his apology, as if in that poor lost mind of his he knew that he had striven only to fail. The reaction was such that I, too, felt the strength drain from me, and when Roger Frampton and Tom came into the room we were drooping side by side as if we had both come to the end of our endurance. Frampton muttered something and knelt beside me, rubbing my hands in his.

"You would not believe me," he said, not angrily, but as if grieving for me. "I would have saved you this."

I shook my head, saying faintly: "I could but try — and for one moment I thought—"

Unable to continue I turned away, fighting to keep back the tears. Beside me I felt Martin stir, as if in discomfort, but he did not speak.

"It was my ruby," I said, regaining control. "He touched it as if he remembered. Then he was gone."

"I know. It has been so all along," said Frampton gently. "But do not lose hope."

Tom, who had been standing beside Martin, looking down at him sorrowfully, cleared his throat and said, "'Put your trust in the Lord. For His mercy endureth for ever.'"

Martin, who had seemed not to listen or understand when I spoke, looked up. For one moment there seemed to be life and interest in his face, then all was as before. But during that moment I believe we three were breathless with hope.

"It may be," I suggested, "that he would be helped if we took him home. In his own surroundings—"

"It is true he cannot remain here," allowed Frampton. "But consider — your house may still be watched, and he is in no condition to escape."

I glanced at the unconscious subject of our talk, now sitting quite patiently, hands lying slackly on his knees, while we disposed of him. It was very hard to see him so.

Tom, who, I believe, was feeling this also, said gruffly: "Mistress Lacey."

Frampton raised his brows, but to me it was as if the mere thought of Henrietta brought relief.

"Indeed, that is the solution," I said eagerly. "She cares deeply for him, and they would not look to find him there."

"That is true." But Roger Frampton did not know Henrietta as I did, and still sounded doubtful. "We must move with care. In those moments when he comes to himself he could betray all. The lady's household—?"

"No danger there. All are devoted to Henrietta and know Martin of old. Believe me, she is our greatest hope."

And turning a little from my own affairs, I thought it might be of help to Henrietta, bringing some purpose to a life just now empty enough.

So it was agreed, also that I should remain in my own home to avoid arousing suspicion, only visiting Henrietta daily. For one more night they would remain here, and I prepare Henrietta, then they could make their way to her after nightfall.

"And you?" I asked. "Are you also remaining?"

He shook his head. "Once your husband is safely settled, I go again. Plans are building in Holland for this poor land. One day I will return to England never to leave it, but that is not yet."

I thought how once again he had risked his life for me and tried to thank him, but he brushed it aside, saying with a smile that it was tit for tat, since I had once saved him, and that perhaps I would now believe that in the past he had not thought of money alone. Growing more serious, he added that in any event his life was none so precious. And for a fraction of time the ghost of Frances, lost and beautiful, seemed to drift between us, and was gone.

Before we left, I laid my hand on my husband's shoulder and kissed him. He submitted, that was all, but for a moment his eyes rested on mine. Again I paused with aching hope, and again that curtain fell. When I looked back from the doorway he had forgotten me, as, indeed, it seemed he had forgotten all the world.

CHAPTER XXVI

If I had thought Roger Frampton over cautious in not allow-
ing Martin to return with me I was to be persuaded otherwise. Early in the morning, even before Henrietta had called,
a horseman rode to the door, and I heard the unmistakable voice of Master Felton upraised, he who had treated my
home and myself with such scant courtesy when he came to
search. So even now it was not over, and I wondered, fearful,
if Martin had been discovered, and was to be taken from me
even before we had found one another again.

At the thought such desolation came that I felt I could
not face this man with his hectoring manner and searching
eyes, but clenching my hands until the nails cut into my
palms I thrust such cowardice aside, and when he came to
me rose with a tolerable semblance of composure to meet
him. With surprise I saw that he was subdued and slightly
ill at ease, and that dealt me a most cruel stab, for I thought
he had come to tell me that the worst had happened and was
actually sorry for me. I had never thought to see compassion
in those hot brown eyes, but it seemed I saw it now.

Forcing myself to speak, to carry on the play, I asked,
"You come to search my home again, sir? You will still not
find my husband here."

He shook his head. "Will you not be seated? This time I come on other business." And again I thought to see that hint of compassion in his eyes.

I did as he said, motioning him to a chair opposite me. And I said in my heart, now he will tell me there is nothing left for me of hope.

He leaned forward holding out his hand. On the broad palm something winked and glittered in the light. I gazed at it vacantly, not speaking. I had been so sure, so terribly sure, of what he would say.

"Do not alarm yourself," he said, with most surprising gentleness. "I did but wish to know if you had seen this before. But you are not well! Shall I call your woman?"

I shook my head and drew a deep breath, for I felt as if I were on a seesaw, now up, now down. At the moment I was dizzily reaching for a star of hope, but at any moment I could come crashing down.

I took the shining thing from him, and my sight cleared. It was a brooch, in the shape of a true love knot, set with diamonds. It had been roughly used. Two of the largest stones were gone, and the setting pulled awry, but I knew it. The last time I saw Frances alive it had glittered at her breast.

"I thought as much," growled Felton, when I told him, his brows meeting in an angry scowl. "It was that damned villain of mine who was responsible. I guessed it from the first, but he went to earth and I could find no trace of him."

"But you have found him now?"

"Oh yes," he answered, with a short laugh. "I have found him, now that it is too late, stabbed, and lying in the kennel, with this hidden in his garments. That was all. I would it had been otherwise, and that he had not cheated the gallows."

"It makes little difference," I said. "Punishing him would not bring her back."

"It would have helped me, since I feel, in a sense, responsible."

I looked at him in surprise, for judging by our last meeting I had not thought to find him a man of sensibility, rather one who blundered through life like an angry bull, not caring who might be trampled in the process.

"It was a man of mine who did it," he said sombrely. "I saw her. She was young, and most beautiful. When I think of her struggling in his grasp—"

I pictured it too and shuddered. Most clearly I recalled her as she left me, alight with triumph, assured that her end was gained. I remembered her in her beauty. I remembered her as they brought her back, and I looked at Felton, and I thought that it was not only on Ralph and Roger Frampton that she had laid her spell.

He said, shaking his broad shoulders as if to remove a burden, and spoke more in his old tone. "Well, there it is. I thought you should know."

"Thank you," I said. "I will see that my brother is informed and given the brooch."

"Yes. I fear there is no hope of recovering more. It will have been broken down in some thieves' kitchen long since. The murderers were disturbed before they had time to search him, else this would have gone with the rest." He paused, then, without the slightest warning, said, "Touching the matter of your husband—"

It was, indeed, as if the seesaw had struck the earth, and with so sickening a blow that I could only cower, waiting for the final blow to fall.

"If he is wise, he is overseas, and will remain there. If not, at least let him remain in seclusion out of town, looking to it that he takes no part in politics. If I find him here I shall be forced to take him. Otherwise—" He shrugged his shoulders, still not looking at me, which was as well, since I am assured that my face would have betrayed that I was again whizzing up, up, to reach the stars.

"You are very kind," I said, when I could command my voice.

"Kind? I am a man with work to do, and I do it as best I can," he answered. "But I am sickened with Jeffreys and his like, and I do not care to see men brought to their deaths by false witness and the mockery of justice. I saw Colonel Sidney at his so-called trial, and I tell you, Mistress, it made me — yes, me — know shame." He cleared his throat raspingly, as if to cover his own weakness. "None the less, keep your husband out of my reach, for by God, if I lay hands on him there will be no escape."

On this note, and having, I suppose, retrieved his self-respect, he stamped off, so much after his old fashion that I could not help but smile. But my thankfulness, my wonder that he should be so changed was more than I can say, and I thought it strange that Colonel Sidney should in some measure have helped Martin. To have moved such a man as Felton was no small matter, and I wished he might have known, though this was foolish, since such small triumphs could not touch him now. At least I could tell Henrietta, and please God one day Martin also would know, and remember with sorrow and with pride.

When Henrietta did come she was every whit as moved as I could wish, and from that I swung at once into my flood of news. As I had known, she was rejoiced to give Martin shelter and marvelled again at Master Felton's new kindness. "I think we should follow his advice, at least so soon as Martin is himself again."

"To send him overseas? Oh, I do not think I could bear it now! It has been so long—"

"I know, I know, and you have been a brave wench, and I most proud of you," said Henrietta, smiling into my downcast face. "No, that should not be necessary. But Felton spoke also of retirement from town, removed from affairs. Had you not thought of that?"

"To speak truth," I answered, pushing back the hair from my aching brow, "I have been set in such a whirl that I have scarce thought clearly. First to know that Martin lived, then to find him — so. And when Felton came I was assured that he was taken, then the relief! I fear I have not looked ahead at all."

"I know, I know," said Henrietta again. "And all this when you should be quiet and untroubled."

"I have wondered at times — Henrietta, one hears such tales. The babe will not be harmed?"

"Good heaven, not." Her old laugh filled the room. "Put such beldame's moanings out of your mind. Infants are well cushioned against all."

Looking down at my spreading girth I thought that in a bodily sense she was doubtless right. And I trusted that no distress of mind I had suffered would affect my child. There was misery enough in the world to which it would come. I did not wish to lay any additional burden on it from troubles of my own.

It was hard to keep away from Martin through the day, which was long in passing, but at last I went to my bed knowing that the move had been safely accomplished, and that on the morrow I should see him, and that please God he would see me also with understanding eyes. For surely, if he once made that journey back, despite what Roger Frampton had said, he would not lose himself again? I fell asleep buoyed by hope, but when I woke in the endless hours before the dawn it was otherwise. And when at last I slept again it was broken by a horrible dream, in which I followed Martin through endless corridors, crying piteously on him to wait for me, only to wait. But he went on and on, never so much as pausing, until I was half dead from grief and exhaustion and sank to the ground. Then he stopped and turned. Where his face should have been was a blank, an emptiness, nothing at all.

I awoke drenched with sweat, my heart beating wildly and with a vile taste in my mouth. The room was filled with light, and around me were the sights and sounds of everyday. But it was long before I could shake off the horror of my dream.

Tabitha and Mercy, who knew of Martin's return and of his condition, looked on me with sympathy, and Tabitha made me take one of her herbal draughts, which was bitter, but made me feel more myself. Tom was out of humour as if he, too, had slept ill, and it struck me that he was probably wishing to be with Martin. when I suggested this, however, he said that he knew well that if Martin could give him an order it would be that he was to remain with me.

"Let us hope," I said, "that it will not be long before we can all be together, you, my husband, and I. It would, however, not be here. Would you be content to lead a country life?"

"We will think of that when the time comes," he replied. "You may not have need of me then."

"You know better than that. But it may be you have other plans?"

I thought his colour deepened, but he made no reply, only remarking that if I did not bestir myself I should not be ready. He might have saved his breath, for I was waiting with burning impatience long before Henrietta's coach came for me. I saw nothing of my surroundings, was as one deaf and blind until we drew up and Tom helped me down. Henrietta came to greet me, surrounded as usual by her cloud of cats, tails erect, as if they shared in the welcome, all save Methuselah who, aged and uncertain of temper, sulked apart. In answer to my eager questions Henrietta reluctantly shook her head.

"He came without demur, does what he is told, goes where he is bidden. But no, Catherine, he did not know me. Frampton said it might be so for days, then there could come a space when he would he himself again. We can but have patience."

I clasped her hands, looking up into her kind and troubled face. I knew that she would never deceive me with false hopes.

"Do you think he will ever wholly recover? Is there nothing we can do?"

"My dear," she answered, "I do not know, and only time can give the answer. But you have kept your faith so long I am assured you will not lose it now."

"I will try. But this is harder than all. It is like beating on a closed door."

"I know, my poor child. But some day, please God, the door will open. And, if you will be advised by me, you will not strive too hard. Talk to him as if all was before, but do not press for an answer. He is troubled, dimly feeling that something is wrong. If he can gain serenity I think that will help more than all."

Without more words she took me to that oddly shaped room which I remembered so well. Martin was sitting there alone, gazing into the fire, and I stood watching him, taking in more than I had done that first meeting. His hair was longer than he had been used to wear it, and there were threads of white amongst the brown. Save for that and for his stillness he was so like his old self that all Henrietta's wise counsels were swept away, and before I knew I was on my knees beside him, his hands in mine, and I was calling on his name. He had started violently when first I touched him and gazed wildly at me, but he made no answer. I fell silent, but remained kneeling beside him, still clasping his hands. There was no response in his touch, but he did not draw them away. As if my gaze drew his he looked down at me, that painful frown wrinkling his forehead.

Schooling my voice to calmness I began to talk, soothingly, as if to some frightened creature about at any moment to take flight.

"I am so thankful, dear, that you are here. It is so much better than that miserable inn, and you have your dear Henrietta to care for you. I wish so much, though, that we could be together in our own home again. You — you would wish that also, would you not?"

Against the complete lack of response my voice faltered and died, but, and this at least was new, he still kept his eyes on me, seeming dumbly to beg me for an answer to some question which was torturing him. I raised my hand and gently stroked his forehead, as if to smooth out the lines so deeply graven there.

"Dear Martin, you have been ill and troubled. But now you are with me again, and please God we are not to be parted more. And do you remember, love, how you said you meant to become a grandfather? Well, you are on the way. There is a baby coming, yours and mine."

As before, the words bounced back from his utter lack of comprehension, and I felt, with the taste of failure bitter in my mouth, that I could do no more. My hands dropped away. Awkwardly I pulled myself up, feeling my legs tremble and the strength draining from me. For the first time he moved, rising, and with some instinct of courtesy proffering me his chair. I sank into it, not looking at him, thinking wearily that now he could make his escape, as doubtless he had been wishing to do all along. Well, he could go, and I would not seek to stay him, for I knew myself beaten, and would strive no more. I leaned back and closed my eyes, not in faintness, but in deadly weariness. It was as if I had used up the last of my resources, and there was nothing left to draw on anymore.

I do not know how long it was before some compulsion made me raise my heavy lids to see that Martin had not gone. He was standing close to me, bending slightly forward, his eyes fixed on my face. I gazed back and caught my breath, for his eyes were no longer empty, and on his lips was the shadow of a smile. Raising his hand, rather diffidently, like a child exploring some new yet half-remembered thing, with his forefinger he touched the scar on my cheek. A thrill ran through me, so exquisite that it was almost pain. I could scarcely keep from crying out my joy, my thankfulness, but some instinct of caution held me back. And I thought how strange it would be if the very thing I had long felt spoilt my life should be the means of rending the curtain which held my love from me.

His touch lingered, then fell away. Once again hope had mocked me, and I could almost feel him withdrawing into that grey neverland, where I could not follow him. With a desperate effort to recall him I held out my ruby, since it had

266

seemed to raise a spark before. He only stood slackly before me, the light dying from his eyes. It was more than I could bear. All my patience, my studied calmness, fell away. I called his name, God forgive me, with anger, and was stopped from saying more by a great lump rising in my throat. Against my urgent desire to do otherwise I was shaken by a storm of sobs.

For the first time he spoke, saying in a troubled voice: "Do not weep. Why do you weep?"

"Because I am Catherine, your wife, and you do not know me!" I cried, unable to control myself. "Do you not understand? I am Catherine, Catherine, Catherine!"

I had not known that I was screaming until the sound echoed shockingly in the quiet room, and I was ashamed when I saw him flinch, and put up a hand as if to ward off a blow.

He said hoarsely, his tone questioning: "Catherine?"

The sound of my name on his lips at last was so sweet, so utterly unexpected that I forgot my tears, and waited, scarcely breathing.

"Catherine?" he repeated, this time more loudly. And all in a moment he was on the floor beside me, his arms around me, his face buried in my breast. He was shaking, and I held him and murmured over him as if he were a child. He neither looked up nor spoke, only clung to me in a kind of desperation, as if here lay his only hope.

I leaned my wet face on his bent head and murmured foolish loving things with little meaning, waiting for the moment when he would look up at me. His grip gradually slackened and fell away. He did raise his head. And I saw that it had been only an interlude, and that he had gone from me again.

CHAPTER XXVII

I look back on the days which Martin spent with Henrietta and they seem to me like a sombre tapestry, lightened here and there by flecks of gold. For most of the time he did as he was bidden, always with that heart-breaking patience, so unlike Martin, but when, for however short a space he found himself it brought the keenest joy. One day, we told one another, it would be the period of remembrance which lasted. One day the other would be only a dark memory, an ugly dream.

There was the moment when he called Henrietta, asking if he had been ill, and how he came to be there. Quickly as she tried to tell him he lost the thread before she had come to an end. Then once he spoke quite clearly to Tom, bidding him care for me, and saying, actually in his old fashion: "Cross-grained as you are, I know I can trust you." And there was the time when he came out of a long silence to say, though not to us: "You are kind, and I wish I could repay you, but those damned rascals have stripped me bare." He added, sadly: "But what use to talk — you cannot understand me, nor I you."

He did not seem to suffer bodily ill, though he was much thinner than of old, and we had found a great scar on his head, just above the right ear, usually covered by his hair. I wondered if it were that which caused his malady, for it had certainly been a terrible blow, and even the bone seemed indented. Now and again his hand would wander to the place, which was what made us notice it first. Henrietta spoke of a physician she knew, who would be discreet. I did not think a physician would heal Martin, since here was no matter for bleeding or draughts, but when one is at the end of hope one catches at straws.

He came, and I wished he had not, for he brought us no cheer, only telling us what we already knew — that the blow had been of great force, doing some damage to the brain.

"You say he comes to himself at times?" he asked, sipping his wine, and seeming more interested in its flavour than in Martin.

"Yes. That is a good sign, is it not?" I asked eagerly.

He pursed up his lips and shook his head. "Who can say? I fear I can give you little hope. There is some pressure, which time may heal. On the other hand, it may increase, in which case—" he shrugged, and spread his smooth hands palm upwards, as if by that gesture he consigned poor Martin to endless oblivion. I turned blindly away and could not speak when he made his farewells. It was not his fault, but I almost hated him, since it seemed to be a matter of supreme indifference to him whether Martin recovered or not.

"Do not be downcast," said the voice of Henrietta from behind me. "He was a good man once, but now is a pot-bellied fool, and I wish I had not brought him here."

"I suppose he did his best," I said wearily. "But he seemed to take away what little hope we had." And when I went to Martin I found no cheer there, since it was one of the days when his withdrawal was complete. I kissed him and came away, since I could do nothing. If he felt the touch of my lips he made no sign.

Henrietta, accompanying me to the door, asked a silent question. I shook my head.

"There is always tomorrow," she said gently. "Yes. 'Tomorrow, and tomorrow, and tomorrow.' And if this is all they mean to him—" I could not end the sentence, could not speak what was in my mind, yet the words hung heavily between us.

"No!" said Henrietta strongly. "Never so much as think it. While he lives there is hope — never forget that. But you are weary and out of spirits, and who can wonder? Go home, my dear, and rest."

I tried to smile my farewell, for her kind face was deeply troubled, but I was in the very pit of despair. There might, as she said, be hope while Martin lived, but could one call it living in truth, this mindless, almost blind existence? I seemed to see the years stretching ahead for him, grey and shadowy, bereft of purpose or meaning, and I thought if he were given the choice he would prefer to die. Sidney, for all his suffering, had known the better part, as had that long-ago ancestor of his, who gave his life away with a cup of water. They, at least, could be remembered with pride, while Martin—!

When I reached home I had no desire for food, and went straightway to my room, and there, lying on the wide bed, I was lost in misery. I felt selfish, since the sorrow was for myself. It seemed to me that what fate gave with one hand it took away with the other. I might as well have remained at the Grange subject to Frances and to her evil creature as to have escaped finding happiness only for it to end thus. At least if you never touch the heights you have not so far to fall. Oh, I revelled in my bitterness like a drunkard in his cups, and I look back on myself and am ashamed.

It had been a day of heavy cloud, with a piercing wind. Now, for the first time, a pale glint of sun broke through. I turned away from it, and my locket, which had slipped to one side, pressed painfully against my breast. I took it in my hand, and as if it had been an amulet slowly, slowly, the black mood fell from me. I seemed to return to a life which, cruel though it might be, had yet something to redeem it. Martin, poor Martin, was as he was, yet what we had found together had been so pure a happiness that it could never be wholly forgotten. Someday, please God, the darkness would lift from his mind. Some day he would see our child. I traced the words he had set on my gift and thought remorsefully how I had missed their meaning. 'Now and forever' — good days and bad, not like the sundial telling only of sunny hours, but bidding me face all that might come with courage born of love.

I smoothed my tumbled hair, straightened my gown, and went downstairs. And though I was many times disappointed, often unhappy in the days to come, I was never again completely lost in darkness. And it seemed most wonderful that the following day Martin held the locket in his hand, for one moment looked on me with understanding and repeated the words which had saved me before he went from me again.

Days passed into weeks. Christmas was over and a new year upon us when there came snow followed by such a frost as had not been in living memory. I did not feel the cold, bitter though it was, but for three weeks I was unable to get to Henrietta or she to me. Tom managed some days to flounder there, reporting little change in Martin, and I was driven all but frantic by being so near yet out of reach. The great river was a sheet of ice, and we heard tales of high junketing on the surface, ox roasting and the like, of medals struck to commemorate so unusual a happening. It did not interest me. I longed only for it to end, and the days dragged cruelly, despite all there was to do with preparing for my baby's entry into the world. Already Henrietta had brought me a wooden cradle, and the pile of biggins, lace-edged caps, cradle cloths and the like steadily grew, and I wished I had spent more time at my needle in the past.

Inexpert as I was, I looked on the result of my efforts with some pride, and there was a faint pleasure in seeing Tom, for all his iron face and solemn speech as head over heels in love with Tabitha as any green boy. Mercy, encouraged by this behaviour, with some defiance introduced a red-faced fishmonger, a Master Roan Burbidge, as her own acknowledged swain. These matters brought me some interest, but I was

271

consumed by my anxiety to reach Martin, and at last I told Tom flatly that if he would not take me I would go alone.

"To slip and fall, maybe killing yourself and the child," said he, scowling. "Have you no patience?"

"None," I answered, setting my lips. "And you will see I do not fall."

He looked from me to Tabitha and Mercy — we were all, I recall, in the kitchen, where we spent most of our time, it being the warmest room in the house. Mercy shook her head, but Tabitha told Tom, "Indeed, I do not think you will prevent her."

"Not he nor anyone," I agreed.

"I shall come also," said Tabitha, again speaking not to me but to Tom. "With one of us on either side—"

"So as we can make the larger heap when we all go down together," said Tom sourly. "The Lord preserve me from a pack of forward wenches!"

He muttered all the while we made our preparations, the girls muffling my bulky figure, and pulling long woollen hose over my shoes that I might not slip, I submitting in a fever of impatience. Tom took a heavy staff in his hand, and we set out like a band of pilgrims. The snow lay frozen where it had fallen, pure and dazzling when first we set out, but as we neared the haunts of men it was defiled by all manner of filth. The going was hard and the still air bitingly cold, but after my long imprisonment I faced its icy touch with gratitude. My sprits rose, and I even laughed, the first time I had done so for many a weary day, when Tom gave a majestic stagger, and we all but subsided with him. He righted himself and us, observed that the laughter of fools was like thorns crackling under a pot, and we went on. The sky was leaden as the surface of the river, and a lazy flake or two drifted down clinging like feathers to our garments.

"The old woman is plucking her geese," said Tabitha.

Tom snorted. "And a fine thing it will be if we are held up and unable to return. Had you thought of that?"

I had thought of nothing, as he well knew, save that I would be kept from my husband no longer. I bore with his grumbling, since his arm upheld me like a bar of iron. I could have kissed his gloomy countenance when at last we stood in the narrow space cleared between the great banks of snow at Henrietta's door.

"If you think the storm will be heavy it would be best if you took Tabitha back now," I said. "You know that I shall be safe here."

They glanced at one another swiftly, then looked away. Tabitha said nothing, but Tom remarked grudgingly that it might be as well, else Mercy could well find herself alone. They waited to see me enter, then, closely linked, went their way, and I felt that they had been given some reward for their care of me. Henrietta's man had admitted me, and now went to call his mistress. I heard her voice raised in amazement and she burst upon me, crying: "Catherine! Good God, you have never ventured here alone!"

I think I have said that her voice was of an impressive quality. Now it fairly echoed through the house, and as at a signal chaos broke loose. The cat Methuselah lost his footing on her shoulder and fled upstairs, swearing and spitting as he went. At the same moment a door was flung open and Martin appeared at the top of the stairs, looked wildly at us, and started to rush down. About three steps he had taken, while we stared open-mouthed, when Methuselah met with him. There was a furious squeal from the cat, and an oath from Martin. For a moment he staggered, grasped at the air, lost his balance and came crashing down, his head thudding against the wall. He lay in a crumpled heap, quite still.

Henrietta and I had both cried out. Now, for an instant, there was a silence which struck terror to my heart. I could not so much as move, and it was she who bent over Martin, thrusting a hand inside his shirt. Servants came running and clustered round. I alone stood still.

"Stand back, stand back," cried Henrietta impatiently. "Give him air. Malachi, fetch wine."

I had been assured that Martin was dead. Now new life seemed to surge through my cramped limbs, and I moved to

Henrietta's side. She looked up at me, saying cheerfully, "A pretty kettle of fish, but small harm done."

Even now I could scarcely bring myself to believe he lived. I whispered: "Are you sure?"

"See for yourself," she said.

I knelt beside her, looking down on my husband. His face was bloodless, and he had made no movement, but when I touched him I felt, as Henrietta had done, the beating of his heart.

"He has cracked that unfortunate head of his, but I do not think there is much damage," she said, feeling his limbs. "I wonder what possessed him? He has not moved with such haste since the day they brought him here."

"I think he heard you call my name," I said. "And if so—"

I could not go on. So many times we had hoped, only in vain. But in that moment when he set off to meet fate in the shape of Methuselah and I had glimpsed his face it had held more life and feeling than I had seen in it since the day we said farewell.

"I have heard tales," said Henrietta obscurely. "We may yet find, please God, that this is a blessing in disguise."

As if to show his agreement Martin uttered a faint groan. I raised him, and Henrietta held wine to his lips. He took a little, and opened his eyes.

"What has happened?" He asked faintly. "Oh God — my head!"

I said, leaning close and speaking gently: "You fell, and hit it. Do you remember?"

He raised a hand weakly, touching his head and wincing. "There is a lump as big as a hen's egg. That damned cat!" he said.

If he had spoken words filled with beauty and power we could not have received them with more joy. I could have hugged Methuselah to my breast, claws and all.

"Someone called on Catherine," said Martin, trying to rise. "I thought—"

"Hush, dear, and do not try to move," I said, trying to hold back my exultation. "Catherine is here. All is well."

He sighed, and looked up into my face, peering rather painfully.

"I never had a squint before, but now I see double," he complained.

A sudden memory struck me. "But you did once before, that time when we were children, and the branch of the elm gave way. You fell cracking your head, and after you said you could see two of me. Do you remember?"

"I remember," he said.

There was a sound beside me, half sob, half laugh. I turned to Henrietta and could not see her clearly, for she seemed, solid as she was to float in a golden haze.

They got Martin to bed, and after a while he was violently sick. I remembered that it had been so that other time long ago, and that he then had yawned consumedly and grown heavy with sleep. This, too, followed, and he slept the afternoon away. Even in sleep, unless I deceived myself, he looked more his old self, and somehow I was convinced that he had truly found his way out of the dark valley at last. True, it had not been as I expected. Vaguely I had imagined him murmuring my name in thrilling accents, clasping me to him as would have befallen in a romance. Instead he had spoken with some discontent of seeing double. Little bubbles of laughter rose to my lips, and when Henrietta came in she said that it was good to see me looking my old self again.

"I thought you would warn me not to expect too much," I said.

She shook her head. "It may be that I also am wrong, but I am convinced that this time he is recovered, and for good. Catherine, Tom is here. He came to take you home, but I told him you would wish to remain."

"If you will allow me. But could I see him? He is so attached to Martin — I should wish to tell him." And indeed, I could have cried it from the housetops, so sure and so happy was I.

When Tom came in, he actually spoke no word of discouragement, and even smiled, a thing unusual with him.

"Praise be to God for His great mercy," said he.

I thought how strange a blessing Methuselah, enraged and spitting had been, and my lips twitched, though heaven knows my heart also sang in praise.

"Mistress Lacey says you remain here?"

"Yes. I must be with my husband when he wakes. I am sorry to have brought you back for nothing."

"It was not for nothing," said Tom.

When he had gone, saying that he would return on the morrow, I thought, with wonder, how confident we all were, Tom, Henrietta, and myself. It was a most lovely feeling, and I hugged it to me, gazing down at the peaceful face on the pillows as the quiet hours passed by. Henrietta brought me food and stayed with me from time to time, but I think she had the feeling that when Martin opened his eyes he and I should be alone. As I remember, I felt no impatience, only a deep content. Looking back that seems strange to me, yet so it was.

The room was growing dark when the sleeper stirred, murmured something incoherent, and burrowed more deeply into the pillow. But now he was restless, jerking his limbs under the coverings, muttering fretfully. For the first time my confidence was shaken, and I prayed silently, dear God, let it be as we have hoped. Let him not look on me with empty eyes.

Martin turned, flung out an arm, and said quite clearly: "Catherine."

I bent over him. "I am here Martin."

He opened his eyes, winced as if the light, poor though it was, hurt him, and gazed up at me. He looked puzzled, somewhat out of temper, and completely himself. And he said peevishly: "Catherine. Why the devil are you up and dressed?"

CHAPTER XXVIII

I awoke from the sleep following pain and a struggle which had left me exhausted, and for a moment wondered what I was doing in my bed in the broad light of day, and why there were faces smiling down on me. Then I remembered, and smiled back, saying weakly but with pride and joy: "My babe?"

"Here, my lamb. A beautiful girl," said Henrietta, and she bent over me and laid a swaddled bundle in the crook of my arm. I looked down at the red face of my baby, crumpled as if in indignation at her entry into the world, and she opened a mouth surprisingly large and uttered a loud wail. We all smiled again, rejoicing in her surpassing cleverness.

"A lovely child," said Tabitha, who had attended me throughout, and had some cause for pride.

"The image of her father," said Mercy.

"She knows what she wants," said Henrietta, nodding.

I put the baby, for the first time, to my breast. She jerked impatiently, found what she wanted, nuzzled to me, and her outcry suddenly ceased. For a space she fed with purpose, then was still. Looking down I saw that she had fallen asleep.

"She has taken so little," said I, somewhat troubled.

"It is sleep she needs now. She is warm and comfortable, and will not put herself about as yet. Do not be alarmed. She will be greedy enough soon enough, take my word," said Henrietta, laughing.

"I wonder how long it will be before Martin is here?" I said, resting my chin on the tiny head.

"It will not be long. Tom set off at the first hint that matters were on the move, long before your pains began. And now you must rest again, my love. We will leave you for a space," said Henrietta.

They went, and I lay with my baby warm against me, and I thought of all that had happened since that day when Martin came crashing down the stairs and back to life. Such things are beyond my understanding, and whether the new knock on his head did indeed relieve that pressure of which the doctor spoke I do not know. Henrietta, who said that she had heard of like cases, held firmly to that belief. For myself, I am not wholly convinced, and have wondered if at that moment when he heard my name and came rushing from his room he had already found himself again. However that may be, it matters little, since his return was no passing affair, but God be thanked for always. One period only was lost to him. From the moment when something came crashing down on him aboard that ship to the time when he heard Henrietta crying my name he recalled nothing, nor, indeed, do I think he ever will. It is like a book from which certain pages have been torn to be for ever lost. It has not marred our happiness.

I lay there in the March sunshine and lived again these days we spent together before we persuaded him, most unwillingly to leave London and be removed from danger. It was very hard to part with him, and in my condition and the state of the roads it was not possible for me to accompany him but having once found him again I walked in fear lest he should be discovered, and at last, as I say, he went. But before that we had talked and talked, as if we must needs repay ourselves for that period of silence. Not that there were not also times when we did not need to speak at all.

It was not until the second day that he asked a question which I had been dreading and spoke Sidney's name. He still lay abed, since the fall had left him somewhat giddy, and I hoped to postpone the time when he must know. But Martin could ever see through any effort of mine to dissemble, and with a sinking heart I knew he must be told. Try as I might to soften it for him, I could see that each word struck a cruel blow, yet he heard all in silence, only the hand lying outside the covers slowly tensed and clenched into a fist on which the knuckles showed white.

"Dear God!" he said, when I had made an end. "If I could but have been there!"

"Martin, Henrietta was there, with Tom. She will tell you all. And there is a letter for you," I said.

"A letter? At that time he could think of me?"

"Yes, love. He was convinced you lived, and when Henrietta saw him in the Tower he wished for our happiness. Martin, he would not now wish you to grieve."

I thought how empty the words sounded as I spoke them, and was not surprised that he made no reply. He listened silently when Henrietta told him of those last moments as she had told me, and laid his friend's letter in his hands. We went out together, leaving him to read it alone, and even then, unworthy as it was, I was forced to stifle a pang of that old jealousy.

"I wish he could have been spared this."

"He had to know," Henrietta replied. "And he will find cause for pride, as we have done." Her words so steady that I remembered her own suffering and was ashamed. I took her hand humbly, and she smiled on me with kindness, and I knew she understood.

When I returned to him Martin was lying with his back towards the door, and I felt with pain that he did not need me. We had been apart for so long that I fear I grudged any moment given other than to myself. But hearing my footstep he turned, spoke my name in a muffled voice, and held out the letter to me.

"Read it," he said. "It is as if he were here, speaking to me."

And when I saw the short and simple lines which a man had taken time to write on the threshold of death, I, too, felt him near. He spoke of Martin's friendship and what it had meant to him, touched on his arrest, and concluded.

> *My trial was a mockery, my judge perverted and out on any pretext for my blood, the jury packed, the evidence hearsay and a sham. But it was only what I knew I must expect lest the plot should burst like a bubble. For it was plainly said that I must die or the plot must die. Since I had no hope I was not disappointed. I wrote my appeal to the king simply to make matters clear, as is my conscience when I go forth to die.*

Martin flung an arm over his eyes. My voice trembled, but I continued.

> *Therefore, dear lad, grieve not for me. In my life are many pages which I could wish unwritten, but of these final ones I am not ashamed. I trust that my God will give me strength to bear myself with courage at the last. I am confident that He will do so.*
>
> *And now, before I bid you farewell in this world, you know what my request will be — that you see to it that my* Discourses Concerning Government *are made public, though I need not ask since I already have your word. Thus though I am gone something of me shall live on.*
>
> *May God bless you and yours, and have you for ever in His keeping.*

The writing had grown somewhat illegible towards the end, but the signature stood out bold and clear. I saw that Henrietta had come quietly into the room, and that her eyes were shining.

"He did bear himself with courage. All men know that," she said.

Martin turned his face away. She said steadily. "You have much to remember, Martin, and his last desire to carry out."

"Yes. There is that, at least," he said.

"Oh, Martin!" I began and could say no more. The thought of those papers silently rotting in the river ooze, the knowledge of what I had done made me speechless.

"What is it, child?" asked Henrietta quickly.

Martin turned to look at me. I gulped, and twisting my hands together, told the tale.

"Indeed, I was at my wits' end. We — Tom and I — did what seemed best at the time. But now they are gone, through me, and you will not forgive me—"

"Now, here's a tale of woe!" said Henrietta, with a laugh. "Take heart, my poppet, and you, Martin, need not look as if the end of the world had come."

"It was the last thing, the only thing he asked of me. I fail in that as in all the rest," said he, with such bitterness that I could have wept.

"Good God, can you not understand plain-speech?" demanded Henrietta angrily. "Am I not telling you? There is another copy."

I think Martin and I both cried out in disbelief. She shook her head, half exasperated, half in sympathy.

"Algernon was pleased to have my opinion of his work, strange though it may seem. 'Tis a rough draft, and may not be too easy to decipher in parts, but the gist of the matter is there, and I have it safe enough."

"Thank God," said Martin. "Thank God."

"Yes. I will go now and fetch it, that you may see for yourself. And in the meantime spare a thought for your wife, who looks in need of comfort."

She went out muttering, and Martin stretched a hand to me. I laid my cheek against his, and told him I was sorry, and hoped he did not blame me.

"Blame you?" he echoed, with a deep breath. "It seems to me that you had much to contend with, while I ran off like a dog with its tail between its legs. I do not blame you, my sweet, but it is damnably hard to forgive myself."

"Oh, Martin," I said, half sobbing. "Do not torture yourself. You could not have saved him, and it was his wish that you should go."

"I know," he answered heavily. "But that makes it no easier."

I said in a choked voice, "It is not easy for me, either."

He sat up suddenly and turned my face to his. He was very pale, and his lips were set, but there was a look in his eyes which sent the last shred of that unworthy jealousy for ever to the winds.

"Do not heed me," I said quickly. "Dear Martin, I know your grief, and I grieve for you. I should not think of myself just now."

He held me closely. "My dearest love, I will spend the rest of my life thinking of you and of your happiness. And I promise you I will put bitterness aside, and only be proud that he was my friend. But — it may take a little time."

"I know, dear heart," I said. "I understand."

* * *

I lay there with my baby sleeping beside me and recalled all this, and much more. It was as if I floated on a quiet sea, which had been hard to reach, but which now surrounded me with wellbeing. Out of our troubles had come so much that was good — the devotion of Tom, Tabitha and Mercy, the steadfast love of Henrietta, the selfless help given us by Roger Frampton. Despite those past moments of jealousy, too, there had been that about the spirit of Martin's friend which made me also proud to have known him.

It all went back to the day when Ralph brought Frances home. With a kind of wonder I thought how little I had guessed what was to come when I stepped forward unwillingly to meet her. Frances. I could feel some pity for her, slave of her passion as she had been, but for that other, her evil genius, even now I could find only a shrinking repugnance. My thoughts turned to Ralph, feeling myself so blessed beside him. I hoped he was not drinking himself to death, and was pulling the shreds of his life together. The neglected estate, surely, could give a man occupation, if not happiness. A picture of the countryside came to me so vividly that I could almost smell the fresh air, the scent of living things longing to burst their bonds after the cruel winter's imprisonment. I closed my eyes, and thought the hazel catkins would be dancing already, that soon the meadows would be golden with buttercups, wild parsley frothing by every path, trees decked in that fresh green which came each year yet each year was a miracle. It was there I wished our child to grow up, not in this great smoky town, where grandeur rubbed shoulders with misery, and vice peered from the fairest exteriors.

With joy I recalled my husband's words. "We are country folk, my wife and l." He would be of my mind, unless he still longed to play a part in politics and intrigue, and could not bear to be out of the swim.

For the first time I was troubled, and as if she sensed the change in me, the baby stirred, woke, and set up a wail. The tiny face was crumpled with indignation, and one tiny hand had somehow escaped from its wrappings and waved outspread fingers, as if to proclaim ill-usage to the world. I remembered Mercy and tried to find a resemblance to Martin but could not, though already the creature seemed to have her father's tenacity of purpose. I satisfied her wants, feeling pride in my ability to do so, and quite soon again she slept.

Henrietta and Tabitha came to tend me, and she slumbered on. I was bidden to do likewise, but now was wakeful, wondering if Martin could be with me before nightfall, knowing that it was probably not possible. The hours of darkness were still too long, although the days were drawing out. I began to fret that he might ride foolishly without due care, all the dangers of the road coming into my mind. Or

Tom might have fallen into difficulties, and Martin not even know yet that he was a father. I gave a foolish sob and found Henrietta at my side.

"Now, now, this will never do," said she bracingly. "There is another for you to think of now, remember. You are bound to be low-spirited from weakness, but you must not give way. When Martin comes he will wish to see you smile."

"I wish he were here," I said.

She smoothed back my hair and told me to have patience, for he would be here the first possible moment, and when I spoke of my fear of footpads and the like, told me these were foolish fancies, and that I was not half so well-behaved as my child. She cheered me, despite myself, and I drifted off to sleep again whether I would or not. The babe woke me once in the night and I fed her, still half drugged with sleep, and after that I knew nothing until it was broad day.

The room was empty, and the babe gone from my side. I felt stronger after my rest and very hungry and was glad when Tabitha brought me eggs beaten in milk, and disposed of them speedily. Mercy followed her sister proudly bearing the swaddled baby, now, she observed, dry and clean, and not before time. We were laughing together when Henrietta entered, first ordering back her cats, which seemed desirous of joining us.

"I think," she said, having embraced me, "that we will cleanse you also, and tie your hair. Visitors must see you at your best."

"Visitors!" I echoed, seeing that she was smiling. "You mean—?"

"Wait a while," said she, nodding and pursing up her lips. "We shall see." And not another word would she say until all was to her satisfaction.

"Now," she said, "Martin is on his way, and his family ready to receive him."

On the words she stepped back, and before I had time to take in what she said, Martin was at my side.

He said in a loud voice, as if he thought childbirth had made me deaf: "Well, my love! So I find myself a father, do

I? Tom — Tom, where the devil are you lurking? Come and see what we have here!"

I heard him with speechless indignation, saw the half sheepish look of pride on his weary face as he held out my babe to be admired by Tom. There they were, all of them, clustered round the bundle which Henrietta had placed in her father's arms, and I might have had no part in it at all. I gave a loud and angry snort, and Henrietta turned quickly.

"Away with you all," she said briskly, putting the babe, which had begun to wail, beside me. "Martin, you may stay, but not overlong. Do not weary her."

I snuggled my baby to me, and she lay quiet. I looked down at her ignoring her father who, it seemed to me, had not risen to the occasion. His eyes were on me, I knew, but I kept my own obstinately lowered.

"Catherine?" he said, with slight discomfort. "Are you weary? Do you wish me to go?"

"As you will," I said, adding angrily, "I wonder you put yourself about to come at all."

He laughed, and came to the bedside, leaning over me. I turned my head away.

"Listen, my Catherine," said he, still with an undertone of laughter, "When I came, having travelled day and night, I saw you pale, fragile, unlike yourself. Now I know that you are my Catherine still, temper and all."

"What did you expect? I lay here longing for you to come, and when you did you had scarce a word for me."

"As a father I am very new. I did not know what to say or do. But now—"

"Well?"

"If you will but turn your head I will show you," he said coaxingly. And as I remained obstinate he spoke my name in a tone which swept all my foolish grievance away. I turned to him, and he said nothing, but it was all as I had hoped it would be, and more.

Sometime later I said: "Martin."

"My love?"

"What are your plans for the future? It is still not safe for you to remain here, but would you — could you — be happy in the country?"

"You mean," said he, "taking no further part in politics? Taking no part at all, letting the government of the country be what it will so far as I am concerned?"

"Yes," I answered, but my heart sank.

"That is what you would wish?"

"I would never try to stop you from doing what you thought right," I said steadily. "Only it seems to me that if all men did as well as possible what lay near at hand, then in time, great affairs might also right themselves."

"And that is your opinion?"

I thought his voice was cold, but I said, "Foolish or not, it is."

He bent to kiss me. "Now, here's a fortunate turn of events! My wife and I see eye to eye, for I had come to much the same conclusion myself. Mind, I do not go as far as you. Not all men can turn to their own affairs and let the world wag as it chooses. One day you will read his writings, and see what could be."

He spoke no name, but for a moment his face was shadowed as he remembered his friend. Then he smiled down at me. "For myself, I will become a Dorset squire with all my heart. Locke, the steward, is old, and a sick man. Good farmland has gone to waste — there is much to do. And with your help, to the best of my ability, I will do so. The roads are none so bad, considering the winter. How soon will you be fit to travel?"

I laughed from relief and happiness. "I do not know. But as soon as I may I will come. I hope Martha still lives so that she can see our babe. She is most beautiful, Martin, is she not?"

His look was somewhat guarded.

"Mercy says she is the image of you!" I said indignantly.

"Good God!" said Martin.

I could not help laughing, but I shook my head at him, and he gave me that look of his in mock repentance.

"You are not vexed?" I asked him.

"At what? At Mercy's opinion of my looks?"

"No! That she is a girl."

He looked down at me, not teasing now. "If she is as her mother is, my sweet, then I am well content."

* * *

It was all a long time ago. We are old folk now, Martin and I, and shake our heads over the behaviours of the young, although to us our youth seems none so far away, and the tale I have told is clear and fresh in my memory, the faces of those who have left us as real as those which surround us today. We have had four children since our firstborn, Henrietta, and three of them are boys, while Martin has achieved his ambition to become a grandfather four times as yet. We are, I fear, the most besotted grandparents in the world, and our children say we indulge their offspring as we never did our own. This we indignantly deny, but I know that my heart is as wax in those baby fingers, while Martin would bring down the stars from the sky to be their playthings if he could.

We live at the manor still, from time to time visiting London, where Mercy and her fishmonger keep the house by the river ever ready to receive us. Tom and Tabitha are with us, and considering his old ways he has taken to married life and fatherhood with remarkable composure, not to say unregenerate pleasure. Our trips to town have been less frequent since our dear Henrietta died, full of years and not sorry to go. I thank God she lived to hear the name of Colonel Sidney cleared before the world, and to see his writings made public even as he had wished. Whether under Anne, the queen, he would feel the country to be better ruled I do not know. Some things are for good, some otherwise, and I suppose it will be so until the end of time.

We saw many changes, Martin and I, in those first few years of our marriage — the death of a king, the short reign of his brother, the rising of the Duke of Monmouth with all that followed it. Roger Frampton did return to England never to leave it again, even as he had said, since he fell with so many more on that bloody field at Sedgemoor, from which the man for whom they gave their lives had fled. Martin, for all his intention of leaving such matters to others would have been there also but for an attack of fever which laid him low, and for which I have never ceased to thank God, though at the time he was near death. It was not only those who fell in battle, for they had the better part, but Jeffreys, that same who had made a mockery of justice to send Algernon Sidney to his death, turned the West Country into a charnel house, leaving a desolation which will not be forgotten, and making his name an abomination. But his day passed with that of James, the king whom he had striven to please, and there came the moment when he craved for pity and found none, even as Henrietta had wished.

Ralph, too, was desirous of joining Monmouth, but he has married a wife of whom he stands in awe, and she would not let him go. A widow, well-to-do, she has presented him with a brood of apple cheeked boys, all with voices that rival even their father's, and he is mightily proud of them. He has become, if not sober, a steady landowner, and is not allowed to stray from such paths as Sarah thinks fitting. She is a notable housewife, as great a contrast to Frances as could well be imagined, and if Ralph's thoughts ever turn to that brief period when he lay under her spell, it is known only to himself.

Martha, Joan, and others of the old servants finished their days with us and are gone, like so many more. As I say, Martin and I are long past our youth, and look back on more years together than there are to come. The days have not always been serene, and even now there are moments when we anger one another, and hurl insults with every intent to wound. I fear, though we should know better, we shall never outgrow it now. But the words graven on my locket have proved true, since out of the pattern of our days has grown an affection deep and abiding, so that for both of us the only home is at the other's side, and the first thing he does on entering the house is to call my name. Nor am I ever slow to answer him.

THE END

ALSO BY MARGARET SCUTT

STANDALONES
CORPSE PATH COTTAGE
SIXPENNY HOLDING
NOW AND FOREVER

Thank you for reading this book.

If you enjoyed it please leave feedback on Amazon or Goodreads, and if there is anything we missed or you have a question about, then please get in touch. We appreciate you choosing our book.

Founded in 2014 in Shoreditch, London, we at Joffe Books pride ourselves on our history of innovative publishing. We were thrilled to be shortlisted for Independent Publisher of the Year at the British Book Awards.

www.joffebooks.com

We're very grateful to eagle-eyed readers who take the time to contact us. Please send any errors you find to corrections@joffebooks.com. We'll get them fixed ASAP.

DX PLAINER: Where does AIB fund
loans under tracker mortgage issue - 17

Lifting cahs on Benkars Pay now
would Be a Bycycle Kick of a Pal
own goal - mark panl 17

Businesses must do more to help
Consumers 17

quarry owners dong side deals
with Home owners 17

Civil Servant distances himself from
Controversial appointment to state housing
agency
banad leader warns... Robert 17

Printed in Great Britain
by Amazon

81568555R10171